THE
DEAD
MAN

THE DEAD MAN

JOEL GOLDMAN

PINNACLE BOOKS
KENSINGTON PUBLISHING CORP.
www.kensingtonbooks.com

PINNACLE BOOKS are published by

Kensington Publishing Corp.
850 Third Avenue
New York, NY 10022

All Kensington titles, imprints, and distributed lines are available at special quantity discounts for bulk purchases for sales
promotions, premiums, fund-raising, educational, or institutional use. Special book excerpts or customized printings can
also be created to fit specific needs. For details, write or phone
the office of the Kensington special sales manager: Kensington Publishing Corp., 850 Third Avenue, New York, NY 10022,
attn: Special Sales Department; phone: 1-800-221-2647.

This book is a work of fiction. Names, characters, businesses,
organizations, places, events, and incidents either are the
product of the author's imagination or are used fictitiously.
Any resemblance to actual persons, living or dead, events, or
locales is entirely coincidental.

ISBN-13: 978-0-7860-2040-9
ISBN-10: 0-7860-2040-7

First printing: April 2009

10 9 8 7 6 5 4 3 2 1

Printed in the United States of America

For my brothers and sisters,
Barry, Madeline, Susan, Tom, Stuart, and Tensy.

ACKNOWLEDGMENTS

Thanks to Jim Born for his help with firearms, to Doug Lyle for his help on forensic matters, to Doug Stone for his explanation of parabolic curves, and to Rick Shteamer for reminding me that the more you do the more you do. Thanks also to Starbucks for reserving my table and not raising my rent and to Jott.com for helping me remember all the brilliant insights that came to me when I was walking instead of writing.

This book, like everything in my life, would not be possible without my wife, Hildy, whose love, support, patience, and encouragement spring from a bottomless well. As always, my agent Meredith Bernstein gave invaluable advice and my editor, Audrey LaFehr, sharpened, shaped, and shepherded the story, both making a good book better. I am grateful to all of them.

Chapter One

December 1959

Sheriff Ed Beedles grabbed the barrel of his shotgun, yanking it from the rack in his patrol car. He knew Charlie Brennan well enough to know better, but there he was, standing in front of his brother's farmhouse not fifty feet in front of him, covered in blood, one arm wrapped over his ten-year-old niece, Maggie, clutching her like she was a hostage, the girl wearing nothing but a nightgown, shivering in the cold. The dispatcher had taken Charlie's call thirty minutes ago, Charlie screaming at her that Sam and Gretchen were dead and that he had Maggie.

The Brennan place was twenty miles south of the sheriff's headquarters in the Johnson County courthouse in Olathe. He'd made good time, taking advantage of the new highway, Interstate 35, that had opened earlier in the year, making it to Spring Hill in twenty minutes, then heading west and busting it over the last few miles of rough county road. He fishtailed making the turn into the Brennans' property, tires spitting gravel and ice laid down in last week's storm, siren blaring, his heart riding in his throat the last quarter mile to the farmhouse. He was first on the scene, his deputy Tom Goodell, and two ambulances five minutes behind.

It had been three weeks since the Clutter family had been slaughtered in their farmhouse near Holcomb. That was a good four hundred miles west, but there had been no arrests and every lawman in the state was on edge, scared the killers would strike again.

Still, Beedles knew it was more likely that Charlie had killed his brother and sister-in-law than some faceless maniacs, most murders being committed by people who knew their victims. He'd heard talk of trouble between the brothers, something about the land their parents left them, but as far as he knew, it was just talk.

He opened his car door and stepped out, keeping the door between him and Charlie, the shotgun invisible at his side. The farmhouse sat on a rise, sheltered on three sides from the wind by stands of maples and oaks. It had been daylight for an hour, the sky heavy and close with leaden clouds, the wind cold and stiff enough to make a man deaf.

"Let her go, Charlie," Beedles shouted.

"They're dead! Both of them." A rose mist floated off of Charlie, fresh blood mixing with the frozen air.

"Then we can't do anything for them but we can take care of Maggie. Now let her go."

Beedles didn't see a weapon in either of Charlie's hands but that didn't mean he was innocent or un-armed. He could be both and also be unhinged by what he'd seen, making him dangerous in another way.

Beedles started a slow walk toward Charlie and Maggie, keeping the shotgun aimed at the ground. His deputy and the ambulances would come storming into the yard any second, no way to tell how Charlie would react to the added commotion.

"It's no good," Charlie said, tightening his grip on the girl. "They're dead! Cut to pieces!"

"And that's a terrible thing. Let's not make it any worse."

Beedles closed the distance between them, leveling the shotgun at Charlie. Though he couldn't shoot Charlie without shredding Maggie with buckshot, he knew the sight of that gun pointed at Charlie couldn't help but make him focus on his mortality.

Charlie stared at the shotgun. "Ed, you don't think I killed them, do you?"

They were ten feet apart. Charlie's hands, arms, and chest were soaked in blood. Maggie's face was streaked with crimson, honey-colored bangs falling over her eyes, her lips blue, her nightgown blood splattered. Beedles stepped closer, raising the shotgun at Charlie's face; Charlie's eyes opened wide like day lilies under the sun.

"I don't think anything, Charlie. I just want to have a look at Maggie, make sure she's okay. Then you and I can talk about what happened. That be all right with you?"

Deputy Goodell's cruiser skidded to a stop, flanking Beedles, Charlie, and the girl. Using his open car door for cover, he drew his handgun, taking a two-fisted aim at Charlie Brennan.

"We okay, here, Sheriff?" Goodell asked.

"How about it, Charlie, we okay?" Beedles asked.

Charlie hung his head. "Yeah, we're okay."

Beedles lowered his shotgun, reaching for Maggie with his free hand. "Come here, sweetheart," he said.

Maggie slipped out from under Charlie's arm and put

her hand in his. Beedles squeezed her hand and she squeezed his, surprising Beedles with her calm strength, as if the blood on her fingers was nail polish.

Over the next hours and days, Charlie Brennan told his story again and again to Sheriff Beedles, the district attorney, the polygraph examiner, and his lawyer, never changing a word, sentence, or paragraph. He and his brother had put their hard feelings behind. He'd come to pick up his brother so they could repair a bad stretch of fence they shared. No one answered when he rang the bell. The door was unlocked so he went in and called out for Sam and Gretchen. When they didn't respond, he went looking and found them stabbed to death in their bed. He got their blood on him when he cradled their bodies in his arms, going crazy at the sight of them. He found Maggie hiding in the bushes beneath her second floor bedroom. The polygraph examiner said that Charlie was truthful in all measures and no charges were filed against him.

Maggie Brennan's story corroborated her uncle. She said that she was awakened by cries coming from her parents' bedroom. Then she heard footsteps coming toward her bedroom. It was dark. Someone grabbed her but his hands were too wet and slippery with blood to hold her. She freed herself and ran onto the balcony off her bedroom, jumping over the rail, her only injury a sprained ankle. She ran into a nearby field, staying there until daylight, coming back and hiding in the bushes beneath her bedroom, too frightened to go inside the house, remaining there until her uncle found her. She spoke without tears; a doctor who examined her explained that she was too shocked to cry, assuring Beedles that it was best if she buried the memories of that night.

Beedles walked through the Brennan farmhouse

dozens of times, re-creating the killer's path, tracing the blood trail from Sam and Gretchen's bedroom to Maggie's. He opened the French doors onto her balcony, stood at the rail, and marveled at the courage of a ten-year-old girl to escape from the killer and jump from such a height.

Charlie Brennan sent Maggie to live with his sister in California. He never set foot on his brother's farm again, selling it in the spring and sending the money to his sister to pay for Maggie's upbringing. That night, he got drunk and was killed when he drove his pickup truck into a concrete culvert.

When Richard Hickock and Perry Smith were arrested for the Clutter family murders, Beedles drove to Garden City to question them. They denied the killings and there was no evidence to link them to the Brennan case.

No murder weapon was ever found. No one was ever charged with the murders of Sam and Gretchen Brennan. It wasn't the only unsolved crime during Beedles's years as sheriff but it was the one that woke him up at night until the day he died.

Chapter Two

January 2009

Maggie Brennan had been waiting to die for fifty years so when the lights went out while she was working late at night and the bell hanging on a hook above the front door jingled as it opened and slammed shut, loosing icy winter wind into the farmhouse, and heavy, steady footsteps trudged up the stairs toward her bedroom, she didn't call 911, cry out, or grab a letter opener to defend herself.

She'd dreamed of this moment often. The image of the killer was as hazy as it had been when she was ten years old, painting her cheeks with her parents' blood before she hurled herself off the balcony outside her bedroom, the killer never caught, never forgotten.

Her work as a neuroscientist researching the toll of trauma on the brain was a constant reminder of that night. Her nightmares affirmed her unspeakable certainty that she would leave this life the same way as had her parents.

She rose from her chair, her voice quiet and calm when her killer appeared in the doorway. "What took you so long?" she asked.

French doors opened behind her onto the balcony, the frozen earth two stories beneath sloping away from the house, rough and rocky. She swung the doors wide, stepping onto the balcony, her feet bare, frigid air rippling through her thin nightgown, pickling her skin. Branches of an oak tree just beyond her reach swayed in the starless night, the eaves above her whining, complaining of the cold.

Her back was to the bedroom. She felt him approach, felt the wooden planks of the balcony sag, then felt a hand slide down the length of her neck, settling into the base of her spine, the push firm as she went over the rail and the unforgiving ground rushed to meet her.

She awoke, as she always did, the instant before impact, her mouth coated with bile. Why, she wondered, was it so easy to kill and so hard to die.

Chapter Three

"Jack, this job is perfect for you."

"I haven't had a perfect job since Sue Ellen Erickson asked me to carry her books home in the fifth grade."

Simon Alexander and I were having coffee late Friday afternoon on the Country Club Plaza, the gray day giving way to full night, snow coming down sideways. The after-Christmas sales were over and the quarter million multicolored lights that turned the Plaza's shops and restaurants into Disneyland from Thanksgiving through mid-January had gone dark. The sidewalks were empty. People with sense were home or on their way.

"You can set your own schedule, spend as much time as you want, take a break whenever you need to, you know . . ."

"Stop shaking."

"Yeah, that."

The FBI had retired me at age fifty because of a movement disorder that makes me shake, sometimes bending me in half, sometimes strangling my speech, sometimes leaving me the hell alone. The cause and the cure are both mysteries, the symptoms a capricious mix of hiccups and hammer blows. The more I do, the more I shake but a friend once told me that the more you do, the more you do. So I put as much into my days as I can, accepting that it will rattle my cage. Some days are diamonds and some days are stones.

Simon was in the technology security business. He called me when his clients' problems got more complicated than a string of ones and zeros.

"I keep telling you, Simon, you don't have to dance around it. I shake. It's not a big deal." A flurry of mild tremors stutter-stepped my automatic denial. "Tell me about the job."

"You've heard of Milo Harper?"

"Kansas City's hometown billionaire. He offered Kate Scranton a job but she turned him down, says she doesn't trust him."

"She'd do better reading astrology charts than her facial action coding system. If someone winks when they should blink, she thinks they're guilty of something they haven't even thought of doing."

"Trouble is, she's usually right. What else should I know about Harper?"

"We grew up together and were roommates at Stanford. He dropped out during our sophomore year. I stayed and got my degree while he left and got rich. Created one of those social networking sites and sold it for a couple of billion. I've done some work for him since he came back to Kansas City."

"You and a billionaire? I don't see it."

"Who knew? He was the tall, good-looking guy with wavy hair, a square chin, and pecs he could make dance. I was the short nebbish geek with early male pattern baldness whose idea of a good pickup line was would you like to play Simon says."

"How'd that work out for you?"

"It was the ones who said yes that scared me."

"Harper plowed a bunch of the money into that place . . . what's it called?"

"The Harper Institute of the Mind."

"He keeps trying to recruit Kate. She keeps telling him no but he keeps asking."

"That's Milo. He can charm you if he wants to but he doesn't care what you think about him as long as you've got talent. And he doesn't take no for an answer. He says the brain is the last frontier. He's recruited some of the top people in the field, except, apparently, for Kate."

"What does he want from me? Is he short on guinea pigs?"

"No, but I told him you were available in case the lab rats got a better offer."

"Nice. Then what is it?"

"He's worried about one of his projects, something having to do with dreams."

"Who's having nightmares?"

"He is. Two of the volunteers participating in the project have died in the last month. According to the cops, one death was accidental and one was suicide."

"Bad luck, but what's that got to do with Harper and his institute?"

"Hopefully nothing, but the families have hired a lawyer named Jason Bolt who has sent Milo the proverbial get-out-your-checkbook-or-prepare-to-die letter. He wants someone to take another look. I suggested you."

I'd heard of Bolt. He'd made a fortune taking down corporations for everything from defective products to defrauding shareholders. He was one of a handful of lawyers who could force a settlement on the strength of his reputation.

"A billionaire takes your advice?"

Simon laughed. "I was the one who told him to quit school."

"What else did he tell you? Why does Bolt think these deaths could be tied to the institute?"

"I'm Milo's friend, not his priest. He doesn't tell me everything. He asked me for a name and I gave him yours."

"You know him. What's your sense of this?"

"Milo is a passionate guy. He loves the institute. The look in his eyes, the way he talks about it, you'd think it was his child, like the walls were papered with his DNA. When he called me, he sounded like a parent whose kid had gone missing."

I knew that fear, how it leeches into your bones, like poison with an eternal half-life. But the Harper Institute of the Mind didn't have dimples, skinned knees, or a smile that could light up a room and break your heart at the same time. It was bricks, mortar, and money.

"Is he married? Does he have kids?"

"Neither. He's married to the job. His first kid was the business he built and sold. Now he has the institute. It's not an accident that the abbreviation for Harper Institute of the Mind is HIM."

My doctor told me that the only way I could control the shakes was to change my lifestyle, to slow down. That was fourteen months ago and I still hadn't found the sweet spot between alive and dead. The work Simon sent me tilted the scale toward alive but sometimes it's better to let the scale swing the other way. Rich people who substitute the things they build, create, and run for the relationships they never had can be more irrational than any overprotective parent.

"I think I'll pass."

"Why? Because of Kate Scranton? Give me a break. I was there for your last fight. I'm surprised there were any survivors."

I laughed. "We're a work in progress. I'm having dinner with her tomorrow night. The problem is that she sees things in me that I don't always want her to see."

"The micro-expressions that she claims give away your secrets?"

"Yeah. It's how her brain is wired. Sometimes I don't handle it very well but I still respect her judgment. Plus, rich guys like Harper who think they can buy people the same way they buy buildings can get crazy when things don't go their way and I don't do crazy."

"At least talk to him. I told him that you would call him tonight. All you have to do is check out this dream project and he'll take it from there."

"I load the gun and he pulls the trigger."

"Just like when you were at the FBI and the U.S. attorney made the call. Why the attack of middle-age angst? You've spent your whole life going after bad guys."

"I always knew whose side I was on and I was a lot better at figuring out the truth. Those lines aren't as bright when a billionaire draws them."

"There was a philosopher who claimed that it was impossible to determine whether some things are true or false. He proved it by saying that all men are liars. If he was telling the truth, then he was a liar."

"Yeah, but that doesn't make not knowing any easier."

Simon took a breath, leaning toward me. "This isn't about Wendy."

Wendy was my daughter. She died early last year, twenty-plus years after her brother Kevin was murdered by a sex offender masquerading as a trustworthy neighbor. Every FBI agent in the Kansas City office attended the funeral, some out of respect, others because Wendy had been a fugitive, the last suspected member of a drug ring I'd helped take down before the Bureau kicked me to the curb, the only loose end being five million dollars that had disappeared into the ether. They were convinced she stole the money.

I never stopped thinking about her, wistful memories sometimes crossing into haunting flashbacks so real they stopped me in my tracks or dreams too vivid for sleep. A snatch of conversation, a familiar fragrance, even a sad-eyed junkie could put me back with her, replaying the moment, hoping for a different ending.

"I know that."

"Then talk to him. That's all I'm asking."

Simon had been good to me. I owed him that much. "Okay."

"Great." He leaned back in his chair. "So, how you doing with the . . ."

"Shaking? Every day is an adventure."

"How about that group of retired cops you told me about? You still get together with them?"

"We have lunch once a month. Somebody presents a case. Maybe one that was never solved or one where maybe be the wrong guy took the fall. We play cop again, trying to put it together."

"Any cold cases get solved that way?"

"No, but a lot of beer gets put away so everyone goes home feeling good about that."

My cell phone rang, the caller ID reading *Private*. I flipped the phone open.

"Hello?"

"Mr. Davis, this is Milo Harper."

"Hang on a second." I covered the phone. "It's your roommate. I thought he was waiting for my call."

"I forgot to tell you. He's a little impatient. I gave him your number."

Simon headed for the door. I put the phone back to my ear.

"Call me Jack."

"For now, I'll call you late. I've been waiting to hear from you."

I gritted my teeth. I'd promised Simon I would talk to Harper. I didn't promise to be nice. "Simon just finished telling me about your situation."

"Fine. I'll meet you for dinner at McCormick and Schmick at seven-thirty and don't be late."

Chapter Four

Milo Harper was waiting for me in a booth, juggling screens on his Mac laptop while talking into a wireless headset, one hand darting in and out of an open briefcase on the seat, glancing at papers, jotting notes in a pocket-size journal. He motioned me into the booth, not breaking his multitasking stride. I slid in across from him, reached over the table, and closed his laptop. He clicked off his headset, scanning me with penetrating, dark eyes that didn't miss, the corner of his mouth twitching with what passed as a smile.

"That's called confirmation bias. What you did, closing my laptop. As predictable as the rising sun."

"You're clairvoyant?"

"Not necessary if you know how the mind works. My phone call primed you to dislike me. You didn't want to come here, especially on a miserable night like this, but you came anyway, probably out of a sense of obligation to Simon. Instead of greeting you at the door like the hero he makes you out to be, I'm sitting here making good use of my time. But you see that as further proof that I'm a rude jerk. That's confirmation bias."

"It wasn't just the phone call."

"What else?"

"Kate Scranton sends her regards."

Harper straightened. He still had the wavy hair and square chin. If he still had the pecs they were hidden under a bulky sweater. He was near my height, six feet, though thinner with a long angular face washed out with an indoor pallor earned from a lifetime spent in front of a computer screen. He hadn't shaved for a few days. The salt and pepper growth that gave actors a patina of cool clung to his sallow cheeks, aging him.

"Interesting. A woman who turns down my job offer trumps a man who thinks the only thing you're missing is a cape and a red S on your chest."

I leaned back against the booth. "I'm here but that doesn't mean that Kate's wrong or that Simon is right."

"No, it doesn't. And, I didn't believe Simon anyway." He pointed to a menu. "You want to order?"

I shook my head. "I'm not staying. Tell me about your problem. I'll tell you if I'm interested."

Our server appeared, asking for our order and his tip with a smile, not saying a word. Harper laid his menu on the table, traced his finger down the selections, stopping at the lobster, raised his eyebrows at me, giving me another chance. I shook my head, Harper shrugged at the waiter and the waiter shrugged back, closing the curtain on our pantomime with another smile before leaving.

"Three people, three brains, not a word spoken, a million . . ."

I raised my hand. "I get it. A brain is a terrible thing to waste."

Harper grinned. "I can't help it. The human brain is the greatest evolutionary achievement and the mind, which is what the brain does, goes it one better. Spend some time with me and you'll learn to appreciate the mental organs. We study everything from basic brain anatomy, structure, and chemistry to behavioral disorders, genetic disorders, and anything else having to do with how the brain and the mind work and don't work. Most places that do brain research focus on one or two things. I'm trying to do it all because it's all connected, one neural miracle."

"Including dreams," I said.

"Including dreams and memory. I've got PhDs like Anthony Corliss who specialize in something called lucid dreaming. It's a way of recognizing when you are dreaming and then learning how to control your dreams."

"Can he make dreams come true?"

"Not yet, but he's trying. He's working with Maggie Brennan, another PhD, who's an expert on memory and posttraumatic stress disorder. The brain makes memories, decides which ones to keep and which ones to toss out. Memories, especially traumatic ones, get a workout in our dreams. We're researching whether people can learn to control their nightmares and manage their traumatic memories through lucid dreaming."

Maggie Brennan's name had the nagging familiarity of something I had heard, forgotten, and now wished I hadn't. It would come to me, probably in the middle of the night, waking me up, only to be forgotten again by morning.

"Simon told me that two people who've participated in the project have died."

"Tom Delaney shot himself and Regina Blair fell off

the top ledge of a three-story parking deck that was under construction. Both had responded to an ad we placed for volunteers."

"What did they have to do?"

"Talk to us about their dreams. Fill out questionnaires. Spend a few nights sleeping in our lab wearing an electro-encephalograph skullcap so we can monitor their brain activity while they're dreaming. Learn lucid dreaming techniques and participate in some additional lab studies, brain scans, and group discussions to measure how they respond."

"Doesn't sound too dangerous."

"It isn't, but this is America and when bad things happen, people hire lawyers. The Delaney and Blair families hired Jason Bolt. You ever hear of him?"

"I have. He carries some weight."

"A lot of weight. He calls himself Lightning Bolt."

I laughed. "Nobody does that! He hits that hard?"

"Worse. Lightning never strikes twice. Bolt does. He tagged me for eight figures a few years ago in a shareholder lawsuit. He called to tell me that he's going to sue me, the institute, Anthony Corliss, Maggie Brennan, and their two research assistants."

"What makes him think Delaney's and Blair's deaths have anything to do with the institute?"

"Volunteers are videotaped describing their dreams. Some of them are pretty graphic nightmares. Those are the ones our researchers are particularly interested in studying. Delaney's and Blair's dreams came true."

"How so?"

"Both of them died the way they dreamed they would. Bolt claims he has an expert witness who will testify that lucid dreaming breaks down inhibitions against dangerous behavior and causes people like Delaney and Blair to act out their nightmares."

"I assume the police investigated both deaths. What did they come up with?"

"Delaney was a suicide and Blair was an accident."

"Did the police know about the videotapes?"

"Not the first time around but Bolt stirred things up so they took another look. A detective named Paul McNair asked to see the tapes and we made them available."

I'd worked with McNair on a joint task force a few years ago. He was a clock watcher, putting in his time until retirement. Not someone who'd be anxious to turn an easy case into a tough one.

"What was McNair's take?"

"That Delaney killed himself and that Blair got too close to the edge and fell."

Chapter Five

I nodded, knowing how little use cops, including ones that weren't lazy, have for dreams when we can make our cases with smoking guns, DNA, and confessions. "Did Delaney leave a note?"

"No. McNair said that not everyone who commits suicide leaves a note."

"He's right. About twenty-five percent don't. What was Regina Blair doing on the parking deck?"

"She was an architect for the general contractor for the three-story garage and an adjacent office building. Both were under construction. The police said she was inspecting the top floor of the garage when she slipped and fell."

"Anyone see it happen?"

"Not according to Detective McNair. It happened early on a Sunday morning." He fished McNair's business card out of his briefcase and handed it to me. "He can tell you more about it than I can."

"Where do I fit in?"

"I need to know as much as I can about Delaney and Blair—anything that will help us prove we had nothing to do with their deaths."

"What do you know about them so far?"

"Delaney was thirty-two, lived alone, and was a newspaper distributor for the *Kansas City Star*. Got a Purple Heart doing two tours in Iraq with the National Guard. He was the oldest of three kids. He went to high school at Rockhurst."

"The private Catholic school?"

"Right. He cut a wide swath there. He played football and basketball and he was on the debate team. His parents have established a scholarship there in his honor. Bolt says they're going to contribute anything they get in the lawsuit to the scholarship fund."

"What about Regina Blair?"

"She was thirty-five. She and her husband live up north at Riss Lake. She had a baby last year. They were active in their church and she volunteered for Big Brothers and Sisters. Her husband teaches at Park University."

"A boy scout and a girl scout. Not much chance I'll find anything in their backgrounds that you can use."

"I'm not looking for dirt. I want to know more about them than their credentials for getting into heaven. I want to know why Delaney dreamed about killing himself and what made Blair so afraid of heights. That could help us."

"What if your institute is responsible?"

"Then we'll pay what we owe and fix what's wrong with our project."

"Don't you have lawyers and an insurance company to take care of that?"

"We have a ten-million-dollar deductible and the right to control the investigation and handling of any claim.

I've got the lawyers but I need you for the investigation.
Your title will be director of security. You can start Monday
morning. I'll pay you double what you were making at
the FBI. Your office will be down the hall from mine.
You'll have free rein to go where you want to go and talk
to whomever you want. When this is over, I'd like you to
stay but that's up to you."

Before I could respond, a spasm twisted my head sideways and down, locking my chin against my raised shoulder. I waited for it to pass, time and my body both held
hostage, the cycle repeating twice more in a twisted game
of catch and release.

"I've got a . . ."

"Movement disorder called tics. Simon told me. The
brain can be a real bitch. It's okay."

"You aren't concerned that I'll shake when I should
shoot?"

Harper smiled. "Superman was allergic to kryptonite
and things worked out for him."

He reached into his briefcase again and slid a skinny
black binder onto the table. "These are summaries of
the projects we're working on, plus the names and contact information for the people running each one."

"Why do I need to talk to everyone when this case is
only about the dream project?"

"I want to make certain we don't have problems with
any of the work we're doing, not just the dream project,
and I don't want to broadcast that we may be getting sued
so I told the project directors that I hired you to review
our internal security procedures to make certain our intellectual property is protected. I sent everyone a
memo telling them to cooperate with you."

"I haven't said yes."

"Why wouldn't you? Kate Scranton won't work for me but Simon Alexander will. I'd call that a wash in the who-do-you-listen-to sweepstakes."

"I listen to my friends but I make my own decisions. You might not like that. You don't like people telling you how to do your job. Same goes for me. I start looking for one thing and I may find another you don't want found. You need to be in control and something like this doesn't want to be controlled."

"Open the binder. Read the tabs out loud."

They were organized alphabetically by subject matter. He interrupted me when I got to Alzheimer's.

"Makes tics look like a walk in the park."

"It's not about the work you're doing. I'm sure it's all important."

"Some more important to me than others."

I looked at him, saw how his eyes changed from lively to hot, how his face darkened.

"You? You're what—forty?"

"Forty-one. Six to ten percent of Alzheimer patients are under age sixty-five and that number is only going to go up. A few are younger than fifty and the youngest on record was twenty-nine."

"I don't know what a person your age who has Alzheimer's is supposed to look like, but you act like you're on top of your game."

He held up the small journal he'd been writing in when I arrived. "I try to write everything down in here on my laptop or my iPhone. I even use a Web service called Jott. I call a phone number and record what I want to remember and they send me an e-mail with my verbatim message and, if I want, a text message reminder. Even with all of that, I'm one step away from pinning notes to my sweater and leaving bread crumbs to find my way home. The trouble with memory loss is that you don't remember what you've forgotten until it's too late."

"Who else knows about your condition?"

"For now, no one besides you and my doctors. The institute is only one of my investments. I've got a lot of balls in the air and I don't know how much longer I can keep juggling them."

"I'm sorry."

He flattened his palms on the table, his fingertips arching, hanging on. "People are always sorry but that doesn't change what's happening to you or me. You're going to shake for the rest of your long life but I'm going to spend the rest of my dwindling years disappearing one brain cell, one memory at a time until I won't recognize you or me. The research we're doing might, just might, stop all of that, if not for me, then for someone else, and I'll be damned if I'm going to risk people's lives or the future of the institute. I don't care what I have to do. I thought you would understand that better than anyone."

Harper was right. I had been primed not to like him whether it was because of Kate or his phone call or the rotten weather or the fear of putting myself on the line again, a shaking and shaken man uncertain if I could do more so I could do more, too concerned about myself than fellow travelers like Milo Harper. I closed the binder, tucked it under my arm, and stood.

"I do. I'll see you Monday morning at eight."

Chapter Six

The hooded light over my front door was on when I came home, bathing the snow that had fallen during the day and drifted onto the porch in soft yellow. More light shone through the curtains in the living room that fronted the house and around the edges of the blinds in the bedroom on the east end of the second floor. The bedroom window looked down on the driveway where I was parked.

The lights had been off when I left earlier in the day. I lived alone except for my dog, Ruby, who knew when it was time to eat but not how to flick a switch. Ruby is a cockapoo—half cocker spaniel, half poodle—a breed that dilutes the poodle's high canine IQ with the cocker spaniel's indiscriminate affection, the combination a perfect antiwatch dog. If someone were robbing me, Ruby would help him pack up my stuff.

I sat in the car, studying the front door and windows. No one peeked at me. It had stopped snowing. My headlights bounced off the white powder and ice crystals swirling in the wind like frozen dust mites.

I wondered who had been in my house and if they were still there; the effort stalled when the day caught up to me. No one knows what causes tics. In terms I can understand, there's a short somewhere in my brain's wiring that does more than kick me from the inside out as if something is trying to escape. At times, it blurs my brain, gumming up the neurons and hijacking the synapses, feeling like a burst of fever that slows me down to a crawl. I leaned back against the car seat, squeezing my eyes closed, waiting for the fog to lift, my body shuddering with aftershocks when it did a few minutes later.

I looked at the house again. Nothing had changed. I got out of the car, the cold air picking me up. There were footprints in the snow leading from the curb, through the front yard and to the door. The street was empty.

Lorraine Trent owned the house. She was a biology professor who was spending a year in Africa doing research. She had needed a tenant and I had needed a furnished place to live after my divorce. When I signed the lease, she gave me the only key. I doubted that she had come back eight months ahead of schedule.

The house is in Brookside, a friendly midtown neighborhood with well-kept houses built fifty years or more ago and shops and restaurants you can walk to, including a dime store with its original creaky wood plank floor. For all its charm, Brookside wasn't immune to crime.

Two kinds of thieves leave the front porch light on while they rob a house. The first kind wants the neighbors to think that nothing unusual is going on while they're in the house. Those thieves are smart enough to have transportation and there was none, unless the getaway driver was waiting to be summoned from around the corner. The second kind is too high to think straight, content to get out with whatever he can carry. Either way, I had to assume that the thief was armed.

I would have felt better if my gun was holstered against my back instead of locked in a case on a shelf in my bedroom closet. Both Kansas and Missouri allowed concealed carry and I had a permit. After I left the Bureau, I quit carrying unless I had a reason. Seemed like a good idea at the time. At the moment, it was a bad idea, increasing the odds that I might get shot with my own gun.

Part of being an FBI agent is having the balls to kick in the door even if it's your own door. Another part is having the sense to wait until someone can watch your back when you put your heel to the door jamb. Part of being an ex-FBI agent with a bad case of the jumping beans is missing kicking in doors so much that you decide not to wait for help.

It was my door and I missed it that much. I was standing on my driveway, ankle deep snow seeping into my shoes, calculating the odds that I could take whoever had invaded my house and not liking the numbers. My days were manageable, my nights not so much. I flipped open my cell phone to call the cops, hearing the conversation in my head before I dialed.

"You say the lights are on in your house?"

"Yes, Officer. Over the front door, in the living room, and one of the upstairs bedrooms."

"And you're afraid to go inside your house when the lights are on? Most people, it's the other way around."

I stuck the phone in my pocket, cut through the snow, and stopped at the front door, which was opened a crack, enough that I could hear a man and a woman shouting at each other. Another woman shrieked *he's got a gun!* I slammed my shoulder into the door. My momentum carried me inside, my snow-packed shoes flying out from under me as I slid across the hardwood floor into the bottom of the stairs leading to the second floor.

A woman had been sitting on my landlady's couch, her feet on my landlady's coffee table, eating my popcorn and watching my landlady's television. The images on the screen were frozen, two women and a man struggling over a gun. She'd stopped the action with my landlady's remote control and bolted to her feet.

She looked to be in her early thirties, lean and muscled with light brown curly hair framing a round face, her eyes wide open and curious but not afraid, her arms hanging loose at her sides, a compact light featherweight. She shifted her weight, subtly setting herself for a confrontation. I recognized the automatic response of someone who been trained and under the gun.

"Who the hell are you?" she asked me.

Ruby sprang off the couch and into my lap, planted her front paws on my chest, and licked my face, cleaning my chin and both cheeks.

"I'm Jack Davis. I live here. Who the hell are you?"

"I'm Lucy Trent and this is my house."

"I don't think so. I mean you may be Lucy Trent but this isn't your house. I rented this place from Lorraine Trent."

"She's my stepmother."

I pulled myself off the floor, taking a breath and holding onto the stairway banister.

"She's my landlady."

Another burst of shakes whipped through me.

"Are you okay? Why are you shaking?"

"It's what I do."

"All the time?"

I walked into the living room. Lorraine Trent had

called it the living den, the house not big enough for both a living room and a den. She'd bragged about the new hardwood floors, the fresh paint, and the new appliances that justified the rent she was charging me.

"No. Not all the time."

I was within arm's reach of her but Lucy didn't back up or relax, telling me with a wry smile that she didn't consider a middle-aged man with the shakes to be much of a threat.

"Well that's a relief. I'd hate to put someone on the street who shakes all the time."

Chapter Seven

"Don't be in such a hurry. Follow me," I told her. I kept the lease in the top drawer of a desk in the kitchen. I showed it to her. "Like I said. It's my house for another eight months."

She skimmed it, nodding at the signatures. "My turn."

She led the way to the bedroom that overlooked the driveway. A duffel bag and backpack lay on the bed. She rummaged through the backpack, handing me an envelope. I opened it. Inside was a copy of the deed to the house naming Lucy Trent as the owner.

"Lorraine didn't say anything to me about this."

"Don't feel bad. She didn't say anything to me about you but, then again, we don't talk much. My father left my mother for her when I was ten. Kind of chilled the whole stepmother-stepdaughter bonding thing. Dad's will provided she could live in the house for five years after he died. Then the house went to me. The five years was up four months ago. I wasn't ready to move back until now."

"She said she was a biologist, that she was going to Africa to do research for a year."

"With luck, she'll lose her passport."

I sat on the bed, another tremor rippling through me. My ex-wife, Joy, and I bought a house in the suburbs when the FBI transferred me to Kansas City. We sold it when we got divorced, the proceeds paying our debts and our lawyers and putting a small stake in both our pockets. Either of us could have left, picked a place without the raw memories of our failed marriage and dead children, but Kansas City was a good place to heal. The pace was easy, the people friendly. The city was comfortable and comforting, like a soft sweatshirt on a cool day.

The house I'd rented was part of that fabric. The fireplace, the overstuffed furniture, and the trees that towered over the front and back, home to enough birds and squirrels for Ruby to chase until she was exhausted, were all part of the balm.

"I'll buy it. The house, I mean. Plus the furniture, everything."

She laughed. "If you could afford that, you wouldn't be renting."

Ruby found us, first jumping on Lucy who was standing in the middle of the room, then leaping onto the bed, sticking her nose in my face.

"That doesn't sound like no. It sounds like how much."

She put her hands on her hips. "All it sounds like is that I'm not going to kick you out tonight."

"Suppose I come up with enough money to make you an offer to sell?"

"I have a rule, Jack. I only deal with what's in front of me."

"Fair enough."

My cell phone rang. I flipped it open and recognized the voice.

"Jack, it's Ammara Iverson."

Ammara had been one of my agents when I ran the Violent Crimes Squad in the FBI's Kansas City office. Most of my Bureau friendships had faded once the shared work that held them together ended. Ammara was different. Though we hadn't seen each other very often, the bond was still there.

"Hey, it's great to hear your voice. What's up?"

"You doing anything?"

"Just trying to decide whether to buy a house or get evicted from it. Why?"

"I've got a dead man wants to talk to you."

The dead man was what my squad called the scene of a homicide, the scene telling us what the victim couldn't. Ammara knew that I trusted the dead man more than anyone or anything but that didn't explain why she was calling me.

"Tell the dead man I'm retired."

"You might wish you weren't when you talk to this one. You better get over here." She hung up after giving me the address and directions.

The FBI had rules for everything including the handling of crime scenes. Preserving the integrity of the physical evidence was critical to solving a crime and getting a conviction. Access to the scene was tightly controlled. Ex-FBI agents didn't qualify. Whatever her reasons, Ammara wanted me inside the yellow tape.

Lucy watched me throughout my brief conversation, making no pretense of not listening.

"Who's the dead man?"

"Inside joke. I've got to go meet a friend of mine."

"What are you retired from?"

"The FBI."

"Your friend with the FBI?"

"For someone who's throwing me out of my house, you ask a lot of questions."

"Best way I know to learn."

"Find another teacher."

I stood for an instant before muscle contractions jack-knifed my head to my knees. I reached for something to hold onto, finding Lucy's arm, her steady grip stabilizing me.

"I'll drive," she said. "You're in no shape."

Some lessons are forced on me. One of them is accepting help when I didn't have a choice. I was in worse condition than the snow-packed streets. If Ammara needed me, my first concern was getting there, not who drove. The contractions released me.

"Okay, let's go."

Chapter Eight

Kansas City covers a lot of territory from the airport north of the Missouri River, to the NASCAR track across the state line in western Wyandotte County, Kansas, to the Truman Sports Complex in eastern Jackson County, Missouri. There are better than forty municipalities spread over five counties and two states, enough for everyone to claim a fiefdom yet many will tell a stranger that they live in Kansas City rather than Raytown, Prairie Village, Independence, or Overland Park.

The southern reaches aren't identified with an iconic landmark. On the Kansas side, they are defined by large, new, and expensive rooftops sheltering more per capita disposable income than many of the country's zip codes, extending beyond the eye's reach much as prairie grasses must have in another time. The rooftops on the Missouri side are smaller, older, and modest, covering the working middle class. The address Ammara gave me was for one of these.

Despite its reach, you could drive from one edge of

the metropolitan area to the other in forty-five minutes, sixty in traffic. Snow changed that. The storm had singled out midtown where six inches had fallen. As we crept south, the accumulation was less, the streets more navigable. The slow drive gave my body time to stuff the clown back into the jack-in-the-box. My breathing eased, my muscles relaxed, my head cleared. I was back in control.

Lucy limited her questions to the directions Ammara had given me. I watched her as she drove, turning into a skid when ice grabbed the tires, grinning as we spun. I wondered how she had earned her swagger. She carried herself like someone who came from my world, someone who was trained for the perpetual scrum between the good guys and the bad guys, someone who knew the dead man.

Uniformed cops had established a perimeter, closing off traffic at both ends of the block. They let us through after checking with Ammara. Lucy pulled into a driveway across the street and opened her door.

"Stay in the car," I told her. She held onto the door handle, one foot on the pavement, sizing me up again, her eyes hard, her mouth firm, the look letting me know that she'd damn well go if she wanted. "Listen, I appreciate that you drove. But you have to wait here. This isn't your show."

She eased back and smiled. "You're right. Sorry."

"Habit?"

"Yeah."

"Thought so."

The house sat back from the curb on a slight rise, the front door shrouded by a low-pitched roof jutting over a deep set front porch, most of which was screened in, an irregular wall of bushes and stunted trees, leafless in winter, dividing the far property line from the neighbor to the west. Stout pillars of inlaid Missouri limestone supported both front corners. Two dormers poked out of the roof, signaling an attic long ago converted to bedrooms.

A walkway led from the driveway across the middle of the lawn, three steps completing the journey to the narrow front door. The storm had petered out by the time it reached this part of the city, dusting old snow with a sprinkling of new. Patches of dark ice hid on the walk, waiting patiently for hurried, careless feet.

Ammara was waiting for me on the front porch, standing next to another uniformed cop in charge of the crime scene sign-in sheet taped onto the front door. Her black leather jacket was open, her FBI shield hanging on a chain around her neck, a green turtleneck sweater highlighting her ebony skin. She had the height, reach, and power to have been an All American volleyball player in college, traits she'd used to her advantage during ten years with the Bureau, the last three in Kansas City.

I hadn't seen her since Wendy's funeral. She hugged me long and hard that day, skipping the platitudes that time healed all wounds and that heaven was a better place and that Wendy was finally at peace because we both knew they were total bullshit. That day was personal. Today was business and we both knew the difference.

"Thanks for coming, Jack."

"You made it sound irresistible. What do you got?"

"Walter Enoch. Fifty-four years old. Worked for the post office as a mail carrier."

FBI agents, cops, DEA, it didn't matter, we all liked to tell stories. There was no fun in cutting to the chase whether the news was good or bad so there was no point in pushing her.

"What happened to him?"

"He died. Probably yesterday, probably of natural causes but we won't know for certain until we get the autopsy results."

"So why the yellow tape and why did you call me?"

"Come inside."

Mail was stacked like cord wood in the entry hall. More stacks narrowed the passage on the stairs to the second floor.

"The guy was a mail carrier but he never opened his mail?" I asked.

"No. The guy was a mail carrier who stole other people's mail, which he didn't open. It'll take a month or more to sort through all of it, figure out what to throw away and what to try to deliver. Some of this stuff goes back years. A whole lot of people are going to find out whether better late than never really is better. This is just part of it."

We walked into the dining room. The table was buried under a mountain of magazines and catalogs. Foothills made of unopened bills, checks, coupons, sweepstakes, and credit card offers spread from the dining room into the kitchen. Unread love letters, thank-you notes, demands, denials, rejections, acceptances, rants, raves, promises, apologies, and more were piled in silent drifts against windowsills, yellowed and coated with dust.

More mail sealed off bookcases, a fireplace, and a television in the den. The ceiling light was yellow and faint, the walls paneled with dark pine.

Walter Enoch's body, rank with the rotten, gaseous odor of decomposition, was slumped in a recliner upholstered in a blue and red tartan plaid shoved against one wall. His gray, bloodless face was hairless, rutted and ribbed with flesh bunched into ridges around his eyes, stretched thin around his mouth, his cheeks pocked and mottled, the residue of severe burns. A large plastic bin with U.S. POSTAL SERVICE stenciled on the sides sat next to the chair.

"Who found him?" I asked.

"His supervisor came to check on him when he didn't show up for work. When no one answered, he called the cops. They forced the door and the supervisor identified the body. There was no sign of foul play but KCPD treated it as a crime scene because of the stolen mail. That makes it federal so they called the Bureau. I was the first agent on the scene and I found this in his lap."

She handed me a plastic evidence bag containing an empty square-shaped pink envelope, the kind that would be used for a greeting card or personal stationery. It was addressed to me at the house I had lived in before the divorce, the handwriting so familiar it hurt. A postal sticker forwarding it to my new address was pasted beneath the old one. A burst of shakes bolted from my belly to my breast, my question stumbling out of my mouth.

"What was inside the envelope?"

"I don't know. It was empty when I found it. The only name in the return address is the initials MG. Any idea whose initials they are?"

I took a deep breath. "Yeah. MG stands for Monkey Girl. It was a nickname I gave Wendy when she was little. She had a stuffed animal, a monkey that she never let go of. She called it Monkey Girl too. The handwriting is hers."

I didn't tell her that Wendy kept Monkey Girl until the day she died or that I had claimed it as my inheritance. I had pictures of Wendy growing up taken at birthday parties, holidays, and for no reason at all. They chronicled her life, visual confirmation of moments in time. Monkey Girl was more than that. Its fake fur and rubber face was a link between the two of us, an indelible reminder of silly names and games, happy times and infinite possibilities.

"Then take a look at the postmark."

The postmark was hard to read because the ink was smeared and the plastic bag made it look like it was underwater. I held it close, angled it in the light and stopped breathing. The envelope and whatever had been inside it had been mailed to me from New York City a month ago, ten months after I buried my daughter.

"You said that the envelope was empty when you found it."

"And, it was in Enoch's lap."

"Maybe he was reading whatever was inside the envelope when he died," I said.

"Then we should have found it on him or next to him and we didn't. We haven't been through everything in the house, but we didn't find anything on the surface of this mess that matches up with the envelope. And none of the rest of the stolen mail has been opened."

I looked at Ammara, now understanding why she had called me. An empty envelope addressed to me by my deceased daughter was cause enough for an investigation. Finding it in the lap of a dead man whose job was to deliver the mail and whose hobby was stealing the mail but not opening it was a bonanza of coincidences. I hated coincidences. They deceived you with their convenient explanations for things that weren't so easily understood.

"You think someone took whatever was in the envelope?" I asked.

"What do you think?"

I surveyed the mail in the den, thought about the unopened stacks and piles I'd seen in the rest of the house.

"I think that makes the most sense based on what we see so far."

"So do I. If we're right, whoever took your mail could have been here when Walter died."

I nodded. "Most people would have tried to help him, called an ambulance, done something."

"Unless they wanted Enoch to die," Lucy Trent said.

Chapter Nine

Ammara and I were facing Enoch's body, our backs to Lucy, unaware she was watching and listening. We turned around. She was standing in the entryway from the dining room to the den, one hand in her coat pocket, the other at her side, palming her cell phone, rotating it in a slow arc, the cell phone camera capturing the scene with faint whirrs and clicks. I glanced at Ammara to see whether she realized what Lucy was doing but her eyes were fixed over Lucy's shoulder, searching for the soon-to-be-demoted street cop that let Lucy past the yellow tape.

"There's always that," I said, wondering why Lucy was photographing the scene and why my instincts told me not to bust her.

"I got bored waiting for you in the car," Lucy said.

"Who's she and what's she doing in the middle of my dead man?" Ammara asked me.

"It's complicated," I said.

"Not really," Lucy said as she slipped her phone into

the purse slung over her shoulder. "I'm Lucy Trent. I own the house where Jack lives until I kick him out, which could happen sooner rather than later the way things are going. I drove him out here because he was shaking too badly to do it himself. That's not so complicated."

"This is a crime scene," Ammara told her. "Authorized personnel only and you aren't authorized."

Lucy smiled and nodded. "So that's what the dead man means. Crime scene. I like it."

Ammara took two steps toward Lucy. I cut her off, my back to Lucy again. "It's okay."

Ammara leaned in toward me, her voice hard but too quiet for Lucy to hear us. "What do you mean it's okay? This is my scene, not yours. Your invitation didn't include a date."

"Understood," I said, my voice matching hers. "I'll handle it."

"Good. Do it now. I don't want your landlady polluting my crime scene."

I raised my hands in surrender. "No problem. One thing. I'd appreciate it if you'd keep me in the loop."

She took a deep breath. "You know the rules, Jack. You're a civilian. I'll tell you as much as I can without compromising the investigation."

"Which means you think that whatever was in that envelope has something to do with the money the Bureau says Wendy stole. You were at her funeral. You saw the date on the postmark. What? You think she rose from the dead and took the bus to New York so she could mail a letter to me confessing to being a thief and telling me where she hid the money?"

"You can make it sound crazy, Jack, but it's what you

taught me. Collect the evidence. Follow where it leads. Let someone else higher up the food chain decide what to do with it."

We stared at each other, her face impassive, our friendship trumped by the job, another thing I had taught her. I nodded, conceding the moment.

"Let's go," I told Lucy.

We gave Walter Enoch's gargoyle death mask a last look.

"He was somebody's nightmare," Lucy said. "Glad he wasn't mine."

"What was that about?" she asked me when we were back in the car.

"The dead guy was a mailman who stole mail instead of delivering it."

"What's that got to do with you?"

"He stole my mail—at least one letter anyway. The envelope was found on his body but it was empty. Ammara Iverson, the agent you pissed off, thought I might know what was in it."

"Did you?"

Weak light filtered through the car as we passed strip centers, street lamps and oncoming traffic, shadows flickering across her face like a grainy silent movie. The effect was jarring, fogging my brain.

I was used to the visual triggers that could unleash spasms or inexplicably weaken my legs, sending me to the floor unless I grabbed on to someone or something. Two hours at the movies watching the latest action flick or five minutes in the florescent lighting aisle at Lowe's was a ticket to the funhouse. I'd have to add a black and white strobe light show to my list of things to avoid in the twenty-third hour of a day when my daughter speaks to me from the grave. I closed my eyes. Lucy let her question drop.

I declined the arm she offered me when we got home, using the banister to steady myself on the stairs going up to my bedroom. Ruby followed behind me, scratching the cushion of the easy chair where she slept, curling up without complaining that I was out late and without asking questions I didn't want to answer.

The dog had her bedtime routine and I had mine. One of the last things I did was check my gun even on days when I never took it out of its case. Guns are one of the few things it pays to be obsessive about because they do not forgive mistakes. Mine was always loaded, the safety always on, the case in the corner of the eye-level shelf in my bedroom closet, one end against the wall, the other flush against a stack of books laid flat with the spines facing out that I promised myself I would read before I die. I wedged the gun against the books, making it impossible to retrieve the gun case without disturbing the books. Wendy's stuffed animal, Monkey Girl, claimed the other end of the shelf.

After checking the gun and putting it away, I always restored the alignment of the books, the precision reassuring me that no one else had touched my gun. It was a safety habit I'd developed when my kids were young and curious about a father they sometimes confused with heroes on TV and in the movies who ate bad guys for breakfast and spit them out with the bullets they caught in their teeth.

The second book from the bottom, a Doris Kearns Goodwin biography of Lincoln, was angled away from the ones above and below. The angled book was a small thing, something I may have dismissed in my fatigued state, except for the gun case. It too was an inch out of place, the dust outline marking its spot on the shelf a testament to my housekeeping skills.

I opened the case, the smell of gun oil reassuring and familiar. The magazine of my Glock 23 was full, the safety on; the barrel smooth and polished as if I had just cleaned it. Except that I hadn't. Not since I'd last fired it two weeks ago at the Bullet Hole shooting range. Since then, I'd checked it every night, not concerned that I'd left smudged fingerprints all over it.

I put the gun away, unanswered questions worming their way into my head like snatches of song lyrics that burrow in your brain and won't stop playing. Lucy Trent was the only person who could have been in my closet. What was she doing with my gun? Why did she ignore my instruction to stay in the car? Why did she take pictures of the crime scene at Walter Enoch's house? And, as long as I was making a list of things to keep me awake, how did she get into the house when I was the only one with a key? I lay in bed in the dark as a final flurry of shakes had the last word, forcing me to put these questions off until tomorrow.

Maggie Brennan's name tugged at me in the halfway house between consciousness and sleep. I heard a voice say her name, calling her unbelievable. It was Tom Goodell, a retired sheriff from Johnson County, one of the beer-drinking cold case crew. He'd presented his case at lunch one day last year. It was about a couple that was murdered in their sleep and the daughter that survived. Though I couldn't summon the details, I was glad to have solved the puzzle of her name. Even if she weren't the same Maggie Brennan, I'd at least have an icebreaker to use when I met her.

My last waking thoughts turned, as they did most

nights, to my lost children: Kevin, dead at the hand of a predator whose last and only decent act had been to blow his brains out, and Wendy, whose drug overdose had been a long-time-coming self-inflicted death. After all these years, my memories of Kevin were a comfortable touchstone from a better time when nothing seemed out of reach. My memories of Wendy, always hovering behind my eyes, were a raw reminder of how I had failed her.

Tonight, Walter Enoch's warped face was the last one I saw, whether he died of causes natural or felonious, why he was holding Wendy's envelope when he died, and what had happened to the envelope's contents were the last unanswered questions of a too long day.

I'd spent my life answering questions such as these, chipping away at the mystery of murder. The one thing I had learned was that the real mystery was not about who lived and who died or even who did it. It was about how we lived, why we died, and what difference we made.

Chapter Ten

Lucy's purse was on the kitchen table when I wandered in the next morning, bleary-eyed, blinding sun glancing off the snow in the backyard, ripples of liquid light washing over the windows. A bag of fresh bagels stood next to her purse. The binder Milo Harper gave me was next to the bag, spread open, poppy seeds trailing across a page titled *Executive Dysfunction Using Behavioral Assessment of the Dysexecutive Syndrome in Parkinson's Disease.* Reading it made my hair hurt.

Ruby went outside through the doggie door from the kitchen to the backyard, excavating snow and chasing latent scents and stray birds. I watched her for a few minutes then walked to the foot of the stairs, listening for Lucy, running water rattling in the pipes telling me she was in the shower. I opened the front door. She had shoveled the walk and the driveway, leaving only the packed tracks the car had made the night before, the car now parked on the street, steam rising off the still-warm hood.

It was seven thirty-five and Lucy had already accomplished more than I probably would the rest of the day. I went back to the kitchen, bit into a bagel, and stared at her purse, last night's questions demanding answers, glad that I didn't need a warrant to get them. I emptied her purse onto the table.

She had a Maryland driver's license, the address in Gaithersburg. Her birthday was April 10, thirty-two years ago. She was five-seven, a hundred and twenty pounds, the photo on the license capturing her in one of those is-it-a-smile-or-is-it-gas grimaces.

I found a library card, a Costco card, a photograph of an older couple holding hands, the woman a future image of her, and four twenties, two fives, and a one. There was a receipt from a Starbuck's at Baltimore-Washington International Airport dated yesterday, a pack of Stride chewing gum, a pen, an assortment of other odds and ends, and a single key on a steel ring.

Looking around the kitchen, I found my keys hanging on a hook next to the light switch. The key in Lucy's purse matched my key to the house. The finish on mine was dull from years of use while her key was shiny. I ran my fingers across the teeth, examining my skin for any loose metal shavings from a newly cut key, perhaps made at the drugstore in Brookside that was next to the bagel shop, opened at six A.M. and had a self-service key machine but there were none.

"Find what you were looking for?" Lucy asked.

It was the day after Wendy's fifteenth birthday. She was on probation for a minor in possession charge and had been out all night, breaking her curfew and her probation. Her purse was stashed under a pile of dirty clothes on the floor in her bed-

room. I waited until she was in the shower to go through it, finding three joints in a plastic bag.

"Find what you were looking for?" my daughter asked.

She was wrapped in a towel, hands on her hips, the bathroom door across the hall open, the shower running.

"Where'd you get the dope?"

"You're treating me like a criminal. How do you think that makes me feel?"

"Ashamed and right."

I didn't know how to be both a cop and a father. We had that conversation too many times to count as she migrated between rehab, school, and halfway houses and back to her mother and me.

"I said, did you find what you were looking for?" Lucy repeated.

"Where'd you get this key?" I asked Lucy.

Dressed in jeans and a turtleneck, her hair damp and her eyes on fire, she snatched the key from my hand, scooped everything else back into her purse, and jammed it under her arm.

"From my father. He sent it to me when he knew he was dying. Now get out of my house."

She wasn't Wendy. I was embarrassed but not ashamed at being caught, my gut telling me that I could still be right.

"Get a lawyer. What were you doing snooping around in my bedroom?"

"I don't know what you're talking about."

She didn't look away and her cheeks didn't turn red but she swallowed hard and blinked like I'd slapped her.

"You're sloppy. You didn't straighten the books after

you opened my gun case and you wiped the gun down. You should have left it the way you found it."

She squared her shoulders, arms tight across her chest. "It's my house. I'm entitled to know who's living in it."

"Why were you taking pictures last night?"

She bit the inside of her mouth. "I didn't think you noticed."

"You're lucky I did and Ammara Iverson didn't. She would have ground you and your cell phone under her boot if she'd caught you."

"But she didn't. And I knew you wouldn't bust me." Her aggravation gave way to a satisfied smile that spread across her face.

"How did you know that?"

"An ex-FBI agent gets called out to a crime scene. There's got to be a reason. Odds are the feds won't tell you everything even if they want your help. That's the way you guys roll. I figured you'd want to know why and that the pictures might help. I downloaded them to my computer. Give me your e-mail address and I'll send them to you."

I studied her, coming up with more questions than answers, then tore a corner off the bagel bag and scribbled my e-mail address on it. She grinned again and stuffed it in her pocket.

"Why take a chance like that to help someone you don't know and who you're kicking out of your house?"

"I don't have a job and I can use the rent money. Besides, I wasn't going to kick you out until I caught you going through my purse. How's that supposed to make me feel?"

Wendy's voice echoed in my head. Lucy's anger was genuine and justified and her read of last night's situation was on the money. The combination was disarming.

"You're not the only one who wants to know who they're sharing a roof with. You show up out of nowhere. I've got questions too."

She pulled a chair away from the table, sat, and stretched her long legs out. "Like what?"

"Like who are you? You act like you've been on the job. What's your story?"

"Montgomery County Maryland Sheriff's Department. I was a deputy for five years."

"Why'd you quit?"

She stood, folded her arms across her chest, and aimed her chin at me. "They're real picky. They make you quit when they send you to prison."

When she bounced off the couch the night before, loose, ready, and confident, I thought that she'd been on the job. Her eagerness to go behind the yellow tape and her refusal to be intimidated by Ammara confirmed it. I saw those things because they were familiar and because it was all she showed me until now. Her eyes narrowed, hard and cold, into a prison yard stare, daring me to push.

"For what?"

"Stealing diamonds, loose stones I found lying on the floor next to a dead body. Victim was a jewelry salesman. Put up enough of a fight to get killed. I got there first. Stuff was scattered all over the room. I didn't think anyone would notice if a few rocks stayed lost."

"But somebody noticed."

"Somebody usually does. The employer had a detailed inventory. We caught the perp the same night before he had a chance to unload any of it. Took all of twelve hours before it got back to me."

"How long were you gone?"

"Thirty-eight months at the Jessup Correctional Facility for Women. Another six months in a halfway house in Bethesda. Plus, I did another year of supervision, peeing in a cup and looking for someone who'd hire an ex-cop, ex-con thief. Not a lot of demand for that. Got my full release last week and decided to come home, start over."

"Why'd you do it? You don't look the type."

"What's the type supposed to look like? One thing I learned on the job and in the joint is that the only thing you need to screw up is a pulse. I was there. The diamonds were there. I knew it was wrong. I knew what I was risking. And then I picked up the stones and got a rush that shut down every rational cell in my brain. It was easy. Next thing I knew, the scene was swarming with deputies and the rocks were burning a hole in my pocket."

"So now what?"

She shrugged. "They say that America is the land of second chances. All I want is mine."

It was an all too familiar refrain that confused need and hope for commitment and effort.

"What happens when that second chance turns out to be another easy score and you want the rush more than the chance?"

The light drained out of her eyes, her mouth quivering. "That's what scares the hell out of me."

Chapter Eleven

The pictures Lucy took at Walter Enoch's house testified to the limits of surreptitious cell phone photography. They were off-centered, grainy, and focused like the camera's eye was half-opened. Enoch's body was recognizable but the pictures showed little else of interest. I put that case aside for the one I'd been hired for.

The police reports on Delaney's and Blair's deaths would be the best source of information about how they died. Despite my misgivings about Harper, I was glad for the chance to do what I knew how to do and there was no reason to wait until Monday to get started. I found the business card for Detective Paul McNair that Milo Harper had given me. He answered on the third ring.

"Homicide. McNair."

It was Saturday afternoon, not a prize shift. McNair sounded distracted. I heard a basketball broadcast in the background, probably a radio on his desk.

"It's Jack Davis. I don't know if you remember, but

we worked a joint task force a few years back. I was with the FBI."

The radio broadcast faded but McNair didn't perk up. "Yeah. Bunch of meth labs out in eastern Jackson County. Couple of crank heads shot each other up."

"Right. Been a while. How you doing?"

"How you think I'm doing? I'm in here jacking my meat on a Saturday afternoon instead of being home watching Kansas kick Missouri's ass up and down the court."

"That's why you get the middle money."

"You got that right. What can I do you for?"

"I'm retired from the Bureau. Doing some private work. I'd like to get a look at the reports on a couple of incidents you investigated."

"Depends. Which incidents?"

"Tom Delaney and Regina Blair."

"Yeah. I remember them. Delaney, he blew his brains out and the Blair chick, she fell off a goddamn parking garage, of all the fucking stupid ways to buy it."

"Those are the ones."

"You working for Milo Harper or Jason Bolt?"

"Milo Harper. That a problem?"

"Nah. That ambulance chaser has taken more money out of here on false arrest and excessive force cases than the taxpayers put in. I'll be here all afternoon unless I get a better offer, like my proctologist had a cancellation."

Kansas City's police headquarters was at Eleventh and Locust on the east side of downtown, a limestone tower built during the Depression. Homicide was on the third floor, the detective's desks arranged back to back in a bullpen, higher ranks in private offices along the wall. McNair was alone, everyone else on duty finding a reason to be out.

He had at least twenty years on the job, his face more jowls than cheeks and chin, his neck and hair faint memories. He was attacking a slab of ribs, ignoring the sauce that speckled his shirt, and listening to the second half of the basketball game between Kansas and Missouri. He was right about one thing. The Jayhawks were putting another beating on the Tigers.

"Hey, Davis," he said, wiping his hands on his pants. "Been a while."

"A few years."

"This is what I got." He pointed to two folders lying on the vacant desk that backed up to his. "Make yourself at home."

I hadn't recovered from the day before. I could feel the shakes getting ready to bust out like runners down in the blocks, waiting for the starter's gun, and I didn't want them to run their relays in front of McNair.

"Okay if I make copies? That way I can get out of your hair."

"Like I got any left," he said, patting his dome. "Knock yourself out. Copy machine is down the hall."

I loaded Regina Blair's file into the copier, skimming the Delaney report while I waited. Delaney lived in an apartment building at Thirty-eighth and Wyandotte. A neighbor reported a bad odor. The manager recognized the smell and called the cops.

Delaney's body was found slumped in a chair. He didn't leave a suicide note.

The gun was on the floor. Most people who shoot themselves hold on to the gun.

The autopsy report noted that the bullet's angle of

entry was downward. Most people who shoot themselves in the temple aim level or up.

The entry wound was in Delaney's left temple. Delaney was right handed. A right-handed person was much more likely to shoot himself in the right temple than the left. Delaney would have had to turn his head all the way to the right to expose his left temple to the gun. Killing yourself is hard enough without adding a gymnastic degree of difficulty.

Photographs showed Delaney's body in the chair, the location of the gun on the floor, and close-ups of the wound. There was also a series of photographs of his apartment.

The entry wound was described as a hole with a compact area of stippling, a surrounding area of charring, and a bright red hue to the wounded tissues. Based on that, the coroner concluded that the muzzle was less than six inches from the victim when the gun was fired. Most suicide wounds are contact wounds, muzzle pressed against the temple. The distance wasn't typical of suicide but was more likely if Delaney had turned his head to the right and stretched his right hand around to the left side of his head, which could also explain the downward angle of the entry wound. The question was why he would go to such trouble.

Delaney's fingerprints were found on the gun, a Beretta 92F .9mm pistol registered in his name. It had a ten-shot magazine that had been loaded with jacketed rounds. The gun and the ammunition were nothing fancy; typical of what someone would buy off the shelf for home and personal protection.

There were also two unidentified partial prints, one on the handle and one on the barrel. They were smudged enough that there were no clear ridges or whorls, raising the possibility that they had been made by someone wearing a latex glove. The only thing for certain was that these prints didn't rule out anyone or anything.

Powder burns were found on Delaney's right hand, confirming that he was holding the gun when it was fired. Two rounds were missing from the magazine. Only one bullet was recovered from Delaney's body. The missing round was not recovered or accounted for, and Claire Wilson, the investigating officer, concluded that the gun's magazine must not have been full when Delaney fired the gun.

The neighbor who reported the smell coming from Delaney's apartment and the building manager were the only people interviewed and their statements did not expand on the basic facts. Neither knew Delaney and had not seen him in the days prior to his death.

McNair's supplemental report described his meeting with Milo Harper and his review of Delaney's dream video. McNair wrote that the video in which Delaney talked of killing himself confirmed the coroner's determination of suicide and that there was no evidence to justify further investigation.

Milo Harper was worried about being liable for Delaney's suicide but another possibility jumped off these pages even though it wasn't there in writing. Delaney may not have committed suicide. He may have been murdered.

Someone wearing latex gloves could have shot Delaney, then put the gun in his hand and pulled the trigger a second time, firing the gun into something to muffle the sound and then recovering the second bullet to make it appear that Delaney killed himself. The Beretta and the jacketed ammunition would do the job.

That would account for the gun being on the floor, the absence of a suicide note, the downward angle of the entry wound, the wound being on Delaney's left temple rather than the right, the distance of the muzzle from Delaney's temple, the questionable partial fingerprints, and the missing round from the magazine. The combination was enough to raise questions.

The file on Regina Blair was thin, devoid of anything that raised a homicide red flag. A homeless man found her body early on a Sunday morning in an alley between an unfinished parking garage and adjoining office building under construction on the northeast corner of downtown. Cause of death was massive head wounds from the fall. She was wearing jeans, a sweatshirt, and a down parka. A leather folio embossed with her name and containing architectural drawings was found on the partially enclosed top level of the garage three stories above where her body was discovered.

The coroner ruled that her death was an accident caused when she came too close to the edge of the uncovered portion of the garage's third level that was not protected by a guardrail and somehow lost her balance. He noted that it had sleeted during the night and that the exposed concrete surface was wet and slick with traces of ice.

No other witnesses were identified in the report signed by Detective Matt Culpepper. McNair's supplemental report after his meeting with Harper was also brief, noting that Blair admitted in her dream video that she was afraid of heights and that she feared she would one day fall to her death, adding that nothing in the video suggested her death was not an accident.

The photographs showed her body where it was found, views from the ground to the upper deck and from the upper deck to the ground and the area from which Blair fell.

I finished copying both files and made my way back to McNair's desk.

"I don't see any witness statements in Delaney's file besides the neighbor's and the building manager's," I said to McNair.

McNair wiped sauce off his chin. "That's cause there weren't any other witnesses."

"No one heard a gunshot?"

"Uniforms knocked on some doors. Nobody heard nothing."

"What about Delaney's family? Had he threatened suicide before? Was he depressed?"

"His parents said he'd been treated for depression since he got back from his tours of duty in Iraq. I watched that goofy video he made for Harper's people. All the guy talked about was killing himself. Finally got around to doing it."

"Any chance it wasn't suicide?"

"What you mean? You think someone killed him?"

I gave him my take. "Any reason someone would have wanted to kill him?"

McNair shrugged. "Delaney was a newspaper distributor for the *Kansas City Star* which meant he worked middle of the night until mid-morning. Only people mad at him are the ones who didn't get their paper on time. Who's gonna want to kill him? Look," he said, hunching over his desk, "the guy offed himself. That's what the coroner's report says. That's what he dreamed of doing. End of story."

"What about Regina Blair?"

"Dizzy bitch. She's the goddamn architect on this building, which includes the parking garage, and she's scared of heights. So what's she doing standing on the edge three stories up, especially when the concrete was slippery as goose shit. You tell me that? OSHA fined her firm a thousand bucks for not putting up barriers, like it was their fault she was an idiot. Load of crap, you ask me."

"Any chance hers wasn't an accident?"

"Not unless she jumped and she didn't leave a note."

"Neither did Delaney. There are no witness statements in her file either. Did your uniforms bother to knock on any doors on this one?"

McNair swept the remains of the ribs into his wastebasket and turned the volume down on his radio. He stood, planted his palms on his desk, and hung his head, smiling the thin, tight-lipped smile of the trod upon, then turned on me.

"Listen, hotshot, these weren't my cases. I got them when Jason Bolt called the chief and told him to reopen the cases or get sued. The chief promised he'd have someone take another look so I took another look and I didn't see anything new because there wasn't anything new to see."

"You didn't think it unusual that Delaney and Blair both died the exact same way they dreamed they would within a month of one another and that both were participants in this dream project?"

"What? Bolt wants to collect from your boss on these cases and you want to turn them into murder so he don't have to pay? The hell with both of you! Those two had death wishes and they made their wishes come true. You tell me what you would do if you were in my shoes, someone tells you a cockamamie story like that."

"I think I'd ask some more questions, knock on some more doors, and do the job right."

McNair straightened, yanking his pants over his belly.

"I showed you these files as a professional courtesy and all you can do is bust my chops. Delaney was depressed and shot himself. Blair was stupid and fell off the edge of a concrete slab three stories up where she had no business being on account of there was no safety barrier and she was afraid of heights. That's not just me talking. That's what the prosecuting attorney and the coroner said. You want to turn that into murder, be my guest but do it on your time. Now get the fuck out of here!"

Chapter Twelve

My ex-wife, Joy, divorced me after twenty-eight years of marriage. I didn't blame her. When our young son, Kevin, was murdered, she anesthetized her pain with booze and I buried mine with work, each of us blaming the other for our daughter Wendy's problems. Twenty-plus years after Kevin died, she came out of her fog and realized that it was time for both of us to move on. I didn't argue. We'd done enough of that.

Some people keep the war going after they split up. Joy and I went the other way. At first, she blamed me for what happened to Wendy, but in time she let that go too, shouldering more of the responsibility than was right. We had what I called an easy peace, both of us reconciled to what we had had and what we had lost.

I met Kate Scranton while I was married, lying to myself that my crush on her was merely the admiration of one professional for another. She was a forensic psychologist and jury consultant, blessed or cursed depending on the moment, with a unique ability to diagnose involuntary microfacial expressions that she claimed were the true windows into our hearts, minds, and souls. Together with her father, Henry, and ex-husband, Alan, both also psychologists, she had built a successful jury consulting practice, reading jurors with uncanny accuracy.

I justified our long lunches as networking, denying Joy's allegations that I was cheating even though our marriage had been dead by any definition of intimacy for a long time. I didn't know what an emotional affair was until Wendy called me on it.

Kate gave me a second chance after the divorce. She was ten years younger, a difference that peeled years off me without aging her. Tall and slender with shimmering black hair and blue eyes to get lost in, she had the sleek, confident beauty that caught other men's stares but stopped my heart. That she wanted me was an enduring mystery I didn't try to solve.

Reality chilled our fantasy of love lost and found. There were reasons we were both divorced. She could be unyielding and just because my body did contortions didn't mean that I was flexible. She could read me when I didn't want to be read and, more to the point, she couldn't help it.

Her teenage son, Brian, was struggling to find his place in a world of divided loyalties where I was one more competitor for his mother's affection. Alan wanted her back and Henry was rooting for him. She didn't want to leave their firm, didn't want to encourage Alan, and didn't want to alienate him for fear of how that would affect Brian. Both told her I was a bad bet.

She said that I cared too much whether people thought my movement disorder was real or bad enough to cost me my career since I didn't shake all the time or whether people thought it was all in my head, making me a crazy freak instead of just a freak. I worried that my world was too small for her, that she would come to resent that I couldn't do all the things that she was used to doing and enjoyed, the travel, the nights out at the theater, the symphony, or the ball park. We weren't there yet, she said, and besides, it was her life and that decision was up to her.

We navigated our way around these land mines, stepping on a few, staying together because what we had was so much better than what we'd come from and we knew too well what it was like to be alone, both of us struggling with being in love.

Kate had been on the road the last few weeks pitching prospective corporate clients, so busy we'd not seen each other or said more than good night or good morning over the phone. I was glad to see her when she picked me up for dinner at seven Saturday evening. I preferred not to drive at night when I was more likely to spasm and contort my way into a plaintiff's lawyer's payday.

"I made a reservation at Axios," she said when I got in her car.

"That place off of Fifty-fifth and Brookside?"

"Yes. It's French. Fine dining encourages two things we haven't had enough of lately—quiet conversation and intimacy."

"We can talk all you want but they better have a hell of a dessert menu because I prefer my intimacy served at your place or mine."

"Brian is with his father this weekend so you might get lucky if you clean your plate."

We sipped the wine, lingered through dinner, and

talked. It was quiet and intimate. I led off, telling her about Lucy Trent, Ammara Iverson, and the envelope from Wendy.

"What do you think was in the envelope?" she asked.

"I've got no idea. Could have been anything from a card to a confession."

"I'm sure Ammara will tell you if they find it."

I nodded. "Trouble is, she'll wait until it's all over before she tells me."

"And you don't like being shut out in the meantime."

"Not so much."

"But you have to accept that because the FBI has the people and resources to do the job and you don't and you don't need the stress."

"Not so much," I said with a grin that she didn't reciprocate. "Okay, yes."

"I know it's hard, but it will be easier on you if you let Ammara handle it."

Her concern was legitimate and genuine but that didn't make it welcome. It was another reminder of limitations I resented more than I accepted. There was no point in having this argument since we both knew that I couldn't and wouldn't sit on the sidelines. I decided to change the subject before telling her about my job for Milo Harper.

"How's Brian?"

She let out a long sigh. "His grades are down and his barriers are up. I want him to see a therapist but his father says to give him time to figure things out on his own. I'm the disciplinarian and Alan is the laid back retro-hippy. Guess which one of us Brian prefers?"

"No contest, but take it from me, you can't make a teenager do anything. Any luck on your trip?"

"No. Our business went into the tank six months ago and isn't getting any better. I've spent the last three weeks smiling while being turned down."

"The economy catching up to you?"

"Maybe. We've reduced our salaries and laid off some staff but if things don't get better soon, I don't know how long we can keep the doors open."

"What would you do if you didn't have the firm?" I asked her.

She reached across the table, taking my hand in hers, caressing my fingers like worry beads. "I don't know. Teach, probably, or do what I've been doing only on a smaller scale, work from home. Neuromarketing is a hot new field. It's all about how the brain influences decision making. My skills are transferable to that field. I might put out some feelers."

"You could talk to Milo Harper, take his offer."

"I'd rather starve."

"Why? He seems okay."

She withdrew her hand. "And you know that how?"

I told her about my conversation with Simon, my meeting with Harper, and that I had accepted Harper's job offer.

She folded her arms across her chest. "When were you going to get around to telling me?"

"I thought I'd wait until we finished your list."

She frowned. "Sorry. I'm whining."

"Nope. Not your nature. You worry, argue, and dissect but you don't whine. So why is working for Harper worse than roaming the streets rummaging through trash cans?"

She parked her elbows on the table, locked her fingers together, and rested her chin on her hands and studied me. I knew her well enough to know that she was thinking about more than her answer. She was anticipating the conversation that would follow, mapping it out in her mind.

"I don't trust him."

"You've told me that before. Why not?"

She took a deep breath. "He is not an honorable man."

"That's two conclusions and zero facts. Convince me," I said.

"I saw it in his face when he tried to recruit me."

"You didn't like his involuntary facial expressions? What did he do, flash a secret smirk or stick his tongue out at you?"

She wadded her linen napkin and threw it onto the table. "Don't demean what I do, Jack."

"I'm not demeaning it one bit. I know your track record but you're not infallible. Give the guy a chance."

"That's the point. I gave him a chance when there was nothing on the line. He told me about his vision for the institute, how the brain is the last frontier and how he needed someone with my expertise."

"And you thought he was blowing smoke?"

"No, I'm sure he believes every word."

"Then what?"

"He asked me what it would take for me to come work for him. I told him there was nothing he could do because I was happy with my firm. He asked whether I would reconsider if there were no firm. I told him that we were doing quite well and I couldn't imagine that happening. That's when he told me that life is uncertain and that he could imagine anything happening. When he said that, he revealed part of his hidden self. His expression was ravenous, like a wild animal."

"He's a billionaire, for Christ's sake. They're all ravenous. That's how they got so rich."

"He's a billionaire who sits on the boards of three of our biggest clients—all of whom quit using us after I turned Harper down. That was six months ago."

"I thought you said it was the economy."

"That's what the general counsels of each company told me. Then I found out that they hired our competition."

"You think Harper is sabotaging your practice so you'll accept his job offer? C'mon."

She ran her fingers through her hair. "I think he's sabotaging my practice because I didn't accept his offer. You can work for him if you like, but I won't."

I leaned back in my chair. Kate was right more often than she was wrong but this was thin.

"I need this job," I said.

She grabbed the edge of the table with both hands. "Why? So you'll feel useful and validated? So you won't feel disabled? Jack, you're so much more than that. You can't spend the rest of your life trying to go back to who you used to be. You've got to be who you are now."

"That's not enough," I said, the words catching in my throat as the shakes claimed me.

Kate took my hand, waiting for the tremors to fade. "I think we can both use some dessert. Let's go. My place."

Chapter Thirteen

Lucy was on the couch when I came home Sunday morning, reading the newspaper. Ruby raced in from the kitchen, trailed by another cockapoo, this one dirty white with a faint honey stripe down her back, both of their snouts frosted with snow. The dogs barreled into me, leaping on me until I kneeled to the floor, letting them lick my hands and nip at my nose.

"I've no idea where the white one came from," Lucy said. "Ruby went outside this morning and brought her back."

"Her name is Roxy. She belongs to my ex-wife, Joy. Roxy stays here when Joy goes out of town. I forgot that she was leaving today for a week. Joy left Roxy in the backyard, figuring she'd come in through the doggie door."

"Bad marriage, worse divorce?"

"Bad marriage, good divorce. She knew it was time even if I was late to the party. She's a good person who deserved better than she got from me."

"That's noble. Did you deserve better than you got from her?"

I took my time, not because I didn't know the answer but because I was surprised Lucy would ask the question and that I was okay with telling her.

"Yeah, we both deserved better."

"And you each got a dog in the property settlement?"

"Nope. We each got our own dog after the divorce unbeknown to the other. Go figure. We take better care of them than we did our kids."

"The dogs always go crazy like that when you come home?"

"They do that whenever anyone comes in the door. They are trained to quit jumping up as soon as they are too tired."

"Looks like you had a nice time last night," Lucy said. I'd told her I was having dinner with a friend and that she could use my car if she wanted to go out.

"I did."

Lucy sat cross-legged on the sofa, patting the cushion next to her, inviting me sit. "So? Who is she? What's the story?"

I joined her. "What are your plans now that you're back in Kansas City?"

"No dish, huh?"

"No dish."

"Well, I need a car and I need a job. I haven't gotten any further than that. How about you? What do you do?"

"I do some security consulting."

"For who?"

"Right now. The Harper Institute of the Mind."

"What kind of security does a place like that need?"

"The confidential kind."

"You left that binder in the car Friday night. It didn't say top secret so I checked it out yesterday. I took another look this morning and saw those incident reports. The suicide looks sketchy. You think he was murdered? Can't tell about the other one. But since they were both involved at your institute, if the guy was killed, you'll have to take another look at the woman. Need any help?"

"No, and next time you find something lying around this house that doesn't have your name on it, leave it alone."

"I'll try but I can't make any promises. Let me ask you a question. How long have you had this gig?"

"I start on Monday."

She rolled her eyes. "I've got another one. When was the last time you worked a full day without shaking?"

I didn't answer.

"When was the last time you were scared to get behind the wheel because you were shaking so bad, not counting Friday night?"

I didn't answer.

"And, last but not least, how are you going to shake and bake your way through a new job at the same time you investigate whatever it is your friend at the FBI won't let you in on? And don't tell me that's not what you are going to do. I was a cop and I saw the look on your face when I asked you what was in that envelope."

Lucy reminded me too much of Wendy. She was smart, funny, and tough and afflicted with a bad judgment gene that had sent her off the rails once and would likely do so again. Landlord or not, I didn't want to sign on for the ride.

"What kind of car are you looking to buy?"

She leaned into the sofa. "You don't give anything

up, do you? I'm trying here. I really am, but you're not working with me."

"What are you saying?"

"I'm saying you need a place to live and I need your rent money. You need help and I'm willing and able but you won't give me a chance. We're stuck with each other. I'm trying to make lemonade out of this and you won't even admit we've got lemons."

"We may have problems, but they aren't the same ones. You can borrow my car on Monday after you drop me off at the institute."

The Harper Institute of the Mind sits on ten acres that was once home to a hospital. Harper tore the hospital down and built a 600,000-square foot facility for three hundred million dollars. It dominates the landscape, dwarfing any of the buildings on the nearby campus of the University of Missouri at Kansas City. The Nelson-Atkins Museum of Art stands in the near distance to the north, its closest architectural rival.

Lucy dropped me off in the circle entrance beneath a roof sheltering a courtyard and a fountain that had been turned off in deference to the freezing weather. I walked inside, stopping to admire a twenty-foot transparent sculpture of the human brain that hung suspended from the four-story ceiling. The surrounding circular walls were painted in varying shades of aquatic blues and greens, lighter colors ascending toward the ceiling, catching the natural light pouring through glass walls, creating an image of a vast sea.

On the far wall, etched beneath the institute's name, was a rhetorical question that joined the images of water and brain. *How Deep Is Your Ocean?* The metaphor made clear Milo Harper's vision of the institute. Understanding our minds required plumbing our depths. If the question was meant to be a guide to the perplexed, it was a success, inducing a sudden sensation that I was in over my head.

A stout, middle-aged woman wearing a name tag identifying her as Nancy Klemp sat behind a high round desk at the rear of the lobby, the elevators visible over her shoulder. Anyone wanting to go farther had to get past her. One of the best ways to secure a place like the institute is to staff the entrance with someone who will demand your firstborn male child as the price of admission. Nancy struck me as such a person. She wore a dark brown, nondenominational uniform that commanded attention without any obvious rank or authority. Her straight-backed, steely-eyed appraisal of me as I approached evoked all the authority she required. I liked her already.

"May I help you?"

"I'm Jack Davis. I work here but I don't know where. Today is my first day."

She picked up a phone and announced my presence to whoever answered.

"Ms. Fritzshall will be down in a moment."

"Thanks, Nancy. By the way, I'm the new director of security. I like the way you handle yourself."

If she was flattered, she kept it quiet. "I know who you are. Ms. Fritzshall told me to call her when you arrived."

"And who is Ms. Fritzshall?"

"Sherry Fritzshall. Vice president and general counsel," she said, her mouth twisting as if she'd swallowed sour milk.

"Mind if I ask, Nancy, how long have you been here?"

"Since we opened, two years ago."

"You're at this desk every day?"

"Eight in the morning until five in the afternoon. Every day."

"I'll bet someone in your job sees and hears a lot, more than most people realize."

She raised her eyebrows, uncertain of my intent. "I do my job. I pay attention."

"I have no doubt about that, Nancy, none at all. I look forward to working with you."

I reached across the desk and offered my hand. She hesitated for a moment and then took mine. Her grip was firm, her hand warm even though a smile was not part of her uniform.

"Yes, sir."

One of the six elevator doors opened. A woman emerged wearing a charcoal gray suit, her black hair pulled tight against her head, her fingers manipulating a Bluetooth earpiece. She shared Milo Harper's long, lean look, the resemblance most apparent in her sleek nose and intense, feverish eyes. She swept around Nancy's desk and looked me over like she was comparing my appearance to a wanted poster.

"Mr. Davis?"

"Still."

"Come with me."

I glanced at Nancy whose attention was fixed on something in the distance. I turned around, following her line of sight across the lobby, through the front doors, and onto the circle drive where Lucy stood, arms folded on the roof of the car. She nodded, got in, and drove away. Nancy looked at me for an explanation.

"My mom. She thinks it's my first day of school."

Nancy ducked her head, hiding a giggle. I really liked her.

As I followed Sherry Fritzshall toward the elevator, I heard Nancy mutter a fragment of the Twenty-third Psalm, *yea tho I walk in the valley of the shadow.*

Chapter Fourteen

Riding in the elevator, Sherry Fritzshall welcomed me to the institute with a perfunctory recitation of its history while she fiddled with her earpiece, stamping her foot at its poor reception. She was a disinterested docent, making certain I knew that she had better things to do than escort me. Once we reached the eighth and highest floor, she deposited me in my office and promised to come back, saying it in such a way as to make it clear I wasn't to leave until she returned.

A young man dressed in jeans and a sweatshirt brought me a cup of coffee and said his name was Leonard and that he had been assigned to me, which was handy because his desk was right outside, and to let him know if I needed anything. He gave me a directory of institute personnel with office locations and telephone extensions and a sealed envelope that he said contained my user ID and password for the computer on my desk, making me promise to shred the contents after I memorized them.

Moments later, a young woman wearing wool slacks, a sweater set, and an institute ID badge hanging from a gold chain around her neck appeared at my door sporting a cheerful grin. She had piano player hands, her fingers long and delicate, a diamond engagement ring sparkling on her left hand.

"I'm Anne from HR," she said.

"That's some last name."

She giggled. "My last name is Kendall but everyone calls me Anne from HR."

I pointed to her engagement ring. "Looks like you won't be Kendall much longer."

Her smile vanished along with the light in her eyes as she made a fist with her left hand, burying the ring against her side. "Well, I guess I'll still be Anne from HR."

She gave me a stack of papers to fill out and instructions to return them to Leonard when I was finished. Filling out the forms, I got hung up on the question asking why I had left my previous employment. I had been forced out of the only job I ever wanted, told that the FBI would not take a chance on an agent who thought shaking was an aerobic exercise.

The diagnosis of my movement disorder is more description than explanation, the last neurologist I saw for yet another opinion apologizing that he couldn't help me. The shaking, muscle spasms, and contractions fit the tics diagnosis, he said. But, he added, the disconnected sensation in my head, a sort of visceral cognitive dissonance, brought on by fatigue and visual triggers, sometimes accompanied by weakness and loss of use of my legs, was not related to tics, was not some concurrent seizure disorder, and neither he nor anyone else could explain it. His only suggestion, made without enthusiasm, was a class of drugs known for their profound and sometimes irreversible side effects. When I declined, he said he understood and comforted me with the faint praise that I certainly was an interesting patient.

I couldn't argue with the FBI's decision to declare me physically unable to perform but that didn't make it any easier to accept. Not when the job was who I was. Not when I had chosen it over my wife and children only to lose them as well. Not when I rationalized those sacrifices in the name of the people I saved and served, especially those who'd been murdered whose silenced voices I had vowed to make heard.

The forms Anne from HR left me didn't have room for all of that. So, I scribbled my least favorite one-word answer: *retired.*

Since retiring, I'd done little more than wander, restless at being an otherwise healthy middle-aged man whose day consisted of roaming the aisles at the sporting goods store, taking in a matinee, or working out in the middle of the afternoon at 24-Hour Fitness, the youngest member of the cardiac rehab set, while the rest of the world worked. My one connection to my former life was the informal lunch group of retired cops. I stumbled whenever someone asked what I did; my confession to retirement sticking in my throat, grateful when the work Simon Alexander sent me changed my status to consultant. I took those jobs for the same reason I took the one Milo Harper offered. I only knew how to do one thing and I had to do as much of it as I could in order to breathe.

It didn't matter that those jobs reminded me why the Bureau had shown me the door. Or that they answered the questions Lucy had asked and I had refused to answer. Yes, I shake everyday but not all the time, more often than not giving no hint of my condition. And, yes I am scared to get behind the wheel when I'm vibrating and my head is fogged. I live each day like an acrobat on a high wire, always on the verge of losing control. I needed a safety net and, although Lucy volunteered, I wasn't convinced she would catch me when I fell.

Sitting behind my new desk, looking out my new window, watching the muddy water in Brush Creek meander through its channel across the street from the institute, I felt restored. I wasn't retired. I wasn't a consultant. I was an employee, for however short a time. I marveled at the curative power of work, the validation of being needed and the comforting structure of W-4's, group health insurance, and profit-sharing plans until Sherry Fritzshall knocked and interrupted my meditations.

"Here's your schedule," she said, handing me a sheet of paper.

It was a list of appointments with the institute's project directors. Sessions were scheduled in thirty-minute increments in a conference room on the eighth floor beginning at 9:30 A.M. Lunch was at noon with her in the institute's private dining room. The last meeting on the schedule was at 5:30 with Milo Harper.

"Whose idea was this?" I asked.

She tightened her jaw, holding back her first response. "Mr. Harper said you should speak to each of the project directors."

"Yeah, but whose idea was this?" I waved the sheet of paper at her.

"Mine. These people are quite busy. Scheduling your meetings was the most efficient way for you to meet with them."

I stood and handed the paper back to her. "I'm sure it is. Cancel the appointments."

Her face colored, either because she was angry with me or embarrassed at having to inform the staff that the new kid on the block had overruled her. I couldn't tell which and didn't care.

She brushed imaginary lint from her suit, the gesture calming her as she cleared her throat. "All of them? What about the one with Mr. Harper?"

"Especially that one."

Hands balled into hammerheads and jammed onto her hips, she fired back. "And our lunch?"

I cocked my head, gave her my most apologetic grin. "No, let's do lunch."

I escorted her to the door.

"Where are you going?" she asked.

"For a walk. By myself."

Her cell phone rang and she turned away, taking the call. I left her in my office, waving to Leonard who jumped out of his chair.

"Hey, Mr. Davis! You can't go anywhere without this."

He handed me a Harper Institute of the Mind ID card threaded through a lanyard so I could wear it around my neck. My picture was pasted in the center. It was a headshot that included the shirt and tie I was wearing but no one had asked me to say cheese since I walked through the front door.

"It's a key card and an ID card," Leonard explained. Swipe it on the sensors to get access to the other floors. Mr. Harper said to make it a master. It opens every door in the whole place. Anne from HR forgot to give it to you. When she brought it back, you were busy so she left it with me."

"If she's Anne from HR, what's that make you, Leonard from the Eighth Floor?"

"It makes her hot and me horny."

"Steady, son. She's wearing an engagement ring."

"Yeah, but she's not wearing a wedding ring. Got to keep hope alive."

Anne had acted like she'd been sentenced to a hard forty when I mentioned her pending marriage, making me wonder whether Leonard's hope was built on inside information.

"Hope is good. So, who took my picture?"

"There's a video camera in the wall behind Nancy's desk in the lobby. HR freezes the frame and pulls it off to make the ID card. Saves having to stand you up against the wall for a photo shoot."

I had noticed the camera but not given it much thought. "Not bad. Who was in charge of security before I got here?"

"I was," Sherry said as she left my office. "See you at lunch."

Chapter Fifteen

I hadn't done any due diligence about my new employer either in my meeting with Harper or since then and it was showing. I hadn't considered whether I had taken someone's place and what impact that might have. All I had done was skim through the binder Harper gave me and piss off Detective McNair. None of that told me where the land mines were buried and I had just stepped on one.

Wendy was my best excuse for not focusing on my new job. I didn't think she had risen from the dead to confess to having stolen the drug ring's money because I hadn't stopped believing that she was innocent. I held onto the hope that if she was guilty of anything, it was of not being strong enough to contain her addiction, that her last couple of years of sobriety had given way to a final, fatal binge, making her vulnerable to the people behind the drug ring.

If I were wrong, what I had learned in twenty-eight years as an FBI agent would prove true once again.

While there are more unintended consequences than conspiracies, more careless acts than crimes, and more people with good intentions than evil motives, crooks, even the ones you love, will never cease to amaze and, too often, break your heart.

Lucy was right that Ammara Iverson would cut me out of her investigation. I couldn't allow Ammara or anyone else to pass final judgment on my daughter and would fight to save whatever was left of her memory. Milo Harper was afraid that dreams could kill. I was focused on the other side of the equation, keeping my dreams of Wendy alive.

Sherry Fritzshall's resentment toward me was palpable. She had instructed Nancy to hold me in the lobby until she arrived and then made certain that Leonard and Anne from HR tied me to my desk until she could hamstring me with a day of interviews, tossing in lunch with her and a meeting with the boss in case I didn't know what to with my free time. Tomorrow, she'd probably ask me to take inventory of the office supplies, promising me a key to the men's room if I found the missing paperclips.

I would meet with the project directors but not on an assembly line that guaranteed canned responses regardless of whether their answers matched my questions. Interviews were much more productive when the subject hadn't spent the day rehearsing.

I needed to get a feel for the institute on my own without being fed forms, schedules, and histories. The best way to do that was to walk the halls and listen to the chatter that bubbles up everywhere there are people who are convinced they are underpaid and underappreciated, which describes everyplace with a clock that gets punched twice a day.

I stepped onto the elevator, activating the buttons by swiping my key card across a sensor. No card, no access. It was a basic security measure to prevent the kind of walk-in traffic that liked to wander hallways looking for unguarded purses and laptops or assault women in the bathroom. I punched the button for the fifth floor, a random start.

Office buildings are office buildings. There are only so many windows, corners, and cubicles. Toss in rooms for files, breaks, supplies, conferences, and toilets and they all look alike after a while. This one also had labs, libraries, auditoriums, and lots of locked doors. I decided not to use my master key card during business hours since barging in unannounced wouldn't win me any friends.

I stuck to the open areas occupied by support staff and the break rooms, practicing my skills as a conversation stopper. People acknowledged me with a nod; a few stealing glances at my ID card to catch my name and waiting until I had passed before resuming their conversations. They were not a welcoming bunch though they appeared intent on doing their jobs and mindful that what they were doing was important enough to be protected from strangers like me.

Less than an hour after I started, I was back at Leonard's desk. He was sorting through mail.

"Tear yourself away?" I asked him.

"Sure thing."

He had one of those perpetual eager, ear-to-ear smiles, the kind guaranteed to exceed expectations on his annual review. He followed me into my office. I booted up my computer and entered my user ID and password.

"What's online here?"

"Everything."

"Meaning what?"

"Depending on your level of authorization, you can access every personnel file, every research project, every everything. You just have to know what you're looking for. What are you interested in?"

"I want to read up on the institute's research projects."

"Here, let me show you." He walked me through a quick tutorial, showing me how to access information. "As you go deeper into certain files, you'll be asked to reenter your user ID and password to make certain you are authorized to see those materials. It's all pretty intuitive."

"Thanks. I'll let you know if I run into trouble. Close the door on your way out."

Leonard was right about the system being intuitive. I found my way into the files of the lucid dreaming project, reentering my user ID and password as the security level increased from file to file. I bypassed the basics explaining the project, giving a cursory glance to Anthony Corliss's biography though I took the time to read Maggie Brennan's.

Her photograph showed a woman with gray hair cut short and straight, no makeup, full cheeks sagging past a down-turned mouth, eyes fixed in the distance—a woman not given to joy. She graduated from Berkeley with a degree in biology and went on to UCLA where she obtained a PhD in neuroscience. A string of academic appointments followed with matching publications in journals and texts, all focused on posttraumatic stress disorder and memory. She joined the Harper Institute a year ago. Her bio began with her college education as if she was born at age eighteen, fully formed. It was a professional résumé, stripped of any personal references to family, faith, friends, or a cold murder case.

I followed the prompts to the dream project videos, entering my ID and password to verify that I was authorized to view these materials, clicking the box promising not to copy or otherwise disclose the videos without the prior written consent of the project director or use them for any other purpose other than the use for which they were intended.

The next page was a search page. I entered Tom Delaney's name. A message appeared stating zero matches found. I tried Regina Blair's name and got the same result. I scrolled back to the search page and selected the option to view a list of research subjects to make certain that Delaney's and Blair's names were both included and that I had spelled them correctly. There were ten pages of names, twenty-five names to a page. Delaney's and Blair's names were missing but another name on the third page caught my eye. Walter Enoch.

Chapter Sixteen

Words that are heavy with nothing but trouble:
"Tinker to Evers to Chance."

Franklin Pierce Adam's poem about the famous Chicago Cubs infielders and their ability to turn the double play was one of my favorites, these final lines sticking with me. The poem reminded me how round the world was, how one thing inevitably led to another, and that very little in baseball or life happened by chance.

I substituted the names, making it *Delaney to Blair to Enoch*, wondering whether their deaths were inevitable the moment they volunteered for the dream project or whether their shared fate was nothing more than serendipity, the circle widening from Walter Enoch to capture Wendy and me. The first line of the poem echoed in my head as I stared at Walter's name on my computer screen.

These are the saddest of possible words.

My cell phone rang before I could open Enoch's

video. I recognized the number displayed on my screen even though I hadn't received a call from the FBI's Kansas City regional office since I left the Bureau.

"Jack, it's Ammara."

A sharp flutter of shakes swept through my neck and head.

"What's up?"

"We'd like you to come in."

The FBI gives answers over the phone but asks questions in person. Invitations made in the first-person plural come from people who give orders to agents like Ammara. I could ask her who wanted to talk to me and why but I knew her answers wouldn't tell me anything I didn't already know.

It was an article of faith in the Bureau that Wendy had stolen the drug ring's money. A few hard-liners suspected that she had reached out to me before her death and that I had covered for her, maybe even helping her hide the money. They were waiting for me to buy a car, boat, or house I couldn't afford on my disability payments. It had been less than seventy-two hours since Ammara had promised to tell me what she could. Her call reconfirmed that the Bureau had convicted Wendy and named me as an unindicted coconspirator.

"I don't have any wheels. I loaned my car to Lucy Trent."

"We'll send someone. Are you at home?"

"No. I'm at the Harper Institute of the Mind."

"Why? Have you lost yours?"

Ammara's sense of humor made this easier on our friendship but not a lot easier.

"I'm considering the option."

"Wait until we're done with you. I'll have a car there in ten minutes."

I didn't know when I would get back to the computer. Tom Delaney's and Regina Blair's video files were gone. I was certain that Anthony Corliss and Maggie Brennan would have an explanation for what happened to their files and that it might even be true.

Not willing to take a chance with Walter Enoch's file, I downloaded it to the desktop and again to the flash drive I carried on my key ring. My exercise in belt-and-suspenders backup reminded me that tics and obsessive-compulsive disorder sometimes ran together, which wasn't always a bad thing.

"Where you headed?" Leonard asked before I could clear his desk.

"Out."

He nodded, his grin locked in place as if a plastic surgeon had hit a nerve, leaving his face happily paralyzed.

"Out. Got it. Will you be back in time for your lunch with Sherry?"

I glanced at my watch. She was expecting me in an hour. "Tell her not to wait up."

"She'll be pissed, big time, if you don't show."

"Promises, promises."

Turnover was a fact of life in any FBI office. In the months I'd been gone, many of the agents I'd worked with had been reassigned to other parts of the country. Intergovernmental task forces staffed by FBI agents and personnel from other law enforcement agencies that worked out of the regional office had been shut down, restaffed, or replaced by other task forces, introducing another wave of new faces. Support staff had undergone normal attrition. All the personnel changes made the place feel foreign even if the walls were familiar.

Knowing that I couldn't go anywhere without an escort confirmed that I was an outsider.

The regional office sat on high ground on the southwest edge of downtown. Ammara led me to a conference room from which I could see the squiggly steel sculptures atop Bartle Hall and, east of them, the reflective glass walls of the Sprint Center where Garth Brooks had performed for eight straight nights when it opened. In between was the Power & Light entertainment district, the heart of Kansas City's revitalized downtown.

She introduced me to the people who had issued my invitation.

"James Kent and Everett Dolan, say hello to Jack Davis."

Hands were shaken, smiles exchanged, all of them cold. Everyone stood.

"Agents Kent and Dolan are from DC," Ammara explained. "They're following up on Wendy's case."

She didn't have to give me their résumés. I'd known guys like them. Kent and Dolan were lifers. Their hair was a gray brush cut, their guts were soft, and their eyes were hard. They were tailors, first cousins to the guys who followed behind the elephants at the circus, carrying shovels. Their job was to wrap up the loose ends the FBI couldn't stand to leave hanging, especially when the threads were wrapped around their own people.

"Sorry about your loss," Dolan said.

I nodded. "What can I do for you?"

"Have a seat."

"I'm good."

Kent tossed Wendy's envelope onto the table, the plastic evidence bag sliding across the smooth surface. "How many other letters did you receive from your daughter after she disappeared?"

"None. And I didn't receive this one either."

"But you did hear from her before she died." It was Dolan again.

I'd gone through this when Wendy disappeared and again after she died. These two were no better or worse than their predecessors but repetition hadn't dulled the ache.

"About three months after she disappeared, I got an e-mail from her. Out of the blue. It was one of those electronic birthday cards. I traced it back to a computer at the New York City Public Library. I went to New York and found her just after she overdosed. She died in my arms. You know all that because it's in the file and I'm betting you guys can read. So what do you want?"

"You talk to any of her friends when you were in New York?"

This time it was Kent. If I closed my eyes, I couldn't tell them apart.

"No. All I did was bring her home. I didn't know she had any friends. If she did, they didn't come to the funeral."

"She ever mention someone named Jessie Mercado?" Kent asked.

"She never mentioned anyone. She just died. That's all."

Dolan and Kent looked at each other, then at Ammara, then at me. Ammara broke the silence.

"We found Jessie Mercado's fingerprints on Wendy's envelope. She's a small-time drug dealer in New York. Turns out she and Wendy were friends."

"You know what good friends junkies and dealers are," Dolan said. He grinned, begging me to take the swing we both knew I wanted to take.

"Yeah. Kind of like you and Kent."

Dolan took a step toward me but Kent grabbed his arm. "You've got no call," he said to his partner. "And, neither do you," he said, letting me know which one was the good cop and which one was the bad cop.

I ignored both of them. "What did Jessie Mercado say about the envelope?" I asked Ammara.

"She said that Wendy used to crash at her place. A month or so ago, she was moving out and found the envelope and some of Wendy's personal effects while she was packing. She sold what she could and put the envelope in the mail. Thought she was doing you a favor. Said she never opened it and didn't know what was inside it. You remember that we gathered Wendy's DNA samples from her apartment?"

"Yeah. They match the saliva on the envelope?"

"All the way," Ammara said. "We got one decent print too. Jessie Mercado's story holds up."

"So we know how the letter got here," Kent said. "What we need is your help figuring out what was in it."

"How would I know what was in it?"

"Why do you suppose it was the one piece of stolen mail the dead mailman opened?" It was Dolan.

"Who says the mailman opened it?" I asked.

"You're saying someone else was there, opened the envelope, took whatever was inside and left it on the dead guy?" Kent asked.

"I'm saying you don't know what happened so until you do, don't act like you've got it figured out. How did Walter Enoch die?"

"The coroner says he had pretty bad asthma. Says his lungs went into spasm causing him to suffocate and have a heart attack," Dolan said.

"The coroner have any idea what caused the spasm?" I asked.

"Yeah," Dolan said. "Someone put their hand over his mouth and nose so he couldn't breathe. Enoch fought back hard enough that he broke his nose. Makes me think the killer was looking for whatever it was your daughter mailed to you."

"Which puts you right where you've been from the beginning," Dolan said

"Where's that?" I asked.

"In the middle," Dolan said. "Now, let me see you shake."

Wendy was ten. It had been a year since we'd lost Kevin. The death of a child is a tragedy but losing a child the way we lost Kevin was an unspeakable tragedy. So, to our everlasting sorrow, Joy and I didn't speak of it, especially around or to Wendy.

She carried the knowledge of her brother's abduction, abuse, and murder inside her until it began to erupt in ways large and small. She didn't eat or she ate too much. She cried too often or not at all. She lashed out at her teachers or she didn't speak. And she shook, trembling like she would come apart.

We made the rounds with pediatricians, psychologists, and psychiatrists, one assuring us that it would pass, another softly encouraging her to release her bottled emotions. Now, let me see you shake, he told her, but she refused to perform for him, claiming her pain as her own. I never loved her more than at that moment.

"You'll have to do better than that," I said.

Chapter Seventeen

"Don't let those guys get to you," Ammara said, as she drove me back to the institute.

"I hear you. They're just doing their job the only way they know how."

"Exactly my point," she said. "DC won't let this one go, you know that, Jack, especially when something like Wendy's envelope shows up. They're going to keep coming at you until they find that money."

We were stopped at a traffic light at Summit and Southwest Boulevard in the heart of the west side Hispanic neighborhood where Mexican restaurants and bakeries held sway.

I looked at her. "Why not let it go? Why not leave Wendy and me alone? It's not like they are going to return the money to the people who bought the drugs even if they do find it. They'll deposit it in the Treasury and the growth in the national debt will slow down for a nanosecond."

"You know why. It's the only way the Bureau can re-move the stain. One of our people did this."

"Colby Hanson wasn't the only one."

"Yes, but he was the only one who was one of ours."

The light changed. We made our way south on Sum-mit, snaking onto the Southwest Traffic Way.

"Not according to Dolan and Kent. They think I know what happened to the money. Hell, they probably want me for killing Walter Enoch."

Ammara dipped her chin and laid on the horn at a driver who shifted into our lane, though his car was two-lengths in front of ours.

"Assholes," she said, pounding on the steering wheel, refusing to look at me.

The other driver was alone, his offense imaginary and not warranting her outburst. The assholes she was curs-ing were Dolan and Kent, the message clear. I wasn't just in the middle. I was in their crosshairs.

As crazy as it was, it made more sense than my at-tempt to link Walter Enoch's murder to the deaths of Tom Delaney and Regina Blair. The police had investi-gated their deaths and found no evidence of homicide. The only thing the three of them had in common was their participation in the dream project, something they shared with two hundred and forty-seven other people.

My daughter had been in love with a rogue FBI agent who was involved in a drug ring. She disappeared when we took the operation down and later reached out to me in a way designed to keep her whereabouts secret. I found her, as she knew I would, though not in time. Every FBI agent I ever knew would believe that she told me what happened to the money before she died. If

Wendy hadn't been my daughter, I would have joined the same church.

I wouldn't take the odds that Wendy had mailed me a confession and treasure map but neither would I bet against it. There were several possible explanations why her envelope was the one piece of stolen mail that was found opened. The seal was old and may have given way. Walter Enoch could have decided after all those years of hoarding the mail to start reading it and chose Wendy's as his first. I knew that neither of these was likely.

The most plausible explanation was also the simplest. Whoever opened that envelope knew where to find it and was willing to kill Walter Enoch to get it. Dolan and Kent had a long way to go to prove that I knew the envelope existed or that I knew that Enoch had stolen it. None of that mattered because they knew the one thing that mattered most of all. I was the only person they could think of who wanted to know what was inside it more than they did.

Ammara pulled up in front of the institute. Her shoulders were hunched over the wheel, her hands still strangling it. She knew the score as well as I did, her conclusions and mine no doubt the same. This morning's session had been well orchestrated, complete with her assignment as my return driver. She was the ultimate good cop, my friend and former colleague, the one who would soften me up with appeals to old times and reason. She was supposed to tell me to make it easy on myself and give Kent and Dolan what they wanted, even if it was my head. I liked that she couldn't bring herself to do it.

"It's okay," I told her. "I get it. You're just doing your job too. The difference between you and Kent and Dolan is that you don't like it. It's what gets those guys out of bed in the morning. Tell them that you gave it your best shot but that I'm the one who is an asshole. And tell them I don't know what happened to the money and I didn't kill Walter Enoch."

She nodded, staring through the windshield. "I'll tell them but it won't do any good."

Chapter Eighteen

"Sherry is waiting for you in the private dining room," Leonard said when I got back to my office.

I looked at my watch. It was one-fifteen. "Really?"

"Totally. It's on the other side of the elevator. Double door."

The dining room was actually several rooms fronted by a small lobby whose walls were paneled in teak and hung with important art. I knew the art was important because each piece was illuminated with a strategically placed light and accompanied by a brass plate announcing that it was on loan from the Milo Harper Collection of Contemporary Art. I studied one piece that was all wild color painted with wilder brush strokes and splattered with globs of black, deciding that I had a greater appreciation for the artistry of converting on third and long than for anything in Milo's collection.

A woman in a sleek-fitting green dress greeted me. Her porcelain makeup and high swept blond hair belonged on a runway.

"It's one of a kind," she said, pointing to the painting.

"Me too. I'm Jack Davis. Sherry Fritzshall is expecting me."

"Of course. Right this way."

I followed her down a corridor until we reached a door at the end of the hall. She knocked once, waited a beat, then held the door open, closing it behind me, sealing the windowless room like an air lock. More teak paneling, more important art, thick plush carpet, and padded walls made it a soundproof inner sanctum with a privileged intimacy that screamed I was lucky to be invited inside these walls.

Sherry was seated at a round table that was draped in ivory-colored linen, empty, food encrusted china and silver shoved to one side, reading from a stack of papers in front of her. She set the papers down, giving me a disappointed look as if I was her teenage son dragged home by the cops in the middle of the night.

"I'm sorry you missed lunch. It was salmon. The chef made a superb sauce."

I took a seat opposite her. "Something came up."

She chewed her lip, rearranged her papers. "Let me give you some advice. Don't underestimate me."

"I don't have an estimate of you."

"Oh, but you do. You think I don't know what I'm doing because I scheduled the meetings with the project directors without consulting you. And you think I resent that you took my place as director of security."

"Okay. I do have an estimate of you. Why am I wrong?"

"I have an MBA from Wharton and a JD from Harvard. I was Milo's chief operating officer before he sold his company. I know how to make things run efficiently."

"And I have a PhD from the FBI. We do security differently than they do at Harvard and Penn."

"Business and organizational management principles have universal application, including for security. There has to be a plan and a system to implement the plan and accountability for execution of the plan."

"All the business systems and management principles in the world won't do a bit of good if you don't have an advanced degree in crimes and criminals. Milo Harper knows that or he wouldn't have hired me."

"My brother is a romantic. He likes to dramatize everything from his perch thirty thousand feet above the rest of us. I operate on the ground where things happen, running this institute and protecting my brother."

"Protecting him from what?"

"From anyone and everything that might harm him."

"You can't do that. No one can."

"I'm his only family. No one will do a better job than I will."

"Which is reason enough for you to resent me."

"That's where you underestimate me. I grant that you have expertise that I lack. It's obvious that you lack what I have to offer, which is an encyclopedic knowledge of this place and my brother's complete trust. If Milo wants you to direct security, then direct it you shall, but you will not shut me out and you will not succeed without my help."

"Why do you think Milo hired me?"

She stiffened in her chair and straightened the papers in front of her. "He's afraid of Jason Bolt. We had to pay him off once before and he's worried we'll have to do it again."

"Have you read the police reports on Delaney and Blair?"

"Detective McNair showed them to my brother and me."

"That's not the same as reading them."

"I'm sure I did but I didn't memorize them," she said, shuffling her just straightened papers.

"Anything jump out at you in the Delaney report?"

She raised one eyebrow. "Apart from the fact that it was suicide?"

"Suicide is a conclusion, not a fact. That report is full of facts that support another conclusion—that Delaney was murdered. And if he was murdered in a way to make it look like his nightmare came true, I've got another conclusion for you. The killer may be someone who works for you and your brother. If I'm right, Jason Bolt is the least of your worries. Thanks for lunch."

I left Sherry picking her chin off the linen tablecloth. I'd tell her about the missing videos and Walter Enoch after I had a better idea where she fit in this universe.

I closed the door to my office, making it to my chair as the shakes claimed me. My back arched and my neck hyperextended over the top of the seat, giving me plenty of time to count the ceiling tiles if my eyes had been open. I gripped the armrests while my abs convulsed, crunching me forward then back, grunting like I was chasing Dante through the Inferno. The tremors eased, my choppy breath catching up and slowing down. I had made it through the day without shucking and jiving in front of Agents Dolan and Kent and, now, Sherry Fritzshall but I'd wound the spring so tight something had to give.

Leonard burst through my door. "What the hell was that? You okay?"

"Never better. I shake sometimes. That's all."

"Are you kidding me? You sounded like a remake of *Halloween*."

"I'll try to keep it down. I'm okay."

"Next time, give me some notice. I'll sell tickets."

People don't know whether to laugh, hide their eyes, or call 911 the first time they are exposed to my physical and vocal contortions; the more profound my outburst, the more intense their discomfort. Leonard's perma-smile was upside down and his eyes were wide with concern that felt real. His joke harbored none of Agent Kent's malice. I returned his smile and waved him away.

"As long as I get ten percent of the gate."

"I'm cool with that," he said and left me alone.

In the old days, I would have spent the rest of the afternoon and evening knocking on doors, catching the project directors off guard, digging up what I could, stirring up the rest until I could sift it out. I wouldn't have started with Anthony Corliss and Maggie Brennan because I didn't want them to think I was focused on them. I would work my way around to them, letting word of my interrogations filter through the hallways, goosing the anxiety that might make them slip—if there was reason for them to slip.

These weren't the old days. I couldn't make it through a day with this much in-your-face face time without getting wobbly and I didn't want to take someone on when the brain fog was rolling in. It wasn't three o'clock and I was done, frustrated that I couldn't even keep banker's hours. Lucy was right. I needed help from someone who knew how to ask the right questions and could go the distance. I left her a message on her cell phone to come and get me.

My body settled and the synapses in my brain re-opened for business while I waited, giving me time to make a mental to-do list. My ex-brothers and sisters in the FBI were building a murder case against me con-structed out of fear and loathing. All I had to do to ex-onerate myself was give them the five million dollars they thought Wendy stole while convincing them that I'd known where the money was all along so they would believe that I had no reason to kill Walter Enoch. At least they wouldn't charge me with murder.

None of this made much sense, and some of it wouldn't make sense even when it was all over. That was the trouble with murder. It made things weird.

Chapter Nineteen

Milo Harper opened my door without knocking, the interruption finishing my to-do list. His sweater hung tentlike from rounded shoulders, his cargo pants sagged from his waist to the floor. He had a slight sheen on his forehead as if he'd ran up three flights of stairs but his gray pallor made it more likely that he was fighting a fever.

"Busy?" he asked.

"Not for you."

He took a seat across from my desk. "You look like you've taken a punch that you didn't see coming."

I laughed. "It's the shaking and it doesn't matter if I see it coming. You don't look so good yourself."

He sighed. "Three hours of sleep will do that to you after a while."

"So dial it back. You must have people who have people who can do whatever it is you're doing between midnight and six A.M."

He ran one hand through his hair. "Actually, I've got

more people than that but none of them are on my clock. You know what I see everyday when I look in the mirror? I see the light in my brain getting dimmer. I'm not going to waste any of the time I have left before it goes dark."

"I've got to say it again. You don't look or act like anyone I've ever seen with Alzheimer's. You don't miss a trick."

"I can still navigate but I know what's coming and I'm not going there. I won't end up lying in bed, weighing eighty-five pounds with a feeding tube waiting for a nurse to wipe my butt not knowing who or what I am. I'll check out on my own terms long before then."

I had no answer to that and no idea why he was in my office. I waited for him to tell me.

"Sherry came to see me."

"I was late for lunch. She didn't like that."

"No, she wouldn't like that. She says you think one of our people murdered Tom Delaney. Is that true?"

"It's possible," I said, running through the anomalies in the Delaney report.

"You've got to go to the police with this."

"I did that. McNair likes his closed cases to stay closed."

"Go over his head. I'll call the chief of police."

"He'll back up his people unless we've got something better. Plus, Jason Bolt will scream cover-up if he finds out you pressured the department."

"So what do we do?"

"You do your job and I'll do mine."

"I can do mine a lot better if Sherry isn't in my office every five minutes complaining about you. Do me a favor, work with her."

"I can do that as long as I know where she fits in."

"She's my older sister. Practically raised me. She's smarter than me and she's my eyes and ears. When you have as much money as I do, someone always wants something. She keeps all that away from me."

"But, you didn't tell her that you've got Alzheimer's. Why not?"

He grinned. "Because she would drive me absolutely, fucking nuts. She'd make me go to every doctor on the planet who could spell Alzheimer's."

"I never had a big sister but I get the picture. It's not because you don't trust her?"

"Hell, I love her but that doesn't mean I trust her with everything in my life. The first lesson in the billionaire's manual is to know what to give up and to who and what to keep to yourself."

"What's the second lesson?"

"Do what has to be done. Don't look back and don't second-guess. You've been on the job half a day. What else have you got for me?"

"I logged onto the dream project to look at the videos of Tom Delaney and Regina Blair describing their nightmares. Their videos are missing and their names don't show up on the list of participants. It looks like they've been erased from the project records."

He nodded, processing the information without a visible reaction I could detect. I wished I had mastered Kate Scranton's talent for dissecting the involuntary facial flickers she claimed shined light on our true selves.

"What else?"

"You heard about the mailman who stole the mail?"

"Yeah. It was all over the news."

"Except for the part about him being a participant in the dream project."

His face remained flat while he absorbed the additional data as if an internal algorithm suppressed his emotions, keeping him focused on the problem, not the people. "How did you make the connection?"

"The mailman's name was Walter Enoch. I ran across it when I was searching for Delaney's and Blair's names on the list of project volunteers."

"The paper said he died of a heart attack."

"He had help."

Harper looked away for an instant, hiding his face, then came back to me, his eyes narrowed. "He was murdered? If you're right about Delaney, he's the second dream project volunteer to be killed. My God, what if Regina Blair's accident was staged too? How do you know about Enoch?"

"People I used to work with at the FBI told me this morning."

"Will they help us?"

"No."

"Then why would they tell you?"

"That's my business."

"Not as long as I'm paying you."

"You hired me, you didn't buy me. I'll tell you what I can when I can."

He stared at me, waiting for me to fold. When I didn't, he stood and reached for the phone on my desk. "Let's get Anthony Corliss and Maggie Brennan up here and find out what's going on with those files."

"Not so fast. I'd rather get to them on my schedule. No point in letting them know what we know until we're ready."

"Corliss's computer has software that tells him whenever anyone at the institute goes into his files. You were logged on to the system. Believe me, by now he knows that you were on and what you were looking at."

"Then I'll go see him. I don't want him to think he's been called to the principal's office."

"I'll go with you," he said making it a decree, not an offer.

I stood. "That's okay. I'd rather talk to him alone."

"Why? He'll know that you're going to tell me whatever he says."

"I can't help what he thinks. If you're there, it will change the dynamic. He'll be more concerned about you than me."

"He damned well better be more concerned about me than you. I sign his check and yours for that matter. Both of you work for me, something you keep overlooking."

His impassive façade gave way, his face coloring from pale to pink to red. Kate's belief that he was trying to ruin her business as revenge for her refusal to work for him didn't seem so far-fetched. I had warned him when we first talked about the job that he and I would get to this moment. There was no reason to duck it.

"Your sister tried to run me as soon as I walked through the front door. I don't know whether that was her idea or yours. When she couldn't, she ran to you. I get that. Now you have to decide what you want to give up and to who and what you want to keep to yourself because you're not going to run my investigation or me. I'll tell you when I've got something or when I need something. Until then, this stays between you and me so just sign my check or get someone else."

We measured one another across my desk; neither backing down until he conceded with a cracked grin.

"We've got the same problem, you and me," he said.

"What's that?"

"We're both losing the one thing we can't afford to

lose—control. You over your body and me over my mind. I don't know why you won't tell me about the FBI but I gather you've got something else at stake, something personal. I could get anyone I want to do this job but I like having someone with a lot on the line. I'll stay out of your way but I want results or I will get someone else."

"What if you don't like the results?"

"That's tomorrow's problem. The question is whether you can do this today."

More than the shaking or the brain fog, I resented that my condition compromised my choices, forcing me to accept weakness as normal, walking away instead of pushing on as unavoidable. If I was going to give in, I might just as well quit. The FBI forced me to do that and the bitter taste hadn't gone away.

Simon Alexander was wrong when he told me that this would be an easy gig, a job I could do on my own schedule, and I was right when I told Milo Harper that something like this doesn't want to be controlled. Neither mattered now. What mattered was whether I was going to answer the bell or pack it in, taking the rest of the day off because I felt like I'd gone ten rounds or rattle Anthony Corliss's cage, knowing that the surest way to chill an investigation was to wait until it was convenient for me.

"It's no hill for a climber," I told him.

Chapter Twenty

The personnel directory Leonard gave me listed Anthony Corliss's office on the fourth floor and Maggie Brennan's on the third. I tried Corliss first. He answered on the first knock.

"Door's unlocked."

The lights were turned off, the blinds drawn, the only illumination coming from a desk lamp and a flat panel television mounted on one wall. Corliss was leaning back in his chair, feet on his desk.

Two people, a woman and a man, their backs to me, occupied chairs in front of his desk. I stepped to one side, giving me a view of their profiles. Both looked to be in their midtwenties, the guy wandering from the screen to his iPhone to the books on the wall. The woman leaned forward, arms across her middle, eyes narrowed on the television, a legal pad in her lap filled with notes.

I recognized Maggie Brennan from the photograph in her bio. She was sitting on a small sofa and turned toward me, her brows rising, her eyes flaring like I'd snuck up on her in the dark. She shifted her weight, giving me her back and facing the screen.

Corliss held a finger to his mouth, telling me not to speak. They were wrapped in the shadows, watching the television.

I put Corliss in his early forties, enough mileage in the wrinkles and folds on his face to separate him from his youth but not enough that it was all in his rearview mirror. Though he was Milo Harper's contemporary, he had an easy energy about him in contrast to Milo's urgency, the difference no doubt owing to the distance on their horizons. His sandy brown hair was cut short, framing a full face. He was shorter than me, creeping past stocky with a black sweatshirt bunching over his belly.

He'd frozen the image on the television when I opened the door, now waving the remote at the screen where a young man, maybe twenty, sat in a chair, the camera in tight, his face locked in a blank stare, the soul patch beneath his chin more like a mud smear. Corliss clicked the remote and the image jerked to life. The man rocked back and forth, palms on his knees, then squared up to the camera.

"Go on," an off-camera female voice said, the tone anxious and encouraging. The young woman with the legal pad was mouthing the words that I assumed were hers.

"Man it was crazy. Scared the shit out of me," the man on the screen said. "I had to get home but it didn't matter which way I went, it was wrong. The streets didn't go where they were supposed to go and then the road disappeared and I was falling."

"What happened next, Quentin?"

"I stopped falling but I never hit the ground. Then I was running, trying to get to class to take a final but it was too late and I flunked out of school. I tried to find the professor, but this giant snake jumped up and the next thing I knew I was sucking my own dick. That's when I woke up," he said, biting his lip to stop from laughing.

"Thanks, Quentin, that's all for today," the woman's voice said and the screen went blank.

"Janet," Corliss said to the woman with the legal pad, "you think that boy is for real?"

Corliss spoke with a soft Ozark twang though his good-old-boy manner stiffened Janet rather than put her at ease.

"His dream had some of the features we're looking for," she said to her pad, not meeting his gaze.

"What do you think, Gary?" Corliss said, swinging his feet to the floor and his attention to the man sitting next to her.

Gary raised his head, glancing first at Janet then at Corliss like he'd been woken from a nap. "I don't know. The guy seemed legit."

"Children," Corliss said, "that boy is why you all got to do a better job screening these subjects before you sign them up. We're paying these people good money and I don't want to throw it away on some kid's jack-off fantasy. Now, get out of my office and find me some nightmares that are worth a damn."

Janet and Gary nodded, rose, and brushed past me, Janet turning on the lights as they left. Maggie watched them leave. She sighed, folded her hands in her lap and looked at Corliss.

"I'm Jack Davis, new director of security for the institute."

Corliss pointed to one of the empty chairs. "Take a load off, Jack, and say hello to my partner in crime, Maggie Brennan. Milo said you'd be coming around to see us. What can we do for you?"

I ignored his offer. His chair was raised higher than either of the other chairs or the sofa, giving him the visual advantage of looking down on his guests, an edge I preferred to keep since I couldn't pee in the corner to let him know I was the new sheriff in town.

"Milo tell you why he hired me?"

"Yep. He said you're going to protect our intellectual property."

"You have any that needs protecting?"

"Matter of fact, we don't. We do pure research, trying to get a handle on nightmares and posttraumatic stress disorder. We've got nothing to patent or trademark and the stuff we publish is copyrighted as soon as the ink is dry."

"Well, then, is there anything else you think we should talk about?"

He leaned back in his chair, putting his feet on his desk again, his hands banded across his belly.

"Can't think what it would be."

Cops categorize people caught up in a murder investigation as victims, witnesses, and suspects. The dead are known, while witnesses may be eager and helpful or scarce and reluctant.

Suspects are labeled as much by circumstance, bias, and behavior as the facts. Some liked to dance, flirting with the facts and playing hard to get, confident that they are too clever to be caught. Others liked to wrestle, flexing their muscles and taking their shots, certain they were too tough to be taken down.

Corliss knew I had accessed his project files and that whatever I'd seen had brought me to his door. That was enough to make him suspicious and wait for me to tell him why I was there rather than offer his conjecture. It didn't make him guilty of anything, but it did make him dance and I liked to make dancers wrestle.

"You know the funny thing about bullshit?" I asked him.

He gave me an ear-to-ear grin. "I don't but I got a feeling you're gonna tell me."

"Everyone thinks theirs doesn't stink."

He laughed, but there was no joy in the sound. "You are right about that. I'm guessing that you're catching my scent."

"Like a feedlot on a hot day. Is your Nashville act for real?"

"I'm not the first one of my people to come down out of the hills but I am the only one with a PhD. They'd be proud of me too if they had any idea what it is I do."

"Try explaining it to me."

He put his feet on the floor and pulled up to his desk.

"Like a lot of science, it's easier to describe than it is to explain. Bad things happen to people all the time and, by the way, it doesn't matter a bit if you're good or bad, shit happens and forgive and forget is overrated. The bad memories take root in the brain and poison our dreams. Digging them out is harder than yanking out a tree stump with a pair of tweezers. Isn't that right, Maggie."

She nodded. "We fill our dreams with the things we can't cope with when we're awake," she said. "The things we are afraid of, ashamed of. The things we want but believe we don't deserve. The things we'd like to say and do that we lack the strength to make real and the things we've said and done that could bring us down. All those things run wild in our dreams. They are beneath the surface but not so far that we can't learn to control them so they don't control us, so we can make peace with them."

"And you can teach people how to do that?"

"We're trying real hard," Corliss said. "Our brains have to process and manage traumatic memories so we can live with them without beating our kids, robbing banks, or just plain going nuts. A lot of that work is done in our dreams. Maggie and I are studying how that work gets done and how we can learn to do it better. We think that if people can learn to recognize when they're dreaming, they can learn to control their dreams and flush out their bad memories. If we're right, a lot of shrinks will have to find another line of work."

"Any side effects from what you do?"

"Like what?"

"Like people shooting themselves in the head or falling off buildings."

Maggie Brennan flinched, her chin snapping down to her chest, then up to the ceiling. If tics were contagious, I'd have thought she had caught it from me. Corliss shot her a hot glance; his eyes and mouth narrow darts.

"The police," she said, her voice so soft I wasn't certain she'd spoken until she said it again. "The police looked into what happened to Tom and Regina. It had nothing to do with our project."

"What Maggie means," Corliss said, "is that Tom Delaney committed suicide and Regina Blair slipped and fell. It's a sad coincidence that both of them were volunteers, but that's all it is."

"You're not troubled by the fact that both of them died in the same way they dreamed they would die, dreams that you were teaching them to control?"

"Hell, yes, it bothers me. It bothers me more when people like you come around trying to blame it on us. Look, every volunteer signs a waiver acknowledging that we are not treating them for any mental or physical condition and that they should consult their own doctor, whether psychologist or psychiatrist or podiatrist, before participating in the project. We are not responsible for their choices or their carelessness," Corliss said.

"Delaney's and Blair's families have hired a lawyer named Jason Bolt. He's got both of your names on a lawsuit. And he's got an expert witness who will testify that you are responsible."

"Lawyers and lawsuits don't intimidate me, Jack. That's what insurance is for and I'm betting Milo Harper has a shit-bucket full of insurance."

"Insurance will buy you a lawyer and pay a claim but it won't keep your name out of the paper. How do you feel about that, Dr. Brennan?"

She looked at me without feeling or expression. "When you've seen the things I've seen, the things people do to one another, it numbs you to something so trivial as a lawsuit. No one knows my name. If it's in the paper, it will be forgotten soon enough."

"If neither of you are impressed by Jason Bolt's lawsuit, why did you erase Delaney's and Blair's records from your project files?"

Maggie Brennan repeated her head bob, facing me. "We didn't do that."

"Who did?"

"Sherry Fritzshall," she said.

There was another label I left out—person of interest. It was reserved for people who hadn't earned the suspect label but had demonstrated great potential to make the jump. Sherry Fritzshall had moved to the top of that short list.

"When did she do that?"

"Right after the police finished looking into everything," Corliss said.

"Why did she do that?"

Corliss shrugged. "You'd have to ask her. My guess is she was afraid Delaney's or Blair's family would sue the institute, waiver or no waiver."

"What about Walter Enoch?"

Maggie Brennan fixed her eyes on her lap. Corliss shook his head.

"Wasn't he something? I about fell out of my chair when I read about him in the paper," Corliss said. "Squirreling away all that mail. Damn!"

"You keep losing volunteers, you're going to have to start drafting them."

"Hey, Walter was my mailman," Corliss said. "I talked him into volunteering. He went through the intake process, did the video, the initial EEG and fMRI testing, and then he quit before he ever did any of the lucid dreaming training."

"What did he dream about?"

"Walter had nightmares, not dreams. Nightmares are bad dreams that wake you up screaming at the demons," Corliss said.

"Suffocation," Maggie Brennan whispered. "He couldn't breathe. That's what he dreamed about. He was terrified to go to sleep."

"That boy was something else," Corliss said. "I wonder if he stole any of my mail."

Corliss thought he was a better dancer than I was a

wrestler. He was trying to slip away before I could get a grip, let alone win the best two out of three falls.

"I imagine the FBI will want to know too."

Corliss's eyes popped. "The newspaper said that the postal service was responsible for returning the stolen mail. What's the FBI got to do with it?"

"Walter Enoch was murdered. You be sure to hold on to his file."

Chapter Twenty-one

Corliss's office was in the middle of the floor across from a maze of cubicles that occupied a third of the interior space. Down the hall from his office, away from the elevators, was the entrance to a break room. That's where Janet and Gary were standing when I left Corliss's office. She was lecturing him, her back stiff against the wall, punctuating with her hands, chopping and circling the air, bouncing fingers off his chest. Gary stood at her side, nodding while looking at me.

Janet was full-figured and short enough that she had to look up to make eye contact with Gary as she brushed her shoulder length auburn hair to one side and then poked him to get his undivided attention. He was big and soft, a few strands of his finger-combed, tousled brown hair hanging down his forehead, his cheeks and chin flecked with a patchy scruff.

He broke her rhythm, tilting his head at me. She spun my way, peeled off the wall, and grabbed his hand.

They walked past the break room and into an office, closing the door.

I couldn't tell whether they were waiting for me or avoiding me. Either way, I wanted to talk with them. Corliss hadn't wasted any of his charm on them. Some people who are embarrassed by their bosses in front of others are reluctant to trash them behind their back, too afraid their rant will get back to their boss; others can't wait for the chance.

I knocked and opened the door. It was a cramped, windowless office, two desks pushed together, a crowded bookshelf on one wall, file cabinets against another, journals stacked on top of the cabinets, room carved out for a framed photograph of the two of them, Janet in a wedding dress, Gary in a tux. They were sitting at their desks, silent, their faces tense and expectant.

"I didn't get a chance to introduce myself before," I said, letting the door swing closed. "I'm Jack Davis."

Gary looked at Janet, nominating her. "I'm Janet," she said. "He's Gary."

One wall was papered with their undergraduate diplomas from Indiana and master's degrees in psychology from Wisconsin. The dates on the sheepskins put them in their mid-to-late twenties.

"You're Casey and he's Kaufman," I said, reading their last names. "Married too," I added, pointing to the photograph.

"Married too," she said.

"Kids?"

"No kids, dogs, cats, or birds. Just us," she said.

"I'm new here," I said. "Just trying to get to know people. Matter of fact, today is my first day. What's it like working here?"

Janet let out a sigh, raising her eyebrows, passing the question to Gary.

"Depends on whom you work for and what you do," he said. "We're researchers. We stick to our project and don't really have much to do with any of the other stuff that goes on."

"You guys work for Anthony Corliss and Maggie Brennan. How's that?"

Gary shrugged. "Maggie's okay."

"She gives me the creeps," Janet said. "She wears that same gray coat and scarf every damn day, hot or cold, rain or shine, it's like a shroud. The woman is in serious need of some color in her life."

"What do you do?" Gary asked.

"My title is director of security."

"What is that?" Janet said. "You're like Homeland Security? Are we going to have to pass through metal detectors and put our liquids in three-ounce containers?"

"Not unless we turn this place into an airport."

"What then?" Janet asked, giving me a microscopic look, daring me to be straight with her.

"Depends on the situation. Could be something as simple as making sure the institute's intellectual property is protected. And, it could be more complicated, like making certain that no one who volunteers to participate in an institute research project gets hurt."

"Like Tom Delaney and Regina Blair," Gary said.

I nodded. "Like them."

Janet slammed her palm on her desk, glaring at Gary. "I told you we shouldn't have come here."

He threw his arms up. "Like we had another choice."

"What am I missing?" I asked. "Were you drafted or did you enlist?"

Gary answered. "You have any idea how hard it is to get into a decent graduate PhD program in psychology? Let me tell you. It's harder to get in to than law school, medical school, or business school. The numbers will make you faint. Plus, you apply to work with a specific professor as much as the university. We were lucky. Corliss took both of us to work in his lab at Wisconsin. The odds against that happening were astronomical."

"And then he left Wisconsin to work here," I said.

"Exactly," Janet said. "And we were screwed. We'd finished our master's but we still had another three years for our doctorates."

"Couldn't you have stayed and worked in another lab or transferred to another school?"

"Not after what happened."

I waited for one of them to volunteer the details, letting the uneasy silence ask the question. Gary filled the void.

"We were doing the same kind of research at Wisconsin as we're doing here, running the same kind of subjects, doing the lucid dreaming training. All the subjects were undergrads. They did it for extra credit. One of the volunteers, a girl, drowned in Lake Mendota. Her parents claimed she committed suicide and sued the university, said we should have known she was suicidal and referred her for treatment. The university wrote a big, fat check to her parents and shut down Corliss's lab."

"Where's Lake Mendota?"

"Not far from Madison, where the university is."

"Did she leave a note?"

Janet answered. "No. No note."

"You said you used the same protocols at Wisconsin as you do here. Did that include videotaping subjects about their dreams?" They both gave me sharp, questioning looks. "Anthony Corliss told me about the videos," I said, hoping that would satisfy them.

Gary leaned back in his chair, hands in his lap. "Yeah."

"Tell me about the girl's dream. Did she dream about drowning?"

Janet looked at Gary, nodding. "Yeah, she did. That really freaked us out," he said.

"Afterward, nobody at Wisconsin wanted anything to do with us and no other schools would touch us, even though Gary and I had nothing to do with what happened. We weren't named in the lawsuit, only Corliss was. On top of everything else, her parents claimed Corliss was screwing their daughter," Janet said.

"That part was bullshit and you know it!" Gary said. "There was never any proof."

She crossed her arms over her chest, her eyes flaring and then turned toward me. "We owed over a hundred thousand in student loans, our lab was gone, and we couldn't get a job selling shoes. Corliss got a good deal to come here that included bringing us along."

"Well, the good deal may not be so good," I said. "Delaney's and Blair's families are suing the institute, Milo Harper, and your bosses, Dr. Corliss and Dr. Brennan."

"Oh, crap!" Janet said.

"I'm afraid there's more," I said. "You guys are getting sued too."

"Us!" Gary said, slamming his fist against the wall. "What the fuck did we do?"

"We came here," Janet said.

"Well, maybe we'll all get lucky and the lawyer who's suing us will die too," Gary said.

Janet sat upright. "Christ, Gary! Don't say that."

"Why not?" he said. "We're all going to die. What difference does it make if a few people here and there go ahead of schedule?"

"Two people are dead already. That's enough," Janet said.

"Three," I said. "Another one of your volunteers, Walter Enoch, is the third." Janet's chin dropped, her hands gripping the edge of her desk. "I gather you don't read the paper or watch TV."

"We don't own a TV," Gary said.

"And, nobody reads the paper anymore. Everything is on the Web," Janet said. "What happened?"

"He was murdered. Died just the way he dreamed he would."

Gary didn't say a word. Janet put her head on her desk.

"Shit," she said. "We are so totally screwed."

Chapter Twenty-two

I was doing my drunk walk by the time I got back to my office, legs buckling, playing tag with the walls and furniture to stay upright. Leonard followed me into my office as I stumbled into my chair.

"What is up with that?" he asked.

"I'm in training for *Dancing with the Stars*. Find Sherry and tell her I want to see her in my office. Now. And close my door."

Corliss had brought some heavy baggage to the institute. I wondered what Milo Harper knew about Corliss when he hired him. Harper surely had enough money to hire people who hadn't been run out of town at their last job.

Lucy hadn't returned my call. I opened my cell to try her again and saw that she'd left me a message. I hadn't heard the phone ring so her call must have gone straight to voice mail. Her message said that she'd pick me up in an hour.

Leonard knocked and opened the door. "Sherry didn't answer. Her secretary says she's in a meeting."

"Tell her secretary to interrupt her."

"I did. I told her to tell Sherry that you wanted to see her immediately. She told Sherry and Sherry told her to tell me to tell you that something came up and she'd talk to you tomorrow."

I smiled, appreciating that Sherry was pimping me with my own excuses.

"Where's her office?"

"Opposite corner from here. What are you going to do?"

"Interrupt her ass."

Leonard's eyes got as big as his grin. "Can I watch?"

"Sorry. You're not old enough."

I kept close to the wall, bracing my hand against it as I walked to Sherry's office. I didn't knock. Her office wrapped around the south and east corners of the building. The Harper art collection was on display, in sharp contrast to the subtle shades of deep lavender and pale yellow in the furnishings. Her desk dominated one wall, a black granite surface resting on twin steel pillars, adorned with a tall red vase holding fresh-cut flowers.

She was sitting at a round table in one corner with two male staffers who had the fresh look of recent college grads and the slumping posture of subordinates. They looked up when I came in, Sherry glaring, the boys staring as I groped my way to an empty chair at their table, grabbing it for balance.

"Get out," I told the boys.

"You have no business . . ." Sherry said, but I cut her off.

"Oh, I do." I turned back to the boys. "I said, get out."

They looked at me and then at her. She nodded and they left.

"Are you crazy, drunk, or both?" she asked.

"I have a movement disorder that makes me shake. When I get tired, I do my drunken sailor act. I toss in crazy for free."

She folded her arms over her chest. "Must be hard to play the tough guy when you can't stand up straight."

"I manage."

"I could have had you thrown out."

"You could have tried."

She sighed. "I didn't want to embarrass you any more than you'd already embarrassed yourself. Let's get this over with so I can get back to work. What do you want?"

"Did you delete Tom Delaney's and Regina Blair's files?"

"The police said their deaths had nothing to do with us. They were no longer part of the project. There was no reason to keep their files."

"So you deleted them?"

"I give orders. I don't push buttons."

"Who pushed the buttons?"

"Someone in IT whose job is pushing buttons."

"If their deaths were unrelated to their participation in the dream project, why erase their records? What were you afraid of?"

"Oh, c'mon Jack. Be a grown-up. People file lawsuits if they get a blister. These two died and Milo has the deepest pockets in six states. It would be hard to find a bigger target."

"Jason Bolt has put the institute on notice that he's going to sue you. Aren't you worried about destroying evidence?"

"The files were deleted in accordance with our document retention policy before we received Bolt's letter. The decision had nothing to do with a lawsuit."

"That's not what you said."

"That's how I'll testify."

"And if I won't back you up?"

"I'm general counsel for the institute. This conversation is protected by attorney-client privilege. The court won't let you say a word about it and, if you do, we'll sue you and collect every last disability and pension check with your name on it."

"Just leave me gas money so I can come visit you when you're in prison for obstruction of justice in a murder investigation. Now what was so disturbing on those videos?"

She stood and circled to her desk.

"I didn't watch them."

I nodded, giving her credit. "So you can testify that your decision to destroy the tapes had nothing to do with their content since you never saw them."

"Nightmares are powerful and frightening. They can make people do strange things even when the nightmares belong to someone else. I didn't want to take that chance with a jury. I told you. I'll do whatever it takes to protect my brother."

"Your brother said that he'd do anything to protect the institute and you'll do anything to protect him. There has to be a limit to how far either of you will go."

"We're not even close."

* * *

I didn't have to throw anyone out of Milo Harper's office. He was alone, surrounded by stacks of reports, binders, and papers. Three flat-screen computer monitors ringed his desk. A sixty-inch plasma TV hung on one wall, soundlessly tuned to CNBC. The blinds were drawn, the light subdued, as if he didn't want to know what day or time it was.

I dropped into a round-backed chair opposite his desk.

"What's up?" he asked.

"Did you know about Anthony Corliss's adventures at the University of Wisconsin when you hired him?"

Harper smiled. "You mean the girl who died, the lawsuit, and the rumors that he and the girl were having an affair?"

"Yeah. That."

"Corliss told me what happened the first time I talked to him. He put me in touch with his attorney who put me in touch with the university's attorney. My attorneys talked to the police in Wisconsin and reviewed everything. They told me that the university caved to avoid bad publicity and that Corliss got a raw deal. Wouldn't be the first time a lawsuit was settled for those reasons."

Harper was right but that didn't mean his lawyers were. Still, he'd done his due diligence and I had to give him credit for that.

"Who runs your IT department?" I asked.

"Frank Gentry."

"Invite him to join us."

Harper made the call and went back to what he was doing while we waited for Gentry as if I wasn't there. I took the time to survey Harper's office. The walls were lined with bookshelves crammed with technical and scientific books. There was no room for the Harper art collection.

Five minutes later, Frank Gentry was at the door. He wore a jacket and tie, the only old-school person I'd met at the institute. He was slim, well into his sixties, with a buzz cut etching the boundaries of a receded hairline. He stood ramrod straight until Harper looked up and waved him in.

"Frank, say hello to Jack Davis. Do whatever he asks you to do." He selected a paper from the stack on his desk, ignoring us.

"Mr. Davis," Gentry said, giving my hand a firm shake.

"Someone in your department deleted a couple of video files from the dream project. Can you retrieve them?"

He bristled. "We have a strict protocol on file retention. Nothing gets deleted unless I sign off on it. I don't recall approving the deletion of any video files."

"Well, they're gone. Sherry Fritzshall says she told someone in your department to do it."

Harper leaned back in his chair, forgetting everything else. Gentry pursed his lips, hesitating to respond. He looked at Harper.

"Sir, it's hard to keep my people in line if your sister keeps going around me."

"I'll remind her. Can you retrieve the files?"

"It depends on how deep the purge was. Whose files are we talking about?"

"Tom Delaney and Regina Blair," I said.

"I'll see what I can do. Anything else?"

"Couple of things," I said. "Anthony Corliss has software on his computer that tells him whenever anyone accesses the dream project files. I want that software deleted from his computer. If it's on anyone else's computers, I want to know whose and I want it deleted from their computers as well. Then I want you to put it on my computer and my laptop. I'll bring the laptop in tomorrow morning."

Gentry nodded, looking at Harper who nodded in return.

"One other thing," I said. "I want a log of everyone who has accessed the dream project files in the last six months. And I want you to do all of this yourself. Don't delegate it to anyone and don't discuss it with anyone other than me."

"Yes, sir, Mr. Davis. I should have this taken care of for you by noon tomorrow."

"Take care of the alert software before you leave today and call me when you're finished with that." I gave him my cell phone number. "Tomorrow is fine for the rest."

"You going to tell me what that's all about?" Harper asked when we were alone.

"I want to see those videos. I'm going to be spending a lot of time looking at the dream project files and I don't want Corliss looking over my shoulder. I want to know who has been in those files and I want to know who looks at them going forward."

"That sounds like the makings of a list of suspects."

"Not suspects, not yet. Just people who may know something."

"Why did my sister have those files deleted?"

"To keep Jason Bolt from getting them."

"Should that make me sleep any better?"

"What's the difference? You don't sleep anyway. I've got one more question. I'm going to need some outside help. Don't ask me who or what. You'll have to trust me. What's my budget?

"Whatever it takes."

Chapter Twenty-three

I headed to the elevator when Lucy called, saying she was waiting in the circle drive. Maggie Brennan got on when it stopped on the third floor. She was a head shorter than me but solid, thick without being heavy, bundled in a gray overcoat, her head wrapped in a gray scarf, just as Janet Casey had described. A black purse was slung over her shoulder, the monochromatic outfit making her invisible on a cloudy day or dark night. Even were the sun shining, she evoked anonymity, someone passersby would neither notice nor remember. She glanced up at me and then lowered her head, reminding me of her reaction in Corliss's office.

"Have we met before today?" I asked her.

"I don't believe so."

"It's just that when I walked in on you and Dr. Corliss, it was like you knew me and not in a good way."

"You'll have to forgive me. I startle easily. I meant no offense."

"None taken. It's a small world. I used to be with the FBI. I have lunch with a group of guys, all retired law enforcement. We kick around cold cases, the ones we didn't solve. One of the guys, a retired sheriff, had a case where a couple was killed. They had a daughter named Maggie Brennan, same as you."

"I googled my name once. There were too many Maggie Brennans to count."

It was a politician's response, neither admitting nor denying. I knew many victims of crime who, like war veterans, wouldn't talk about their experiences, especially to strangers.

"So, how do you do it?" I asked her.

"Do what?"

"Teach people to control their dreams."

She raised her head a fraction. "The short explanation is that we use external cues during REM sleep such as recordings and tactile stimuli like special lights that alert the subject to the dream state without interrupting it."

"I've never heard of that before. It sounds impossible."

"Don't confuse the unfamiliar with the improbable," she said.

"Does it really work?"

"I'm an agnostic. We don't have enough data yet. But if we can't answer that question soon, Milo Harper will cut off our funding and we may never find out."

"What do the volunteers tell you?"

"Some subjects tell us that they are able to recognize when they're dreaming and then direct their dreams. Three-fourths of dream content is negative, frightening, and scary. These people say they can make their dreams more pleasing."

The elevator doors opened and I followed her into the lobby.

"What's that do for them when they're awake?"

She stopped, raising her head to mine. Her eyes were dark pools, anxious and sad.

"Dreams allow us to overcome inhibitions so we can do the things we fantasize about when we're awake. People who can control their dreams may be better able to break free of their inhibitions."

I wondered whether she would change her mind when she found out that Jason Bolt's expert witness agreed with her. "Does that make them better or worse?"

"It depends on the inhibition. Overcoming an inhibition to assert yourself can make you a better employee. Overcoming an inhibition about sex can make you a better lover."

"What about the inhibitions that protect us from our worst impulses?"

"It should be obvious that overcoming those inhibitions can have unfortunate consequences."

"Like suicide?"

"I'm a neuroscientist. I study the effects of psychological trauma on the brain. Dr. Corliss is a psychologist. He deals with behavior."

"How?"

"By helping people overcome their inhibitions."

"Even if it kills them?"

"You'll have to ask Dr. Corliss."

"I'm asking you. Did Tom Delaney and Regina Blair die because Corliss taught them to overcome their inhibitions?

"You are asking a question I cannot answer."

"Can't or won't?"

"Can't. Who can say why such things happen?"

"But if that is what happened to Delaney and Blair, their deaths would be powerful proof of your theories. Harper might even keep funding you if no one found out that your study had a fatal flaw."

"Those are Dr. Corliss's theories, not mine."

"I thought you were partners in this project."

"He is the lead investigator. We have different responsibilities. I'm concerned with memories, the input, if you will, of dreams. He's concerned with dreams and their effect on behavior, the output from those memories. That said, if what you suggest is true, it would be powerful proof, though I admit it raises ethical questions I leave to philosophers. As for the funding, well, I don't share Anthony's ambitions. I'm tired and I'll be relieved when my work ends."

"That's a pretty casual attitude about an experiment that may kill people."

"Perhaps, but I suppose I'm too used to death. I've studied many people who were perpetrators or victims of violence and I can tell you one thing I've learned. Killing is easy. Dying is hard."

"How about you? Have you learned to control your dreams?"

Her eyes searched mine and I saw in them a shared pain. We both knew the aftermath of violent death.

"Nightmares, Mr. Davis. I have nightmares that never leave me and no one can control. If you'll excuse me, I have a long drive. I live in the country where roads don't get plowed and the snow stays until it melts."

She pushed the Call button for the elevator to the parking garage.

"It's possible that Delaney didn't commit suicide but that his dreams still caused his death," I said.

The garage elevator opened. She stood, her back to me, as three people stepped onto the elevator, turning around when the doors closed.

"You're suggesting he and Walter Enoch were both murdered?"

"And maybe Regina Blair, though I've got nothing to go on there except that she was a dream project volunteer like Delaney and Enoch."

"And was it their dreams or their participation in our project that proved fatal?"

"It could be both," I said.

"You look as though you are concerned about more than that. Are you worried about me? Do you think there is a madman at work who might threaten me because I have nightmares?"

"There may be."

"You needn't worry. I've known for a long time how my life will end."

"You sound like a fatalist. I thought scientists were rationalists."

"I know what I know," she said.

"Knowing how you'll die is one thing. Knowing when is another."

"The when will take care of itself," she said. In the meantime, will you protect me?"

"Yes."

She patted me on the arm. "Then I won't worry. I'll leave that to you."

Chapter Twenty-four

Nancy flagged me as I passed the front desk.

"You leaving already?" she asked.

"Hell, I'm lucky they haven't fired me yet."

She laughed. "I don't think luck's got anything to do with it."

"Are you a religious person?"

"I know that Jesus Christ is my Lord and Savior, if that's what you mean," she said.

"I heard you reciting the Twenty-third Psalm this morning. I couldn't tell whether that was a prayer or a warning."

"A little of both."

"Should I be worried?"

"I'd worry if people who come in here keep on dying. I heard about the mailman on the news. He's the third one in a month. People better wake up and pray."

* * *

Lucy was waiting in the circle drive. I slid into the passenger seat. Before I could buckle the seat belt, I was shaking and grunting, my back arched and rigid, my neck wrapped around the headrest. Concentrated activity, like the day I'd put in, held the tics at bay but when I took a break, they swarmed. The guerrilla attack didn't last long, maybe ten seconds, but it made time stand still.

"How about if I drive?" Lucy asked when order had been restored.

I appreciated her pragmatic response. It took me a long time before I was able to shake off the shakes like water off a duck's back, but Lucy got it right, acknowledging my condition without dramatizing it.

"Great idea. So, how was your day? Did you find a car?"

"Drove past some dealerships," she said, pulling into traffic.

Though not yet dark, drivers crept along, leading with their headlights, wary of slick spots on the pavement though much of the snow had been pushed to the curb. We got caught in the aftermath of a six-car chain reaction rear-end collision that turned a ten-minute drive from the institute to our house into a thirty-minute crawl.

"Didn't see anything you liked?"

"Didn't look."

"What did you do all day?"

"I took a tour."

"What kind of tour."

"The dead man tour. It was great. No waiting. I started at Walter Enoch's house, then swung by Tom Delaney's apartment, and finished up at Regina Blair's parking garage."

I should have been surprised but I wasn't. She'd told me that she had read Delaney's and Blair's incident reports. I could yell at her, tell her to mind her own business. I could make her pull over, give me the keys, get out, and call a cab. I could move out of her house, stay at Joy's while she was out of town, and look for a new place if that's what it took to get rid of Lucy. But I didn't do any of that because she had done what needed to be done, knowing that I couldn't and that I was too bull-headed to ask for her help.

"How'd that work out?"

She flashed me a grin that showed her molars. "Fair to middling. I'll show you what I've got when we get home."

While we were stuck in traffic, I called Kate Scranton.

"You busy tonight?" I asked her.

"Nothing too important. Catching up on paper-work."

"Come on over and bring your laptop."

"What about my toothbrush?"

"Absolutely. And dinner for four wouldn't hurt either."

"You're having a party, I'm bringing dinner, and laptops are included?"

"It will be good for your bottom line. And don't scrimp on dinner. I've got an expense account."

"Who was that?" Lucy asked.

"Kate Scranton. She's a jury consultant and a psychologist and she's an expert in reading facial expressions."

"I'm no expert, but from the 'cat-that-ate-the-canary' look on your face, she's more than that," she said, the flush I felt in my face egging her on. "She's the one, isn't she? Your friend from Saturday night."

I nodded. "Am I that easy?"

"Make it tougher on me next time, keep your tongue in your mouth."

"I'll try to remember that."

My next call was to Simon Alexander.

"It's payback time," I told him.

"What did I do?"

"Hooked me up with Milo Harper. I need you at my house. Bring your laptop, a couple of printers, and a lot of paper. Kate's bringing dinner."

"What's the name of the game we're playing?"

"The dead man."

Chapter Twenty-five

Roxy and Ruby jumped us when we came home, forcing us onto the kitchen floor to play with them. Lucy and I sat opposite one another, our backs against cabinet doors. Roxy settled into Lucy's lap, raising her head so that Lucy could stroke her neck and belly in one continuous motion. Ruby planted her front paws on my chest, her eyes boring into mine until I conceded her dominance.

"That dog owns you," Lucy said.

"I could do worse."

I lifted Ruby off the floor, spun her onto her back, rubbed her belly, and let her go. She scrambled to her feet, ready for the best two out of three falls. Roxy sprang to life, not wanting to be left out.

"You're on your own," Lucy said. "I'm going upstairs and clean up."

"Dinner," I announced to the dogs, clapping my hands.

Ruby eats at the speed of light. Roxy dawdles while

Ruby watches, waiting for a chance to poach her food, forcing me to stand guard to make sure Roxy doesn't go hungry. I grabbed my laptop and loaded Walter Enoch's dream video from my flash drive so I could watch it while the dogs ate.

The doorbell rang as the video finished downloading. Roxy bolted for the front door. Ruby froze, torn between greeting company and raiding Roxy's bowl until I picked it up. She gave me a dirty look and then raced after Roxy.

I opened the door. It was Kent and Dolan. Cockapoos are known for their indiscriminate affection and weak bladders when they are excited and nothing excites them more than greeting someone new. The dogs clambered over both agents before they could cross the threshold, peeing on their shoes.

"Goddamn mutts," Dolan said.

He kicked at Roxy and Ruby. They dodged his shoe and retreated into the house behind me.

"You touch my dogs and I'll shoot you with your gun."

"Easy. Easy. We've got a search warrant," Kent said, reaching into his overcoat and handing it to me.

The warrant was for any written or electronic communications to or from Wendy Davis.

"You've also got dog piss on your shoes. Take them off."

"Give me something to wipe them off with," Dolan said.

I stuffed the warrant in his hand. Dolan wadded it into a ball and reached for me when Kent stepped in front of him.

"See what I'm doing," Kent said. "I'm taking my shoes off." A vein in Dolan's forehead throbbed as he faced his partner. "Take yours off and we'll get what we came for and get out of here."

"Goddamn mutts," Dolan said, as he kicked off his shoes, leaving them next to Kent's on the front stoop.

They didn't take long with their search, rifling through drawers and pulling books off of shelves, fanning the pages and waiting for incriminating evidence to fall out. I followed behind them as they went upstairs, Dolan catching Lucy's bedroom door with his chin when she came out while he was going in.

"Son of a bitch!" Dolan said. "Who the hell are you?"

"Who the hell are you?" she asked.

"We're FBI agents," Kent said. "We're executing a search warrant. Please identify yourself."

"It's okay," I said. "The dogs peed on their shoes."

Lucy giggled. "Really? Roxy and Ruby peed on their shoes?"

"Golden rain," I said.

"I love those dogs," she said. "I'm Lucy Trent. This is my house."

Kent looked at me. "That right?"

"She's my landlady."

We finished the search as a foursome, ending in the kitchen.

"That your laptop?" Dolan asked, pointing to my computer sitting on the kitchen counter next to Roxy's dinner.

I nodded. "You can search the dog food too if you want."

He tucked the laptop under his arm. "Warrant covers electronic communications. We'll let you know when you can have it back."

The dogs stayed in the kitchen, letting me escort Kent and Dolan to their shoes.

"What was that about?" Lucy asked after we watched them drive away.

"The envelope Ammara Iverson found on Walter Enoch's body was from my daughter Wendy. She used the initials MG for the return address, which stands for Monkey Girl. That was my nickname for her."

"I didn't know you had a daughter."

"She died ten months ago."

"I'm so sorry. What happened?"

We sat on the sofa in the living den, a dog in each of our laps, and I told Lucy about Wendy, just the broad strokes, how she struggled, how she rallied only to fall back, how her addiction claimed her, and how her mother and I failed her.

"The FBI is convinced Wendy stole five million dollars from the drug ring. They think that whatever was in the envelope had something to do with the money and that I know where it is. They also think I found out that Walter Enoch had stolen Wendy's letter so I killed him when I stole it back."

"How do you know that's what they think?"

I told her about my meeting with Kent and Dolan and Ammara Iverson and my conversation afterward with Ammara.

"Do you know where the money is?"

"No."

"Do you know what was in that envelope?"

"No."

"Did you kill Walter Enoch?"

"No."

"Do you have an alibi for when he was killed?"

"I don't know when he was killed other than it was a day or two before his body was found. I can account for where I was and what I was doing but I don't have witnesses who can vouch for every minute."

"Why didn't you ask Dolan and Kent when Enoch was killed?" Lucy asked.

"It wasn't important to me. I didn't think I was a suspect."

"Yeah, but they may not see it that way. They may have expected you to ask, figuring if you didn't it was because you already knew. That's the way I'd see it."

Her cop logic was sound enough to make me shake. I'd made the mistake of acting like an innocent man, which was the surest way to arouse suspicion. Lucy pressed me again.

"Do they have any proof that you know where the money is or what was in the envelope or that you killed Walter Enoch?"

"Not until they get a look at my laptop. Enoch volunteered for the Harper Institute's dream project. They made a videotape of him describing a nightmare in which he suffocated to death, which happens to be how he died, with an assist from the killer. I found the video today in the dream project computer files and copied it to my flash drive. I had just finished loading it on my laptop when they rang the doorbell. Once they find the video, they'll go nuts."

"Why? You can explain why you had the video and when you got it. The timing has nothing to do with Enoch's murder."

"But the fact that I have it fits with their larger narrative."

"Oh, shit! That isn't all they'll find on your laptop. I e-mailed you the pictures I took of Enoch and his house with my cell phone. They'll love my explanation of that."

I'd seen the pictures. They were no use to me but Dolan and Kent would treat them as further proof that I was guilty of crimes ranging from conspiracy to murder no matter how I explained them. They were the kind of cops that shoved the facts into their theories no matter how square the pegs or how round the holes.

"The video and the pictures are enough to make them keep coming after me. When they see that you e-mailed the photographs to me, you'll be in the soup too."

"So let them keep coming. You're innocent."

"Lucy, you were a cop. You know how guys like Kent and Dolan think. They've already convicted me. Being right matters more to them than the truth."

Chapter Twenty-six

Frank Gentry called, confirming that he'd deleted Anthony Corliss's alert software and installed it on the desktop computer in my office and that no one else was using the software. I caught Simon while he was still at his office, telling him to bring an additional laptop for me.

Lucy left and came back carrying pads of poster-sized Post-its and a fistful of markers in a rainbow of colors. Her cheeks were red from the cold and her eyes were dancing and bright, fueled by our chase of the dead man.

She stripped the living den walls, papering the empty spaces with blank Post-its. I needed to rest so I sat in the recliner watching her work, genuflecting with intermittent spasms.

"I learned under a great homicide detective," Lucy said. "She taught me that the best way to put a case together is to visualize it. Put it on the walls, let the facts paint the picture."

"I do it the same way. Put each case on a separate wall. Start with what we know about each of the victims and how they died. Then we'll fill in what you saw at each of the scenes. We'll also have to keep track of witnesses, evidence, and questions we need answered, plus links between the cases."

She turned toward me, hands on her hips. "Gee, great ideas. I never would have thought of any of that."

We mirrored each other's grins, both glad to be back in the hunt, realizing how much we had missed it.

"Okay, okay. I get it," I said, the words staggering out of my mouth like drunks leaving a bar at closing time. My neck arched and stretched, shoving my head upward and back, raising my chin like the open end of a drawbridge and locking me in the pose until the spasm passed. "I guess this isn't your first time."

"No. But it's my first time in a while, same for you. We need to check each other's work. Shake the rust off."

"Might as well. I'm shaking everything else."

She stood over my chair, looking at me with soft, sad eyes and laughed, giving me a quick hug. "You are something, you know that. Tell you what. I'll write. You edit."

"This isn't the first essay I've ever written, Dad," Wendy said.

She was applying for college. The application included an essay on the highs and lows of her life and what she'd learned from them. She said her lows were the death of her brother and her addiction and her highs were staying straight and sober for over a year and graduating from high school. She wrote that she learned the same thing from the highs and the lows. You

*can't always choose what happens to you but you can choose
how you deal with it.*

*"Are you sure you want to put yourself on the line like
that?" I asked her when she showed me a draft and asked for
my comments.*

"This is who I am. What else would I write about?"

"Something that doesn't label you as high risk."

*She laughed. "Are you serious, Dad? High risk is tattooed
all over me. I can't run away from that. Tell you what, I'll
write, you edit."*

"Works for me," I told Lucy.

She made her way around the room, using different
color markers for different topics: black for victims,
blue for witnesses, green for evidence, red for the crime
scene, though she labeled it THE DEAD MAN in all
caps, winking at me over her shoulder as she wrote. Her
handwriting was hurried, her shoulder and neck muscles bundled and flexed as she worked.

She didn't look like Wendy. She was taller and her hair
was shorter and darker. She was cocky while Wendy was
leery. In spite of their differences, I sensed in her the
same urgency about life Wendy had shown, as if they
knew that they'd closed more doors than they'd
opened and that they were running out of doors. There
were no words for how much I missed my daughter.
There were only memories Lucy was bringing to life,
making me realize that this could be the land of second
chances for both of us.

Chapter Twenty-seven

Kate rang the doorbell while Lucy was still hanging the new wallpaper. When I introduced them, Lucy leaned into Kate, whispering something in her ear that made them both giggle like schoolgirls, look at me, and laugh again.

"What?" I demanded.

"Oh, nothing," Kate said.

She was holding two bags of carryout from Bo Ling's. She handed one bag to Lucy as they locked arms and headed for the kitchen.

When Simon arrived a few minutes later, he stared at Lucy's handiwork, then looked at me, his mouth open.

"Everything will be illuminated," I said. "After we eat."

I spread out dinner in the kitchen while Simon set up an office in the dining room. The dogs, exhausted from the parade of people, slept under the kitchen table, waking long enough to scavenge for crumbs.

When we finished our fortune cookies, I laid everything out for Kate and Simon.

Simon pushed back from the table, his eyebrows raised. "Lucid dreaming sounds like junk science to me."

"Maybe, maybe not," Kate said. "The work I do is all about what's going on beneath the surface. Dreams are part of that so I stay current with the research, which is all over the place. Freud thought dreams were the way we fulfilled our forbidden aggressive and sexual wishes. Later, people thought that dreams were the cognitive echoes of our efforts to work out conflicting emotions. Now some researchers will tell you that dreams are just epiphenomena."

"Translation, please," Simon said.

"Sorry," Kate said. "They think that dreams don't mean anything at all, that dreams are just the mind's attempt to make sense of random neural firings while the body restores itself during sleep."

"So, dreams are noise the brain makes while it's doing its homework?" Lucy asked.

"That's exactly how one researcher at Harvard explains it. But there's other research that suggests that dreams are a training ground where people rehearse survival behaviors. I read a report by one psychologist who said he helped a patient reframe his nightmare by rehearsing alternatives to the most frightening part while he was awake. Eventually, the nightmare went away. That doesn't sound so different from what Anthony Corliss is trying to do."

"Except for one thing," I said. "Instead of helping his subjects reframe their nightmares, he may be helping to turn them into reality."

"Why would he do that?" Lucy asked.

"It's the rule of unintended consequences. It's not what he's trying to do but it's what happens," I said, repeating Maggie Brennan's explanation that lucid dreaming may help people overcome their inhibitions, causing them to do things they would otherwise never do.

"Do we know if anyone else is doing this kind of research?" Kate asked. "Maybe they've had similar experiences."

"I don't know about that, but this has happened before with Corliss," I said, telling them about the girl at Wisconsin who drowned.

"If Milo Harper knew about that, how could he have hired Corliss?" Kate asked.

"Corliss told him all about it and Harper's lawyers talked to the lawyers for Corliss and the university. They say Corliss got hosed."

"Of course that's what they would say," Kate said. "They didn't talk to the lawyer for the girl's family. They made their mind up after hearing only one side of the story. Harper wanted to hire Corliss. His lawyers knew that and they made sure their client got what he wanted."

"You don't know that," I said.

"I know Harper and I know lawyers. That's enough for me," she said.

"I'm a software guy," Simon said. "I can program a computer but I don't believe you can program someone to kill themselves. Besides, you said the mailman was murdered."

"Jack, Simon's right," Kate said, "and assuming you are not a mad dog killer and thief and that Anthony Corliss and Milo Harper aren't crazy, what's going on?"

"Let me take a crack at it," Simon said. "The way I see

it, there are a few possibilities. First, Delaney and Blair weren't murdered but Enoch was, making for one crime. Second, Delaney and or Blair were murdered, making for two or three crimes that are potentially connected. Third, all three were murdered, which, given their participation in the dream project, increases the likelihood the murders are connected."

"Which is a nice way of saying that they were committed by the same person. And, if they were, the killer may not be finished," Lucy said.

"Are you talking about a serial killer?" Kate asked.

"It's possible," Lucy said. "By definition, a serial killer has at least three victims and they usually share things in common. These victims were all volunteers in the dream project. And, they died—or were killed—over a short span of time with a shorter time between the second and third murders than the first and second, which is typical of a serial killer on a spree."

"What's the timeline?" Simon asked.

"Blair died on December tenth, Delaney on January ninth, and Enoch died last week on the twenty-third. The interval between Delaney and Blair was thirty days. It was fourteen between Blair and Enoch. If I'm right, another victim will turn up in the next few days."

"So the killer must be someone involved in the dream project," Kate said.

"Whoa. Slow down, CSI," I said. Though I'd raised the same prospect with Maggie Brennan, I didn't want my makeshift team running wild. "We're a long way from profiling a serial killer. They usually commit ritualized murders with a heavy sexual component. The murders look alike from how the victims were killed, to the letters spelled with words cut out of magazines and sent to the local newspaper. Apart from Delaney's, Blair's, and

Enoch's participation in the dream project, we don't have any of that here. Plus, a serial killer doesn't account for Wendy's envelope."

"The thing about the letters to the newspaper," Kate said, "that's just an example, right. You don't mean every serial killer does that."

"No," I said. "My point is that serial killers operate in a pattern. They keep body parts as souvenirs. They like to taunt the police, maybe even insert themselves in the investigation because they think they're too clever to be caught. There's no evidence of a sexual component in any of these deaths. None of the bodies was mutilated and there have been no communications from the killer."

"It's not like baking a cake. Just because it doesn't fit the pattern so far, you can't rule it out," Lucy said.

"Agreed," I said. "But that doesn't mean we only focus on single white men in their twenties and thirties who live alone and are sexually dysfunctional."

"And who set fires, abused animals, and wet their beds when they were kids," Simon added. "Hey, I watch TV too."

I sighed. "Try more Food Network and less *Law and Order*."

"What do you want us to do?" Kate asked.

"Help me fill in the blanks. There are two hundred and fifty volunteers in the dream project. Each of them was videotaped describing their dreams. I want you to take a look at the videos and tell me if anyone jumps out at you on the secret psycho scale. I'll give you my ID and password for the institute's computer system."

"Two hundred and fifty videos. Sure thing. Let me call the office and tell them I'm quitting my job."

"Don't tell them that. Tell them you just got a huge

piece of work at a premium rate. My budget is unlimited."

Her smile lit up her face. "That I can tell them."

"Simon, I want you to run background checks on the volunteers and the staff that had access to the dream project files. I'll know tomorrow which ones actually got into the files. Let's see who's had a restraining order entered against them, who's been arrested, and who's late on their mortgage."

"How soon do you want all this?" Simon asked.

"Now would be just fine. Is that a problem?"

"Were you serious about the unlimited budget?"

"Milo said I could spend whatever it takes."

"In that case, now is not a problem. It's impossible, but it isn't a problem."

"What Kate and Simon are going to do may not be enough," Lucy said. "A lot of serial killers are charming people like Ted Bundy or the BTK killer in Wichita. That guy was active in his church and was a Cub Scout leader."

"Look," I said, "we aren't going to make the same mistake Dolan and Kent made and assume we know anything until we can prove it. Why would a serial killer take whatever was in Wendy's envelope?"

"One reason," Lucy said. "The killer was picking his next victim."

Chapter Twenty-eight

"I don't buy that," I said. "It's too random. It doesn't fit the pattern."

"Don't underestimate the rules of randomness," Simon said.

"What are you talking about?"

"He's talking about the world," Kate said. "We like it orderly but it's mostly disorderly."

"From coin tosses to baseball to the stock market, the world is random," Simon said. "Hitters and stock pickers have hot streaks but over time, they regress to the mean. In the end, randomness rules."

"What's that got to do with murder?" Lucy asked.

"Everything," Kate said. "Einstein said it is a magnificent feeling to recognize the unity of a complex of phenomena which appear to be things quite apart from the direct visible truth. We're looking for an explanation that accounts for everything we know but if we limit ourselves to what's most obvious or most likely, there's a good chance we'll be wrong."

"Maybe so, but the direct visible truth is what I know. There are facts in common, that's it. Even if they added up to a pattern, I don't fit into it. I'm not a participant in the dream project."

"You are as connected to the Harper Institute as Delaney, Blair, and Enoch were, maybe more."

"If you widen the net that much you make every institute employee a potential victim, which doesn't tell you anything," I said.

"It's just as dangerous to make up your mind too soon that the case is one thing as it is to decide that it isn't something else," Lucy said.

"She's right," Kate said. "It's called the Endowment Effect. People attach more value to the things they own just because they own them whether they're coffee mugs or opinions. That's why we overvalue our houses so much we can't sell them and it's why we have such a difficult time changing our minds."

"Okay, I won't argue with that," I said. "I'll keep an open mind but I still don't buy that a killer has put my name on a list. Let's get to work."

Simon and Kate took over the dining room and Lucy and I went back to our poster art. She took the floor and I settled into the recliner.

"Take me on the dead man tour," I told her. "How'd you get into Enoch's house?"

"The back door. Flimsy lock. I have a set of picks."

"Possession of burglary tools," I joked.

"To be a crime, the tools have to be used to enter an occupied structure for the purpose of committing an offense therein. Enoch's house was not occupied and my motives were pure," she said, sticking her tongue out at me.

"All charges are dropped. What did you find?"

"Not that much, to tell you the truth. There were no signs of forced entry, which suggests that Enoch knew his killer."

"With all the stolen mail sitting around his house, he wasn't going to let a stranger in. It had to be someone he trusted."

"Or someone who forced his way in once Enoch opened the door. Easy enough if the killer had a gun."

"Could be the same person either way. Enoch may have known the killer well enough to open the door but not let him in. That's when the killer pulls a gun. Best bet is that Enoch knew the killer. What else?"

"Not much. The feds had emptied the place except for his clothes and furniture and there wasn't much of that. I checked the drawers and I went through his clothes but I didn't find anything helpful. When we were there the other night, it was like walking around in a giant storage closet jammed with junk. Today, you could hear echoes. He didn't have any pictures of family, friends, or dogs and cats. His television didn't work. He didn't have any books, magazines, or newspapers. This guy didn't just live alone. He was all alone."

"You took pictures?"

"With my digital camera. You want to see them now or later?"

"Later. Did you break into Delaney's apartment too?"

"Nope. I told the manager I was looking for a place to live. I had her show me empty units until we got to his. When I told her I was interested in that one, she told me that the last tenant had killed himself in the apartment. I told her I wanted to spend some time in the apartment by myself to see if that creeped me out so she left me there."

"Any luck?"

"Nada. I went over every inch of the place looking for a bullet hole the crime scene techs may have missed."

"You picked up on the missing bullet they couldn't account for."

"Hard to miss that when I read the incident report. It could be the key to everything else. The angle of the entry wound, the whole gun in the right hand and wound in the left temple, all of that bothered me. I figure the shooter popped him, then put the gun in Delaney's hand and fired a second time so Delaney would have powder burns on his gun hand."

"But you didn't find another bullet or bullet hole."

She shook her head. "Just like Enoch's house. It had been sanitized by the time I got there."

"The gun was a Beretta 92f loaded with jacketed .9mm rounds. A thick book would stop one of those rounds before it got to the last page. The scene photographs show some bookshelves. We need to find someone who was in the apartment while Delaney was alive and can look at those pics and tell us if any books are missing."

"What are the odds of that?"

"Zero if we don't try."

"I can go back there tonight and knock on some doors. Better chance that I'll find people at home now than during the day."

"Run me through the Blair scene first."

"She was found in an alley between a garage and office building, both of which are connected by covered walkways at each floor level. If she was pushed, the killer could have come from any floor of the building or the garage."

"You find anything that suggests she was pushed?"

"Maybe," Lucy said, putting a blank Post-it poster on the wall. "It's a simple physics problem." She drew a two-dimensional sketch of the profile of the parking garage and the alley, using a stick figure to represent Regina Blair. "Initial velocity is everything. If Regina slips or intentionally steps off the parking deck, her initial velocity is relatively low. She'll probably drop almost straight down. Depending on how she responds to falling, she could even land feet first," she said, drawing an X to mark the impact near the base of the parking deck.

"What if she's pushed?"

"Her initial velocity will depend on how hard she was pushed and where on her body the push was applied. If she was hit fairly hard, say between the shoulder blades, her initial velocity would carry her farther out from the deck and she'd follow a nice parabolic curve to the bottom, something like this," she said, drawing a curve out from the deck and down to the midpoint of the alley. "And if she was pushed, there's a good chance she was startled and would have been swinging her arms and legs in midair, which could widen out the curve, carry her farther across the alley."

I picked up the incident report and studied the diagram of the scene. "Regina's body was found ten feet from the base of the parking deck. The sketch shows her lying at roughly a forty-five degree angle to the deck."

"I'd say that's consistent with her being pushed," Lucy said.

"Except we don't know if the homeless guy who found her moved the body. It's also possible that she didn't die on impact, managed somehow to stand up and then fell over and died."

"That doesn't work with her injuries. She had massive head wounds. You don't get that falling over. You get that falling three stories and landing on your head."

"What did you get in physics?"

"An A," she said, smiling.

"Well, I got a C but I agree with you. It looks like Regina was pushed. Were there any security cameras in place?"

"None. Probably will be once the construction is finished but not before."

"Were the entrances from the garage to the building locked?"

"No, but I was there during working hours. The construction crew was still on the job."

"More people to talk to. Find out if anyone saw someone."

"Delaney's neighbors tonight, construction crew tomorrow. Don't wait up," she said, grabbing her coat and my car keys.

"Where's she going?" Simon asked from the dining room when Lucy left.

"Delaney's apartment building. Looking for witnesses. How are you guys doing?"

Simon and Kate exchanged glances, each waiting for the other to take the lead. Simon raised his hands, palms out, in a you-first protest.

"I found a log of the videos," Kate said. "They range anywhere from five to twenty minutes. Best guess is that they average around ten. Setting aside the Delaney, Blair, and Enoch videos, that leaves two hundred forty-seven videos times ten minutes which equals twenty-four hundred and seventy minutes which is a little over forty-one hours of viewing time. And that doesn't allow any time for replay, slow-motion, frame-by-frame analysis, or just plain thinking."

"It's the same story with the background checks," Simon said. Entering the search requests for all those people, plus any of the staff you toss into the mix, will take me a few days. Then I have to match the hits to the volunteers, make certain I've got the right person. If something interesting turns up in the first cut, I have to dig deeper. Until I know what I've got, there's no way to predict how long this will take."

"Then," Kate said, "we've to cross-reference the videos to the background checks, see if there are any videos we need to revisit based on the background checks or vice versa."

"And your point is?" I asked.

"Unless you can narrow this down, we need help," Kate said. "A lot of help."

I shrugged. "So get the help. Milo will pay for it."

"I'm a one-man band," Simon said. "I don't have minions at my disposal. Plus, we're dealing with confidential information and a murder investigation. I can't just call a temp agency and tell them to send over ten people who won't ask questions and who will keep their mouths shut."

"What about you?" I asked Kate.

"My father taught me how to read microfacial expressions. Alan isn't bad at it but he's not as good as Dad and I are. They're the only ones I'd trust with this."

"Henry and Alan? Your ex-husband wants to drop the ex and your father wants to give away the bride. On top of that, they hate me. That's who you want me to hire?"

"They only hate you because they think you almost got me killed," she said.

I didn't blame them. I'd let Kate push her way into Wendy's case and she had almost gotten killed. She had given up trying to convince her father and Alan that it was her fault, not mine, but people hold on the hardest to the beliefs that get them through the night. Now I was asking for her help again and she wanted to ask them for theirs.

"You think they'd be willing to help?"

"Our cash flow is tighter than last year's pants. If we don't take this work, we could all be looking for jobs. And, we've got half a dozen staff people whose families are counting on their paychecks and health insurance. Simon can keep them busy. Dad and Alan will do it for the employees if nothing else."

I looked at my watch. It was nine o'clock. "Do they work nights?"

"For premium rates?" they asked in unison.

"Ultra premium."

"I'll meet you at your office in an hour," Simon said to Kate.

He packed his laptops, leaving one for me, and left. Kate took her time. I stood behind her, rubbing her shoulders. She leaned into me and I wrapped my arms around her waist. She turned, hugging me, lifting her face to mine, kissing me. I started to shake, my head sliding down her neck to her shoulder, her grip tightening as my knees weakened.

"I can stay. I brought my toothbrush," she said.

"I'm fine. Besides, you have to get things up and running at your office."

"Okay, but I'm leaving my toothbrush here."

"Good. At least I'll have something to cuddle with."

"Roxy and Ruby will be jealous."

Chapter Twenty-nine

There were times when I knew that the job could get me killed, when the people on the other side of the door might be high enough, stupid enough, or scared enough to shoot instead of surrender, or when the creep I helped send away might try to make good on his threat to get even when he got out. Those risks came with the territory, like living in Kansas City where the blaring of tornado sirens was a rite of spring sending throngs of people outside with their video cameras searching the sky for twisters instead of taking shelter in the basement.

The possibility that a serial killer had plucked my name from the top of Walter Enoch's dead letter pile lay closer to the odds of being sucked into oblivion by a tornado than it did any risk I ever took as an FBI agent. But no matter how remote the chance, I'd learned one thing people living in trailer parks knew about tornados. It was human nature to tease the bear and curse God when the bear did what bears were meant to do.

In the four days since Simon Alexander had bought
me a cup of coffee, it was possible that I'd gone from
being a some-time security consultant to being both a
murder suspect and serial killer target, depending on
whose paranoid flavored Kool-Aid I drank. I had one advantage over Kent and Dolan and Walter Enoch's killer.
Shaking made it easier to look both ways and see who
was coming at me.

It wasn't only my status that had changed. So had the
other volunteers in the dream project and, for that matter, Maggie Brennan's, all of whom could be targets if
we were dealing with a serial killer. Tom Goodell never
missed a retired cops' lunch and the next one was on
Wednesday. I hoped he could close the loop between
my Maggie Brennan and his.

The house was quiet and the dogs were sleeping. I
reached in my pants' pocket and retrieved the flash drive
that held Enoch's dream video and that Kent and Dolan
would have taken along with my laptop had they bothered
to search me. I loaded the video on the computer
Simon had loaned to me, expanded the image to full
screen, and turned up the volume.

The video began with the credits: *Harper Institute of
the Mind, Dream Project, Anthony Corliss, PhD, Project Director, Maggie Brennan, PhD, Assistant Director.* Bold yellow
font identified the subject as Walter Enoch and the date
of the video as January 12.

Enoch's face filled the next frame, the camera shooting him from the neck up, magnifying his moonscape
features. The dark paneled wall behind him was familiar. The camera pulled back a few inches, enough to reveal patches of blue and red tartan plaid fabric,
confirming my memory. The video had been shot in

Enoch's house. He was sitting in the chair where his body was found.

I froze the video, ran upstairs, and dug my Bose headphones out of the bedroom closet, not wanting to miss anything. Back in the kitchen, I took a deep breath and clicked play. Anthony Corliss's voice filled my ears.

"Before we talk about your dreams, Walter, tell me about your accident."

Walter's hand found his chin, crept over his mouth.

"I don't like to talk about it."

"Why? Because it wasn't an accident?"

Walter shuddered, looking away from the camera.

"No reason to talk about it."

"Walter, c'mon now. Look at me," Corliss said from behind the camera. And Walter did. "It's just you and me here, nobody else, and we've known each other a while now. We're friends, you and me, and I'm a doctor. A psychologist. You know that. I've told you about all the people I've helped who've suffered so bad for things they didn't even begin to deserve, things you wouldn't wish on a dog. I can help you if you'll let me."

Walter shifted in his chair. "You should go. I should never have let you in the house. Now you know what I've done."

Corliss ignored the request. "I'm glad you let me in, Walter, because now I can help you. I'll find you a lawyer and I'll testify for you. Tell the judge what a bad time you've had. After what you've been through, they'll go easy on you. Right now, though, you've got to tell me about your dreams. They've got to be terrible. You tell me about them and I'll help you find some peace."

Walter blinked his thin, stubby, pale eyelashes. His chest heaved as he struggled to breathe. "I am what I am. I got no need to make peace with you or anybody."

"I'm not talking about me or anybody else, Walter. I'm talking about you. Your pain is written in the scars all over your face. Let me help you."

Walter turned his head to the side, pressing his cheek into the back of his chair. "I'm fine. I don't need nobody's help."

"Something like your face, it was probably your mother. Fathers use their fists or a belt. Mothers use water. It's a subconscious connection to the womb. That's why when they go crazy some mommas drown their babies. Others boil them."

Walter ground deeper in the chair, a trickle of tears rolling over his ruined face. Corliss let the silence hang, waiting for him. The dead air lasted a couple of minutes, the camera detailing Walter's squirming anguish. He broke the silence, his head burrowed into the cushion, muffling his sobs.

"My mother poured boiling water on me. I was eight years old. She said I was a monster."

"Were you?"

"Not yet."

"I believe that, Walter. No way you deserved that. No way at all. But that's what she did and here we are. Can't un-ring that bell, can we? So let's concentrate on the part we can do something about starting with your dreams, Walter. Let's you and me get a handle on that."

Corliss's hand appeared in the frame, handing tissues to Walter who wiped his eyes and blew his nose, rolled his shoulders back and down and faced the camera, red eyes and blue lips the only colors in his washed-out face. He coughed, wet and raspy, gulped air, and nodded at the camera, his voice at first soft, gathering strength.

"It's the same dream. Not every night, but most nights. Ever since she burned me. She's running away from me and I'm chasing after her, calling her but it's like she don't hear me because she never stops. Not till I get lost. Then I'm caught up in these dark green vines and they're climbing all over me, pulling me down in the ground and I'm crying for my mother but I'm not making any sounds so she can't hear me. She doesn't know I'm in trouble and I need her. Then the vines, they turn into a big pond and the water's up to my neck and I see my momma in the middle of the pond and the water is shallow there cause I can see her, all of her except for her feet. She's smiling at me and I know she wants me to swim over to her so I start swimming and the closer I get the hotter the water gets and it's getting deeper, not shallower, and I can't touch the bottom. Then the water gets in my mouth and nose and I can't breathe and I'm sinking like a stone. Momma reaches down in the water and grabs me and I tell her I'm so sorry for whatever it was that I did. She calls me a monster, says the devil is in me. Then she shoves me down deeper in the water and the water is burning me. I can't breathe cause I'm swallowing the water and my insides feel like they're on fire and I know right then that I'm gonna die."

"But you don't die. You wake up," Corliss said.

"I don't want to. I want it to be over."

"It will be, soon, I promise you," Corliss said.

The screen went blank but I couldn't take my eyes off it until I realized I was the one holding my breath, the effort shattered by a fresh round of spasms and whiplash, thinking as much about Anthony Corliss as I was about Maggie Brennan. She struck me as a vulnerable mix of steel and sadness. I remembered the promise I'd made to protect her and hoped I could keep it.

I lumbered into the living den on unsteady legs, staring at the wall Lucy had designated for Walter Enoch, wanting to add my answers to the questions she had written. But the gears in my brain had gummed up and all I could do was collapse into the recliner. I promised myself that I would rest a few minutes and then try again, a promise that was broken when Lucy woke me and put me to bed.

Chapter Thirty

Lucy and I sat at the kitchen table, sipping coffee and picking at stale bagels. I looked out the window where barren trees, mud-streaked snow, and an iron skillet sky blended into a dull tintype. I was having a herky-jerky morning and felt as flat as the weather.

Ruby was dozing on the floor while Roxy scratched my leg, wagging her tail, which was code for will work for belly rub. I ruffled her beard and she dropped to the floor and rolled on her back, spreading her legs in a pose that mimicked Britney Spears at her most overexposed but for Roxy was charming. I rubbed and Roxy wagged, both of us agreeing that no one could ask for more from a relationship. Her unconditional enthusiasm gave the day hope.

Lucy had struck out at Delaney's apartment complex the night before. A few people knew who he was but none claimed him as a friend and no one had ever been in his apartment. She'd gone to the *Kansas City Star*'s distribution center, found the night shift circulation manager, and gotten the same story. Delaney picked up his papers on time, delivered them on time, and didn't cause any trouble. The manager said he was quiet and kept to himself.

I played Walter Enoch's dream video for her. She drained her coffee and shoved her bagel aside.

"Okay. Now we know that Enoch let Corliss in his house for the video," she said. "It's not likely that he opened the door for anyone else. That puts Corliss at the top of the list of people he could have let in to kill him."

"There's more. I talked to Corliss about Enoch yesterday. He admitted knowing him and recruiting him for the dream project. He said that Enoch had been his mailman but he acted like he didn't know anything about the stolen mail until he read about it in the paper. He lied to me and I want to know why."

As I spoke, my head rotated hard left and down, my left ear meeting my raised left shoulder in a fighter's clinch while my right shoulder dropped and my torso pivoted to the right. The spasm held me for a three count then released and repeated. I let out a long breath.

"You should try that," I said. "Works the lats, the obliques, and the core."

"I'll keep that in mind. So, how worried should I be?" Lucy asked.

"About Corliss?"

"Right. That's exactly who I'm talking about, you moron." She reached across the table and thumped me on the arm. "I'm not going to keep putting you to bed unless you tell me what's going on."

I had awakened lying on top of my bedcovers, wearing yesterday's clothes. A night's sleep, a shower, and clean clothes were not enough to squelch my seismic activity.

"Hey, you didn't even tuck me in."

"You want turn down service, talk to Kate. Seriously, Jack. I'm worried about you. I want to know what's the matter with you. After all," she said, straightening and giving me a tongue-in-cheek glare, "I am your landlady. That gives me rights."

It was a fair request. We were living under the same roof and working on the same case. She'd not only taken risks for me, she had taken care of me. I hoped her concern wasn't over whether I could pay the rent; that I was filling some of the void in her life in the same way she was filling mine.

"I have a movement disorder called tics."

"What a lousy name," Lucy said. "The ones that are hard to pronounce have better telethons. Tics sounds like something you get walking in the woods."

"I'll give you that. It's a neurological disorder, cause and cure unknown. You've heard of Tourette's?"

"Sure."

"Well, it's similar to that. In my case, the more I do, the more I shake. Doesn't matter if it's work or working out, reading a book or going to the movies. There are medications that help some people but they didn't work for me, and the side effects were too intense. I have to manage it by regulating my activities and keeping a balance between what I do and how much I shake."

"Except you do more than shake. Cirque du Soleil would die for some of your contortions. Last night, you were walking around here like your legs were made of spaghetti. When I came home, you had a glazed look on your face like your brain was on a slow motion loop."

"My doctors can explain some parts of it better than others, like the problems with my legs. They tell me the weakness in my legs isn't caused by tics but they can't tell me what is causing it. All the MRIs, EEGs, and other tests come up negative. The good news is that, whatever it is, it won't kill me."

"As long as you spend your time taking walks in the park. I'm not so sure about chasing the dead man."

I shrugged. "I tried walking in the park and walking in the mall and just walking around. It's not enough. It's not who I am."

"I hear that. Changing who you are is harder than it looks. Trust me, I know."

"Besides, it's too late to walk away from this one even if I could."

"At least you've got backup. Simon strikes me as one of the good guys, cute in a nerdy way but smart and steady. Kate is smarter and she's in love with you even though she says you can be a pain in the butt, like I didn't know that after living with you for four days."

Kate didn't wear our relationship on her sleeve. She didn't carve initials in a desktop or tree trunk and I couldn't imagine her opening up like that to Lucy the first time they met.

"She told you that?"

Lucy grinned. "The pain in the butt part?"

"No, you moron." I returned her thump on the arm.

"Oh, the in love part. Not in so many words but my advice is don't piss her off too many times. You're not likely to do any better any time soon. Same goes for me."

"How's that?"

"I've got your back too. I may not have a fancy degree but I'm kick ass in the clutch. First killer puts you on a list, I'll shoot him."

"You're a convicted felon. Where are you going to get a gun?"

"Your closet. Lord knows you shouldn't carry. Last thing we need is for you to start shaking and shoot yourself."

"No way. You leave that gun where it is. You get caught with it and you'll go back to jail. Then who's going to put me to bed?"

She rose from the table and gave me a peck on the cheek. "Nice to know you'd miss me. Time to go to work."

Lucy pulled to the curb in the circle drive at the entrance to the institute. It had been a quiet ride, neither of us bothering with small talk.

"What will you do with the money if you find it?" she asked.

I had unbuckled my seat belt and was about to open the door. Her question stopped me. I hadn't thought about it because there was only one answer.

"Turn it in."

She nodded and took a breath, picking up speed as she spoke, gesturing like a manic conductor. "Why? I mean, I know why. The money isn't yours. It's dirty. The FBI already thinks you know where it is. If you find it and start spending it, they'll be all over you in a heartbeat. You could go to jail. I know all that. But, what if you could keep it without getting caught? Five million dollars is a lot of money. Don't you ever think about that?"

Her face was flush, her breath quick. I knew the look. It was the rush of the impossibly possible, the one in a million shot that breaks the rules that shouldn't apply just this one time and that will fix everything forever but never does and always makes things worse. In that moment, she was Wendy at her most maddening.

"No. Not now. Not ever."

"Well, hey, you're right. Me neither," she said, slapping the steering wheel. "You know what else I've been wondering. How did the mailman end up with Wendy's letter in the first place? If he was Corliss's mailman, was he yours too?"

"That's a question worth asking. Put it on your list after you talk to the construction crew. Finding someone at the post office who will talk to you may be a little tricky."

"Not with my charm. What are you going to do?"

"I've got a lot of ground to cover today but I'm going to start with Anthony Corliss, give him a chance to come to Jesus with me before Kent and Dolan find their way to his office. Once they see Enoch's dream video, they'll have a tough choice to make."

"What's that?"

"Who to arrest first, Corliss or me."

Chapter Thirty-one

We reveal ourselves in many ways, denying, confessing, and rationalizing our faults while exaggerating or diminishing our glories. We embrace and chase those we love and covet, rejecting and denouncing others that threaten us. Our involuntary blinks, nods, winks, grimaces, and squints may flesh out our hidden selves, but nothing says more about us than what we do in the moments that test us, whether it's the hungry, homeless man with his hand out or that which tempts us when no one except God is looking and we aren't convinced He's on duty.

Lucy's question about the money revealed her needs rather than her faults. She had already told me what she'd done, what it had cost her, and how afraid she was of what she might do the next time. Now she was reminding me that she needed backup as much as I did. I hoped I would be kick-ass in the clutch for her.

* * *

"Morning," Leonard said. "Frank Gentry was up here looking for you. He waited in your office for a while but he gave up."

"Great. Call him. Tell him I'm here now. I need to talk to him right away."

"No good. He said he'd be tied up in an IT staff meeting until at least eleven and don't ask me to interrupt him."

"Why not?"

"He was in the Special Forces. When those guys give you an order, you don't argue. They'll break your legs just to hear the sound it makes. Me, I'm a conscientious objector."

"To the military?"

"To pain, especially mine."

"Fair enough."

The message light on my phone was blinking. It was a message from Gentry telling me that he'd left the report I'd asked for in the top left-hand drawer of my desk. I found the report in an envelope stamped confidential. It contained the list of staff people who had accessed the dream project files. Gentry had been thorough, alphabetizing the names and including columns identifying each person's position at the institute, their contact information, and the dates on which they had accessed the files. There were thirteen names on the list, including mine.

The least surprising names were Anthony Corliss, Maggie Brennan, and their research assistants, Janet Casey and Gary Kaufman. Four of the people on the list were identified as directors of other projects. I had no idea how their work related to the dream project but added that question to my to-do list. Gentry had included his name since he had accessed the files at my request, his access occurring last night.

The remaining names—Milo Harper, Sherry Fritzshall, and Leonard Nagel—registered on a scale somewhere between interesting and baffling. It took a moment for me to realize that Leonard Nagel was my Leonard. Gentry identified his title as administrative assistant to director of security, adding a footnote that Leonard's access was not authorized and that Gentry was continuing to investigate how he had breached the system security. All three were regular visitors, having accessed the dream project files before and after the deaths of Delaney, Blair, and Enoch.

Leonard's desk was across from my open office door. I watched him as he worked, tapping his Bluetooth earpiece as calls came in, flexing his irrepressible grin. He shuffled papers and scrolled through screens on his computer monitor, a combination pep squad leader and perpetual motion machine. He glanced my way, saw me watching, winked, and went back to work.

I called Simon, gave him all twelve names, and told him to make those background checks a top priority.

"Including Milo and Sherry?" he asked.

"Including them. Nobody gets a pass."

"You going to tell Milo that you're investigating him?"

"Depends on what you come up with. I know he's your buddy. I need to know if you can do this."

Simon hesitated. He was a loyal and devoted friend and I was putting him between those conflicting demands.

"I don't like it," he said.

"What do you think Milo would tell you to do?"

This time, Simon didn't hesitate. "Whatever it takes."

"Those are the words the man lives by."

"Milo's a celebrity. Sherry gets some press but not nearly as much as he does. There will be a ton of stuff on both of them. This will take awhile."

"Focus on what's not in *People* magazine. And don't forget about Leonard. He's my assistant. The dream project files are password protected and he wasn't supposed to have the password. Find out if he's a got a track record of snooping or peeping."

I got to Anthony Corliss's office the same time he did. He was wearing a waist-cut down jacket, jeans, and hiking boots damp from the snow. His cheeks were red, his hair matted against his scalp. He was holding a knit cap and scarf in one hand and a backpack in the other.

"Hey," he said. "Back for more?"

"Just a few questions."

"Damn, I'm sweating like a stuck pig," he said as he unlocked the door. "Walked to work. Seemed like a good idea at the time and it's either exercise or die. I hate exercise but I'm not ready to die."

"Where do you live?"

"Over in Crestwood, a couple of miles from here. Not a bad walk on a nice day but it was a bitch in this cold."

I followed him into his office. He hung his coat, cap, and scarf on a hook on the back of his door, tossed the backpack on the couch, and dropped into his desk chair. I sat in a chair across from him.

"That's a little north of me. I'm in Brookside."

"Well, then, I guess we're neighbors. That mean we're gonna be friends?" he asked, leaning back in his chair, flashing a smile.

"No reason we can't be. I need you to educate me."

"About what?"

"For starters, the girl at Wisconsin who drowned."

His smile vanished. "You were a cop, right?"

"FBI."

"Like I said, a cop. You ever make a mistake? Arrest the wrong man? Ruin someone's life, maybe send them to death row?"

"I did my best and trusted the system to get things right."

"Well, bully for you, brother, because the system sucks. I had nothing to do with that girl's death. The university didn't ask my permission to settle that lawsuit. They gave away their money and my reputation. Now you want to talk about the dream project, I've got time. You want to dredge up what happened at Wisconsin and I'm busy."

Ask any con on a cell block and he'll tell you he's innocent, that his lawyer screwed up his case or that the guy in the next cell confessed that he did it. Ask anyone who's ever paid big bucks to settle a lawsuit and they'll point you to the fine print that says the settlement is not an admission of liability, which liability is expressly denied, thank you very much, adding that they settled so that everyone could get on with their lives.

Then there are the people who do terrible, inexplicable things and convince themselves they didn't because that's the only way they can look in the mirror. Mixed in with all of them are the ones who are innocent and blameless. Picking those hapless ones out of the crowd is dicey at best. I hadn't made up my mind about Corliss.

"Walk me through the process your volunteers go through from how they are recruited until you're done with them."

"It's pretty simple. We're not like research programs at universities. When I was teaching at Wisconsin, we got all the volunteers we needed from students who wanted extra credit for participating in psychology studies. They worked for free. Here, we have to pay people, just like the drug companies doing trials. We put ads in the local papers, things like that. They fill out a questionnaire, we do the brain scans, the EEGs, we make the video where they tell us about their dreams, and we teach them about lucid dreaming. That's the quick and dirty."

"How much do you pay?"

"Couple hundred bucks. Not enough to give up their day jobs. It's more to get their attention. The real hook is the chance to get past their nightmares. That's what these people are looking for. Some of them are flat out scared to go to sleep."

"You recruit many people on your own, like you did Walter Enoch?"

"Walter was the exception. He was too good a candidate to pass up."

"Tell me about the videos. How does that work?"

"We got a room here we use. My research assistants shoot most of them."

"What about Maggie Brennan? Does she take any of the videos?"

He shook his head. "Maggie isn't what you'd call a people person. Getting subjects to open up about their nightmares isn't in her skill set. She can read an fMRI or an EEG like nobody's business, tell you what part of the brain is lighting up and why, but that's where it begins and ends for her."

"And you?"

He laughed. "I am a psychologist. If I didn't like people, I'd have to find another line of work."

"How many volunteers have you videoed?"

"Not more than a few. I fill in if the research assistants aren't available or if they think the subject is particularly interesting."

"Like with Walter Enoch?"

"He was a mess, wasn't he? Can you imagine going through life with a face like that? People are afraid to look at you or can't stop staring. What a burden. Don't get me wrong. I'm not saying he's better off dead. People can adapt to all kinds of things. But he wasn't exactly living the good life."

"Can I get a look at the room where you and Walter made the video?"

"Didn't do it here. Walter was real shy. Hard to blame him. It took me forever to talk him into volunteering. He didn't want to come down here, so I said we could do it at his house and he said okay."

"I watched his video last night."

"You always go to this much trouble just to trip someone up? If you watched that video you knew where it was made."

"And I knew you lied to me yesterday when you acted like you didn't know that Enoch had stolen all that mail. You want to be friends? Friends don't lie to friends."

"Course they do, all the time. Hell, lying is one of the necessities of friendship. Your friend asks how do I look and you say great even if you'd never leave the house looking like that. That's what friends are for. I promised Walter I wouldn't turn him in. That was the only way he'd talk to me. Maybe that was a mistake. If it was, I wasn't going to give myself up to you on our first date. I didn't know you from Adam when you walked in that door or what you were after."

"I think you had a pretty good idea what I was after. The alert software on your computer told you that I had accessed your files."

Corliss flattened his palms on his desk, looking first at the floor then at me. "You do your homework. I'll give you that."

"Why did Enoch agree to do the video at his house? Having company would have been the last thing he wanted. It would have been safer to do the video at your house or the institute."

"Doing it at his house was my idea. I wanted to know more about him. Best way was to see where he lived. Took me a while, but he finally trusted me enough to let me in. That was a big step for him."

"How many times were you in Enoch's house?"

He sat back in his chair, arms crossed. "Just the one time. When we made the video."

"Did you take anything from the house?"

"No. Why would I do that?"

His phone rang. He answered and listened, his face turning pale. "Okay," he said and hung up. "Two FBI agents named Kent and Dolan are here. I wonder why they want to talk to me."

I decided to let Kent and Dolan tell him, not wanting to step on their interrogation. He would tell them about our conversations and I didn't want to give them any more ammunition for obstruction of justice or witness tampering charges.

"Don't worry," I said. "You look great."

Chapter Thirty-two

I could keep some parts of my investigation from Milo Harper but I couldn't let him be blindsided by the FBI. His door was open. He was standing behind his desk, rifling through papers, opening and slamming shut drawers, his hair disheveled, his eyes wild. I knocked and waited.

He looked up, stared, and squinted as if to bring my face into focus, tapping one hand against his thigh. "What?"

"We need to talk."

He waved me in. "Sure, sure."

He pursed his lips, squinted some more, and pounded his fist on his desk. "Damn it! I can't remember your fucking name!"

People walking by his office slowed, rubber-necking like they were passing an accident on the freeway. I closed the door and met him at his desk.

"It's Jack Davis. I'm the director of security."

"I know what you do. I hired you for Christ's sake,

but I lost your name. Frustrates the living daylights out of me. Same with this mess," he said, pointing to the papers scattered on his desk. "I write myself notes in a little spiral notebook—reminders of what I'm supposed to do, who I had lunch with today and who I'm having breakfast with tomorrow. I used to keep that stuff on my iPhone but I was making so many notes, it was just easier to write them down. I came in this morning and I can't find the damn spiral. I don't know what I did with it."

I looked around his office. The spiral pad was sticking out from under a pile of papers that had fallen to the floor under his desk. I picked it up and handed it to him.

"This what you're looking for?"

He took the pad and let out a deep sigh, patting it against the palm of his hand. "Thanks. This is a thin reed to hold onto. Have a seat."

It was the first time I'd seen any indication that he had early stage Alzheimer's. I understood his frustration and anxiety. They were side effects of losing control, knowing that his inability to remember my name or the things he wrote on the pad or what he'd done with it weren't minor outbreaks of the benign dementia called Can't Remember Shit. They were steps on the downhill slide and there was no getting back to the top of the hill.

"You ever get used to the shaking?" he asked me.

"By now, I feel like I've always been this way. My old life of going to work every day, chasing crooks, having a few pops with my squad, that was someone else. It doesn't seem real. This life does. Maybe that means I'm used to it."

"Well, I'm not. I'll never accept it and I'll never get used to it. I'm going to fight it all the way."

"I don't give advice, especially when I'm not asked, but I'll tell you this much. It's a lot harder to fight a secret war. I tried that. I was dumb enough to think that no one had noticed anything different about me. But people knew something was wrong. They were just afraid to ask. You can let people wonder and whisper or you can let them help you."

"I want to do this on my own terms."

"You may not get the chance. Same thing may be true for this investigation. Two FBI agents are downstairs right now interviewing Anthony Corliss about the murder of Walter Enoch."

His eyes exploded, wild again, as he smacked the arms of his chair with both hands.

"How could you let that happen? You should have told them to get lost unless they had a warrant. What the hell am I paying you for?"

My father had Alzheimer's. It changed his personality more than his memory; it made him volatile, hostile, and so nasty at the end that he had to be drugged so that he'd stop taking swings at his caregivers. I didn't know whether Harper's outburst was the residual effect of the morning's frustration or the beginning of something more insidious. The more aggressive my father got, the calmer I got, making it easier for him to hear me. It worked with him. I hoped it worked with Harper.

"They don't need a warrant to talk to someone. I know these guys. Their names are Kent and Dolan. If I ran interference for Corliss, they'd be back with a team of agents and cops and they'd spend the next two days carrying boxes out of here under the watchful eye of the media. You want to lose control of the situation, that's the best way to do it."

He took a deep breath, hugged himself, and apologized with a weak smile.

"You're right. You're right. Why do you think they're interested in Corliss?"

"For starters, he recruited Walter Enoch for the dream project and convinced him to take the video at Enoch's house which means that Corliss knew about the stolen mail and didn't turn Enoch in. On top of that, there were no signs of forced entry and that suggests that Enoch knew his killer well enough to let him in the house. Given the stolen mail, Enoch wasn't likely to let many people in his house. Corliss may have been the only one. Toss in what happened with the girl at Wisconsin and I'm not surprised that the FBI is real interested in talking to him."

"You're saying they think Corliss killed Walter Enoch?"

"I'm saying they've got good reasons to talk to him and we've got no good reasons to make their job any harder."

"Do you think he did it?"

"I think I'd be doing what Kent and Dolan are doing."

Harper settled back in his chair, looking past me, digesting what I had told him.

"Do you think Corliss had anything to do with what happened to Tom Delaney and Regina Blair?"

"There's too much we don't know to answer that question."

"Like what?"

"Like why you, your sister, and my assistant were logging onto the dream project files like it was your home page."

He laughed. "We're all suspects, is that it?"

"I don't have any suspects but I do have a lot of questions."

"It's how I keep tabs on my projects. I don't have time to meet with everyone as often as I'd like and the project directors don't keep the hours I do."

"Makes sense. Leonard wasn't authorized to have access to the dream project files. Frank Gentry is figuring out how he did it."

"Fire Leonard. Today. Now."

"I'd rather wait. I want to know how he did it and, since we know he's doing it, we can monitor him. We'll learn a lot more than if we kick his ass out of here. What about your sister? Why would she be poking around in these files?"

"Let's ask her," he said, picking up his phone.

The door to his office flew open as he dialed. It was Sherry, her arms clamped at her sides, her hands balled into fists, her mouth trembling.

"Nancy Klemp called me from the front desk. One of the maintenance people found a body stuffed in a utility closet in the sub-basement."

Chapter Thirty-three

The institute had two sets of elevators. One serviced the floors above the lobby. The other was for the parking garage and the basement levels beneath the garage. There were no surveillance cameras in the elevators and I hadn't seen any on the floors except for the one behind the front desk in the lobby. I didn't know about the parking garage.

"What kind of surveillance do you have in the building?" I asked Milo and Sherry as we got on the elevator on the eighth floor.

"There's the camera at the front desk and we also have cameras on each level of the parking garage and inside the elevator lobbies at each level of the garage," Milo said.

"What about the basement levels?"

"None."

"Does anyone monitor the garage cameras in real time?"

"No," Milo said.

"Why not?"

Sherry answered. "It wasn't necessary. A key card is required for garage access. We trust the people who work for us."

"Then why have the cameras in the first place?"

"In case something happens," she said.

"How long do you keep the video?"

She swallowed hard. "The cameras record over the previous day's video beginning at midnight."

"Who figured out that system?" I asked.

"I did," Sherry said. "It was the most cost-effective way to do it. This is a research institute, not a police state."

"It's also a security system without any security. If something is caught on camera, it's gone before anyone knows it happened," I said. "What about the key cards? Is a record kept of the dates and times people go in and out of the garage?"

Milo looked at Sherry, waiting for her to answer. When she didn't, we both knew how deep the shit we were in was getting.

"Well?" Milo asked her.

Sherry crossed her arms, shooting daggers at her brother. "We used to keep those records. Frank Gentry sent me daily reports with all kinds of crap, including that. I had too much paperwork to get through and I couldn't get anything done. I finally told him to quit sending it to me. He asked me what to do with it and I told him to get rid of it at the end of every day. He said there's no point in tracking it if we're just going to get rid of it so I told him to quit tracking it."

Milo stared at her like he was seeing her for the first time. She ignored him, her arms folded across her chest, her jaw clamped, and her eyes fixed on the descending floor numbers on the elevator display. I let it ride. She'd been in over her head and neither of them knew it. Making them both feel worse wouldn't make me feel any better.

The maintenance man was waiting for us when we got off the elevator in the sub-basement. He was Hispanic, bony, and older than me with close-cut silver hair and a matching moustache. An institute ID identifying him as Carlos Morales was clipped to a shirt pocket that held a pack of cigarettes, his hand involuntarily reaching for a smoke he couldn't have.

"This way, Mr. Harper," he said.

We followed him through a warren of concrete hallways painted white and marked by overhead pipes interspersed with pale florescent tubes, giving the subterranean space a dispassionate chill. We passed equipment and storage rooms until we reached the utility closet in a corner of the basement.

Nancy Klemp was standing in front of the open door, her face a quiet mask, her eyes unfocused and brimming. Carlos hung back as I shouldered past Milo and Sherry.

"Stay back. No one goes inside the closet."

Nancy nodded and stepped away, giving me a clear view of the body. It was Anne from HR.

The closet was wide and deep, at least six feet to the back wall where her nude body was propped up, her knees bent and legs splayed open, a broken shaft of wood stuck in her vagina, dried blood staining her inner thighs and the floor. Her head hung to one side, resting on her shoulder, eyes open, purple bruises ringing her neck. Her clothes were folded on the floor, her purse and shoes on top like paperweights.

I didn't see the ID badge and gold chain she was wearing around her neck when she gave me the set of new employee forms to fill out the day before. I doubted that the chain was sturdy enough for the killer to have strangled her with it, though he could have taken it if he was afraid it might have captured his DNA.

Her hands were at her sides. The ring finger on her left hand was missing, a bloody pair of wire cutters lying next to her. A bank of electrical boxes was mounted in the middle of the closet wall to my left. A tool chest sat beneath the boxes, one of the drawers open.

I turned to the others. "Nancy, have you called the police?"

"No. I called Ms. Fritzshall soon as Carlos called me. Then I came down here."

"I'm glad you did but I need you to go upstairs and call the police. I'll stay until they get here."

"I knew her," Nancy said. "She was a good girl. Real good. She was supposed to get married in June. Her boyfriend used to work here. I watched them dance at the Christmas party."

I put my arm around her. "I'm so sorry."

"Yes, sir." She hurried away, wiping her eyes.

"Carlos, when did you find the body?"

"Not more than fifteen minutes ago. I came down here to get some tools. I opened the door and there she was. Man, I couldn't believe it."

"Did you go in the closet?"

"No. I was too scared."

"Did you touch anything? Did you touch her?"

He was a small man, a lifetime of hard work written in the lines worn into his leathered face. He filled his chest and rolled his shoulders back, daring me to insult him with another question.

"I would never do such a thing."

"That's good to know. Wait back at the elevator for the police. Show them the way."

"I didn't touch her," he said, his dark eyes burning. "I wouldn't. I've got a wife and two daughters."

"I didn't mean anything by it," I told him.

"I'll tell the cops the same thing," he said, marching off, his back stiff, his head high.

"What about the FBI agents?" Milo asked. "Shouldn't we get them down here?"

"Not their jurisdiction," I said. "This looks like a sexual assault and murder. Kansas City PD will handle it."

"What FBI agents?" Sherry asked. "There are FBI agents in the building and nobody bothered to tell me?"

"There's a dead body in the closet," I said. "That trumps the FBI agents."

"They're talking to Anthony Corliss about Walter Enoch's murder," Milo said. "They think he might have had something to do with it because Enoch let him in the house to take the dream video."

"Milo," Sherry said, her hands on her hips, "you can't leave me out of the loop like this. Things are getting out of control and if you think you can handle this without me, you're out of your mind."

"I wasn't leaving you out of anything but after the way you mangled our security, that may have to change," he told her. "I'll be in my office," he said to me. "Anything I can do to help?"

"Yeah. Have HR pull Anne's file and put it on my desk."

"Done."

"What about me?" Sherry asked. "What am I supposed to do?"

"I don't care," Milo told her. "Just don't screw it up."

Chapter Thirty-four

Crime scenes are like people. Some are a confused, chaotic mess, tormented by misplaced passion or uncontrolled rage. Others are organized and well ordered with little left behind that would lead to the offender's capture and conviction. And some, like this one, are staged to give the dead man a voice that screams look what I did and there's nothing you can do about it.

An autopsy would reveal the time and manner of Anne's death, though several things were likely. The bruising around her neck was evidence that she'd been strangled. The sexual assault could have occurred before or after she was dead, or both. The killer may have raped her with the piece of wood because he was impotent or because he didn't want to leave his semen.

The killer probably worked at the institute now or in the past since someone else would not have been familiar with the sub-basement. He probably knew Anne, or at least had seen her and singled her out, though she may not have known him. Several hundred people worked at the institute, enough that he could have stalked her without her ever having a hint that he existed until their one and only encounter. However, it would have been easier for him to get her onto an elevator headed for the sub-basement if she knew him and wasn't afraid of him.

Most murder victims know their killers, spouses and partners most likely to kill the ones they love. Anne's fiancé had worked at the institute and would need a tight alibi.

I thought of all those possibilities as I studied the scene from outside the closet. The other scenario I had to concede was that a serial killer was working his way through the ranks of people affiliated with the institute. A pattern was beginning to emerge.

Regina Blair had been first, pushed off a ledge, maybe even on an impulse. Tom Delaney was next, the killer becoming more proactive, staging a suicide, ratcheting up the violence with Delaney's gun. Walter Enoch's murder had been more intimate—a hand pressed over Enoch's nose and mouth, squeezing the life out of him in a careless effort to disguise the homicide as something else.

It was a pattern marked by the increased violence and boldness of Anne's murder. The careful staging of her body meant that the killer was in control of the moment of death but the pattern meant the opposite. The killer was losing control, taking less time between victims while becoming less clever and more savage. If I was right, Anne was the latest, not the last, victim.

"Step away from the closet, sir."

Two uniformed officers had arrived. Both had seasoned, steady eyes. I nodded, taking note of their name badges, Sanchez and Grant. Sanchez had given the order. Carlos Morales was a step behind Sanchez.

"It's all yours," I said. "I'm Jack Davis, director of security. Carlos here found the body. Nancy Klemp called it in. She was the next person on the scene. Both of them told me that they stayed out of the closet and didn't touch anything. Milo Harper and Sherry Fritzshall were with me when I relieved Nancy. Their offices are on the eighth floor. So is mine. Let me know when you're ready to talk to them and I'll set it up."

Grant wrote it down and Sanchez followed me back to the lobby which was swarming with uniformed cops, the circle drive filled with squad cars, their red, white, and blue lights richocheting off the glass walls, television crews setting up shop in the near distance. Sherry Fritzshall stood in the center of the lobby, directing traffic as the cops asked her questions. Nancy Klemp held her ground at the front desk.

"How's she doing?" I asked Nancy as we watched Sherry work the room.

"She'll be all right. She's a hard one to run over."

A sedan snaked into the packed circle drive, finding a seam between squad cars. Detective Paul McNair jumped out of the passenger side, the detective who was driving close on his heels. They aimed for Sherry and I met them there.

"Well, Davis, you got a real homicide this time?" McNair asked.

"The victim is a young woman. Looks like she was strangled and sexually assaulted. The killer left her nude and staged the body to make a lasting impression on whoever found her. Does that qualify?"

"Good enough for me," McNair said.

"Does that mean we get a real investigation?"

"I'd like to see some identification," Sherry said, not wanting to be left out.

"I'm McNair. This is Quincy Carter. We're KCPD homicide," he said, both of them showing her their badges. "Who's in charge here?"

Carter was black, his shaved head, broad shoulders, and fresh, eager eyes a sharp contrast to McNair's sloped back and pasty face. Carter was about getting it done and McNair was about getting it over with. I wanted to ask them the same question, hoping that Carter was the one who answered.

"I'm Sherry Fritzshall and I'm in charge."

McNair looked at her then at me, waiting for me to confirm or deny. I looked at Carter, giving him an opening. He tilted his head at McNair.

"What do you need from us?" I asked McNair.

"You know the drill. There's a lot of people in this building we need to talk to and I don't want to have to chase any of them down."

"Follow me," I said, walking back to the front desk. "Nancy, do we have a PA system?"

She handed me a microphone and pushed a button on the control panel built into her desk. "Goes all over."

"May I have your attention," I said into the microphone, pausing and looking around the lobby as my voice reverberated. People stopped what they were doing and stared at the speakers hidden in the ceiling.

"This is Jack Davis, director of security. We have a police emergency. No one is in any danger and the building is secure. You may go about your regular duties but remain in or near your offices until the police have an opportunity to talk with you. Please give them your complete cooperation."

"Thanks," Carter said. "I'd like to put people at all the exits just in case someone decides to go home early."

"Nancy, give the police any help they need finding their way around," I said, pointing to the control panel. "Can you program the elevators so they can use them without a key card?"

She nodded and pushed another button.

"Sanchez can take you downstairs where the body was found," I told McNair. "I told him what I know, which isn't much. The victim's name is Anne Kendall. I'll have a copy of her personnel file when you're ready for that."

"We'll need that to find out who to notify," McNair said.

"I called her boyfriend," Nancy said. "I told him to come over but I didn't tell him why. He's on his way."

"Boyfriend?" McNair asked. "What's his name?"

"Michael Lacey. He used to work here. They were supposed to get married in June," Nancy said.

"Were they living together?" McNair asked.

"I think so," Nancy said. "Everybody does anymore."

McNair turned to Carter. "Find out if Michael Lacey made a missing person's report on Anne Kendall."

"There he is. You can ask him yourself," Nancy said, pointing to the circle drive where a man in jeans and a parka was waving his arms at the uniformed cop blocking the front door.

"You got some place quiet where we can talk to the boyfriend?" McNair asked.

Sherry answered. "There's a conference room on this level. I'll show you."

"Sanchez, go get Mr. Lacey and take him to the conference room," McNair said. "Don't ask him any questions and don't answer any. Just babysit him until we get the rest of this circus organized."

"If this is the circus, does that make Jack Davis the clown?" asked Agent Dolan, his face split with a toothy grin. "My partner and I heard your announcement, thought we'd see if you needed any help. You guys were so busy solving the crime, I didn't want to interrupt."

"Who's this asshole?" McNair asked.

I hadn't seen him get off the elevator. "His name is Dolan but he'll answer to asshole," I said.

"FBI," Dolan said, waving his ID.

"See, I told you he'd answer to asshole."

Carter turned his head to cover his laugh. McNair didn't bother.

"We've got this, Dolan," McNair said. "It's a homicide. Nothing here for the feds."

"Funny thing, we've got one too. And we think one of our suspects is in this building," Dolan said, giving me a long look that turned McNair's and Carter's eyes my way.

McNair nodded. "That is a funny thing. You got some time, why don't you go with me and Carter and the three of us will have a look at the body in the basement. Nancy, show us the way. Davis, you go wait in your office. We'll be by to see you in a little while."

Chapter Thirty-five

McNair, Carter, and Dolan fell in line behind Nancy, disappearing into the garage elevator. Sherry stood by me, waiting for Sanchez to retrieve Michael Lacey from the cops at the front door.

"That FBI agent sure gave you a look," she said.

"He has a crush on me."

"That wasn't a man love look. That was an accusation look. You said the FBI is questioning Anthony Corliss about Walter Enoch's murder. It sounds like Dolan thinks you're a suspect too."

"Thinking isn't in his skill set."

"Well, he has a badge and you don't so he must be doing something right. And I'm certain my brother will want to know if you are a suspect. I think that would be quite a conflict of interest for you. I don't know how you could continue working here."

I wanted to tell her that thinking wasn't in her skill set either but that wouldn't advance the ball so I ignored her and watched Lacey as Sanchez herded him toward us.

He was jabbering, searching for a question Sanchez might answer, his head swiveling as his eyes darted around the lobby, the fact that he was the only civilian being escorted by the cops and what that might mean dawning on him. He stopped as if to turn back but Sanchez cupped his elbow, keeping him in line as he stumbled, the solid ground on which he'd built his life giving way.

Close up, he wasn't a bad looking guy, the slight crook in his nose offset by the cleft in his chin, a combination some women would call quirky and cute. No one would say that he looked like someone who would strangle and rape his fiancée until after he was convicted. Then people would say that they knew it all along, that they saw it in his eyes or the way he walked or the way he chewed his food. Until then, they'd say he looked normal, like the rest of us.

"This conversation isn't over," Sherry said to me as she led them toward the conference room.

I would have shot a snappy comeback at her but I shook instead, a belly to the brain temblor that jacked my head up and back like I'd been hit with an uppercut.

"Can't wait," was all I could manage.

Leonard jumped me when I got back to my office.

"What the hell is going on? People are going crazy up here. There's all kinds of rumors about a dead body being found."

The police wouldn't start canvassing the floors until

after McNair and Carter were finished in the sub-basement and could brief their troops on what questions to
ask. Anything I told Leonard now would be rebroadcast
in e-mails, text messages, and phone calls, distorted by
the time it reached the second set of eyes and ears, in-
decipherable by the time it reached the last, confusing
people about what they knew and how they knew it.
Since McNair couldn't find his foot if he stepped in a
bucket, I didn't want to make his job any harder.

"So let's not start any new ones. When the police
come by, just answer their questions."

He traded in his stick-on smile for hangdog disap-
pointment. "You don't trust me to keep quiet."

I put my hand on his shoulder. "I trust you to be
human."

He brightened at my touch. "That's a start. You've
got company," he said, pointing to my office.

"Who?"

He leaned toward me, his voice a conspiratorial whisper. "Connie Nichols. She's the HR director and a total
bitch. You give a girl a compliment and she'll write you
up for harassment. Word is she's a dyke."

My mother taught me not to drink from a poison
well and not to turn my back on the person who poi-
sons it. She wouldn't have liked Leonard.

"Thanks for the heads-up."

Connie Nichols stood when I came in; a manila file
tucked under one arm. She was middle-aged middle
management, dressed in a dark green pantsuit, her bottle blond hair cut straight and close to her shoulders,
her face grim.

"Jack Davis," I said, shaking her hand. "Have a seat."

"Connie Nichols, HR director. What a terrible thing."

I closed the door and sat in the chair next to her. "What terrible thing are we talking about?"

"My God! Poor Anne!" she covered her mouth and lowered her head, crying. She pulled a tissue from her jacket pocket and wiped her eyes.

I waited for her to stop crying, not surprised that she knew about Anne. Nancy Klemp had called Anne's boyfriend. There was no way to know how many others she had called, though one would have been enough to start a wildfire. Carlos Morales no doubt had done the same, his story racing along a separate upstairs/downstairs network, the two colliding like weather fronts spawning a shit storm. Whatever doubts Connie may have had were extinguished when Milo Harper told her to bring Anne's file to my office. She sat up, red-eyed.

"Is it true, what they're saying he did to Anne? That's so awful it's unspeakable!"

I didn't want to lie to her and I didn't want to fan the flames. "May I see her file, please?"

She handed it to me, taking my request as confirmation, her eyes welling up again. Anne's application and performance reviews were on top, the more recent information toward the back. She was twenty-five years old, graduated from high school in Warrensburg, Missouri, and from Truman State with an English degree. She had worked for the institute for eighteen months and her performance reviews were exemplary. Connie reached for the file, flipping to the last page.

"You should probably take a look at this. She turned it in yesterday."

It was a sexual harassment complaint.

Leonard Nagel began asking me out in November. I told him that I was living with someone and that we were going to get married. He said he didn't care and that he would make me forget my boyfriend. He kept asking me out even though I told him to stop. Since then, he has continued to bother me and has made a number of graphic sexual references that are not welcome. I told him that if he didn't leave me alone, I would file a complaint against him for harassment. He laughed and said that it would be his word against mine and that I would be sorry if I did.

"Who else knows about this?"

"No one," she said, ducking her head, her cheeks red; a silent confession that this too had gone out on the in-house wire. "She left it in an envelope on my desk last night. I was so busy when I came in this morning that I didn't open it until I heard what happened. Then Mr. Harper told me to bring Anne's file to your office. When I saw Leonard, I got so frightened, I started to shake."

"Nothing wrong with a little shaking. Does Leonard have a track record for this sort of thing?"

She nodded, taking a deep breath. "Another woman filed a complaint last year. Same story. Leonard came on to her. She told him to get lost and he wouldn't take no for an answer. She said he'd just show up out of nowhere and tell her what he wanted to do to her and how great it would be. She said she was scared to death of him."

"What was Leonard's story?"

"He denied everything. He said he complimented

her one time about a dress she was wearing and that was it."

"How was her complaint resolved?"

"She dropped it when her husband got transferred out of state. She said that she was just glad she'd never have to see Leonard again. I wanted to fire him but Mrs. Fritzshall said no because he could sue us since we had no proof."

I knew from supervising my staff at the FBI that employees like Leonard could be fired without cause so long as the decision wasn't based on race, gender, religion, age, or sexual orientation. Connie could have canned him without explanation and he couldn't have done anything about it. Sherry had screwed the pooch on building security and personnel decisions. It was a good thing her brother had a lot of money. He would need it to clean up her messes.

"The police will want a copy of Anne's file and the other woman's complaint. Make an extra copy for me. Do it yourself. I don't want anyone else seeing this stuff."

She stood, her back stiff, the veins on her neck taut. "I'll bring the copies right back."

"That would be great. The police will want to have a look at Anne's desk so make sure no one goes near it."

"I'll take care of that. How long will it be before the police arrest Leonard?"

"If and when the police arrest anybody is up to the police. Our job is to let them do their job. It will be up to the court and a jury to decide whether Leonard or anyone else is guilty of anything. Jumping the gun could ruin his life if he's innocent."

Connie grabbed the handle to my door, leveling me

with a hard-eyed glare. "I hope they cut his balls off and feed them to him before they execute him."

I followed her into the hall where she blew past Leonard. He waited until she was out of earshot.

"Did I tell you or did I tell you?" he asked, his be-my-buddy grin back in place, a thin sheen of sweat percolating across his forehead.

"You sure did."

"She say anything about me?"

I didn't want to spook Leonard before McNair and Carter could talk to him. I hadn't wanted to lie to Connie Nichols but I had no compunctions about deceiving him.

"Not a word."

"Good to know. It's just that she's got her favorites and I'm not one of them."

"I wouldn't worry about it. If she doesn't like you, it's probably because of the geography. You're up here on the eighth floor with the top brass and she's downstairs, probably stuck in a cubicle she wishes had windows and walls. Nothing you can do about that so don't let it get to you. Besides, you work for me, not her."

He rose and offered me a fist tap, his grin splitting his face into northern and southern hemispheres. "You got that right, boss!"

I sat at my desk chair, comparing Leonard to Michael Lacey. Their profiles were different: Lacey's long on probabilities and short on facts; Leonard's easier to plug in to what I'd seen in the basement. He'd snooped in the dream project files, made unwanted advances to Anne and threatened her. And, he had a track record.

That was reason enough to put Leonard on the short list for Anne Kendall's murder and to check for any

connections between him and Regina Blair. But his profile didn't put him in the ballpark with Tom Delaney
and Walter Enoch. Looking for a unified theory, one
that captured all the victims with a single killer could be
a mistake, a cop's version of looking for love in all the
wrong places.

Chapter Thirty-six

Frank Gentry materialized in my doorway, his gray suit coat buttoned, his navy and red regimental striped necktie cinched tight and straight against a white, buttoned down shirt. The clock on my desk read five after eleven. I was tempted to stand and salute but waved him to a chair instead.

"Did you find the report I left in your desk?"

"Yeah, thanks. It's a good start, but I need more detail. Can you go deeper and tell me which subfiles each of these people accessed and when?"

"Sure. Are you interested in any specific files?"

"I am. There are videos of the research subjects talking about their dreams. I want to know who accessed the videos for Regina Blair, Tom Delaney, and Walter Enoch."

"Not a problem. You have the report handy? I want to double-check something."

I had tucked the report back into the envelope and put it back in the drawer. I took it out and handed it to him. He studied the envelope, frowning as he turned it over and tapped it against his hand and then got up and closed my office door.

"That's not my envelope. I always write my initials in small letters in the bottom right-hand corner. Habit I got into when I was in the service. My initials aren't on this one. No wonder everyone thinks that little son-of-a-bitch Leonard killed that girl."

I raised my hand. "What do you mean that everyone thinks Leonard killed that girl?"

"That's the chatter. I'm amazed he hasn't been arrested yet the way people are talking. He saw me go in your office earlier this morning. I closed the door because I didn't like him watching what I was doing. After I left, he must have gone snooping, found the report, and then put it in a new envelope so it would look like it hadn't been opened. No way you would have known the difference."

He handed me the envelope as Detective Carter threw my door open, breathing hard.

"Where's your assistant, Leonard Nagel?"

I looked past him at Leonard's empty desk and came out of my chair. "He was right there a minute ago."

Carter lifted the two-way on his jacket collar to his chin. "Attention all personnel. Lock this building down. No one goes in or out. Find Leonard Nagel," he paused, looking at me.

"White male, dark brown hair, five-ten, hundred eighty pounds," I recited, Carter nodding and repeating the description, looking at me again.

"Approach with caution," I said.

Carter added the rest and clicked off the radio. Half a dozen uniformed cops had gathered outside my office. Sanchez squeezed through the crowd.

"We've checked the entire floor, bathrooms, offices, and closets," he said to Carter. "Caught one guy with his pants down but it wasn't Nagel. We're taking it floor by floor. I radioed for a search dog. We'll flush him out of whatever spider hole he's hiding in."

Milo Harper was next, the cops peeling back to make way for him. "What's happening?"

"Milo Harper, say hello to Detective Carter, KCPD homicide," I said. "They want to talk to Leonard Nagel. He was here a minute ago, but now he's gone."

"I told you we should have fired him this morning," Harper said to me.

"Fired him? Why?" Carter asked.

"We found out he was hacking into confidential files on our network," Harper said. "Jack said we should hold on to him until we knew how he got past our system security."

"I'm glad you didn't fire him," Carter said. "Otherwise, he could be on his way out of town by now instead of bottled up inside this building."

"You think he had something to do with Anne's murder?" Harper asked.

"We want to ask him some questions," Carter said.

"About what?"

Carter flipped the question onto Harper. "We understand that the murder victim, Ms. Kendall, filed a sexual harassment complaint against Leonard Nagel. What do you know about that?"

Harper winced, hit by another dropped shoe. "Not a goddamn thing."

"She left it on Connie Nichols desk last night, just before she left," I said. "Connie told me that she didn't see it until this morning. She also told me that another employee filed a complaint against him last year but dropped it when her husband was transferred. She's making copies of everything for the police."

"I just came from her office," Carter said. "What do you know about the earlier complaint?" he asked Harper.

Harper hesitated, blinking as the scope of his ignorance came into focus. "Nothing. My sister handles those things." He took a deep breath. "Is there anything else I should know?"

"Do you do background checks before you hire people?" Carter asked.

"I don't know but I assume you're about to tell me why we should," Harper said.

"I am," Carter said. "When we found out about the complaint against Leonard, we ran his name through the computer. He was charged with date rape in Colorado a few years ago but pled out to a lesser charge. Part of the plea deal was that he had to register as a sex offender, which he did in Colorado, except he didn't register when he moved to Kansas City. Happens more often than we'd like to admit."

Harper's face went slack, his mouth hinged wide, then bounced back. "How can I help you find him?"

"We've got people waiting at the elevators on every floor and at all of the exits," Carter. "And, we've got teams sweeping the stairs and each floor. If he pops open a ceiling tile and gets in the vent system, can he find a way out we don't know about?"

"The best he could do is hide but he can't go floor to floor. The only way he could do that is in the trash chute. It's big enough and there are handholds all the way down for access in case something gets stuck or the chute needs to be repaired."

"Where do we find the chute?"

"There's an interior corridor on each floor. That's how you get to the bathrooms, the break room, the stairs, and the freight elevator. The trash chute runs parallel to the freight elevator."

"Where does it bottom out?" Carter asked.

"At the loading dock on the ground floor. The trash is collected in a Dumpster and wheeled out for pickup."

"When is the trash picked up?" Carter asked.

"That much I do know," Harper said, looking at his watch. "Every Tuesday, about now."

Chapter Thirty-seven

Harper and I caught up to Carter and Sanchez as they got on the elevator. I reached for the door as it was closing.

"We've got it from here," Carter said.

I let go and stepped back, slamming my hand against the wall. I'd spent the morning following procedure, playing the role of civilian bystander, my one concern to stay out of the way and not screw anything up and I was choking on the protocol.

"I may not know half of what's going on inside these walls but this is my goddamn institute," Harper said, "and I'm sure as hell not going to sit on my ass and wait for the all clear to sound. My office, now."

Carter was right and Harper was wrong but wrong felt a lot better than right. I followed him into his office where he stopped in front of a bookcase, pulling back the spine of a book that wasn't a book. The shelf parted in the middle, opening onto an elevator.

We stepped on, Harper laughing. "It's good to be rich."

"You convinced me."

He punched the button for the ground floor and the car plummeted like an amusement park ride. Harper's face lit up. "They're taking the local. We're taking the express."

"Where does this thing land?"

"It goes to the garage where I park but it will stop on the ground level at the back of the loading dock."

"Carter and Sanchez will get off at the lobby and then have to find their way to the dock. We'll be inside before they're on the ground."

The prospect sobered Harper. "Should we be afraid of Leonard?"

"He's running and people who run do stupid things. That makes them dangerous."

"But you can take him, can't you? I mean he's younger, but you were an FBI agent, for Christ's sake."

That was enough to make me look for the stop button on the elevator. Harper didn't know better but I did. He was one of the rich boys who kept score with their toys. The secret express elevator was one and I was another.

"Carter was right. We should let the police handle this."

Harper stared at me. "It's the shaking, isn't it? You're afraid we'll find Leonard and you'll come apart into a million little pieces. Well, you might and I might forget to do something that costs me millions of dollars. That's the road you and I are on but I'm not slowing down or getting off. What are you going to do?"

I asked that question every day, wondering what I'd

lost to my movement disorder and what I'd surrendered. That was the hard part of taking it easy, the balance I sought more of a deal with the devil, my soul for a steady gait, a quiet day for an empty life. Harper could afford to take chances because it was his money and that's all it was, money. I could put myself on the line, but I couldn't take him with me.

"Go play in traffic," I said as the elevator stopped.

The door opened and I swept my leg against the back of Harper's knees, lifting him off his feet and shoving him as he fell. He hit the floor, rolling against the rear of the elevator, banging his head, stunned and breathless. I pressed the button for the top floor and stepped out, the door closing behind me.

The loading dock was a modest space, the twenty-foot ceiling making it appear larger than it was, the length of the walls matching the ceiling height. Surplus furniture was scattered along the wall to my left, the open door to the trash chute cut into the one on my right, overflowing garbage bags littered along the base of the wall.

The Dumpster had been wheeled across the floor and parked against the entrance from the dock into the building. The door swung back into the dock, the Dumpster blocking Carter and Sanchez who were pounding and shouting from the other side.

The overhead garage door, wide enough to accommodate two semis, was raised, icy air filling the dock. A uniformed officer lay crumpled outside the door, unconscious but breathing, the crowbar next to him and the lump on his head explanation enough.

I jumped off the dock, slipped on a patch of ice and scrambled to my feet, catching a glimpse of Leonard beating a path through the snow up a hill rising to the east of the building. He was two hundred yards ahead and I was twenty-five years behind.

"Leonard!"

He threw me a look over his shoulder, stumbling, clawing against the snow with both hands and digging his way up the slope. An irregular line of pine trees ran along the crest of the hill. He grabbed a tree trunk, hoisting himself over the ridge as a news chopper zeroed in on us, the cameraman leaning out the open side.

I ran after him, my street shoes no match for the snow, tumbling twice before I made it to the top of the hill. He was halfway down the other side, running and falling, jumping to his feet, hell bent for the northeast corner of the campus. I swallowed air and shouted.

"Leonard! Stop!"

Sirens and the chopper drowned out my voice, though I tried again as I sprinted after him.

Volker Boulevard ran along the north side of the campus, Troost Avenue bordering on the east, both major thoroughfares. They were clogged with fast moving traffic now that the streets had been plowed, salt and sand grinding any lingering ice into the pavement, people in a hurry making up for lost time.

Across the intersection, there was a wooded area on the right and the wide channel of Brush Creek on the left. Both would give him sparse cover though neither offered a way out. I was closing the gap between us but not fast enough.

When he reached the intersection, he cut to his right, bolting onto Troost, dodging a car and a bus, horns screaming, the driver of a pickup slamming on his brakes, the truck skidding and fishtailing, the back end swatting Leonard like he was a pin ball. He cart wheeled through the air, limp and dead before he hit the pavement, spread-eagled on his back, cars rear-ending around his body in a chain-reaction collision.

I weaved through the tangle of vehicles as people piled out, rubbing their necks and scratching their heads. I kneeled over him. His lifeless eyes were open, his mouth fixed in his signature grin.

Wendy sent me an electronic birthday card a few months after she disappeared, signing it Monkey Girl, the nickname I'd given her when she was little. Simon traced it to a desktop computer in a reading room at the New York City Public Library at 42nd Street and Fifth Avenue. I was on a plane the next day, combing the library, staking out the adjacent Bryant Park, mingling with the crowds on 42nd Street and in Times Square and following the endless streams of people bubbling up from the subway or getting on and off buses.

I found her three days later, staggering from an overdose on the sidewalk next to the park. It was five o'clock in the afternoon, people on their way home, rushing past her as if she wasn't there. I was coming down the library steps on 42nd, elevated enough that I could pick her out in the crowd when a kid on a skateboard sideswiped her, bouncing her off a guy in a suit who shoved her into a lamppost. She stumbled onto 42nd and collapsed, a taxi skidding to a stop inches from her head.

I lifted her head into my lap, her glassy eyes struggling to focus, her voice weak and feathery.

"Daddy?"

"I'm here, baby."

"You found me. I knew you would." She reached for my collar, pulling me close, her breath shallow, her face pale. "It's Monkey Girl."

"I know it's you, baby. Hang on. You're going to be okay."

She squeezed my hand. "No I'm not, Daddy, but I love you and I'm glad you found me."

And she was gone, an improbable smile her last gift.

"Jack! Jack! Are you okay?" I looked up to see Lucy bulling her way through the crowd that had materialized. "Oh, my God! I was on my way to the institute and I saw you chasing him down the hill. Who is he? I can't believe he ran into all that traffic. He didn't have a chance."

As she helped me to my feet, I started to shake, tidal waves ripping through me. I held onto her, my head on her shoulder, my knees buckling. She wrapped her arms around me, keeping me upright as my legs gave way, steering me out of the intersection.

"My daughter, Wendy," I said when we reached the curb and I caught my breath, "I found her in New York just before she died of an overdose. She's drifting down Forty-second Street and a kid blows past her on a skateboard, knocks her into a guy who shoves her into a lamppost, and then she spins into the street, practically melts onto the pavement. I got to her, knelt down, and lifted her head up. She looks at me, tells me it's Monkey Girl, like I don't know who she is."

"Monkey Girl. You lost me."

"It was her nickname when she was a little girl. I gave it to her and she gave it to a stuffed monkey I bought her. Anyway, she says it's Monkey Girl and then she dies, but she's smiling, same as Leonard. Neither one of them had a reason to, but they died smiling. Go figure."

My legs buckled again and another pair of hands grabbed me.

"Let me help," Milo Harper said.

They lifted me, one of my arms across each of their shoulders, and dragged me to a bus stop bench, propping me up. I gulped choppy breaths, aftershocks doubling me over.

An EMT dropped to one knee in front of me. "You okay, buddy?"

I waved him off. "It'll pass. It'll pass."

The EMT looked at Lucy who nodded. "Happens every time he chases someone into an intersection," she said, satisfying the EMT.

"Okay, okay," I said a few moments later when my legs were back and I had stopped shaking. "Let's get out of here."

They hung close to me as we walked around the intersection where crime scene techs were taking pictures and measurements while drivers gave their statements and television news crews made their living.

"Hey, Davis," McNair yelled, making his way over to us. "It doesn't get easier than this, does it? Looks like I'll be home for dinner."

Chapter Thirty-eight

Milo squeezed my arm. "You owe me for that stunt you pulled in the elevator."

"More like you owe me," I said.

He nodded and grinned. "I know."

I filled Lucy in as we walked back to the institute, taking the long way around to the front entrance where reporters swarmed Milo. He and I exchanged shrugs and I left him to work his magic.

"You think Leonard killed Anne or was he running because everyone thought he did and he was afraid of getting busted for not registering as a sex offender?" Lucy asked when were inside the lobby.

"I don't know."

"Is there anything to connect him with Blair, Delaney, and Enoch or is this a stand-alone murder?"

"He hacked into the dream project files but I don't know if he saw their videos. That's all I've got so far."

The lobby was crammed with cops and people waiting for the elevators. Each time one opened, the crowd grew as those passengers joined the throng, finding their friends, hugging and crying, trading can-you-believe-it for I'm-not-surprised.

Nancy Klemp was on duty at the front desk, implacable and unruffled by the chaos around her, answering questions and giving directions.

"What's the latest?" I asked her.

"Ms. Fritzshall went on the PA and told everyone to go home. Said to take the day off tomorrow and come back strong on Thursday. We've got six elevators and eight floors of people. Gonna take forever to clear everyone out of here. I wouldn't be in a hurry to get upstairs unless you feel like walking."

"What happened with Anne's boyfriend, Michael Lacey? Is he still in the conference room?"

"I haven't seen him leave."

Lucy and I navigated through the crowd to the conference room. The door was open. Lacey was slumped over the table, his head on his folded arms. A uniformed cop stood in a corner. Carter tapped me on the shoulder from behind. I hadn't heard him approach.

"You did good out there," Carter said.

"I was too old and too slow. What about him?" I asked, pointing to Lacey.

"I told him he could hang out here until the TV trucks take off. He doesn't want to deal with the cameras."

I stepped farther down the hall away from the door, drawing Carter with me. "You satisfied about Leonard?"

He opened his jacket and pulled out an evidence bag, holding it up for me. Anne Kendall's Institute ID badge was inside the bag, the gold chain smeared with blood.

"We found this hidden in Leonard's desk. That satisfy you?"

"Makes me feel better. Doesn't make me feel good. Lacey have an alibi?"

"Says he was home and fell asleep watching TV. Thought she was working late. Woke up this morning and she wasn't there. Said he started making phone calls and then got one from the gal at the front desk."

"That's thin. Were they getting along?"

"So he says. We'll check it out," Carter said.

"Does that mean you aren't satisfied or that you're just running the traps?"

Carter smiled. "McNair is satisfied, but he's easy. I'm harder to please. Lacey says that Anne told him about her sexual harassment complaint against Leonard. He could have forced her to take him to the institute and used her ID to get in the building, killed her, and planted the ID in Leonard's desk, figuring that plus the complaint would be enough to put the stink on Leonard."

"On that theory, Leonard turning out to be an unregistered sexual offender was an added bonus."

"Better to be lucky than good. Could have gone down that way, but my money is still on Leonard," Carter said. "This Lacey doesn't seem the type. He was blown away when we told him she was dead. I know that doesn't mean much but it felt real to me."

"You interested in another take?"

"Why not? I could use the overtime."

"Let's go upstairs to my office."

"Are you kidding? Have you seen how many people are in line for those elevators?"

"Wait here. I know a short cut."

I found Milo surrounded by a throng of reporters, peeling him away long enough to ask how to summon his private elevator to the loading dock. He pulled out his iPhone, tapped in a number, and smiled.

"Phone activated. It's on the way. How about that?" he said, turning back to the cameras.

The eighth floor was empty when Lucy, Carter, and I reached my office except for the crime scene techs poring over Leonard's workstation. I described the dream project for Carter, walking him through the deaths of Blair, Delaney, and Enoch, and the increasing pattern of violence culminating in Anne's murder.

"You got a whole lot of nothing, you know that," Carter said.

"I don't have a guy who harassed one of the victims, ran when the cops showed up, and had the victim's bloody ID squirreled away in his desk, which, I might add, is the dumbest place he could have picked to hide a souvenir. That's enough for McNair but not for you. I do have three dead people, four counting Anne Kendall, and a lot of questions that nobody seems interested in asking."

"You say that McNair took a second look at Delaney's and Blair's files?"

"So he says."

"Then he did. He's a better cop than you give him credit for. My boss is going to need a good reason to let me or anyone else take a third look."

"Anne Kendall isn't a good enough reason?"

"Not without more proof that Delaney and Blair were homicides and not without something to tie them to her and Enoch. You know how this works. But as long as we're talking, tell me why Kent and Dolan have such a hard-on for you?"

"What did Dolan tell you?"

"Not much. His mother didn't teach him to share. He

had a look at the closet in the sub-basement and went back upstairs. All I got from him was that you were damaged goods."

I had taken a chance on Carter and if I was going to make it pay, I had to go all the way with it. If he took this on, he'd find out about my personal connection to Walter Enoch's murder and would shut me down for trying to sandbag him. He listened as I rolled out the rest of it, telling him about Wendy and my movement disorder. He nodded, asking the right questions at the right time, leaning back in his chair when I was finished, letting out a deep sigh.

"You are the king of the clusterfuck, you know that?"

"Wouldn't be any fun if it was easy," I said.

"This is McNair's case."

"You're his partner, not his butt boy."

"He's not going to like it if I make him look bad."

"McNair doesn't need any help with that."

"My lieutenant won't like it if I get in a pissing match with the feds over one of their cases. Especially if he finds out you're behind it and the feds are putting your tit in the wringer. Doesn't do much for your credibility."

"I can handle Kent and Dolan. And if all four deaths are related, you've got an exclusive claim to three out of four. Your boss can take that to his boss, let the brass run interference."

"All that aside, you've still got a whole lot of nothing. Why would I want to hike up my pants and step in that?"

"To get it right."

Carter studied me, weighing his career. The phone on my desk rang, the name on caller ID reason to hope for the first good break of the day.

"It's Frank Gentry, the institute's IT director. He's been doing some work for me on this."

"Go ahead," Carter said. "Take it."

I picked up the receiver and listened as Gentry told me about the results of his additional research on the dream project video files. I thanked him and hung up.

"Leonard Nagel didn't access Delaney's, Blair's, or Enoch's dream videos," I said.

"That helps my case against Leonard but it doesn't help yours," Carter said.

"So who did access their videos?" Lucy asked.

"Other than Anthony Corliss, Maggie Brennan, and their two research associates?"

"Yeah," she said.

"Just one other person. Milo Harper."

Chapter Thirty-nine

"What do you make of that?" Carter asked.

"Harper says that's how he keeps track of what's going on at the institute."

"If he was concerned about what happened with Delaney, Blair, and Enoch, it makes sense that he'd take a look at their videos," Lucy said.

"After they died, but not before," Carter said, echoing my own concerns. "He's got to be too busy to single out three research subjects for special attention and he's got to be too smart to hire you to investigate Delaney's and Blair's deaths if he had something to do with them."

"We've got Enoch's video but we need to see the videos Delaney and Blair made to get a handle on this," Lucy said.

"Gentry came through on their videos. He e-mailed them to me," I said.

I brought up the e-mail screen on my desktop. Gentry's e-mail was at the top of the list. I downloaded the

Blair video and the three of us crowded around my monitor as the credits rolled with Gary Kaufman doing the narration: *Harper Institute of the Mind Dream Project, Subject—Regina Blair, Date: November 28.*

The video ran twelve minutes. Regina was composed through the first eight minutes, Kaufman explaining the procedure, Regina acknowledging her understanding of the process and her willingness to participate. When Kaufman asked her to describe her dream, she tilted her head back, closed her eyes, and breathed steadily before she answered, keeping her eyes closed. As she spoke, she hunched her shoulders and held herself with crossed arms.

"I'm in a dark place. It's not pitch black but almost. There are shadows and bits of light. I can't figure out where the light is coming from and everywhere I turn, I can't find anything to touch or hold on to. I start taking little steps with my hands in front of me. I'm trying to find my way out and my heart starts beating so fast I can't breathe. I'm sweating and I'm calling for help but I can't hear my own voice and no one answers. Then I start shaking and I feel cold and hot at the same time and then it's just light enough for me to see that I'm standing on a ledge looking down and there's no bottom, no end, and then I'm falling. I don't even know what made me fall but I can't stop and I scream all the way down."

She opened her eyes, tears streaming down her face as she shook. The camera closed in until her face filled the screen before going black.

It wasn't an unusual dream. I'd had dreams of being lost, of falling. Knowing her dream had come as true as any dream could made it feel real, infecting me with a fleeting sense of vertigo.

No one said anything as I downloaded Delaney's video. Corliss's voice provided the introductory narrative, the onscreen credits noting the date as December 22.

"Corliss told me that the research assistants are supposed to shoot the videos but he shot Walter Enoch's video and this one."

The camera was focused on Delaney. Like Enoch, he was sitting in the same chair where the police found his body, an entertainment center behind him, television in the middle, books lining shelves on either side.

"That's Delaney's place," Lucy said. "The entertainment center was still there when I was in the apartment."

"The videos were supposed to be done at the institute. Corliss said he took Enoch's video at the house because he wanted to know more about him. I wonder what his excuse is for taking Delaney's at his apartment."

"One thing is for sure," Lucy said, "both Enoch and Delaney would be more likely to let Corliss in if he'd been there once before and there was no sign of forcible entry at either place."

"And Kent and Dolan were interviewing Corliss about the Enoch case when Anne Kendall's body was found."

"Okay, okay," Carter said, "I'm paying attention."

I'd brought my copies of the incident reports on Delaney and Blair to the institute. I spread out the photos of Delaney's apartment the police had taken on my desk. Delaney's body had been found in a swivel chair, the chair turned with its back to the television. The photographs showed the body from a variety of angles as well as the rest of the room. Two of the photographs included the entertainment center. I froze the video image of the entertainment center and compared it to the photographs.

"Look at the shelf to the left of the television," I said. "In the video, the shelf is full. In the photographs, it's half empty. Something is missing."

"So what?" Carter said.

"So the killer could have shot Delaney, put the gun in his hand, and fired it again into a couple of books. Delaney ends up with powder burns on his hand. The bullet ends up in one of the books and the killer takes the books and the missing bullet with him."

Carter stepped back from the monitor. "That's what you want me to hang my hat on? No disrespect, Jack, but all that shaking you been doing must have scrambled your brain."

"What about the angle of entry of the bullet? You really think Delaney committed suicide by wrapping his arm around his head to shoot himself? That's crazy!"

"Committing suicide is just one of the crazy things crazy people do," Carter said. "I'm out of here."

"At least stay and watch the rest," I said.

"What for? I got enough nightmares of my own. I don't need nobody else's."

"Five minutes. That's all I'm asking. You said you need the overtime."

Carter let out a long breath. "You don't give up, do you, man?"

"Not yet."

I pushed the play button and the three of us watched, shoulder-to-shoulder. Corliss coaxed and coached Delaney through the preliminaries, Delaney agreeing to the videotaping, acknowledging that the video may be shown to others and that Delaney under-

stood that this was for research purposes only and that
no treatment was being given. Delaney showed no emo-
tion throughout the exchange, his face flat, his voice
flatter. Then Corliss steered the conversation to Delaney's nightmare.

CORLISS: How are you feeling, Tom?
DELANEY: Like shit.
CORLISS: Are you sleeping?
DELANEY: Some. Not much.
CORLISS: Why not?
DELANEY: I don't know.
CORLISS: What happens when you sleep?
DELANEY: I keep having the same dream.
CORLISS: Tell me about the dream.
DELANEY: I already told you when I signed up for the
    project.
CORLISS: I know you did. That's why I wanted to make
    this videotape. Your dream is important to the pro-
    ject.
DELANEY: Okay. I'm sitting right here. In this chair. I
    take my gun and put it up against my head, like this.

He lifted his shirt and pulled the Beretta from his
waistband with his right hand and placed the barrel
flush against his right temple.

CORLISS: But you don't pull the trigger in your dream.
    Why not?
DELANEY: 'Cause I'm a chicken-shit loser, that's why."
CORLISS: It's okay, Tom. Put the gun away."

I paused the video, looking at Carter.
"You see what he did with the gun?" Lucy asked.

"Right hand to right temple. No wrap around gymnastics."

"Yeah, I see it," Carter said.

"Still think I got a whole lot of nothing?" I asked Carter.

"I think you got enough for a third look. Give me your cell number." I wrote it out for him and he handed me his card. "E-mail address is on there. Shoot that video to me," he said and left.

Chapter Forty

"Had enough for one day?" Lucy asked.

"Two dead people are two more than my daily limit."

"I had to park a couple of blocks away. I'll get the car and meet you in the circle drive."

"I can walk, you know."

"I know. Makes me feel better if you let me get the car."

I'd learned that it helps some people to help me even if I didn't need the help, a gentle reminder that nothing happens to just one person.

"Fair enough. I'll meet you downstairs in ten minutes."

I watched the rest of Delaney's video. Corliss took him through the dream sequence several more times, but Delaney didn't change a detail. Each time, he pulled out his gun with his right hand, held it to his right temple, and stuck it back in his pants when Corliss told him to do so, Corliss never asking or checking whether the gun was loaded. The more they went through the motions, the more it began to look like they were rehearsing a one-act play though I doubted Delaney realized it would close on opening night.

I e-mailed Delaney's video to Carter, downloaded it to my flash drive, and packed the incident reports into the canvas satchel that passed as my briefcase. The rest of the institute's employees must have taken to heart Sherry's suggestion that everyone go home early because the halls were quiet and empty and one of the elevators opened the instant I pushed the call button. For the second day in a row, it stopped on the third floor and Maggie Brennan stepped on. She had replaced her gray scarf and gray coat with an identical version in black.

"It seems we're fated to make this trip together," she said.

"I could do worse."

She tilted her head at me. "I'm not so certain but thank you for the vote of confidence."

"You're welcome. New coat?"

She raised her arm. "I finally tired of the other one."

"Some day, huh? It's good that everyone gets tomorrow off."

She nodded. "A day of rest suits me. The police talked to me and I heard what happened with that young man. Do you think he killed that girl?"

"He had a reason to run. That could have been it."

"You don't sound convinced."

"Let's just say I'm agnostic on the subject," parroting her uncertainty about the dream project.

She smiled. "Are you teasing me?"

"A little. Truth is I like to take my time before accepting a quick and easy answer to something as hard to figure out as murder."

"Then you would have made a good scientist. I heard talk that the young man, what was his name?"

"Leonard Nagel."

"Yes. Leonard. I heard that he had been in trouble before."

"He had. He may have been guilty or he may just have been running from his past."

"The past is difficult to outrun. It chases us like the sound of the driven leaf."

"You've lost me."

"It's from Leviticus," she said, reciting the verse. "'As for those of you who survive, I will cast a faintness into their hearts in the land of their enemies. The sound of a driven leaf shall put them to flight. Fleeing as though from the sword, they shall fall though none pursues.'"

The elevator stopped on the ground floor and we stepped out.

"What does that have to do with Leonard?"

"He'd sinned and survived. That made him weaker, not stronger, afraid of the simplest and smallest things, like the sound of a driven leaf. Perhaps that's what drove him into that intersection."

"But he was pursued. I was chasing him."

"I've known many people like your Leonard. He wasn't running from you. He was running from himself and none of us wins that race."

Chapter Forty-one

Lucy had parked my car in the circle drive, the passenger window down. She waved as I passed through the doors of the institute, the last of the low-angled sun slicing through the trees, disappearing at my feet. The day, though at its end, had warmed, as winter days in Kansas City will do, turning snow to slush and stoking frozen bones with the promise that spring was around the corner no matter how far the bend in the road.

Gone were the squad cars, fire trucks, ambulances, news crews, and gawkers. Gone too were the frightened and anxious people who worked here, the loss of two of their own seeding their nightmares, leaving them rattled and relieved that they had survived the day. In their place was an empty after-hours quiet. The hum of homebound traffic hung in the air, a white noise reminder that loved ones will be home for dinner, the sun will set and rise, and we will begin again.

That faith in normalcy, that bedrock certainty that there are more good guys than bad, that hard-eyed survivor's optimism, gets us through the night and emboldens us to take on the day. It will allow Carlos Morales to one day go searching for tools in the sub-basement closet where Anne Kendall was murdered without imagining her violated body pressed against the wall and allow Connie Nichols to drive through the intersection where Leonard Nagel died without muttering under her breath that he got what he deserved and not caring whether he did.

Underlying all of that is our shared faith in justice—that whoever takes a life will be called to account by those who have sworn to take up that burden. I took that oath when I joined the FBI and though my badge had been taken from me, I couldn't set that burden down.

A black sedan cruised into the circle drive, stopping between Lucy and me, Ammara Iverson at the wheel, Dolan in the passenger seat, and Kent in the back. Dolan stepped out, opened the rear door, and thumb-jerked an invitation. Lucy jumped out of my car, stopping when I waved her off.

"It's okay," I told her as I unzipped my jacket and cradled my satchel under my arm.

I slid into the backseat, Dolan slamming the door like he wanted to throw away the key.

"We're double-dating? No wonder Dolan's so testy. He's jealous that you're in the back with me," I said to Kent.

"Do me a favor, don't start," Kent said. "I don't need you jamming him every time you open your mouth."

"And I don't need you guys popping up like the Pillsbury doughboy every time I turn around and riding my ass."

Kent let out a sigh. "Maybe we can work it out so we don't have to."

"Right. Next thing, Dolan will tell me he'll respect me in the morning and it's only a cold sore."

Dolan cursed and pivoted in his seat, ready to climb into the back. Ammara grabbed his arm before he could finish the turn and backed me off with a hot look.

"Let's take a walk, just you and me," Kent said, throwing his door open, climbing out of the car and cinching the belt on his trench coat.

We took it slow, following the circle drive toward the street. He rolled his shoulders and twisted his neck, getting loose, making it easier to say what he had to say, the words sticking.

"I'm not going to apologize for how we came at you," Kent said. "Take yourself and your daughter out of it, look at it the way you would have if you'd been us, and you would have done it the same way."

"I don't need an apology but I'd like to think I would have done it different."

"Oh, yeah. What would you have done?"

"Let it go. Wendy is dead and the rest of them are dead or in jail. I lost my daughter and my job. I don't give a crap about the money. Finding it won't change a damn thing for the Bureau or me. You want to work a cold case, find one that matters."

"Brass in DC doesn't see it that way, especially after this whole thing with the mailman. The way that touches you, forces our hand. We got no choice now and you know that."

I stopped and turned toward him. "Look, I don't know what was in the envelope Wendy sent me. I don't know where the money is and I didn't kill Walter Enoch. You tried bracing me downtown with the worst good cop, bad cop duet I've ever seen, though I got to admit that Dolan is born to the asshole role. Then you tried the soft soap with Ammara and now this, a mix of the high-low. What's next?"

Kent gave me a weak smile and gestured toward the street, keeping us moving. "Coroner makes Enoch's time of death sometime between ten o'clock Wednesday night and two o'clock Thursday morning. You got an alibi for that window?"

"I was fast asleep. Alone. Like everyone else whose mail Enoch either stole or delivered. You need more than that. Can you put me at the scene? Can you put me with Enoch? Can you tie me to the money?"

"Wendy contacted you twice we know of before she died. Stands to reason she told you what happened to the money and stands to reason you'd try to protect her memory, maybe even keep the money for your golden years. The letter she sent you ties you to Enoch. And it doesn't matter that the rest of the people on Enoch's mail route don't have an alibi. You're the only one whose stolen mail was opened."

"If it was me, don't you think I'd have taken the en- velope too? And what about Corliss? You must have watched the video that he took at Enoch's house on my laptop. Hell, he talked Enoch into participating in the dream project and into letting him in his house with all that stolen mail. There were no signs of forcible entry. Corliss is a lot better choice than me. Ask him if he's got an alibi and ask him to take a polygraph."

"We did. He says he was asleep, just like you. He turned us down on the poly, says they're unreliable. You and I know better even if the courts won't let the results into evidence. Why don't you take a polygraph? Maybe put this whole thing to bed."

"Last time I offered, they turned me down. The examiner says I shake so much the results wouldn't mean a thing."

We made it to the street. A silver Lexus was parked on the curb, a vanity plate on the front bumper reading *Bolt*, jagged lines of yellow on either side of the name. The driver was short, his head clearing the steering wheel by inches. He raised one hand, giving me a wan salute. I gave him my back, wondering who or what he was waiting for.

"We did watch the video and Corliss told us all about it," Kent said. "Question is what was it doing on your laptop?"

"That guy in the Lexus," I said, tilting my head in Bolt's direction. "He's a lawyer named Jason Bolt. He's making noise about suing the institute for the wrongful death of two other volunteers. Milo Harper hired me to take a look at those cases, help put together a defense. When I found out Enoch was also a volunteer, I got curious."

"When did you find out Enoch was a volunteer?"

I thought of Lucy waiting for me in the circle drive, realizing that Ammara and Dolan were quizzing her. They had worked us, bringing Ammara to lower my guard, separating Lucy and me so they could question us at the same time before we could get our stories straight.

"Yesterday morning."

"So how come you got pictures of Enoch's body on your laptop? Those had to have been taken Friday night when Ammara called you out to the scene only she says you didn't take them. That leaves your landlady, Lucy Trent, who, and I got to confess, this is the part I really like, is another ex-cop that can't resist temptation. You living with a thief that takes pictures of the murder victim on the sly don't exactly help your credibility."

"She's got nothing to do with this."

"Then why was she taking pictures of the dead man?"

There was no answer I could give that wouldn't dig a deeper hole for her or me. "She was playing games. Thought she was being cute."

"That the best you can do?"

"She made a mistake. Let it go."

"That's the kind of mistake connects you and her to Enoch."

"You want a connection, try one between Enoch, the two wrongful death cases, and the woman who was found dead here this morning."

"You telling me all four are connected? What? You want us to go chasing a serial killer so we'll forget about you?"

"It's not as much of a stretch as you trying to make me for Enoch and the missing money."

"That explains why the chief of police reached out to the SAC. There's talk about a joint task force."

"That will tie you and Dolan up for a while."

"Not likely. We'll let the locals have Enoch, probably toss in a profiler and a few forensic people to back them up, if we can get some resolution with you on the drug money."

"What do you want from me?"

"Wrong question. The right question is what am I giving to you?"

"Don't make me wait until Christmas."

"Wise ass. Put this in your stand-up act. You've got forty-eight hours to come up with the money and the letter Wendy sent you. If her letter told you where the money is, we'll give you the benefit of the doubt that you haven't had it all along and you walk. After that, we do things Dolan's way."

"Why the free pass?"

"It's not free. It costs five million and you can thank Ammara for talking the SAC into it. She says you deserve one last chance to do the right thing."

"The Bureau is that hung up on the drug money?"

"You don't get it, do you, Davis. It's never been about the money. It's always been about you. You're the one who isn't dead and isn't in jail. You're the one that got away. That's what the Bureau can't stand. Neither can I."

"I know why you think Wendy told me about the money. I can't help that. But nobody can think I was part of what went down with my squad."

Kent's good guy façade vanished, his eyes hard, his lips pulled back. "It was an agent on your team that went bad, it was your daughter that helped him, and it was you who couldn't hack it anymore and wouldn't own up to it. Anybody else would have been transferred to Sitka or shit-canned. But you shimmy shake your ass into a cushy retirement on a bullshit disability that ain't so bad you can't collect a fat check from Milo Fucking Harper. And nobody, I mean nobody from DC to KC, can stomach that. So you want to buy peace with us, it's gonna cost you five million dollars."

Chapter Forty-two

I watched Kent trudge up the circle drive toward the cars, his head bent into the wind, winter having caught its breath, blowing again, affirming Kansas City's weather reputation—if you don't like it, don't worry; wait fifteen minutes and it will change. I zipped my jacket against my throat and stuck my hands in my pockets, the last thing he said hitting me harder than the fresh blast of cold air.

It was all about me, the punch line to a lame joke turned into probable cause for an indictment. I knew that people in the Bureau were both angry and skeptical about my movement disorder, furious that I hadn't come clean sooner while doubting that it was real or disabling, ignoring that I hadn't quit, that I was forced out, shit-canned instead of sent to Sitka, untroubled by their contradictory complaints.

What I didn't understand until now was how deep the institutional need was for me to take the fall for what had happened on my watch and how deep the re-

sentment was that I had skated on a cluster fuck that
would have torpedoed anyone else's career, taking their
pension down with it. I thought back to Wendy's funeral and the stiff condolences that I had received. In
my grief I had failed to hear what they were really saying, that she had gotten what she deserved. They were
singing from Connie Nichols's hymnal.

And here I was, living what to them was the good life,
collecting disability and a paycheck. Sure, I had the
shakes, whatever that was. But I had stayed on the job and
on the case when I should have put myself on the disabled list, getting away with the unforgivable sin of letting a dirty, rogue agent operate under my nose, aided
and abetted by my daughter, without paying the price
they would impose.

That I might now profit to the tune of five million
dollars was, for them, both unacceptable and unspeakable. That they might be wrong was unthinkable. Facts
may be stubborn things but hate, anger, and disbelief
are deaf, dumb, and blind.

Ammara had negotiated a forty-eight-hour cease-fire,
her tagline that it was my last best chance to do the right
thing telling me she stood farther away from me than I
had hoped. It also told me that Kent and Dolan were
nowhere on Enoch's murder. If they had enough to arrest me or anyone else, they would have done it. This
latest tactic was a desperation squeeze. Either I'd go
belly up, giving them the money and my head, or I'd do
their job and find Enoch's killer, Wendy's letter, and the
money to save my skin. It was an all-in, throw-down bet,
the Bureau's honor for my life.

"Jack Davis?"

I turned around. Jason Bolt was looking up at me. I
hadn't heard him get out of his car. He was short be-

hind the wheel and shorter on his feet, the close-trimmed brown beard running from his jaw line to his chin and his medicine ball belly making him more Keebler elf than courtroom giant.

"Yeah."

"I'm Jason Bolt," he said, keeping his hands in his pockets. "I saw you on TV today. Milo Harper called you a hero for chasing down the guy that murdered Anne Kendall."

I had seen the television cameras but hadn't paid attention to whether they were filming me and I hadn't heard what Harper had said.

"If I was a hero, I would have caught him before he got to the intersection and, as far as I know, the police haven't said whether he killed anyone."

Bolt nodded. "Spoken like a wise man."

"What can I do for you?"

"I assume you know that I represent the families of Tom Delaney and Regina Blair. I'm going to sue your boss and at least four of his people."

"So I hear. Why not leave the staff out of it? If you're entitled to any money, the institute will pay it."

"Accountability," Bolt said. "People have to be held accountable. They can't hide behind their employer's insurance policy. That's why I'm suing Corliss, Brennan, Casey, and Kaufman for punitive damages. Insurance doesn't cover that and an employer can't indemnify for it. I'm going to serve the papers on them myself. I stopped by to get a good look at this monument Milo Harper built to himself since I might end up with the keys."

"Look all you want."

"Just so you know, I'll win no matter what you come up with."

"No matter what I come up with?"

"I do my homework, Jack. When I heard your name on the news, I checked you out. Try doing a Google search on yourself. You had a lot of press coverage last year. Given your background, I assume that Harper hired you to dig up dirt on Tom and Regina so he can blame their deaths on anything but the lucid dreaming project."

"You expect me to respond to that?"

"Not until I take your deposition. But I do have some advice for you. When you're done digging around in Tom's and Regina's past, you might want to take a close look at Harper and company before all the mud starts to fly."

"Why the heads-up?"

"I represent two families who lost their loved ones. We can make the case about why and how they died or we can make it about a lot of other things."

"Like what?"

"For starters, like Anthony Corliss's adventures in dream land at the University of Wisconsin. Hiring someone with his track record is grounds for punitive damages."

Bolt was baiting me again, hoping I'd give him something he didn't already have. When I didn't respond, he threw more chum in the water.

"And then there's Peggy Murray."

"Is that name supposed to mean anything to me?"

"I don't care but it will mean everything to Milo Harper. You tell him that. Remind him what happened the last time he took me on. He'll get a settlement offer from me tomorrow. It will be on the table until the end of the week. Tell him to take it because he'll never have a better chance to put this behind him."

"That's the second ultimatum I've been given in the last five minutes. Must be a special on them today."

"Luck comes in bunches."

"In that case, I can do with a little less luck."

Ammara drove past us, glancing my way, looking past me for oncoming traffic, making me invisible. Kent stared straight ahead. Dolan aimed a finger gun at me, pulling the trigger. The traffic cleared and they were gone.

"Car has government tags and the guy in front has a shitty sense of humor. Must be friends of yours," Bolt said.

"In another life."

"That's what I like about what I do. I only have one life. It's a simple one, dedicated to my clients. I know that sounds like a self-serving, sanctimonious bunch of crap but it's true. They depend on me and I depend on them to depend on me. There's no ambiguity, no shades of gray. We're loyal to one another. I don't have friends from another life taking real or imaginary shots at me and I don't need anyone to watch my back."

"You sleep at night?"

"Like a dead man."

"No worries? No nightmares?"

"Just one. Letting my people down."

"That doesn't sound so simple, all those people counting on you."

"The cases are complicated and the stakes are high but it's a simple life as long as I follow one rule."

"What's that?"

"Do whatever it takes."

Chapter Forty-three

I slid into the passenger seat next to Lucy. She was locked in a thousand-yard stare, hands white-knuckled on the steering wheel, her eyes red-rimmed and full.

"Hey," I said. "You okay?"

"Yeah." She triggered the ignition, put the car in gear, and glided toward the street, taking it too slow like a drunk trying to walk a straight line.

"So, how'd it go with Ammara and Dolan?"

She took a deep breath. "Some things you never get over, you know that?"

"Tell me about it."

She pulled into traffic. I didn't ask where we were going. I'd let her find her way.

"I'd come off a twenty-hour shift when I was busted for the diamonds," she began, reading more into my off-hand suggestion to tell me about it than I had intended. She glanced at me, her raised brows asking if she should continue.

"It's okay. Go on."

She took another deep breath, gathering herself. "My eight hours were up when I found the jewelry guy's body. We were short-staffed. It was a hot case and the thought of going home, taking a shower, and going to bed with those stones under my pillow freaked me out. I never asked for the overtime. I just stayed with the case. It was understood that's what I'd do. The whole time, I'm trying to figure out how to get back in the motel room, drop the stones on the floor, and let someone else find them, but there's no way. First the room is packed with cops, CSI, everybody. After that, it's taped off and I'm on the street with one of the detectives, a drop-dead gorgeous guy named Ricky Brown who I'd been flirting with for a month, trying to get him to ask me out and I think he's interested except he's coming out of a messy relationship only he's not all the way out yet. No way I can go back. Part of me is scared shitless and part of me is so jacked up I can't see straight thinking everything will be okay if we just don't catch the guy that did it. I'm like praying, please God, I know he killed the salesman and I screwed up but how about giving me a break because nothing is going to bring the dead guy back and I'll make it up to you if you let me skate. I'll sell the stones and give the money to the church. I swear on my mother's grave I will. Then, twelve hours later when we catch the guy and he's got the stuff on him and Ricky asks him is that all of it and he says it's all of it except for some diamonds that he left lying on the floor and Ricky looks at me and I choke, I mean I don't say anything but it's like I'm saying everything. Later, when I'm serving my sentence, I talk to this prison chaplain and I tell him the story and that I must have been really screwed up to think God would answer my prayer and the priest says to me that

God answers all prayers, it's just that sometimes the answer is no. Which makes sense so I keep praying that I don't screw up again because I don't think I can handle going back and then Dolan puts me in the backseat of their car and starts grilling me about you and the pictures of Enoch's body I took and they found on your laptop and I swear to Jesus for a few minutes there I was back in that shitty Gaithersburg interrogation room, Ricky staring at me across the table, the diamonds spread out in front of us, him saying what a shame because we could have had something and me thinking my life is over and I want to die. That's how Dolan makes me feel and then he says that he knows about Gaithersburg and that if I help him, maybe wear a wire with you that they'll take care of me. All I have to do is give you up."

"Do whatever it takes," I said, the words becoming the zealous mantra of the true believer no matter the cause.

She pounded the steering wheel, looking at me for the first time since I got in the car, tears pouring down her face. "Exactly. The bastard!"

I opened the console between our seats and handed her a package of tissues. She sniffled and wiped her eyes and nose.

"What did you tell Dolan?"

She smiled at me. "I told him to go fuck himself. Guy like him, it's the only way he'd get any."

She was a mess but a beautiful mess. I stroked her hair and patted her on the shoulder. "You did good, kiddo. So, other than that, Mrs. Lincoln, how was the rest of the play?"

She laughed at the old joke, a small gurgle that blossomed into full out whooping, spreading to me, the two of us howling until she was crying again and I was shaking, our laughter opening our internal relief valves, purging the day's pressures, letting us begin again.

It started with a phone call from Kate.

"We just turned on the news. Are you okay?"

"Never better," I stammered, punctuating my answer with a grunt.

"Right. You sound terrific. Go home and take it easy."

"Make me believe you and Simon haven't come up with anything, in which case I'll have to fire you, and maybe I will."

"Is Lucy driving?"

"Yes."

"In that case, you can come over. We're at my office. See you in a few."

I gave Lucy directions. "Any luck with the construction crew on Regina Blair's project?"

"No. She was on site a lot but no one was working the morning she was killed."

Lucy had classified Blair's death as a homicide. My gut said she was right even though we still couldn't prove it.

"Did you ask the people who knew her about her fear of heights?"

"Yeah. The foreman said she was famous for it. He joked with her about it but he liked her. Said she never got close to the edge of anything unless it was the sidewalk. He gave me a lead, though."

"What?"

"He introduced me to the homeless guy who found her body. You'd be surprised how bad someone can smell in the middle of winter. His name is Vinny and he's equal parts teeth and charm, which is to say he's doesn't have much of either. But, twenty bucks bought me a dissertation on life on the street and a complaint that no one gave him a reward for finding the body."

"He probably went through her pockets before he flagged down a cop."

"That's the thing. He came clean on that at the get-go. He complained that she didn't have anything on her worth stealing."

"Nothing?"

"He said she had a cell phone but that was no good to him since there wasn't anybody he wanted to call. He went through her wallet but the liquor store wouldn't let him use her credit cards and that would just land him in jail anyway. He was looking for cash, jewelry, a watch, anything he could turn into a fifth of gin without a lot of questions. He figured someone got to the body ahead of him and he said that pissed him off more than anything because that alley was his. I don't remember the police report saying anything about her being robbed."

"Maybe she wasn't robbed, not the way Vinny means it."

"Is there another way?"

"It's not the way, it's the reason," I said, picturing Anne Kendall's mutilated left hand, her ring finger snapped off with wire shears. "Vinny was looking for something he could sell. The killer was looking for souvenirs."

Chapter Forty-four

Kate's office was on the second floor of a block long building at Thirty-eighth and Broadway, the north end anchored on the ground floor by a jazz joint called Blues On Broadway. The rest of the street level block was occupied by a dry cleaner, a tattoo parlor, a tax pre-parer, and a comic book store. The second floor was all offices, a dentist on the south end, a lawyer on the north end, and Kate's firm in the middle.

Wilson Bluestone Jr. owned the building and the jazz joint. Kate told me he'd rehabbed it, updating the old dark brown brick exterior with new dark brown brick and green awnings, gutting the office space, and finish-ing it out with twenty-first century upgrades, making it eco-friendly and techno-smart, which Kate translated as hip, chic, and cheap enough.

Not long after I left the Bureau, Kate took me into the bar and introduced me to Bluestone, calling him Blues, which explained the club's name. He had five inches and forty pounds of ripped muscle on me, and

the easy assurance that both attracted and repelled
trouble. Kate said he owed his copper coloring to his
Shawnee Indian ancestors.

She also introduced me to Lou Mason, the dark-
haired, dark-eyed lawyer who was tending bar. When I
asked him if that paid better than practicing law, he said
he was taking a sabbatical from the practice, Blues grinning, saying that sabbatical was lawyer jive for getting
your ticket punched. Mason nodded and grinned back
at him, adding that, either way, bartending beat the hell
out of working for a living. Mason shook my hand and
gave Kate a hug that lasted a beat too long unless they
had a history. When I asked Kate, she said it was a long
time ago, the hug saying it might be history but it wasn't
ancient history.

There was an entrance to the second floor offices in
the center of the block on the Broadway side and another in an alley on the backside. I guided Lucy to the
alley where we parked, taking the stairs to Kate's office,
the door bearing the firm name in bold black, DMC,
and beneath that in a smaller font, Decision Making
Consultants.

Kate's ex, Alan, once told me that he liked the name
because it reminded him of his favorite musical group,
Run DMC. Alan is bald, five-five stretched out, and one
forty-five wet with a sun-starved complexion and a
rhythmically challenged body that's been declared a
muscle-free zone. When I laughed and told him that he
and hip-hop went together like pocket protectors and
crack cocaine, he stopped talking to me. I was too hard
on him but I couldn't help it. Kate had loved him, married him, had a child with him, and still worked with
him. He had something she had loved that I couldn't

see and didn't have. On the other hand, maybe I wasn't
hard enough on him.

Kate described the office as egalitarian. It was all
open space, no private offices, everyone on equal foot-
ing on the geographic food chain, the floor divided
into task zones separated by chest-high partitions,
money that could have paid for show-off furnishings instead plowed into the hardware and software that made
DMC run.

The office was littered with empty pizza boxes,
wadded sandwich wrappers, donut sacks, and coffee
cups. People were slumped in their chairs, a few watching the screen savers on their computer monitors, one
long-haired guy tapping the last drops from cans of Red
Bull onto his tongue before adding them to the pyra-
mid he was building on his desk.

Some of them looked up, nodding as we passed; others were too wiped out to notice. They'd been going
hard for twenty hours. We found Kate, her father, Henry,
Alan, and Simon gathered in one corner.

Henry was sleeping, his thick body nestled in a deep-
backed chair, his legs stretched out, chubby fingers
locked over his chest, breathing lightly. The older he'd
gotten, the longer he'd grown his bushy white hair, letting it hang to his collar.

Alan was standing at the windows, watching the traffic on Broadway, wearing a navy warm-up suit with red
piping, one of several that comprised his casual ward-
robe. Simon, his eyes glazed, was shuffling through a
stack of papers. Kate, her back to me, was watching a video
on a desktop computer, one frozen frame at a time.
Alan saw us first.

"Oh, it's you," he said.

Kate turned around, her face lighting up. She stood, swept her hair off her forehead, and gave me a quick kiss, squeezing my shoulders in a half hug. Alan watched, swallowed, and resumed his traffic survey.

Simon looked up from his papers. "I'm never buying you a cup of coffee again for as long as I live."

The subdued greeting was enough to rouse Henry. He wiped his mouth with his sleeve, sat up straight, and tilted his chin toward me.

"Jack," he said.

"Henry."

It was as close as we ever got to a conversation. Kate sighed, wordlessly apologizing for Alan and her father. I was Alan's rival in a competition that he'd lost years ago and Henry was his second, backing him up and encouraging Kate to give their marriage a second chance for their son's sake.

"Your people look exhausted," I said.

"They are exhausted," she said. "But they've worked their butts off."

"How far have you gotten?"

Simon answered. "The staff just finished the background checks on the dream project volunteers. I did the ones for the people on the list Frank Gentry gave you. "We've generated a lot of paper but I haven't had time to process the content."

"Then send the staff home," I said. "Tell anybody who doesn't feel like driving to call a cab. Add it to the expenses and tell them I appreciate what they did."

"Will do," Simon said, making his way toward the troops.

"What about the videos?" I asked Kate.

"That's taking longer," she said. "Dad, Alan, and I are

about halfway through but we're done in. We can't see straight. We need a break."

"Anything worth talking about?"

She shrugged. "A few, but it's hard to tell without more context. Simon says there's additional material in the institute's files on the volunteers that might help but he doesn't have access to it."

"I'll get what you need from Frank Gentry in the morning."

"Morning would be good. We can be back at it by eight, right, Alan?" she said.

He didn't answer, his hands planted on the glass, his attention on the street.

"Eight o'clock tomorrow morning. Okay, Alan?" she repeated.

"No," he said, his voice quiet but firm.

Kate cringed, bit her lip and took a breath. "Okay. What time do you want to get started?"

He turned and faced us, hands jammed in his pants pockets. "I'm not coming in. I quit."

Kate's eyes narrowed, her mouth slack. "What do you mean, you quit? You can't quit. We took this job and we have to finish it. Our employees are depending on us."

"Kate, you're kidding yourself. The employees finished the background checks. There's nothing else for them to do. Nothing. Not on this project or any other project. They wrapped up what little we had in the pipeline last week."

Her eyes darted past my shoulder to the rest of the floor, lowering her voice to keep the conversation semi-private. "This job will pay us enough to keep going until we get more work."

"You're wrong, honey," said Henry. "I wish you

weren't but you are. This job will let us give everyone two weeks of severance and cover our rent for the rest of the month. After that, we're all in and all done."

She wheeled around, confronting her father, hands on her hips. "You taught me never to quit."

Henry was tall, his height, girth, and flowing mane giving him a mythological cast as he stood, putting one hand on her shoulder.

"I also taught you not to be a fool. It's okay. Our people are good people. They'll find something else. Hard times make for hard choices and, sometimes, choices that are past due being made. Like for me. I'm eighty-three years old. It's time I retired. I'll be here in the morning to tell the staff and help you finish reviewing the videos. Good night, sweetheart," he said, kissing her cheek. "I love you."

"What about you?" Kate said to Alan as her father ambled toward the exit.

"I'm sorry, Kate. I can't do this anymore," he said, waving one hand toward the rest of the office but aiming a finger at me, making his real point, then dropping his arm to his side in surrender. "Anyway, you and Henry are a lot better with the facial action coding system. I'm just in the way."

Kate's color was building, her face red and her blue eyes flashing. "So you're just walking out on me?"

He shrugged, turning his palms up. "You walked out on me a long time ago, Kate. I'm just catching up."

Kate stamped her foot, her hands balled into fists, her arms clamped to her sides. "Damn it, Alan, is that what this is about? Our divorce? Are you kidding me? You've got to move on, Alan."

He picked up his coat, pulled a muffler from one sleeve, draping it around his neck. "I am. I've taken a job with a neuromarketing firm in San Diego. It's good money and I'm going in as a partner."

"San Diego! How are you going to do that? Are you walking out on our son too?"

"I'll commute on weekends until the end of the school year."

"Then what?"

He took a deep breath. "Then Brian and I are moving to San Diego. He'll be fourteen in a month and legally can choose which one of us he wants to live with. I told him about the job and he wants to go with me."

Kate folded over like she'd been punched, stumbling backward. I caught her and eased her into a chair. She put her head in her hands and let out a low moan. Alan left without another word, his head down. I scooted a chair next to Kate's, sat beside her, my arm around her, pulling her close.

"Well, that sucks," Lucy said.

Simon returned, taking in the scene. "What'd I miss?"

"A train wreck," Lucy said. "Where's all the paper you were bragging about?"

"There," Simon said, pointing to a banker's box filled with manila folders neatly tabbed and indexed with names in alphabetical order.

"Grab it and let's get out of here," Lucy said.

Simon picked up the box and his coat. "What about them?" he asked, pointing to Kate and me.

"Good question," Lucy said.

Chapter Forty-five

Death imposes a rough justice, balancing peace and the end of suffering against the loss of all we cherish. I don't recommend it and I'm not in a hurry for it but there are things worse for us than our own death. Or so it seems when we lose a child, begging God to take us, not them, or when we suffer a blow that, in the moment, feels as incomprehensible and fatal.

Kate's son, Brian, was alive and well and would, if the actuarial tables were kind, live his full life expectancy, growing up, going to college, and getting a job. Like many, he will get married, have children, and he and his family will prosper or not as fortune dictates. Kate, like any other parent, will live to see some but not all of that, exulting in the highs and commiserating in the lows. Yet no matter what lay ahead, her anguished cries made one thing certain. This moment of unanticipated rejection, abandonment, and betrayal would always be one of irreducible pain.

The deaths of my children had taught me that com-

fort from others was both necessary and inadequate,
that while we need someone to lean on, we have to remember how to stand. So I stayed at Kate's side until
she gripped the arms of her chair and raised herself to
her feet. I cupped her elbow as she cleared her head
and found her balance and I held her tight when she
turned into me, burying her face against my neck. I
didn't make any false promises that everything would be
all right because I knew too well that some things couldn't
be fixed, but I told her the one thing that I believed
with absolute certainty.

"You will get through this."

She stepped back, framing my face with her hands. "I
know that. I don't have any other choice."

A year ago, Kate had moved from her downtown loft
to Fairway, a Kansas side suburb much like Brookside. She
found a house around the block from Alan's so that
Brian's shuffling from one parent to the other would be
less of a hassle.

We stopped at the Hen House grocery on Johnson
Drive, and picked up simple things even I could make
for dinner—salad from the salad bar, rotisserie chicken,
potatoes, and asparagus—while she went to see Brian.
He had stayed with a friend during her parents' office
all-nighter. She had called him on his cell phone, finding him at his father's.

The table was set, the salad tossed, the chicken
warmed up, the potatoes baked, and the asparagus
grilled when she returned, her face washed out, the
light gone from her eyes. I ate while she picked at her
food, sipping wine.

"Turns out they were planning this for a while," she
said.

"It's a hard thing to do on the fly."

"I can't believe Alan would turn my own son against me."

"You don't know that's what happened."

She slammed her hand onto the table, rattling her wineglass. "And you don't know the first thing about it!"

I kept my voice level and low, making certain she could hear me if she was listening. "You're right. I'm just saying that it's hard to sort anything out right now. This is January. School isn't out until the end of May. You've got time to work it through."

She pushed her plate away. "I'm sorry. I shouldn't have snapped at you like that."

"That's okay. You were blindsided and I've got broad shoulders."

"I know. They're very nice shoulders."

We did the dishes and sat on the couch in her den, finishing the bottle of wine and talking about Alan, Brian, her father, and her firm; no mention of a serial killer. We took a shower. I washed her back and then we rubbed lotion on each other's back after we were dry. We fell into bed and she settled next to me as I shook, her arm draped over my chest until the day's last tremors retreated.

"Thanks," she said. "For staying with me."

A verse from a song I used to sing to my kids when they were little popped into my head. I sang it softly. "It's my job and like it fine. No one has a better job than mine."

She chuckled. "I remember that song. It was one of Brian's favorites when he was little."

"My kids too. I don't remember the rest of it."

I was on my back. She was on her side. We held hands.

"I miss him already," she whispered.

"San Diego is a big place. Has to be more than one neuromarketing firm out there. You can go with him."

"I know," she said, squeezing my hand.

We drifted to sleep. An hour later, she woke me, kissing me and sliding on top of me, our lovemaking as much about our needs as our desires.

We rose early, drinking coffee while scanning the morning newspaper.

"Oh, my God," she said, looking at the photograph of the institute on the front page beneath the headline about Anne Kendall's murder and Leonard Nagel's death. "I've been so caught up in my own world, I didn't ask you about what happened."

I told her about my day at the office. She peppered me with questions about Anne's boyfriend, Michael Lacey, how did he look, what did he say, what facial expressions did I notice, running me through the same gauntlet about Leonard.

"Leonard always had this goofy smile plastered on his face. He was jumpy all morning," I said. "But he had good reasons even if he didn't kill Anne. I don't have a take on the boyfriend. Anthony Corliss is another puzzle."

I described my conversations with him, letting the evidence of his links to Tom Delaney and Walter Enoch speak for itself, the recitation fueling my own suspicion.

"Corliss walked to work yesterday?" Kate said, seizing on a detail I hadn't given any attention. "In this weather? Why would someone do that?"

"He said it was for the exercise."

"There are a lot better ways to get exercise. I would like to have been there for that conversation. People who are hiding something often have to build an elaborate scaffolding of lies to support it. The lesser lies, like why he walked to work in the dead of winter, can be easier to detect because the person telling them is more intent on protecting the bigger secret."

She was right. It didn't make sense. Corliss was a Pillsbury Doughboy, not close to being in shape. He was more likely to get in his licks on a treadmill while watching the Food Channel if at all. There was a better reason for him to have left his car at home. It might contain incriminating evidence, like Anne Kendall's blood. In which case, he'd either get rid of the car or soak it in bleach and hope for the best.

"The institute is closed today. I'll see if I can get a look at his car tomorrow."

She paused, her internal wheels spinning. "Speaking of the institute, what are you going to do about your boss?"

"Milo Harper? What do you mean?"

She set her coffee mug on the table. "He ruined DMC, just like he said he would, and you're still working for him."

When she first told me how Milo had threatened her if she didn't come to work for him, I passed it off as overblown rhetoric. I couldn't do that now, at least not without digging into it.

"I'm too deep into this thing to quit even if Harper did what you think he did. When the dust settles, I'll check it out. If the books need to be balanced, I'll find a way to do it. In the meantime, you might as well get as deep into his pocket as you can. How about I pay your staff a bonus for a job well done? Say, an extra two-weeks' pay on top of the severance they're going to get."

She leaned across the table and kissed me. "That's a good start."

Chapter Forty-six

Kate dropped me off in my driveway. The sky was a mix of sun and clouds, the front yard a quilt of emerging brown grass and retreating gray snow, the sun promising the grass a better day, mild dry air backing up the promise. The weatherman we'd listened to in the car wasn't impressed. He predicted sleet by late afternoon turning to ice by early evening turning to snow by midnight, ending with a day off from school tomorrow.

My cell phone rang before I made it to the front door. Caller ID said it was Quincy Carter.

"Carter, what's up?"

"You got your third look on Tom Delaney."

"And?"

"And CSI found some shredded paper fragments on the floor next to Delaney's body. It was the same kind of paper used for books. Some of the fragments had gunpowder residue on them."

"You telling me McNair ignored that?"

"I told you he's a better cop than you give him credit for. It was in a supplemental report he never saw because it was misfiled. It took me half the night to find the techs that worked the scene, reconstruct what happened, and track down the file."

We both knew that McNair's second look at Delaney's file should have included making certain all the lab work was accounted for but Carter was the kind of cop who'd handle that on his own without bad-mouthing his partner to me. I respected that even if it meant McNair really was a lousy cop.

"Now what?"

"Delaney's file is officially reopened."

"Thanks, Carter."

"No problem. There are some other things you should know."

"Like what?"

"I talked to the detective in Denver that worked Leonard Nagel's case. He said the woman who accused Leonard of rape recanted."

"Then why did he plead? Why wasn't the charge dropped?"

"The DA wasn't sure which one was lying, Leonard or the victim. Leonard's lawyer was a rookie PD, told Leonard the DA could still prosecute. Leonard took the deal rather than risk jail. He registered as a sex offender in Denver and took off. Probably figured he'd left all that behind until Anne Kendall gets murdered. He'd been the subject of one harassment complaint and been threatened with another by the murder victim. He's scared because he hadn't registered as a sex offender in Kansas City. He hears the drumbeats in the hallways and takes off."

"What about the other woman who worked at the institute who filed a complaint against him?"

"I called her last night. She stuck to her story but she said she never felt like he was dangerous, just obnoxious."

"Did you find Leonard's fingerprints on Anne's ID badge?" I asked.

"No. Only print we found was a plain print that could have been made by someone wearing a latex glove."

"Same story with Walter Enoch. Wendy's envelope had glove prints on it too."

"How about that? Enough snowflakes fall and pretty soon you can pack them into a snowball."

"So where does that leave you?"

"I've got a murder victim that made a complaint against a dead guy with a sketchy record and incriminating evidence that the killer could have planted in his desk. It will be a while before we know if there's any DNA evidence to tie Leonard to the murder."

"If it wasn't Leonard, it had to be someone who knew enough about his track record to try and frame him. That should narrow the universe."

"I talked to the HR director, Connie Nichols. She says that records of harassment complaints are confidential but people hear things. Anne might have told someone she was going to file the complaint. That person tells someone or someone else could have overheard them talking about it. Doesn't matter because there's no such thing as a secret."

"What about the boyfriend, Michael Lacey? He knew that Anne was going to file a complaint against Leonard."

"Neighbors tell us they fought like Ali and Frazier," Carter said. "Her parents live in Texas. She called her mom over the weekend, told her the marriage was off, and that she was moving out as soon as she found a place to live."

"What's Lacey say about all that?"

"Nothing. He lawyered up. Not the sort of thing you do when we've got a corpse everyone is ready to hang the murder on. We're getting DNA samples from him and we'll see where that takes us."

"Maybe he's just scared or he's got a lawyer who knows better than to let him keep talking if there's a chance you'll put Kendall's murder on Leonard and close the book. Anything to link Lacey to the other cases?"

"Not yet, but we're looking."

"You've been busy."

"Like I told you, I can use the overtime."

"As long as you don't have enough to do, put Anthony Corliss on your interview list," I said, telling him why Corliss may have decided to walk to work.

"Thanks," Carter said. "You have any other bright ideas?"

"Anne Kendall was missing her engagement ring and the finger it was on. Regina Blair wasn't wearing any jewelry when her body was found. Someone may have robbed her after she fell or, if she was killed, her killer may have been collecting souvenirs. If it was me, I'd want to know if she wore a watch or a ring or a necklace."

"If it was me, I would too. We'll check it out. Listen, I've got to run."

"One last thing. I heard you guys were reaching out to the FBI about a possible task force to work these cases if they're connected. Anything going on with that?"

"Not yet. The feds are dragging their feet as usual. Said they'd get back to us in a couple of days if they haven't closed the Enoch case by then. My lieutenant thinks they might be close. You hear anything about that?"

Now wasn't the time to tell Carter that I had thirty-three hours left on my forty-eight-hour deadline. I could use his help but I had to find Wendy's letter first. If there was anything in it that incriminated me, Carter wouldn't be interested in my explanation any more than Kent and Dolan would be. And, I couldn't rule out the possibility that he was already working with Kent and Dolan and was playing me from the backside.

"The Bureau always says they're close. It's in the manual."

Chapter Forty-seven

I hung up and opened the front door as Lucy walked into the living den from the kitchen carrying a pad of poster-sized Post-its. She had hung new Post-it wallpaper with more names, notes, and questions around the room, taking down or covering up the now outdated first edition. She peeled off the top sheet of her pad and fixed it over an older sheet. This one was titled SOUVENIRS. The list read:

Tom Delaney	*Books*
Regina Blair	*Jewelry*
Anne Kendall	*Finger and engagement ring*
Walter Enoch	*Wendy's letter*

"What do you think?" she asked.

Her list proved the importance of a fresh set of eyes. Dolan, Kent, and I had made the same mistake about why the killer took Wendy's letter. We all had assumed it was about me but Lucy's list came at it from the killer's perspective, which changed everything.

"I think it fits, not well, but it fits."

"What's wrong with it?"

"Delaney's books aren't just souvenirs, they're evidence that the killer staged the murder to look like suicide. Another homeless person could have taken Regina Blair's jewelry, just like your friend Vinny said. I agree that Anne's amputated finger is a classic serial killer souvenir but Wendy's letter would make more sense as a souvenir if the killer took the envelope as well."

"Except for one thing," Lucy said. "We didn't pick up on Delaney's books and Blair's jewelry the first time around. Same with Wendy's letter. If the killer took the envelope and the letter, no one would have ever known. I mean Enoch didn't keep an inventory of the stuff he stole. But there's no way we couldn't know the letter was gone if the envelope was left behind, especially since it was the only piece of stolen mail that was opened."

"So the killer wanted us to know that he'd taken the letter. He's playing a game with us, taunting us. That's what serial killers do," I said.

"The books, jewelry, and letter were more subtle. It took a while for us to figure them out. There's nothing subtle about Anne Kendall's amputated finger. I'd say the killer is getting impatient with us."

"He's telling us how stupid and incompetent we are. We didn't get it the first three times, so he's making it easier on us. That's why Anne's murder was so violent and her body was staged for maximum shock and her finger was amputated," I said.

"And that fits with the shorter time frame between murders. All of which means that there's going to be another victim sooner rather than later if we don't get a lucky break. The first four victims were connected to the institute. Stands to reason the next one will be too."

Anthony Corliss was the one person with ties to all four victims, though his connection to Anne Kendall was less direct than with Delaney, Blair, and Enoch, limited to the fact that he and Anne worked at the same place. Connie Nichols might know whether their paths ever crossed.

I grew uneasy thinking about potential victims, realizing that there was at least one other vulnerable person in Corliss's immediate orbit. Maggie Brennan. I'd see Tom Goodell at the retired cops' lunch today. If my Maggie and his were one in the same, I wouldn't let her suffer the same fate as her parents.

I scanned the walls. There was a Post-it titled DREAM PROJECT VOLUNTEERS with five names I didn't recognize. I assumed that their background checks had turned up something of interest. Another page titled DREAM PROJECT STAFF listed Anthony Corliss, Maggie Brennan, and their research assistants, Janet Casey and Gary Kaufman. A third page had the names of the other project directors that had accessed the dream project files.

Milo Harper and Sherry Fritzshall's names were on a separate page along with another name, Peggy Murray. Hers was the name Jason Bolt had waved at me like a sword. Lucy had circled it in black and underlined it in red.

"Why did you put those volunteers' names on the wall?"

"Just covering the bases. They're the only ones with

anything hinky in their backgrounds. Couple of DUIs, one domestic abuse complaint, stuff like that."

"What about Corliss's research assistants and the directors of the other projects?"

"Janet Casey and the directors are dull, boring academics."

"What about Gary Kaufman?"

"He's got a juvenile record but the details are sealed. Whatever he did, the record was expunged when he turned eighteen."

"Couldn't have been that bad," Lucy said, "if he got into college and grad school."

"His parents could have known the right people," I said. "Keep working on it. Find out what he did."

I pointed at the Post-it with Peggy Murray's name. "Jason Bolt, the lawyer for the Delaney and Blair families, says she's his secret weapon. Where does she fit in to all of this?"

"Hey Jack, you got an extra razor around here?" Simon asked before Lucy could answer.

He had come down the stairs and into the living den, barefoot, wearing yesterday's chinos and an undershirt, rubbing his chin stubble. I looked at Lucy who blushed and kept her eyes on the floor.

"Sure," I said. "Check the cabinet under the sink in my bathroom."

"Thanks. Any chance you got a spare toothbrush to go along with it?"

I nodded. "Same place. Keep the razor and the toothbrush but do me a favor and leave the towels, okay?"

"No problem. Hey, Luce," he said to her. "I'm going to take a quick shower."

He grinned at me, mouthing *Simon Says*, and disappeared up the stairs.

"Luce?" I asked her. "Since when are you Luce? What is he, Sim?"

She took a breath and planted her hands on her hips. "He's nice and really smart, both of which are a change of pace for me so don't give me a hard time. Besides, it's been a while."

"Just tell me he didn't ask you to play Simon Says." She blushed again. "Okay, never mind," I said closing my eyes and covering my ears. "I don't even want to know."

"Luce, honey," Simon called from upstairs. "Can you run up here for a second?"

She took the stairs two at a time. I heard her giggle and a door slam as Roxy and Ruby raced in from the backyard, their paws muddy and wet. They slammed into my legs, ran circles around me, and flew back to the kitchen, a sure sign they hadn't had breakfast.

I followed them, poured their food, and watched them chow down. "Well," I told them. "Life goes on."

They didn't look up. When they finished eating, Roxy nipped at Ruby's hind legs, Ruby chasing her through the doggie door into the backyard. The banker's box with Simon's files was on the kitchen counter, the files still in alphabetical order except for one labeled *Peggy Murray* that lay on top. The names on the other files were typed on labels that had been neatly applied to the folders. Peggy's name was handwritten, proof it was a late entry.

Inside her file were printouts from a blog titled *The Milo Harper Files* authored by Jamie Del Muro who wrote that her mission was to expose the truth about Harper. She gave a laundry list of his sins, everything from stealing the idea for the social networking Web site that made him rich to engaging in insider trading of the stock in his company. The home page of the blog carried a dedication that read *For my sister, Peggy Murray. No Retreat! No Surrender!*

According to Del Muro, Peggy Murray came up with the idea for what became Harper's Web site, building the first version of the site while she was a student at Stanford and dating Harper. They both quit school to work on the Web site. Then Peggy had a bike accident when she and Harper were riding together on a country road alongside a gorge. According to the police report, which Del Muro included on the blog, Harper claimed that Peggy lost control of her bike going down a steep hill and fell a hundred feet to her death. Del Muro accused Harper of running her off the road so that he could have the Web site to himself. Later, Peggy Murray's parents accepted Harper's gift of stock in the company, which proved to be worth more than a million dollars when it went public. Del Muro accused her parents of taking blood money and being accomplices after the fact to the murder of their daughter.

No doubt Harper knew all about Jamie Del Muro and her blog and his lawyers would be ready when Jason Bolt played this card. Under normal circumstances, I expected Harper to brush the whole thing off as the rant of a crazy person. But these circumstances weren't normal. Dead bodies were piling up around Harper and his institute. Bolt was right about one thing. Harper wouldn't want Jamie Del Muro's story hitting the papers where it would get more play than in the blogosphere. And if the public interest got ginned up enough, an ambitious prosecutor might reopen the investigation.

The better question was whether the story was true, whether Peggy Murray was the first victim of Milo Harper's whatever it takes credo. If she were, Harper wouldn't have broken a sweat over ruining Kate's practice. I added those questions to the ones I had about Harper accessing Delaney's, Blair's, and Enoch's dream project files before and after their deaths.

Even though the institute was closed for the day, I was certain Milo wasn't taking the day off. I'd only been on the job for three days but it was time for a performance review. His, not mine.

Chapter Forty-eight

Lucy and Simon were on the sofa in the living den, feet up on the coffee table, bare toes touching, when I came downstairs after showering and shaving. Lucy's hair was wet. Simon's bald pate was glowing, radiating heat.

It was her house. I was just living in it. She wasn't my underage daughter and he wasn't the bad kid who'd led her astray. I knew all that but still felt like I'd walked in on Wendy and the pimple-faced boy who took her to prom so he could get in her shorts; my problem, not theirs.

"Simon, are you still on the clock?" I asked.

He craned his head toward me. "Punched out last night, boss."

I joined them, standing near one end of the sofa. "I read Peggy Murray's file. Did you know her when you were at Stanford?"

Simon sat up, feet on the floor. "'Course I knew her. We were like the Three Musketeers. We had classes together, lived in the same dorm freshman year. She was what we called geeky hot. I had a crush on her but I didn't have a chance against Milo so I settled for swimming in their wake."

"Any truth to Jamie Del Muro's story?"

"Peggy worked on the Web site with Milo. I did too, for that matter. Milo always told me it was his idea. I never had a reason to doubt that."

"And the bike accident?"

"Milo said she lost control of her bike. The police agreed. What else is there to say?"

"Any of that sound familiar?"

"What are you saying?"

"I'm saying that's what the KCPD said about Regina Blair. It was an accident. And they also said that Tom Delaney committed suicide."

Simon planted his hands on his knees, his face coloring. "Give me a break, Jack. Jamie Del Muro is a whack job. She started this crap when Peggy died and she's kept it going all these years. Her parents disowned her, for Christ's sake! You can't paint Milo with that brush."

"Then why did you put all her crap in a file for me to read and why did Lucy write her name on the wall?"

Lucy put a hand on Simon's arm. "We struck out on the rest of the background checks," she said. "You told Simon to dig up anything he could find on Harper. When he told me about Peggy Murray, I told him we had to tell you even if it was bullshit."

"Think like a cop, Lucy, not like someone who just got out of the shower with one of Milo's musketeers, and tell me how you know it's bullshit."

She jumped to her feet, squaring her shoulders. Simon grabbed her wrist and she shook it off. "I know it the same way I know you didn't kill Walter Enoch and you didn't help Wendy steal five million dollars."

"That's isn't what you know. It's what you believe. There's a difference."

Simon stood. "I know Milo and that's good enough for me."

"Well it isn't good enough for me."

I grabbed my car keys and headed for the institute. It felt good to be behind the wheel instead of buckled into the passenger seat.

I passed a grocery on Sixty-third Street. The parking lot was jammed and people were streaming out of the store with full carts, trusting the weatherman's forecast more than the sun-spackled sky, not weighing the difference between what they knew and what they believed about the coming storm before stocking up. They were preparing for the worst while hoping for the best, same as me.

My cell phone rang. I fished it out of my pocket and saw Joy's name on the caller ID.

"Hey," I said.

"Did I catch you at a bad time?" she asked.

It was the same reflex question she asked whenever she called after our son Kevin died, most of those times bad times. After she left me, we softened toward each other until Wendy disappeared, her death another blow to our relationship. In spite of everything that had happened, we both acknowledged a lingering connection, kept alive through Roxy and Ruby. The dogs gave us a safe way to stay in each other's lives, sharing canine custodial duties, neither of us willing to explore why that was important or why we could manage that but nothing else.

"No, this is fine. I thought you were going to be gone all week. Are you back in town?"

"I'm coming home tonight. I'll pick up Roxy on my way from the airport."

"No problem. Where are you anyway?"

"Houston," she said, her voice fading.

"You okay?"

"I'm just tired. My plane gets in around eight."

"Don't count on it. We're supposed to get hammered with a snowstorm."

"Well, I'll get there eventually. How's Roxy?"

"She's great."

She hesitated a beat, her voice hopeful. "Maybe Ruby can come over for a play date next week."

"I'll check her calendar but I'm sure she can squeeze you in."

She brightened, her voice rising an octave. "Thanks, Jack, for taking care of her. I'll see you tonight or tomorrow."

I wasn't surprised to find Milo Harper in his office. He was at his desk, his back to the door. Sherry Fritzshall stood at his side, one hand on his shoulder, both of them staring out the window. They turned when I knocked. His face was grim, hers ashen. I repeated Joy's question.

"Is this a bad time?"

Harper waved me in as Sherry gave his shoulder a final squeeze and walked past me without a word.

"I told her," he said. "About the Alzheimer's."

"Why now?"

"I had to. My latest memory lapse just cost me a couple of million bucks on a deal I thought I'd made but I hadn't. I thought I could outrun it if I just ran fast enough but I can't."

"What are you going to do?"

"A couple of billion dollars complicates life. It will take a while to unwind everything, figure out what to keep or get rid of, and who's going to manage it. Sherry screwed up the institute's building security but she's good at straightening things out and she's all the family I have. I need her so I had to tell her. So," he said with a weak smile, "what can I do for you?"

We jump into the middle of other people's lives, expecting them to be waiting for us, surprised when they're too busy with their own problems to make time and space for ours. In a more perfect world, this would be a time to leave Harper alone but that wasn't the world we lived in.

"I ran into Jason Bolt yesterday. He was parked out in front looking at the real estate like he was getting ready to take over the title."

"What did he want?"

"He said he was sending you a settlement offer on Delaney and Blair that would only be on the table until the end of the week."

Harper laughed. "I give ultimatums. I don't take them."

"Bolt knows about what happened with Corliss at Wisconsin and he said to remind you what happened the last time you took him on and to tell you that he knows about Peggy Murray. He thinks that will motivate you to settle in a hurry."

Harper laughed again, shaking his head. "Peggy Murray! Damn. You know what's funny about Alzheimer's?

The old memories last the longest. Some stuff is just too hard to forget."

"I know about her too."

He straightened, hands on his desk. "Bolt told you?"

"No. Simon did. He's one of the people I hired to help me. I told him to do a background check on you. He printed out the story on Jamie Del Muro's blog."

His eyes widened. "You hired Simon Alexander to investigate me? Why would you do that?"

"I had him run background checks on anyone that had a connection to Delaney, Blair, and Enoch. You're on that list."

"For Bolt's lawsuit," he nodded. "That's what Bolt will do. I guess it makes sense for you to know what Bolt knows."

"I didn't do it because of the lawsuit."

"Then why do it?"

"Delaney, Blair, and Enoch were dead. Anne Kendall was the fourth and Leonard Nagel makes five. I want to know why."

Harper rocked back in his chair, my meaning registering with him. "Everyone is still a suspect, is that it? Including me? Jamie Del Muro is a lunatic."

"Then why haven't you sued her for libel and slander and shut her Web site down and taken every penny she has?"

"I wanted to but my lawyers talked me out of it. All that would do is draw more attention to her. She'd like nothing better than for me to sue her. I'm a public figure which means people can say practically whatever they want about me. Besides, she's not the only one who takes shots at me. Like the song says, money can't buy me love. If I sued everyone who made up shit about me, that's all I'd ever do. Jason Bolt will have to do better than that to bring me to the table. You should be digging up dirt on Delaney and Blair, not me. What have you found out about them?"

"Delaney was murdered. Blair almost certainly was too. Probably by the same person who also killed Walter Enoch and Anne Kendall."

He smiled. "Great! Then I'm off the hook and Jason Bolt can pound sand."

Harper had a singularly egocentric outlook, more concerned about Jason Bolt's lawsuit than the likelihood that a serial killer was working his way through the institute.

"Why did you access Delaney's, Blair's, and Enoch's files in the dream project?"

"I told you. That's how I keep track of the research projects."

"There were two hundred and fifty volunteers in that project. You picked the three that were murdered and you looked at their files before and after they were killed. How does that happen?"

He rose, coming around to my side of the desk, getting in my face. "How do you think it happens?"

"You tell me. Was it an accident like Peggy Murray's bicycle running off the road after she designed your Web site or a coincidence like Kate Scranton's practice going under after she turned you down?"

Chapter Forty-nine

"So that's what this is about? Kate Scranton?"

"It's about a lot of things. She's one of them."

"I hope you're sleeping with her. Otherwise, you're blowing the job of a lifetime for nothing."

"And you're blowing the chance to convince me I should take you off my list of suspects. I'd say that gives you more to worry about than me."

"Me? A murderer? First Peggy Murray and now four more people. I'd have to be one of the all-time great serial killers."

"More like one of the ordinary ones. You have to at least get into double figures to be one of the great ones. Serial killers sometimes go years between binges. It will be easy enough to find out if there were any other unsolved murders around Palo Alto around the same time Peggy died."

He took a step back, squinting at me. "You're serious, aren't you?"

"You're about to find out how serious."

He put his hands up and then wiped his mouth with one, holding me at bay with the other.

"Okay, okay. Peggy first. We worked on the Web site together. It's hard to say who came up with what. We were kids. We didn't know the first thing about intellectual property rights or anything else. Later, when the company took off, I made a deal with her parents, giving them stock for Peggy's contribution to the Web site. They had lawyers and I had lawyers. It was an arm's length deal."

"And what about Peggy's bike accident?"

He stuffed his hands in his pants pockets and circled the room, stopping at the windows overlooking Brush Creek, turning back to me, his voice soft, his throat full.

"We'd been out riding all day. Peggy was as competitive as I was, maybe more, always trying to beat me. Didn't matter if it was about getting the better grade or getting to the bottom of the hill first. She took off down this long steep hill, really kicking it. There was a blind curve at the bottom, no guardrail, and a long drop. It was the first time we'd been on that stretch, so we didn't know. I was drafting behind her. We hit some loose gravel and spun out and both of us lost control. I laid my bike down but she flew off the road. She broke her neck and I got a bad case of road rash."

His narrative matched the police report Jamie Del Muro had posted on her blog. I studied him, looking for the practiced recitation of someone expecting to be accused only to be betrayed by a liar's tics and twitches, seeing instead a face grimacing with pain, gone pale from a memory relived.

"I think about her everyday," he said, his voice a whisper, his eyes wet. "And I have nightmares about the accident two or three times a week. That's why I funded the dream project."

"Maggie Brennan says you threatened to cut off the funding if she and Corliss couldn't prove that people could learn to control their nightmares with lucid dreaming."

"The institute is a not-for-profit but that doesn't mean I'm in business to lose money. I'm rich but not rich enough to fund projects that don't produce results."

"How's the dream project doing?"

"Not great. I tried the lucid dreaming techniques and they didn't help. I met with Corliss at the end of November. I told him he had three months to produce results or I was going to pull the plug. That's why I looked at those videos. I wanted to see whether he was making progress."

"Why Delaney's, Blair's, and Enoch's videos? Why not any of the others?"

"I didn't pick them. I told Corliss I wanted to see some representative videos. Those were the ones he suggested. He said they were a good cross-section of different types of nightmares. After they died, I went back and looked at their videos again."

"Why?"

"For the same reason I built this place—to try to make sense of things. Look at what happened to Delaney, Blair, and Enoch and then what happened to Anne Kendall and Leonard Nagel. None of that makes sense. I don't suppose it ever will no matter how much money I spend."

I gripped the back of a chair to steady myself as a burst of shakes ripped through me, hinging me at the waist, dropping my chin to my chest. I managed my symptoms by staying in a comfort zone of modest and moderated activity. I'd been out of that zone for six days, taking a pounding that would grind me into the ground if I didn't back off soon. I took a long breath as the tremors passed, righting myself as Harper watched.

"And look what's happening to you," Harper said. "I don't know how you do it."

I wouldn't let Harper lump me together with murder victims. I wasn't dead and my movement disorder wouldn't kill me. And I wouldn't let his attempt at sympathy throw me off track.

"What about Kate Scranton's business?" I asked, one arm wrapped around my middle, one hand still gripping the chair, the words stacking up in my throat before stuttering out. "Is that just another one of those things that doesn't make sense?"

He went back to his chair, slumping then sitting up. "I'm a lot of things, Jack. Some I'm proud of and some I'm not. I'm smart, I'm lucky, and I'm a lousy loser. To be honest about it, I wanted Kate for more than her mind. She said no. I'm not used to rejection and I don't take it well. I admit it was a petty thing to do but I made a few phone calls, figured she might have second thoughts if she had fewer options. It was easy. I could fix it just as easily. You tell her that."

I took another deep breath, straightening and steadying myself, letting go the chair. "I'll let you tell Jason Bolt. I think he just got a new client."

He waved a hand, dismissing the prospect. "It's only money. Besides, by the time her case goes to trial, I'll be too far gone to know or care."

"For a lucky guy like you, that may be the best piece of luck you ever have. One last thing."

"What's that?"

"I quit."

He shook his head. "I doubt that. You're not the type even if you go off my payroll. You won't quit until it's over. That's why I hired you in the first place."

Sherry Fritzshall was waiting outside Harper's office, leaning against the wall. Her eyes were puffy, her mascara reduced to black smudges. She walked away and motioned me to follow her, waiting until we'd rounded a corner before she stopped and handed me her business card.

"Give this to Kate Scranton. Tell her to call me next week and we'll work something out and we won't need lawyers to do it. I only met her once but I liked her. Tell her I'm sorry about what happened."

"You can make that happen?"

"Milo agreed to give me power of attorney. By the end of the week, I'll be able to make anything happen."

"What happened to doing whatever it takes?"

She folded her arms across her chest, shuddering. "Sometimes it takes too much. After all this, after poor Anne and the others, after finding out what my brother did to Kate Scranton and how he kept his condition from me, sometimes it just takes too much."

"You surprise me."

She smiled, her face still sad. "I told you not to underestimate me. I hope I haven't underestimated you."

"What do you mean?"

"I'm not accepting your resignation."

Chapter Fifty

I was still employed, the building was empty, and I had a key card that opened every door in the place. The retired cops lunch started in a little over an hour. I could be late as long as I got there before Tom Goodell left.

Everything that I had learned pointed to Anthony Corliss. Both Walter Enoch and Tom Delaney had let him in their homes, making it likely they would have let him in a second time when he killed them.

Harper had threatened to cut off Corliss's funding if he didn't produce results, taking me back to my earlier speculation that Corliss might have killed Delaney, Blair, and Enoch in a twisted effort to use their deaths as proof that his lucid dreaming methods worked. Suggesting to Harper that he watch their videos fit with that scenario even if nothing else about it made sense, as if serial killers were models of rational thinking.

Corliss may have expected to get away with those murders or he may have been playing a game with the police, upping the stakes with Anne Kendall's murder, as Lucy had theorized, Anne's murder the only one that fit the rape-torture-murder stereotype that had made serial killers so feared and so famous. That Corliss's pattern didn't fit the serial killer stereotype reminded me of Maggie Brennan's caution not to confuse the unfamiliar with the improbable.

I took the elevator to Corliss's floor, making a quick and careful circuit. The ceiling florescents were off, the only illumination from faint wall fixtures that cast more shadows than light. Doors to private offices were closed, cubicles empty, no printers, faxes, or copiers humming in the background, no classic rock battling country music from desktop radios, no hallway chatter about last night or next weekend. I knocked on Corliss's door, listening for any sounds from the other side, waiting long enough for him to answer. It was locked. I waved my key card across the sensor, hearing the lock release and opened the door.

Though I didn't need probable cause and a warrant to search Corliss's office, I didn't want to toss it like Kent and Dolan had done when they searched my house. If Corliss were the killer, he'd be alert to anything that was out of place or out of order and I wanted him to keep thinking he was smarter than everyone else. I studied the room, taking note of how his books were arranged on their shelves, how close his chair was pushed in against his desk, how three black pens were scattered at random across the desk while two highlighters, one yellow and one orange, were aligned side-by-side.

I started with the desk, working my way through the three drawers on the right, finding nothing of interest. I slid the desk chair out of my way and opened the pencil drawer in the center of the desk. It was a junk drawer, crammed with pens, Post-it pads, paper clips, rubber bands, and loose change. I massaged the mess, finding a small, single sheet torn from a notepad, folded in half and buried under a tin of peppermint Altoids. I spread it open on the desk reading a handwritten list of initials: RB, TD, WE, AK, the initials too easily translated as Regina Blair, Tom Delaney, Walter Enoch, and Anne Kendall. It was a dead man's list.

I took a picture of the list with my cell phone before calling Quincy Carter, getting his message to leave a message, telling him that I was e-mailing him Exhibit A for the case against Anthony Corliss. I picked the list up by one corner and slid it into an envelope I found in the pencil drawer, sealing the envelope and sticking it in the inside pocket of my jacket. It wasn't a pristine chain of custody but I couldn't take the chance of leaving the list behind and hoping that Carter got a search warrant before Corliss got rid of it, even if taking it meant that Corliss might realize that someone had searched his office.

There were two file drawers on the left side of the desk, files hanging from front to back on runners sitting in grooves on either side of the drawer. The top drawer contained copies of journal articles. I sifted through them, not finding anything secreted between the pages.

The bottom file drawer contained thick files on Corliss and Maggie Brennan, each filled with copies of their résumés and articles they had written, together with thinner files on Janet Casey and Gary Kaufman, whose résumés and publications were shorter and fewer. All their credentials were impeccable and all their articles were inscrutable.

At the back of the drawer I found files for Regina

Blair, Tom Delaney, Walter Enoch, and Anne Kendall. I grabbed Anne's first, looking for the connection between her and Corliss. The file was arranged chronologically, the oldest material at the top. The first item was a printed exchange of innocuous e-mail Anne had initiated last week with Corliss asking if he had time to see her without explaining her purpose, Corliss setting their appointment for last Wednesday at four o'clock.

The e-mail was followed by a dream project intake questionnaire Anne had completed and signed, also dated last Wednesday, which focused on biographical information and medical history, all of which was unremarkable except for the last question that asked why she wanted to participate in the project. She wrote that she was having nightmares that were disturbing her sleep.

Next was a psychological test titled *Minnesota Multiphasic Personality Inventory*. When the FBI was trying to decide whether I had a disabling movement disorder or was just a head case, they sent me to a neuropsychologist who gave me a battery of tests spread over three days, one of which was the MMPI. The neuropsychologist explained that the MMPI is used to identify personality structure and psychopathology, including depression, anxiety, and fears. It made sense that Corliss would ask his volunteers to take such a test.

The MMPI in Anne's file hadn't been completed. There was a handwritten note reading *Anne Kendall, Monday 5:30 p.m.* clipped to the front page, presumably confirming when she was supposed to have taken the test. The note also confirmed the second and last time Corliss had scheduled a meeting with her.

Her file was Exhibit B against Corliss, establishing their connection and putting them together when she got off work on Monday. Corliss was supposed to have administered the MMPI to her the evening she was killed though the test was still in his drawer. No wonder he had refused to take a lie detector test.

The last item in her file was a document titled *Harper Institute Dream Project*, the next line reading *Confidential Dream Narrative*. The fine print below the title assured the volunteer that the narrative would be used only for the research project and not disclosed without the subject's written consent. To further preserve confidentiality, the subject was assigned a number and instructed not to put his or her name on the narrative. The subject number on this narrative was 251. I flipped back to Anne's intake form and found the same designation, confirming that this was her dream narrative.

The handwriting was neat, filling each line margin to margin with delicate looping letters and curlicues, a schoolgirl's cursive.

> *My father died when I was three. My mother remarried when I was five and my stepfather started abusing me when I was twelve. I still have nightmares about him abusing me. In my dreams, he finds me no matter where I am. Sometimes I am in my old bedroom in my mother's house. Sometimes I am in my bedroom at my apartment where I live with my fiancé. Other times, I am at work or in the parking garage or even in a store or on the street. No matter where I am he finds me. I turn around and there he is. At first he acts real nice. He asks me how I'm doing. I can't see his face but I recognize his voice and I smell his aftershave and it makes me sick at my stomach. He takes me by the hand and I try to pull away but he won't let me. He tells me how pretty I am and he rubs my face and undresses me.*

*I try to run away but my arms and legs won't move.
I'm completely paralyzed. I try to scream but nothing
comes out. He rapes me over and over and when he's
done he sticks something in my vagina and leaves me
naked on the ground where everyone can see me. I wake
up and can feel him on me. I take a shower to get rid of
the smell but it doesn't go away. I can't tell my fiancé
about this because I'm afraid he won't want to marry
me. He sees what happens when I wake up in the middle of the night and asks me what's going on. I lie to
him and he doesn't believe me and we end up having
horrible fights. I take antianxiety and antidepressant
medications that get me through the day. Everyone sees
me as perky little Anne from HR but I don't know how
much longer I can pretend that everything is okay when
every night before I go to sleep I pray that I won't wake
up in the morning.*

I put her file down. All I could do was shake.

Chapter Fifty-one

Anne Kendall's description of her nightmare turned my theory of a serial killer whose crimes had grown progressively more violent on its head, replaced by a theory that better matched the facts. The killer had staged each murder to mimic the victims' nightmares. Regina Blair dreamt that she would fall to her death. Tom Delaney dreamt that he would commit suicide. Walter Enoch dreamt that he would suffocate. Anne Kendall dreamt that her stepfather raped her, leaving her naked, violated, and exposed. Though she didn't die in her dream, the killer added his own ending to her nightmare.

Had Anne been the first victim, I would have struggled to explain why the level of violence decreased rather than increased with the subsequent murders. That fact alone may even have been sufficient reason to exclude Anne's murder from the others.

The brain, Kate had once explained to me, organizes information into patterns based on the sequence in which it receives the information so that it can understand and process similar data in the future. She called this reliance on the order in which we learn things sequential or vertical thinking. When we encounter information that doesn't fit the pattern, we need to blow it up, start over, and build a new one that fits all the information using what she described as lateral thinking and I understood as thinking outside the box.

I had pictured a serial killer gradually losing control, taunting us with our failure to recognize what was happening or stop him once we figured it out. But this killer was in control, taking his victims from the dream project pipeline. That meant the killer had to have access to the volunteers and their files, which excluded Anne's boyfriend, Michael Lacey. It also excluded Leonard Nagel because he was a stranger to three out of four of the victims. While he could have stalked and harassed Anne Kendall, neither Tom Delaney nor Walter Enoch would have opened their doors for him. All of which brought me back to Anthony Corliss. I may have misunderstood his methodology but that didn't mean I was wrong about his guilt.

There was still the question of why Corliss chose these victims, whether they shared something in common besides their participation in the dream project. I found the answer in Delaney's and Blair's files. Maggie Brennan had written reports analyzing their test data and interviews she had conducted with them, noting that both had admitted being sexually abused when they were children, Delaney by a Boy Scout leader and Blair by a summer camp counselor. Walter Enoch's mother had abused him, though not sexually, and Anne Kendall's stepfather had repeatedly raped her.

It wasn't a leap of faith to conclude that the killer

had probably also been abused as a child, his rage fueling these murders. Maggie Brennan had told me that she had spent her life studying victims and perpetrators of violent crime. I wanted her take on my theory and I wanted to know whether Corliss had confided in her that he had been abused as a child, questions I needed answered before someone else's dreams came true.

I took my time going over the rest of his office, no longer caring whether I made it to the retired cops' lunch or whether Corliss knew about my search. I would catch up to Tom Goodell and his cold case as soon as I could. It was more important to find the evidence that would close the book on Anthony Corliss. Short of a confession, the best evidence was the souvenirs the killer took from his victims.

I combed the office, pulled books off shelves one at a time, removed desk drawers looking for anything that might be taped to the inside of the desk frame. I put a chair on Corliss's desk, stood on it and popped open ceiling tiles scanning the hidden crawl space, finishing my search an hour later without finding Tom Delaney's bullet punctured books, Regina Blair's jewelry, Anne Kendall's severed finger, or Wendy's letter.

I called Quincy Carter again and left another message, hoping his unavailability meant that he was closing in on Corliss faster than me. That would be both good news and bad news. I wanted Corliss off the streets but I also wanted Wendy's letter so I could deal with Dolan and Kent on my own terms. Corliss's house was the best place to look.

Corliss didn't have a phone directory in his office. I did a search on his desktop computer, finding his address on Cherry between Fifty-third and Fifty-fourth, and entered his phone number in my cell phone. I tucked the Delaney, Blair, Enoch, and Kendall files under my arm and turned off the light. Looking around his office, I had no doubt he would realize that someone had tossed it; any concerns I had about that long since passed.

Crestwood, where Corliss lived, was an area I had considered when I moved in from the suburbs. Its borders were Fifty-third on the north, Fifty-sixth on the south, Oak on the west, and Holmes on the east. Built beginning in 1919 by Kansas City's visionary and legendary residential developer, J. C. Nichols, it was known for its Colonial and Tudor homes. Beyond the architecture, it was another of Kansas City's many long-established neighborhoods of well-kept homes and welcoming families, young, old, and now ethnically diverse.

After Corliss was arrested and when the inevitable television crews showed up, its residents would shake their heads and say that Crestwood was the last place on earth they would expect to find a serial killer. The greater surprise would be if they said it wasn't one of those singular, secure last places.

The 5300 block of Cherry was a five-minute drive from the institute. It was a quiet side street, not providing a shortcut to anywhere; the kind of street you didn't take unless you belonged there and where well-meaning neighbors were serious about the signs posted on both sides of the street proclaiming it a neighborhood watch area.

I circled the block, disappointed that Corliss's driveway wasn't brimming with police and his house wasn't ringed in yellow tape. I didn't see any cars or vans parked down the block or in driveways that were obvious surveillance vehicles. From all appearances, this peaceful street and Corliss's limestone and brown brick

Tudor house, with its detached garage and arched entrance, oak trees made leafless by winter, and six-foot evergreens flanking the front door like sentries, was the last place on earth anyone would look for a killer. On my second pass, I parked in front of a house two doors down and on the opposite side of the street facing away from Corliss's house.

I never forget about my movement disorder but there are times when I pretend that it isn't real as if my mind can trick my brain into calling the whole thing off. Mornings are the best time to play that game when I'm rested and fresh and the day is a blank check and there's no reason I can't do whatever I want. It's harder to pull the trick off when, like now, the blank check bounces and the brain fog rolls in and my muscles stretch my body to a hair trigger pull. That's when I have to choose between backing down and stepping up; between the more you do the more you do and what the hell was I thinking.

I punched Corliss's number into my cell phone and listened to it ring half a dozen times before my call rolled into voice mail. Corliss apologized in his easy Southern drawl that he couldn't answer, asked me to leave a number, and promised that he'd get back to me just as soon as he could.

I stepped out of the car, my body whiplashing while I held on to the door, my knees buckling. No one rushed out of their house offering to help or yelled at me to clear out before they called the cops. I squeezed my eyes shut until the fog cleared and my brain sent me a message. If I was fool enough to keep going, I was on my own.

Chapter Fifty-two

The wind picked up, a fine mist stinging my face. I zipped my jacket and stuffed my hands into my leather gloves. The weather was turning sooner than the weatherman had predicted. That didn't make him wrong; it made him early.

There's no way to sneak up on a house you're planning to break into in broad daylight when it's in a neighborhood watch area if people are serious about watching. The best option is to use the purposeful stride, a brisk walk marked by an authoritative posture, arms hanging loose at your sides, shoulders back and chin out front, the walk telling the neighborhood watchers that you've got every right to do what you're doing so butt out.

I started at the front door, ringing the bell and rapping on the door, waiting a reasonable time before stepping behind the evergreens and in front of the windows to the right of the door, cupping my hands around my eyes and against the glass and peeking inside. The lights were off. I tapped on the window, getting no response. If Corliss had a watchdog, it was deaf.

The garage was to my left, set at the back of the driveway like at my house. The overhead door was windowless and locked. The windows on each side were also locked; the glass dirty and streaked with layers of grime, making them more mirrored than transparent. The best I could tell, the garage was empty.

The backyard was fenced, a rickety, wooden perimeter, with a gate that squealed for oil when I pushed past it. There was a screened-in porch at the rear of the house, its door unlocked. I hesitated. So far, I was a mere trespasser. One more step and I graduated to home invasion. I reached for the doorknob, stopping when I heard a voice behind me.

"Police! Freeze!"

I tried but I couldn't do it. The first tremors shot from my gut to my neck, turning me into a life-size bobble-head doll. My knees were the next to go. I gripped my thighs with my hands, trying to stay upright.

"I said freeze! Keep your hands where I can see them!"

I couldn't do that either and I couldn't talk, my vocal cords twisting into knots.

"Sir, this is your last warning! Let me see your hands! Now!"

I reached out with one hand to balance myself against the porch, my other hand wrapped around my middle and hidden from the cop's view. I made a quarter turn toward him, my hidden hand making his eyes pop. He aimed his Taser at me as I opened my mouth, yelling *nooooo* without making a sound, though he wouldn't have stopped even if he heard me. The Taser pins bit my neck like bee stings, fifty thousand volts putting me on the ground and out.

* * *

The sun was shining in my eyes, making me squint. I shaded my forehead with one hand cutting the glare enough that I could see Kevin and Wendy playing at the ocean's edge, waves running up their legs, the chilly water making them shriek and giggle.

I didn't know how they got there. She was eight and he was four, too little to be in the water by themselves which was why Joy and I had forbidden them to leave the beach house we were renting without us. A minute ago, they had been in the kitchen. Kevin was watching cartoons and Wendy was playing with Monkey Girl, her favorite stuffed animal, while I scrambled eggs for breakfast, one pan runny the way Kevin liked them, and another pan hard the way Wendy preferred.

I ran to the beach, scooping them up in my arms but they slipped out of my grasp and ran away, Wendy holding Monkey Girl's hand, the monkey's feet dangling, leaving a trail in the wet sand. I chased after them, my feet bogging down, baffled at how they skimmed across the surface leaving me farther and farther behind. I yelled their names and they glanced back over their shoulders shouting at me to hurry.

I kept running, catching up to them as the beach became concrete and the ocean transformed into streets with trees and houses and shops, all flashing by in a blur. It began to rain, cold sheets that blurred my vision. I ran on, harder and faster than I had ever run, losing more ground as Kevin and Wendy grew older, their strides quickening and lengthening as they ran. I called their names again and again as they looked back at me, this time crying, begging me to run faster.

Kevin, now wearing the Dallas Cowboy's T-shirt we gave him for his ninth birthday, began to slow and stumble, his arms flailing as the pavement turned to mud. I churned and churned through the muck, getting closer to him; an arm's length back and I could hear his wincing breaths, a foot away

*and the fat rain drops splattering on his back splashed on me,
then inches between us and I could smell him, the way he stank
after a day in the sun, telling us he'd shower tomorrow. When
at last I reached for him, he slipped through my fingers and the
earth swallowed him.*

*Wendy ran on, her voice reaching back to me, saying hurry,
please hurry. She was still clutching Monkey Girl though she
had grown up, her face lean and gaunt, her eyes hollow the
way they were when I found her lying in the street in New York.
The rain stopped. The mud turned into a hard, ridged track,
cracking under a resurgent sun that burned my face as I ran
after her, the rough ground slicing into my bare feet, my footprints bloody. Then she tripped and fell, sprawling and skidding, disintegrating on impact into a million pieces, and
disappeared into the earth.*

*I stopped running, whirled around, and saw Joy standing
next to me, hands on her knees, her chest heaving. She'd been
running alongside me the whole time though I never saw her.
We should have saved them, she said, then looked at me and
asked why we hadn't, but I had no answer. She bent down at
the spot where Wendy had vanished and picked up Monkey
Girl, sobbing and cradling it in her arms and walked away as
I began shaking and crumbled to the ground, praying that it
would claim me.*

Chapter Fifty-three

A blood pressure cuff squeezed my right arm, swelling and releasing, as my dream faded and I rejoined the world, my eyes still closed.

"I've never seen someone keep shaking this long after getting Tasered," a woman's voice said.

"You think he's having a seizure?" another woman asked, her voice deeper than the first one.

"I don't think so," the first woman said. "His vitals are normal. He's just shaking, like the current is still going through him."

The shakes tapered to a few mild ripples and I opened my eyes. "Shaking is what I do."

I was laying on a gurney inside an ambulance, flanked by two female paramedics, stethoscopes hanging around their necks. The one on my left was smiling; her partner on my right frowning, checking the readout on the blood pressure monitor a second time.

I raised my head, glancing around. Quincy Carter was

standing outside the ambulance, one of its two doors open wide enough to let him in and keep most of the cold air out.

"And you're damn good at it," he said.

"Thanks. First time I've been hit with a Taser."

"At least you didn't shit your pants," Carter said. "It makes some guys do that. Makes some guys' hearts stop too. Be glad you didn't do that either."

The shakes stopped and I raised myself up on my elbows. "I don't know whether to write a thank-you note to the cop who shot me or a testimonial to the manufacturer."

"Easy," the paramedic on my left said, cupping the back of my head in her hands. "What kind of meds are you on?" she asked.

"None."

"What do you mean that shaking is what you do?" her partner asked.

"I have a movement disorder called tics. Makes me shake."

"Then I recommend against pissing off any more cops," she said. "Can you sit up?"

I eased my legs off the gurney, the paramedics spotting me in case I wobbled. "So far, so good. What are you doing here?" I asked Carter.

"Your cell phone was ringing when the paramedics got to you. When my name popped up on the caller ID, the officer who stopped you from breaking into Corliss's house answered it. I was returning your calls. The officer told me what happened and I asked him not to Taser you again unless he thought it would do you some good."

"I owe you."

"Don't worry. I'll collect."

Carter and the paramedics helped me out of the ambulance. He held my elbow and escorted me to his car. My first few steps were half drunk but I was walking sober when we slid into the backseat.

"You okay?" he asked.

I wiped my face with me hands. "All things considered, I should have taken the day off."

"Why didn't you?"

"Haven't been on the job long enough to build up any vacation time."

"You're retired from the real job. The one you've got now ends at the front door of the Harper Institute. I won't ask what you were thinking when you decided to break into Corliss's house but I'd be interested in knowing what you were looking for."

"Souvenirs," I said.

"Not the kind you get at the county fair."

"No, the kind a serial killer collects, like Regina Blair's jewelry."

"The FBI passed Walter Enoch's case to us. That letter your daughter sent you and Enoch stole could be another one of the souvenirs."

"You could be right. Have you found anything out about Regina Blair's jewelry?"

He nodded. "Matter of fact, I did. Talked to her husband. He said Regina always wore a tennis bracelet, one of those things with diamonds all the way around."

"Even on Sunday mornings when she was on a job site?"

"He said that the bracelet belonged to Regina's mother. Said Regina never took it off day or night. We searched her house but didn't find it. We went back to the homeless guy who found her body and he denied taking it. Polygraph backs him up. Could have been someone else took it before he found her."

"You don't sound convinced."

"I'm just saying. That piece of paper with the initials on it that you e-mailed to me is real interesting but it doesn't make Regina's bracelet a souvenir. And I need the original of the list."

I nodded, retrieved the envelope containing the list from my jacket pocket, and handed it to him. "There's more." I told him about Anne Kendall's dream narrative.

"You didn't consider telling me about that and waiting for me to get a search warrant for Corliss's house?"

"You have one?"

He sighed. "The prosecutor is a pretty conservative guy. Some people say he's too scared of looking bad and losing, but you didn't hear that from me. He isn't sold on Corliss. Says the list of initials isn't enough to go in front of a judge for a warrant. Kendall's dream narrative will help but he'll want McNair and me to take a run at Corliss first. See if we can break him down or at least get something more solid for the judge."

"Well, Corliss isn't home."

"And when he gets home, his neighbors are going to tell him what happened here today if they haven't already left him voice messages about the guy who tried to break into his house and would have if they hadn't called the cops. That should convince him to get rid of any souvenirs he's collected."

"Okay, I get your point. Waiting would have been better but I don't think he'll get rid of them. They're too important. He might move them, find another hiding place, but he'll hang on to them."

"If he's our guy. In the meantime, we have to find him."

"You think he's on the run?"

"On the run or missing, or hiding, or at the movies, or down at the boats gambling. Who the hell knows? We haven't been looking for him long enough to say."

"I'll let you know if I find him."

"You? You aren't going to find anybody. You're going home."

"Says who?"

"Says me. You're in no shape to drive. I found Lucy Trent's number in your cell phone. I called her and she should be here in a few minutes. I told her to take your car keys away. You shouldn't be driving."

"Why are you so concerned about my welfare?"

"I'm not. I'm concerned about my case and having you running around breaking into my suspect's house isn't going to do me any good."

"Don't worry. I'll stay out of your way."

He turned toward me, his shoulders blocking out the passenger window. The mist had thickened into icy pellets pinging against the roof of the car.

"Jack, I've known a lot of cops like you, guys who can't walk away. Every one of them has a good reason. Maybe it's the case they never closed that eats at them. Maybe it's not having anything else to do that matters. You, I get it. You didn't go out on your own terms. That's got to be hard. I don't know how I'd handle that. But you strike me as the kind of guy who knows better than to go after someone like Corliss on your own."

"I said I'd stay out of your way."

"That's not good enough, Jack. If you're right that Corliss is a serial killer, you've got to back the hell off. I mean all the way off. Stay out of my way and stay out of his way. You're no match for someone like that. I don't want you ending up one of his souvenirs. So do what you're told and don't make me arrest you for attempted burglary. Are we clear on this?"

"Clear," I said as another burst of tremors danced through me.

"Damn, you do shake."

"It's what I do."

Chapter Fifty-four

Lucy and Kate pulled up next to us in Kate's car. Lucy jumped out of the passenger side, leaving her door open as I got out of Carter's, engulfing me in a hug.

"You are so totally grounded," she said. "Hand over the car keys."

"You have to let go of me first."

She stepped back, her hand out. "Okay, let's have them."

I fished the keys out of my jacket pocket and dropped them in her gloved palm. "Thanks for coming to get me."

"Are you kidding? Like I've got time to find another tenant. I'll drive your car. You ride with Kate." She ushered me into Kate's car. "See you back at the ranch," she added, slamming the door behind me.

"You've made quite an impression on her," Kate said, nudging her car down the wet street.

"I'm the ideal tenant. I've got no place else to go."

She laughed. "It's more than that. She's had a hard time. You're filling a void for her."

"Actually, I think Simon's got that one covered."

"So she told me. Good for her and good for Simon. You can walk her down the aisle."

"Aren't you getting a little ahead of yourself? So far, they're a one-night stand. There's a reason neither of them have ever been married."

"Doesn't matter whether it's Simon or someone else. Mark my words. When the time comes, she'll want you to do the honors."

I shifted my weight, the ride and the conversation making me uncomfortable. "I wasn't exactly Father of the Year material. I don't know that I'll do any better as a surrogate father."

"Don't turn your nose up. Second chances are hard to come by."

The ice was sticking to the windshield, building up on the corners outside the wipers' reach. The slick coating made the streets shine. Kate tap-danced her brakes, keeping her car under control.

"She's a good kid," I said.

"Good kids and second chances are both hard to come by."

I knew where this was heading and I wasn't ready to go there. "Children aren't fungible. You can't trade them in for next year's model. Joy and I talked about having another baby after we lost Kevin but we couldn't get past the notion that we were trying to replace something that couldn't be replaced. I know that works for some people and God bless them but it didn't work for us. No one, including Lucy, can take Wendy's place."

"And no one should. But life goes on."

I changed the subject. "How did it go with your staff this morning?"

"Dad is a lot better at those things than I am. He was terrific but everyone still cried."

"It may not be as bad as you think," I said. "You were right about Harper. He did sabotage your practice."

"How do you know that?"

"I called him on it and he told me."

"I hope he rots in hell."

"Don't worry. He's got the whole hell on earth thing going for him," I said, explaining that Harper had Alzheimer's and was turning control of his affairs, including the institute, over to Sherry Fritzshall.

"Well," Kate said, "I'm sorry that he's sick but I'm still going to sue his ass."

"You won't have to. Sherry overheard Harper telling me what he'd done to you. She wants to meet with you next week, no lawyers, and work something out. I think she's sincere."

Her jaw clenched and loosened. "I don't know."

"Don't turn your nose up," I said. "Second chances are hard to come by."

"It's not that. With Dad retiring and Alan moving to San Diego, I don't think I can make it work by myself."

"Sure you can. Sherry's not going to write you a blank check but she'll be reasonable. You'll be able to keep your staff together until you can recruit a couple of partners, maybe merge with another group. You can do it."

She didn't respond, paying more attention to the road then necessary even given the deteriorating weather. Then I realized that I'd missed the point.

"It's not that you can't do it," I said. "It's that you can't do it if Brian is going to be seventeen hundred miles away."

She stopped for a red light and turned toward me. "No, I can't. Like you said, kids aren't fungible."

I nodded. "No, they aren't. So, when are you moving?"

She took a deep breath. "Not until the school year ends. I made a couple of phone calls today. I'm flying out there tomorrow and meeting with some people. It's all very preliminary. Dad will finish reviewing the dream videos for you."

"Tell him that won't be necessary. The smart money is on Anthony Corliss. I was about to break into his house to look for evidence when that cop zapped me. The police are looking for him now. We'll see how that pans out."

"I'm glad you're letting the police handle it."

I gripped my armrests, holding myself in place as a new round of aftershocks rumbled through me, making me stutter. "About San Diego. That's the right decision."

She reached across my seat, her hand on my wrist. "It's not a zero sum game, Jack. You can come too. There's nothing keeping you here."

With her gone, she was almost right. "Who will walk Lucy down the aisle?"

"That's what airplanes are for."

We left it at that until she dropped me off, saying she had to go home and pack. Lucy was waiting inside with Roxy and Ruby who jumped me like they had just gotten out of solitary confinement. I sat on the floor, letting the dogs smother me. Ruby planted her front paws on my chest, demanding to know where I'd been while

Roxy ducked under her chin, knocking Ruby from her perch as she curled up in my lap, the two of them starting over, jockeying for position, settling between my legs, their front paws draped over my thighs, their chins on my knees.

"It's good to be loved," Lucy said.

"Amen to that."

Chapter Fifty-five

The weatherman was right. The sleet turned to ice and the ice to snow and there was nothing to be done except to watch it come down. Ice slapped against the windows, encased tree limbs, and carpeted the ground, the perfect undercoat for the snow—fat, wet, lazy flakes tossed on the wind, piling, drifting, and blowing. The storm blanketed the region, branches and power lines snapping north and south of the Missouri River; roads and schools closed east and west of the state line. Local television gave wall-to-wall coverage with live reports from all the places we were warned not to go, headlights streaming in the background proof that some people couldn't take a hint.

I was one of them. Not that I left the house. Lucy and I were sitting on the sofa in the living den. She grinned and stuck the car key in her jean pocket, daring me to try getting it out. It was Quincy Carter's hint that I couldn't take, the weather and Lucy's protective instincts keeping me homebound for the night.

In that moment, she reminded me of Joy, not Wendy, and of a time when going after the key would have been worth the effort. I hadn't thought of Joy like that for quite a while, flashes of our early years welling up when she had shown more spunk and steel than any woman I had ever known, filling me with longing for past lives. I didn't know what triggered those memories, whether it was Joy's phone call or Lucy's mischievous smile or Kate telling me she was leaving, but they blossomed into a fleeting daydream that I was standing in a circular room surrounded by closed doors uncertain what was behind each: happiness or sorrow, the future or the past, the lady or the tiger.

"Hey," Lucy said, waving her hands a few inches from my face. "Anybody home?"

I blinked and laughed. "Just me."

"Well, don't even think about going out in this weather."

"Not a problem. I'm all in and all done."

"For tonight. Tomorrow will be a better day. You know what I think," she said, taking my hand. "I think our timing is good."

"Me too."

Her cell phone rang, her face lighting up at the name on caller ID. She jumped off the sofa, turning her back to me.

"Hey, you," she said, walking toward the kitchen.

"Tell lover boy I said hello."

She gave me the finger over her shoulder and kept walking as my cell phone rang.

"Jack, it's me," Joy said. "Is this a bad time? You were right about the weather."

I leaned into the soft cushions of the sofa, surprised

at how glad I was to hear her voice. "No, this is a good time. We're really getting hammered."

"Every flight to Kansas City has been canceled. At this point, I don't know if the airline can even get me on a flight tomorrow. I may not make it back until Friday. I hope you don't mind keeping Roxy," she said, the strain in her voice apparent.

"Don't worry about it. Are you okay?"

She hesitated. "Yeah, it's just that I'd really like to get out of here. I'll tell you about it when I get home. Give the dogs a hug for me," she said and hung up.

I didn't believe her but the right to pry and push was one of the things I gave up in our divorce settlement. Lucy came out of the kitchen, took the stairs two at a time, and was back down a few moments later, wearing a parka with her backpack on her shoulder.

"Don't tell me you're going out in this weather?"

"Simon says it's not that bad and he doesn't live far from here. Besides, you aren't going anywhere."

She opened the front door, a mini–snow flurry whistling inside.

"I'll need the car in the morning."

"Sure, sure," she said, shoving the door closed behind her.

Roxy and Ruby were curled back-to-back on an easy chair. They lifted their heads, stretched, and yawned, jumping to the floor and trotting into the kitchen. I followed them. They ignored me, marching single file out the doggie door.

I made a pot of decaf and sat at the kitchen table. Simon's banker box was on the floor. I pulled his file on Anthony Corliss, poured a cup, and broke my promise to Quincy Carter.

Simon had found newspaper coverage about the girl at the University of Wisconsin. Her name was Kimberly Stevens. The article matched the details Janet Casey and Gary Kaufman had given me. Kimberly had been a sophomore. She volunteered for the dream project to get extra credit in her introductory psychology class. She drowned in Lake Mendota. Her parents sued the university and Corliss. The university settled the case, emphasizing that it was not admitting liability. The family's attorney, Eric Abelson, said the family was satisfied with the outcome of the case, though no amount of money could compensate them for their loss.

Kate had criticized Harper's lawyers for only talking with the lawyers for the university and for Corliss and not talking to the family's lawyer. I searched Abelson's name on Google, finding his Web site which boasted that he was available 24-7. It was almost ten o'clock. He answered on the third ring and listened while I explained that I was calling because of the similarity between his case and the one Jason Bolt was going to file.

"You know I've already spoken to Bolt," he said.

"Bolt told me he knows about your case so I assumed he'd talked to you."

"And you should also know that I sent him a copy of my file and I told him I'd do anything I could to help him."

"I know whose side you're on."

"Then why do you think I'm going to help you?"

"Because I'm trying to figure out whose side I'm on."

I listened to dead air while Abelson calculated his response. "You said you were working for Milo Harper. Are you still on his payroll?"

"I am."

"And Bolt is getting ready to sue your boss?"

"I know that."

"And you don't know whose side you're on?"

"It's complicated."

Another pause. "Are you recording this conversation?"

"No. Why would I?"

"Because I don't know what kind of crap you're trying to pull but this smells like a setup."

"It isn't."

"If you're lying to me and a tape of this call just happens to turn up, you and I are going to have some serious shit to sort out, you got that?"

"Understood. I'm not recording our conversation."

"I'll tell you what. How about I record it?"

"Fine by me."

"You're serious?"

"It's late, I'm beat, and I'd like to get past this bullshit so if it will make you feel better to record the call, hook us up," I said, my last words coming out in a tumble.

"What's the matter with your voice?"

"I have a movement disorder that makes me stutter sometimes and, like I said, it's late and I'm beat."

Another pause. "I just ran your name through Google. Are you the Jack Davis who used to be with the FBI?"

He'd been stalling while he ran a background check on me. "Yeah."

"Damn. Hang on. I'm reading the article in the *Kansas City Star* about the woman who was murdered at the Harper Institute. Is that what this is about?"

"Yes."

"The newspaper says this guy Leonard Nagel, the one who was hit by a car and killed when he ran from the scene, did it. What's all that got to do with Corliss?"

"The newspaper got it wrong."

"Where's Corliss?"

"I don't know. The police are looking for him. So am I."

"You think he may be the killer?"

"Right now, he's the leader in the clubhouse."

"In that case, how can I help you nail the son of a bitch?"

Chapter Fifty-six

"Tell me the truth about your case."

"What's that supposed to mean?"

"It means I don't want to hear your opening statement to the jury or the payday speech you made to the university. I don't want to know the opinions of the whores you hired as expert witnesses. They've been paid and so have you. This isn't about Bolt's case and it isn't about money. It's about a murderer, probably a serial killer that's still on the street. I don't care whether you and Bolt have got a hard-on for Corliss. I care whether he's guilty. If he is, I'll do everything I can to take him down. If he isn't, I don't want to get it wrong."

"I was a prosecutor before I went into private practice and I still do a fair share of criminal work. I know the difference between proving a civil case by a preponderance of the evidence and a criminal case beyond a reasonable doubt. I could have won my case against the university seven times out of ten but I couldn't have gotten an indictment against Corliss."

"Break it down for me."

"Kimberly Stevens was an emotional train wreck. She didn't belong in school, let alone as a volunteer in Corliss's dream project. That should have been obvious to Corliss. Instead of referring her for treatment, he took advantage of her."

"You could prove they were having an affair?"

"Her roommate says they were. She says Corliss cut it off and that's when Kimberly killed herself."

"Was there any other evidence of the affair? E-mails, phone records, that sort of thing?"

"She sent him some pretty torrid e-mails but he was smart enough not to respond. If he wasn't screwing her, the e-mails were enough proof that he should have informed the university and recommended that she get therapy. Either way, the e-mails made my case."

"Then why do you say you only had a seventy percent chance of winning?"

"Because any plaintiff's lawyer who tells you he's got a better shot than that in any case is a liar. You can prepare all you want but something unexpected always happens during trial and juries are unpredictable."

"Why no criminal case?"

"Kimberly drove to Lake Mendota by herself the night she died. She went for a swim and never came back. No one saw her go in the water. My experts called it a suicide but—and here I'm giving you the unvarnished truth—we'll never know for sure. It could have been an accident."

"Where was Corliss that night?"

"I don't know."

"How could you not know? That would be the first thing I would have asked him."

"Give me some credit. I didn't get to ask him that or

anything else. The university agreed to settle on the morning I was supposed to take his deposition."

"Corliss told me that he didn't want to settle, that the university made him. What do you know about that?"

"That's bullshit. Corliss was covered by the university's insurance policy. The insurance company had to provide him with a defense, hire a lawyer to represent him, the whole shot. Except the insurance policy didn't cover my claim for punitive damages so Corliss hired a good friend of mine to represent him on that claim. After the case was over, she told me that the university and the insurance company wanted to go to trial but that Corliss was scared shitless about giving his deposition. I had made a settlement demand within the insurance company's policy limits, which meant they could settle the case and get Corliss off the hook for punitive damages. She threatened to sue them for bad faith for exposing Corliss to a judgment for punitive damages if they didn't settle, so they caved."

Abelson's information was like everything else in this case, filling some of the gaps while leaving the most important questions unanswered. Corliss was drowning in circumstantial evidence but there were enough holes in the case against him for any decent defense lawyer to exploit. There were multiple explanations for the incriminating evidence and nothing to place him at any of the crime scenes. If the prosecutor was as conservative as Quincy Carter claimed, he would run from the case, saying it was all shadows and no substance unless Carter or I could come up with something more solid.

"There had to have been a reason Corliss was so afraid to give his deposition. Maybe he was worried that you'd find out something he wanted to keep secret or that you had figured out his secret and were going to drop it on him in the deposition. You checked me out while we were on the phone. You must have done more than that with Corliss. What did you have on him?"

"I hired an investigator who worked backward from the time Corliss came to Wisconsin to the day he was born. He didn't have a track record at the other universities where'd he worked or gone to school. Not so much as a student complaining about a grade. What are you looking for?"

"Four people who were participants in Corliss's dream project have been murdered in the last couple of months. Each of them died the way they dreamed they would die. I think the killer knew about their dreams and staged their murders to mimic their nightmares. Each of them had also been abused when they were kids and the killer may have chosen them because of their history of abuse."

"I handled a serial killer case when I was in the DA's office. I'd say you're looking for someone who was abused when he was a kid."

"More likely than not."

"One of my psychology experts who, by the way is an honest whore, told me to focus on why Corliss became a psychologist. He said that a lot of people are attracted to the field because they want to figure out why they or their family are so screwed up. In Corliss's case, it was both. Turns out his family was a dysfunctional mess and Corliss had his own issues."

"Like what?"

"Like his father beat him, his mother, and brothers and sisters until one day his mother didn't get up off the floor. The father went to jail and the kids went to foster care. Corliss knew all about vulnerable kids like Kimberly Stevens because he'd been one."

"I'd say that made your odds of winning your case a lot better than seventy percent."

"Close as you can get in this business to a sure thing, except nothing makes me more nervous than a sure thing. What's it do for you?"

"Makes me nervous."

Chapter Fifty-seven

The storm died during the night, dawn breaking with the roar of grinding chain saws and the rumble of pavement scraping snowplows. Sunlight flashed across the frozen landscape, rebounding with a blinding glare, ice and snow a convex mirror.

The house lost power during the night, the digital clock in my bedroom saying three A.M., trailing my watch by four hours, when two enterprising kids who lived down the street rang the doorbell at seven, handed me my newspaper, and offered to shovel the driveway and front walk for fifty bucks. They laughed when Roxy and Ruby christened the snow around their boots, one of them exclaiming *awesome, dude,* while the other took video with his cell phone and uploaded it to YouTube. I hired them because my car was nowhere in sight, meaning that Lucy was digging Simon out of the snow instead of me.

I flattened the *Kansas City Star* on the kitchen

counter, the headline above the fold—"Police Suspect Serial Killer"—knocking me back. A color picture of paramedics wheeling Anne Kendall's black-bagged body out of the Harper Institute was bordered on the right by a vertical stack of thumbnail headshots of her, Walter Enoch, Tom Delaney, and Regina Blair and, on the left side, by another stack featuring Milo Harper, Sherry Fritzshall, Anthony Corliss, Leonard Nagel, and me.

Mine was the Bureau's official photo, what we called the yearbook pose, eyes and head straight on at the camera, half-serious, half-smiling, and no toothy-goofy grin. It was the same picture the *Kansas City Star* had used when a reporter named Rachel Firestone did the stories on Wendy and the drug ring. She hadn't pushed when I refused to give her an interview, investigating the same way she wrote—tough but fair.

Rachel had the byline on this story, detailing the murders of Anne Kendall and Walter Enoch without embellishment, knowing that the facts packed all the punch she needed. She reported that the police had re-opened their investigations into the deaths of Tom Delaney and Regina Blair, citing unnamed sources suggesting that they may have been the first two victims of a serial killer that also killed Enoch and Kendall. A police department spokesman called speculation about a serial killer premature but declined further comment, citing the sensitive nature of the ongoing investigation.

Special Agent Manny Fernandez, media spokesman for the FBI's Kansas City Regional Office, said that the Bureau was cooperating with the police department in the Walter Enoch murder investigation while also pursuing leads about another case that were developed based on the stolen mail found at Enoch's house, saying that they were close to making an arrest. Agent Fernandez declined comment when asked if the suspect in that case may be connected to the murders.

Firestone ended her story by reporting that Jason Bolt was filing suit against the Harper Institute for the wrongful deaths of Delaney and Blair, quoting Bolt's allegations that the institute had been negligent in its hiring and supervision of Anthony Corliss and alleging that the dream project was reckless, dangerous, and irresponsible. Bolt was quoted saying that he had been retained by Anne Kendall's parents and would be filing a wrongful death case on their behalf within the next week and that he was trying to locate any surviving heirs of Walter Enoch to make certain their rights were also protected. Rachel gave Sherry Fritzshall the last word, Sherry denying Bolt's allegations and calling the deaths of the dream project participants a tragedy for them, their families, and the institute.

The story stretched onto page two where there were sidebars written by Rachel and boxed in a panel alongside the main story. The first was about Leonard Nagel's criminal record, the second about the lawsuit against Corliss and the University of Wisconsin over Kimberly Stevens's death, and the third announced that Milo Harper had taken a leave of absence from the institute for personal reasons and that Sherry Fritzshall had replaced him as president. Sherry was quoted as saying that these changes had been planned for some time and were unrelated to the deaths of the dream project participants.

The last sidebar was about me, reprising my history with the FBI, the drug ring, Wendy, and my movement disorder. Firestone quoted Jason Bolt saying that the institute had waited too long to hire a director of security and then compounded that mistake by hiring someone whose disability should have disqualified him from the job, describing my hiring as part of the institute's continuing pattern of fatally flawed judgments.

I wasn't surprised by the newspaper coverage. The murders of Anne Kendall and Walter Enoch were sensational enough on their own. The prospect that they were victims of a serial killer was a reportorial windfall. Toss in a billionaire who walked away from the crown jewel of his empire without explanation, a registered sex offender killed while fleeing the police, and an ex-professor and an ex-FBI agent who left their last jobs under a cloud, all of whom worked for the billionaire, and Rachel Firestone must have felt like she'd died and gone to heaven twice over.

She had excellent sources, including, I assumed, Jason Bolt and Eric Abelson. Someone in the police department must have briefed her as well, no doubt off the record and only after Rachel promised anonymity.

The Bureau spokesman, Manny Fernandez, wasn't speaking off the record. He was sending me a message, reminding me that my forty-eight hours were almost up. Kent had promised me that if I didn't turn over the drug money, the Bureau would do things Dolan's way, which was shorthand for getting ugly.

It wouldn't matter whether they could make a case against me. They would ruin me with more than the innuendo hinted at in the newspaper. There would be a news conference. A sober-faced Fernandez would rehash the case, disclose Wendy's letter with the irresistible but unsupported conclusion of its contents, labeling me as a person of interest in the investigation of the missing money and encouraging me to come forward and tell what I knew.

They would bang the drum as often and as long as it took to convince the world that I had betrayed the public trust and gotten away with a crime. My denials and explanations would be footnotes to the story, my reputation the first casualty, my chance to spend the rest of my life doing more than wandering the aisles at the Bass Pro Shop the next. And, if they were lucky enough to find Wendy's letter and leverage it into an indictment, they would force me to spend my disability payments on attorney's fees before sending me to prison.

I couldn't sit back and wait for any of that to unfold, depending on luck and justice, both of which were blind, to get it right. Anthony Corliss was the lynchpin, the only name on my list of suspects whether the list was short or long. He didn't ooze menace like Anthony Hopkins in *The Silence of the Lambs* or any other cinematic thrill killer but evil isn't always obvious. More often it's hidden behind a banal façade, stunning us when it's finally revealed.

No one else fit the profile as well as Corliss. No one else was as connected to the victims, knew their vulnerabilities, and shared their tormented history. And no one else had as many questions to answer.

Lucy didn't pick up when I called and neither did Simon. I was starting to shake from sitting around and doing nothing. I had to get out of the house, clear my head, and find a way to get to Corliss without falling apart.

I pulled on jeans and a sweatshirt, hiking boots and a barn jacket, wrapped a scarf around my neck, and tugged a wool cap around my ears and left the house, paying the teenage snow shoveling crew on my way out. They pocketed the money and cut over to the next block south looking for more business.

A city snowplow had made one halfhearted pass down my block, leaving a slick hardpack on the pavement bordered by a foot high wall of snow shoved against the curb, blocking driveways and imprisoning cars that had been left on the street. I headed east toward The Roasterie Café, a coffee shop a few blocks away on Brookside Boulevard.

I was near the end of the next block when a black SUV turned onto the street from behind me, the driver at first matching my slow pace. Glancing over my shoulder, I couldn't tell whether the driver was looking for an address or just being careful or was following me and not caring that I knew, relying on the fact that I was too far from home to turn back. The windows were tinted, the sun adding an impenetrable glare, making the driver invisible. The car didn't belong to any of my neighbors and it wasn't a typical Bureau surveillance vehicle.

I scanned the street. No red-faced, over weight, out of shape, middle-aged men were shoveling their driveways, auditioning for heart attacks. No kids in mittens and ski caps were launching sleds off the slopes of their yards or rolling a snowman to its feet. No moms in boots and bathrobes were wading through the snow, clutching their nightgowns to their throats while fishing for the morning paper.

I was out in the open on icy, snowy terrain, alone, exposed, and unarmed when the driver accelerated, wheels spinning and whining against the snowpack, the chassis shimmying, tires gaining purchase, the car closing the distance before I could react, skidding to a stop, the front end sliding past me and kissing the snow-bank. The driver lowered the tinted window. It had been months, but I hadn't forgotten Rachel Firestone's volcanic red hair, emerald green eyes, and disarming smile.

"You could have phoned. Would have been a lot safer," I said, pointing at her right fender, buried in the snow.

She threw the car into reverse and yanked it free, then shifted into drive, aiming true east, standing on the brake, and making the SUV shudder and me shake.

"How's that?"

"Better, but you still could have phoned."

"You turned me down for an interview the last time and I wasn't sure you'd take my call after the story in today's paper."

"I'd have said hello."

"But that's it."

"Hello and good-bye," I said and started walking.

She followed, her car gliding alongside me. "It's news. You're news."

"Your luck, not mine."

"Why do you make this so hard?"

I stopped and faced her. She had alabaster skin, her cheeks tinged rose by the cold.

"I'm not interested in selling papers."

"Your luck, not mine. Where are you going? I'll bet to The Roasterie."

"You're a smart reporter."

"I'll give you a ride. It's cold."

I started walking again. "No thanks, I've seen how you drive in winter and I want to live to see the spring."

"C'mon, Jack. I'll buy you a cup of coffee."

"That's all I'm worth? A two dollar cup of coffee?"

"That's a lot on my budget."

"I'll pass," I said.

"Okay, buy your own coffee. Just tell me one thing?"

"What's that?"

"Why does the FBI want your head on a pike outside the village gates?"

Chapter Fifty-eight

I declined Rachel's offer of a ride, using the rest of my walk to think about the bait she'd thrown at my feet.

News stories, like murder cases, are organic, living creatures that grow arms and legs and reproduce. Random chance, chaos, the rule of unintended consequences, and the probability that we are all within six degrees of separation of one another combine to spawn new stories and new cases, the pregnant sometimes the last to know they're with child.

Rachel began with the murders and stumbled onto a parallel track about me, following the road map the FBI had laid out for her. She wanted information about both stories and so did I, but trading for it was tricky, particularly when one party wants to go public and the other wants to stay private, when a good deal may be measured more by what you didn't give up than by what you got.

I crossed Brookside Boulevard. and walked a block south to the café. Rachel's SUV was parked on the street, tilted to port, the starboard wheels resting on a snow berm built by the city's plows. The aroma of fresh ground coffee picked me up before I hit the door.

The Roasterie is Kansas City's homegrown coffee company. The owner started roasting coffee beans in the basement of his house in Brookside. When he outgrew the basement he moved to the city's west side, later opening the café in his old neighborhood. It's as good a place for a cup of coffee as there is, embracing Brookside's laid-back ambience with overstuffed chairs, soft light, and easy music.

Rachel was waiting at a table in a corner near the door, two steaming mugs in front of her. I took the seat across from her, my back to the wall.

"Coffee tastes better in a mug than in a paper cup," she said. "And these mugs feel great in your hand. Your cup is unleaded."

"Good guess."

"It wasn't a guess. I researched your movement disorder when I wrote the stories last year. Caffeine is not your friend."

I took two dollars from my wallet and laid them on the table, raised the cup, and took a sip. "Thanks."

She'd engineered this meeting so I let her take the lead, not wanting to appear too anxious to make a deal, preferring to let her set the floor in our negotiations by going first.

"You read my story?"

"All of it."

"At least admit that we used a decent picture of you," she said.

"I didn't know you had more than one to choose from."

"We have others," she said, setting her cup on the table. "From Wendy's funeral."

"Thanks for not using one of those."

"You're welcome. What did you think?"

"You covered a lot of territory."

"Did I get it right?"

"Too late to worry about that now."

"It's never too late. There's always tomorrow's paper. This story has legs, a lot of them."

"You're good at what you do. You'll get it all by the time it's over."

"I could use your help," she said, leaning back in her chair, twisting the diamond ring on her left hand.

"Getting married?"

She smiled, her eyes flickering with doubt. "Next month, in California. It's what my girlfriend wants."

"That's not exactly an enthusiastic endorsement of the institution of marriage."

She dipped her chin, nodded, and gave her ring another twirl. "Let's just say I have an easier time committing to my work."

"Trust me, it may be harder to commit to the people you love but the fringe benefits are a lot better than the ones you get on the job."

"Voice of experience?"

"Yeah, all of it hard."

"Like what happened to your daughter?"

"Like what happened to her."

She sighed, hunching over the table. "I know you're right but this is such a screwy business, I don't know whether I can't let go of it or whether it can't let go of me. I start out writing a story about the murder of Anne Kendall and the next thing I know there's a serial killer on the loose and my FBI source is whispering in my ear about you and your daughter and this crazy mailman who stole everyone's mail. How does that happen?"

"They're using you."

"No shit, Sherlock. They can use me till they use me up as long as there's a story worth writing."

"So, you'd do the same thing to me, use me till you use me up?"

She grinned, cocked her head to one side, resting her chin on clasped hands. "Only in a good way."

"Is that supposed to make me feel better?"

She planted her hands on the table. "Look, everything I wrote about you last year was straight and true. I didn't use your daughter to make you look guilty or your movement disorder to make you look pathetic. Now you're in the middle of a serial killer story and the one with the mailman. No way I can leave that alone. Neither can the cable networks. I got calls last night from Fox and MSNBC asking me to appear on their morning news shows today."

"You're hitting the big time."

"Right. You're about to be diced, dissected, profiled, and psychoanalyzed by people who think news is a carnival sideshow. So talk to me. Make sure I get it right. Make sure your side of the story gets out there."

"You're all feeding the same beast. They'll gnaw on this story for a day or two until they find fresh meat somewhere else."

"Maybe, but you and I are joined at the hip on this one. I'll be there when the arrests are made and when the jury comes back. I'll write the follow-up stories about the victims and their families and I'll do the where-is-Jack-Davis-now piece in five years. I'm not going away."

"What do you know about the murders that you left out of today's paper?"

"If I tell you, are you going to play fair or take advantage of me?"

"I doubt that I would get very far trying to do that."

"For an ex-cop, you give good flatter. Talk to me and I'll talk to you."

"On or off the record?"

"On."

"No good."

"Okay, off the record. You'll be a source close to the investigation."

"Sorry. Here's my deal. You talk to me now and I'll give you an exclusive when it's all in and all done. Take it or leave it."

"That's not much of a deal. From what I hear, you could be dead or in jail by then. A dead man gives a lousy interview and a defendant can't get past his own lawyer to talk to the press."

She'd given more in that answer than I'd given. "Who wants me dead and who wants me in jail?"

"Ahhh," she said. "I've got your attention, at last. Okay, consider this my good faith offer. Quincy Carter and I go way back. He likes you but thinks you're in way over your head because of your movement disorder. He's afraid you didn't learn your lesson when you got zapped trying to break into Anthony Corliss's house and that you're going to keep going after Corliss even though he warned you to stay out of it, so he's cutting you out of the loop. I wouldn't count on him returning your calls. He doesn't want your blood on his hands."

I nodded, glad to know that Carter saw Corliss the way I did. "That's the dead part. What about the jail part?"

"My sources at the FBI aren't as good but I'm getting a pretty strong vibe that they think you're hooked into the money your daughter stole from the drug ring. I put it to their spokesman, Manny Fernandez, straight up and he denied it with a wink and a nod, which for those Bureau guys is like Tom Cruise jumping up and down on Oprah's couch telling the world he's in love."

"Carter knows more about the murders than I do and I don't know what happened to the money so what could I possibly tell you?"

"A lot. Like what's going on at the Harper Institute? Why did Milo Harper step down? How did two whack jobs like Leonard Nagel and Anthony Corliss get hired there? For that matter, how did you get hired?"

"I can't help you with any of that. I agreed to do a job, not sell newspapers."

I drained my cup and stood.

"Where are you going? What are you going to do?" she asked.

"I've still got a job. I'm going to the institute."

"If you're hoping that Corliss decided to come to work today and is sitting behind his desk, waiting for you so he can confess, you're going to be disappointed. He isn't there."

"How do you know that?"

"I checked. He's not at home either. And I talked to Carter. He says Corliss is in the wind."

"Thanks."

"One other thing," she said, grabbing my wrist. "Carter can't find Maggie Brennan, Janet Casey, or Gary Kaufman. They're all gone, so talk to me."

I held on to the edge of the table, steadying myself as a burst of tremors rattled through me. "When it's over."

Chapter Fifty-nine

I didn't give Rachel a chance to offer me a ride, knowing I'd shake all the way home. If I kept moving, I hoped I could stay a step ahead of the tremors and find a way to keep the promise I'd made to Maggie Brennan that I would protect her.

I didn't think Corliss had decided to go on vacation, taking her and their research assistants along for the ride, and there was no other explanation for their simultaneous disappearances that didn't include a body count. The question was how Maggie, Janet, and Gary fit into Corliss's pattern.

Until now, I believed that he'd chosen his victims because of their shared history of abuse, maybe killing them as a way of killing himself, using their dreams as a template for murder. Maggie could fit that pattern if she was the same Maggie Brennan as in Tom Goodell's cold murder case.

I didn't know enough about Janet and Gary's background to place them in this matrix. They could have

been in the wrong place at the wrong time, they and
Maggie somehow figuring out that Corliss was the killer,
perhaps confronting him and forcing him to take them
out to protect himself. Or Corliss may have decided to
include them in a last binge, making himself the final
victim in a murder-suicide.

If Carter knew that Maggie Brennan was missing, that
meant someone had been to wherever she lived. She
had told me that she lived in the country, which translated to living outside the KCPD's jurisdiction. Carter
would have asked the county sheriff's office to check on
her while he did the same for Janet Casey and Gary
Kaufman who I assumed lived in the city. Cops and
deputy sheriffs would have knocked and, when no one
answered, checked for signs of forced entry, then gone
in themselves looking for dead bodies.

If Rachel Firestone knew that none of the missing had
reported for work, Carter must have also sent a separate
team to the institute to search their offices, the garage
and the sub-basement. Nancy Klemp would have stalled
the cops until she reached Sherry Fritzshall who would
have handled it herself without calling me, glad for the
chance to assert her new authority.

I checked my watch. It was close to nine. Carter had
covered a lot of ground, no doubt working through the
night. Rachel had been right behind him, plying him
for information, double-checking his work before staking me out. There was no reason for me to plow the
same ground. The best way to stop spinning your
wheels is to go in a different direction. Tom Goodell
was my best bet.

I called Lucy again. She didn't answer though Simon
picked up when I tried his number.

"Where's Lucy? Why haven't you guys returned my calls?"

"Take it easy, Pop. Your little girl is a grown-up."

I must have sounded like an outraged father but I couldn't dial back the tone. I was as irritated with Lucy as I was frightened for Maggie Brennan, Janet Casey, and Gary Kaufman. And a week of high intensity shaking didn't help.

"She's not my little girl and if you call me Pop ever again, I'm going to kick your ass into another zip code. I told Lucy last night that I needed my car back this morning and she isn't answering her phone. Now where the hell is she?"

"Sorry, Jack. I was only kidding around. She left here at seven-thirty. I've been working out in my basement. Cell phone reception is lousy down there. I just came upstairs when you called."

"Okay, if you hear from her, tell her to call me."

"Will do. Is everything all right?"

"Not hardly. Did you see this morning's paper?"

"Yeah, but after you bit my head off, I didn't think it was a good idea to bring it up."

I took a deep breath, trying to talk, my vocal cords too tangled to get the words out. I stopped walking and took more deep breaths. "Hang on," I managed as I waited for my throat muscles to relax, trying again, my words still choppy. "The police can't find Corliss. And, Maggie Brennan and their two research assistants are also missing."

"That is very bad, Jack. It sounds like Corliss has gone totally off the rails. What are you going to do?"

"Find them."

"How can I help?"

I punched out the words in spurts, like bursts of Morse code. "There's a retired Johnson County sheriff's deputy named Tom Goodell. He probably lives in Olathe. I need a phone number and an address."

"Piece of cake."

My car was parked in the driveway when I got home. I shoved past the door, stamping the snow off my boots.

"Lucy! Where are you?" I called out, my speech restored to a steady cadence.

She didn't answer but the dogs did. They came flying down the stairs, jumping on my legs, circling and racing back upstairs as I headed for my bedroom. The cream-colored carpet was crosscut with wet dog tracks and boot prints filled with dirt, salt, and specks of fine gravel, the trail going up the stairs, into my bedroom, back out, and down the hall to Lucy's, the mess renewing the suspicions I had when I realized she'd searched my room a week ago.

"There you are," Lucy said from the bottom of the stairs.

I looked over the rail. She was in her stocking feet, carrying a vacuum cleaner. I was on edge, trying to rein myself in and not doing a very good job of it.

"What were you doing in my bedroom?"

She came upstairs, set the vacuum cleaner down in the hall, uncoiled the cord, and plugged it in. "Trying to catch your damn dogs so I could dry their feet off before they tracked up the whole house, but they're faster than me so all three of us left our tracks."

She didn't look away, her sharp tone telling me she didn't care for mine, letting me know that I was pushing her buttons. I gave her a disbelieving look, eyebrow raised, jaw set.

"What? You think I was snooping around in your room? Give me a break. You want to clean up the mess, be my guest," she said, throwing up her hands.

"Where have you been?"

"You know where I've been. I spent the night at Simon's."

"I meant this morning. Where were you this morning?"

"I got some breakfast and went to the grocery store."

"I told you last night that I needed my car today. Why didn't you answer your phone or call me back?"

Her face reddened as she crossed her arms over her chest and turned her back to me, her shoulders rising and falling. She stood like that for a moment and then faced me, her hands on her hips, her even color restored.

"Jack, you kind of remind me of my dad and I get the feeling I remind you a little bit of your daughter. But that's not who we are, either one of us. I'm sorry I didn't get the car back to you any sooner but you can't run my life or chew me out when I come home too late or don't answer the phone every time you call. Look at us. We're a couple of beat-up people who could get through the day a little easier if we cut each other some slack."

I didn't know what to say, even though I knew she was right. I was cranked up; raw, and worried with none of the control she was using to back away from a fight I was starting.

"Where are my car keys?"

She handed them to me and I went into my bedroom, opened the closet, and took down my gun case. I clipped the holster to my belt in the small of my back and was sliding my Glock into place when Lucy appeared in the doorway.

"What in the world are you doing?" she asked.

"I made a promise to Maggie Brennan that I wouldn't let anything happen to her. The police can't find her or Corliss or their research assistants."

"And you can? You know something they don't know?"

I pulled my jacket on. It was cut below the waist, covering my gun as long as I didn't try to touch my toes.

"I know what I'm doing," I said, my knees buckling, twisting me to the side as I held on to the closet door.

"Knowing is only half the battle, G.I. Joe. You sure you can handle the other half? When you're done doing the Twist, maybe you can show me the Mashed Potato."

I sat on the edge of my bed. "I'm fine. I just need a breather."

She came over to me and put her hands on my shoulders. "Give me the car keys, Jack."

I looked up at her. "Why?"

"You need a driver. It's bad enough that you're probably going to shoot yourself. I don't need you wrecking the car while you're at it. I'd hate to have to buy my own ride."

Chapter Sixty

"We're all dressed up with no place to go," Lucy said. "We've got to work this thing before we go running off half-cocked to nowhere." She took my arm, pulling me off the bed. "Let's go. Downstairs."

I threw my coat on the sofa as she paced around the living den, studying the Post-its on the walls. My muscles quit twitching as I watched her think. She was right about us. We were both beat up, too many of our wounds self-inflicted. We needed more than a little slack from one another. We needed a hand up and she'd given me hers.

"Okay," she said, stopping in the middle of the room. "What do we know that we didn't know yesterday?"

"Start with the article in today's paper."

I handed it to her, giving her time to read it, then told her about my conversation with Rachel Firestone.

She tucked the paper under her arm, took another lap around the living den, stopping across from me.

"Working theory—Corliss is responsible for the disappearance of Maggie, Janet, and Gary. Worst case—they're dead. Best case—they will be soon if we don't find them."

"Agreed," I said.

"It's pretty tough to snatch three people all at once," she said. "Especially when two of them are young and could put up a fight, like the research assistants."

"Even if Corliss had a gun, he's got to put them in a car and drive somewhere. He can't do that and watch them at the same time. If he lets one of them drive, he's still got control problems."

"He could tie them up, duct tape them, but that's the kind of thing people in other cars would notice—three people all bundled up and gagged. You can get one, maybe two people in the trunk, but three's a crowd."

"So, he grabs them one at a time," I said.

"Possible, but not likely. Janet and Gary were probably together. Two people are easier to handle than three, but not that much easier. Makes it more likely that he talked them into meeting him somewhere they were familiar with, someplace that wouldn't raise any red flags."

"Could have gone down that way."

"What else makes sense?" she asked.

"He takes them out separately. Kills them where he finds them."

"The most likely place he would have found them is where they live which means the cops would have found their bodies by now," Lucy said. "Besides, that's too spontaneous and Corliss is a planner. Look at how much trouble he went to with Walter Enoch and Tom Delaney, taking the videos where they lived and then going back to kill them. And what about the way he staged Anne Kendall's body?"

"You're right," I said. "Anne came to him about the dream project last Wednesday and she was killed the following Monday. Maggie and I left the institute at the same time on Tuesday. If Janet and Gary were gone by then, I think she would have mentioned it."

"So, he doesn't grab them. He invites them."

"More like he gives them an order. He's their boss."

"He's Janet and Gary's boss, not Maggie's."

"Then he invites her and orders the others," I said.

"That would work. But where's the party?"

"Someplace private, no walk-in traffic."

"Not one of their houses. The cops have been there," Lucy said. "Then where?"

"I don't know but I know where to look. Grab your coat. If Corliss persuaded Maggie, Janet, and Gary to meet him somewhere, there might be something in his office about that location, maybe a calendar entry or a handwritten note like the one with the victim's initials on it. "

The lobby was quiet, as if Tuesday's turmoil had taken place in another dimension of time and space. Nancy Klemp was on duty, nodding as we passed her desk, the starch in her back replaced with a defensive crouch across her shoulders, afraid and ready. Her comparison of the institute to the valley of the shadow of death had been prophetic.

I swiped my master key card across the lock sensor for Corliss's office and swung the door open. It had been stripped bare, desk drawers, file cabinets and bookshelves empty, and his computer gone. There was nothing left but the furniture. I picked up the phone on the desk and called Sherry Fritzshall's office.

"Where are you?" she asked.

"In Anthony Corliss's office. What happened to all of his stuff?"

"The police took it."

"When?"

"This morning. What are you doing in his office?"

"My job. Were you here when they took everything?"

"Yes. They had a search warrant. There was nothing I could do."

"Did the warrant cover anything else besides Corliss's office?"

"Yes. It included the offices of Maggie Brennan, Janet Casey, and Gary Kaufman. They took everything that wasn't nailed down."

"Next time, call me."

"If there's a next time, it will be too late to call you."

We checked Maggie's office and the one Janet and Gary used to be certain no scraps had been left behind. A swarm of locusts couldn't have done a more thorough job stripping a field.

"What now?" Lucy asked.

"The IT department. If Corliss is like most of the rest of the world, he exists as much in cyberspace as he does on the ground. It's impossible to cover all those tracks."

We found Frank Gentry at his desk. He stood, stifling the impulse to salute, instead straightening and tightening his regimental striped necktie.

"I need your help," I said.

"Then you've got it."

"I assume all the institute's computers are networked."

"They are. Desktops, laptops, Blackberries and iPhones,

anything that's wired or wireless. If we provide it, it syncs to the network."

"What about backup?"

"I won't bore you with the details, but if it was done on one of our machines in the last twelve months we've got it."

"Except for everything Sherry Fritzshall told you to dump," Lucy said.

Gentry's face burned but he didn't flinch or duck Lucy's shot. "Except for that."

I said, "The police took Anthony Corliss and Maggie Brennan's computers and the ones that Janet Casey and Gary Kaufman used. I need you to print their calendars for the last year."

"What are you looking for?"

"Meetings they may have had somewhere besides at the institute."

"Then I'll check expense records too. If they spent any money for it, there will be an expense voucher and a reimbursement record."

"Great. How long will all that take?"

He glanced at his watch. "Give me an hour."

It took him fifty-three minutes.

"Here you go," Gentry said, handing me a sheaf of papers. "Calendars and expense records."

"Anything jump out?" I asked, knowing that he would have studied the records before giving them to me.

He plucked Corliss's calendar for October of last year from the middle of the stack and put it on top, reading the entry for the twelfth. "Art gallery, noon, lunch."

"What art gallery?"

"It's not really an art gallery, at least not one open to the public. We just call it that. It's where Mr. Harper keeps the pieces of his art collection that aren't on display here or in one of his homes or that aren't on loan to a real gallery or museum. He also uses it for off-campus meetings and retreats."

"Where is it?"

"In the Crossroad's District near Twentieth and Oak. It used to be a brewery," he said, jotting the address down on the calendar.

"Would Corliss have been allowed to use it?"

"Sure, subject to availability. It's one of the perks for the project directors. All he had to do was make a reservation. There's also an expense record for that day," Gentry said, thumbing through the pages. "Lunch for four people, thirty-eight dollars."

"How would Corliss get in?"

"You need a key card, just like here. There are several of them. Ms. Fritzshall's secretary keeps them."

I called Sherry. "How many keys are there to Harper's art gallery?"

"Why? What's this about?"

"I'll explain later. How many keys?"

"Four."

"Where are they?"

"My secretary keeps them. She hands them out if someone reserves the gallery."

"Ask her if anyone reserved it in the last day or two."

"Hold on," she said, coming back on the line a moment later. "Anthony Corliss reserved the gallery for yesterday. Gary Kaufman picked up the key Tuesday afternoon and hasn't returned it."

Chapter Sixty-one

Today was Thursday. I checked Corliss's calendar for yesterday. He had nothing scheduled. Neither did Maggie, Janet Casey, or Gary Kaufman.

I reconstructed what I knew of their movements over the last two days. I had talked to Corliss on Tuesday morning just before Kent and Dolan took a crack at him but I hadn't seen him since. I rode down the elevator Tuesday evening with Maggie, commenting what a good thing it was that the employees had been given Wednesday off, Maggie replying that a day of rest suited her. Neither had said anything about a meeting at the Gallery. I knew less about Janet and Gary's movements since I'd last talked to them on Monday.

Kent's and Dolan's interrogation may have convinced Corliss that the walls would soon come tumbling down, pushing him over the edge. He could have reserved the gallery by phone and instructed Gary to pick up the key, using the fact that the institute was closed on Wednesday as a reason to meet there.

I got a key to the gallery from Sherry's secretary and called Quincy Carter after Lucy and I were in the car. He didn't answer, confirming Rachel's warning that he had cut me off. I left him a message telling him about the gallery and that Lucy and I were on our way there.

"I know why you called Carter but why make sure he knows that's where we're going?" Lucy asked.

"Motivation. Even if he doesn't think it's a good lead, he'll want to get there before we do. All things considered, I'd rather he go through the door first."

My back arched as I spoke, wedging me against the headrest, spasms genuflecting me in my seat, my gun pressing on my spine.

"Hey, Sparky," she said. "Remember me. Lucy Trent. Kick-ass in the clutch."

"You'd like that, being first through the door, wouldn't you?"

"Damn straight I would."

We were northbound on Main, climbing the long, steep hill from the Plaza. The snowplows had done their best, but the ice was stubborn and cars were stranded on the slope, turning our drive into a slow motion slalom. Lucy goosed and cajoled the car, keeping the tires rolling but not spinning, cresting the hill with a broad smile.

A few blocks later, we did the downhill run on Main, a sweeping descent, the Liberty Memorial on the left, Hallmark Cards' headquarters and Crown Center on the right, Lucy nudging the wheel and working the brakes, turning right on Twentieth, grill smoke coming from the Hereford House cutting the late morning air.

"Stop here," I said, after we crossed Oak.

Lucy eased to the curb half a block from the gallery. We walked the rest of the way. There were no cars, civilian or police, parked along Twentieth. The street had been plowed, obliterating tire tracks that would have been left by anyone going into or leaving the gallery and there were no footprints in the snow on the sidewalk or on the three steps leading to the entrance.

The maroon brick building was narrow across the front, set long and deep into its lot. A heavy wooden door was cut into the brick and shrouded beneath an arch. The parking lot on the east side was empty.

I looked east and west on Twentieth, then north and south on McGee, the next cross street east of the gallery. Traffic was light. I gave Carter a few minutes and then turned to Lucy.

"Showtime."

She held her hand out to me, palm up. "Me first. Give me your gun."

"Carter shows up and sees you with a gun, could be a lot of trouble."

"I'll tell him I took it from you so you wouldn't accidentally shoot yourself."

I smiled. "Kick-ass in the clutch. I can't wait to see this."

I handed her my gun and the key card and followed her to the front door. She tried the handle but the door was locked. She ran the card across the sensor, the lock giving way with a firm click.

Holding the gun with both hands, arms extended down in front of her, she leaned against the door, pushing it open an inch, testing the sound it would make, waiting a beat for a reaction from the other side. The door and the gallery were silent. She looked back at me, one step below her. I nodded and she ducked her chin, slammed her shoulder into the door, and we blew across the threshold. Lucy went to the right and I went to the left, dividing the field of fire for anyone who may be waiting for us.

The door opened into the main gallery, a broad, high-ceilinged hall with smaller rooms on each side. Paintings hung on the walls, interspersed with sculptures mounted on pedestals and the floor. There were no lights on, the only illumination coming through the open door and the windows, leaving the recesses of the main hall in shadow. Wide stairs at the back led to a landing, an additional set of stairs at each end continuing to the second floor.

Anthony Corliss was the only one waiting and he was dead. His body lay across the stairs. He was nude, his chest and belly a torn quilt of stab wounds, his blood running down the stairs into a dark puddle on the floor, his right ear gone, another souvenir, a serrated gash on the side of his head taking its place.

We kept our distance from Corliss's body, not wanting to disturb the scene any more than was necessary to make certain no one else was in the building. Lucy made a quick check of the side rooms and the second floor.

"It's clear," she said.

I walked outside, standing on the front steps, and started to punch in Carter's number on my phone when I saw him turn the corner from Oak, his partner McNair riding shotgun. Lucy came up behind me and slipped my gun back into the holster. I leaned against the wall and shook, the bricks absorbing the tremors, Lucy squeezing my arm.

McNair got out of the car, pushed past us like we weren't there, and into the Gallery. Carter stopped at the foot of the steps.

"Who is it?" he asked me.

"Anthony Corliss. He was stabbed to death. The killer stripped him and cut off his ear."

"Naked and mutilated. Staged for us. Just like Anne Kendall."

"The way it looks."

"It's not being wrong about Corliss that bothers me," Carter said.

"I know. It's being late."

Chapter Sixty-two

Cops, ambulances, news crews, and gawkers came in predictable succession, sawhorses and yellow tape keeping people where they belonged. Lucy and I had found the body so our place was inside the perimeter until Carter cut us loose. He put Lucy in the backseat of his unmarked and me in a squad car. We weren't suspects but he was playing it straight, making certain that he got each of our stories instead of one we'd told each other.

Carter gave McNair the perfect job, one where he could do no harm, stationing him at the entrance of the Gallery, deciding who got in like a bouncer working the rope line at a hot nightclub. McNair was in his element, strutting without straining.

I looked out the window at the gathering crowd. People love a parade. They're drawn by the pomp and pageantry, the marching bands and smiling faces. Fathers hoist little kids on their shoulders, those too big for shoulders climbing lampposts or straddling mailboxes for a better view.

The dead man is just as big a draw, the spectacle of the crime scene offering a dangerous whiff of mortality. Its attraction is hypnotic. Though some people are afraid to look while others can't bear to look away, no one wants to miss any of it. The visceral reminder of our shared vulnerability tweaks a primal fear, leaving us entranced and relieved that this time wasn't our time.

Rachel Firestone jostled her way to a sawhorse directly across from me, waving until I nodded, holding her thumb to her ear and her pinky to her mouth, gesturing me to call her. Jason Bolt tapped her on the shoulder, saving me from responding. Rachel gave me a parting wave and followed him into the crowd.

I settled back against the seat, my assumptions about this case once again upended. Corliss wasn't the perfect fit but he was the best fit I had, not because the evidence against him was overwhelming. It wasn't. It was circumstantial, reinforced by more assumptions predicated on his relationships with the victims, their shared history of abuse, and what had happened to Kimberly Stevens in Wisconsin. My suspicion of Corliss depended as much on what I didn't know as what I did know. The biggest gap in my knowledge was that there was no plausible alternative.

Having guessed right about the Gallery was small consolation, though Corliss's murder had given me that plausible alternative—Gary Kaufman. He had picked up the key to the Gallery from Sherry Fritzshall's secretary. When I talked to him on Monday he was nonchalant about the deaths of Delaney and Blair, saying that we all died, adding that it made no difference if a few people went ahead of schedule. I passed it off as lame humor and even more lame philosophy, though his wife, Janet, had recoiled, admonishing him that two people were already dead, as if to say that was enough. It was a reach to now put the murders on Kaufman, but that's what you did when you guessed wrong and had nothing else.

If Gary Kaufman were the killer, I had little doubt that Maggie Brennan was next on his list. He'd save his wife for last, debating whether to end his spree with a murder-suicide or just another murder. I knew my latest scenario was a castle in the air, the foundation built on missing pieces. I called Simon, hoping he had found some of them.

"What's up chief?" he asked.

"Corliss is dead." I gave him the quick and dirty.

"Since Kaufman had the key to the Gallery, sounds like that puts him at the top of the leader board."

"Only because there's not much competition. You told me he had a juvie record. What did you find out about that?"

"Those records are impossible to get into. Best I could do was check newspaper reports, see if there were any stories that matched the location and time frame."

"And?"

"Kaufman grew up in a suburb of Las Cruces, New Mexico. I found a story in the local newspaper about a kid charged with animal cruelty around the same time Kaufman's record pops up. The kid in the newspaper story was put on probation. The paper didn't identify him because he was a juvenile. A week or so later, there's a letter to the editor from a woman who says it was her cat the kid killed and that he should have been tried as an adult and sent to jail."

"Tell me you found the woman and talked to her."

"Got off the phone with her about twenty minutes ago. She's old and hard of hearing and she slurs her words like she's half in the bag or maybe she had a stroke. Anyway, from what I could make out, she claims the kid strangled her cat, gutted it, and amputated its paws. When I asked her if the kid's name was Gary Kaufman, she started crying."

"Kaufman wouldn't be the first kid to graduate from torturing animals to being a serial killer."

"One weird thing," Simon said. "She asked what kind of trouble Kaufman was in and I asked her what made her think he was in trouble and she says mine was the second call she'd gotten about him. The first one was from a policeman but she couldn't remember his name or where he was calling from."

"I'm betting it was Quincy Carter. How about Tom Goodell? Any luck tracking him down?"

"That's not as easy I thought it'd be. He's not on the grid. No address, no utilities, no credit cards."

"He's an old guy, probably in his eighties and not in the best health. I remember him saying that his son is a cop. Works in Lenexa or maybe in Leawood. Could be he's living with his son. Check it out."

"I'm on it," he said, hanging up.

Carter opened the door and slid in beside me. "Next time, I'll take your call."

"Wouldn't have mattered. We were both late."

"The coroner will figure the time of death but I'm betting Corliss has been dead at least twelve hours."

"Maybe longer than that," I said. "There were no tracks in the snow on the sidewalk or on the steps. The snow probably covered the killer's footprints and it stopped snowing during the night."

"No tracks in front but there's a door in the back. Leads into an alley. We found footprints and tire tracks."

"I guess I'm rusty. I should have sent Lucy around to the back and taken the front myself."

"No. You should have stayed out of it," Carter said. "Like I told you. And I should have known you wouldn't. Would have been better if I had arrested you when I had the chance."

"Don't feel bad. I found a body for you."

"But no killer. Thanks a lot. I've got to admit that Corliss looked like the right guy especially after I got an earful from that lawyer, Jason Bolt."

"He tell you about the coed at the University of Wisconsin?" I asked.

"You too, huh. Even had the lawyer from up there call me. So, I talked to the detective who investigated that girl's death. Said it was accidental or suicide. No evidence it was a homicide."

"Everyone we look at in this case has dirt on them, but not killer dirt."

"Including your boss. Bolt also told me about Peggy Murray, tried to convince me that Milo Harper murdered her. We ran the traps on that one too. Another accident."

"Bolt's doing what lawyers do. Stir up a lot of shit, hope enough of it sticks to turn into money."

"Harper's problem, not mine. I didn't buy him or Leonard Nagel as killers and I started falling out of love with Corliss when we had a handwriting expert examine the list with the victims' initials on it that you found in his desk. Preliminary analysis says it's not Corliss's handwriting. We're trying to match it with handwriting samples from other people at the institute but that will take time."

"Maybe the killer wrote it and planted it in Corliss's

desk, same as he planted Anne Kendall's ID badge in Leonard Nagel's desk."

"Or maybe Corliss found it and knew who the killer was, which got him carved·up. Tell me how you tripped to the gallery."

I ran through it for him. He took notes on a spiral pad, stuffing the pad in his shirt pocket when I finished.

"So Kaufman is in the mix."

"Not just because he had the key to the gallery. He was busted for strangling and mutilating a cat when he was a teenager. That shit is like an advanced placement class in serial killer school."

He looked at me, eyes wide. "I don't want to know how you know about Kaufman's juvenile record."

"Then don't ask. How did you find out about it?"

Carter smiled. "You think I'm sitting on my ass waiting for you to call me? I'm like Santa Claus. I've got a list and I'm checking it twice."

"What's your take on Kaufman?"

He shrugged. "Could be him but the cat story doesn't do it for me."

"Why not?"

"It may not have happened."

Chapter Sixty-three

"What do you mean? A friend of mine you don't want to know about talked to the woman that owned the cat. He got the story from her."

"And I talked to the prosecutor's office in Las Cruces. Had them dig out the file. The woman was a drunk then and she's still a drunk. When Kaufman was a kid he liked to chase her cat. Then, one day the cat disappeared. Except for one of the paws that turned up in the woman's mailbox."

"So, no strangled, gutted cat."

"Right. Kaufman denied having anything to do with the cat but he had a nickel bag of marijuana in his pocket when he was picked up. He pled to a misdemeanor possession charge and the animal cruelty count was dropped for lack of evidence. After that, he stayed out of trouble."

I sighed. "I don't get it. Leonard Nagel is a registered sex offender only maybe he got a bum deal. Anthony Corliss was run out of the University of Wisconsin on a

sexual harassment charge where the victim ends up
dead and, depending on whose lawyer you talk to, he
may have gotten hosed. And Gary Kaufman was a
teenage psychopath except there's no proof of that."

"Like you said, every one of these people was dirty."

I took a deep breath. "Okay, let's look at it another
way. The killer planted evidence in Leonard Nagel's
desk to implicate him in Anne Kendall's murder and
may have done the same thing with the list of initials in
Corliss's desk. For that matter, the killer could have
arranged for Gary Kaufman to pick up the key to the
gallery to make certain we'd focus on him."

"So, the killer is leading us around by the nose, getting us to chase the wrong guys."

"Not just any wrong guys. Each of them had something in their background that would make us suspicious even if it didn't hold up when we took a close look
at it."

"Maybe that was the point," Carter said. "It's a classic
misdirection play. Keep you and me running in a dozen
different directions."

"And the longer we do that, the worse the odds are
that we find Maggie Brennan, Janet Casey, and Gary
Kaufman alive."

Carter nodded. "It's like after a tornado. You start
out looking for survivors but at some point it's all about
finding the bodies."

"The killer had to know what baggage Leonard and
Corliss and Kaufman were carrying."

"I know you've only been at the institute a few days
but who had access to that kind of information?"

"Milo Harper knew about Corliss and he might have
known about the first sexual harassment complaint
against Leonard and he knew what was in the victims'

dream project files but there's no way he could have known about Anne Kendall's sexual harassment complaint or Kaufman's juvenile record."

"The description of her nightmare Anne Kendall wrote for Corliss was about being sexually abused. Stands to reason she might have also told him about Leonard Nagel coming on to her. And Kaufman would have had to explain his juvenile record to get into the grad program at Wisconsin with Corliss."

"That puts some but not all of the information in Corliss's head and he's dead. We're looking for someone who knew all of it."

"One way or another," Carter said, "everything was available to someone willing to dig for it. Your anonymous friend found out about Kaufman. The sexual harassment charges against Leonard were on the office grapevine and the criminal case against him in Colorado was public record, same as the Wisconsin lawsuit against Corliss. Plus, we know that Leonard hacked into the dream project files, which means the killer could have done the same thing to learn about the victims' nightmares. Who at the institute has the skill set to do all that?"

I shook my head, not able to get my mind around what I was about to say. "There's only one person. His name is Frank Gentry. He's head of the IT department."

"You know if he's at work today?"

"He was there a while ago."

"Let's hope he hasn't gone home early."

"I'll go with you," I said.

Carter laughed. "I don't think so. You wait here. I'm going to have someone drive you to police headquarters so you can give your statement."

"I already told you what I know."

"Yes, you did. But you didn't write it down and you know we have to have it in writing."

"I can do that tomorrow."

"No. I don't want to take a chance that you might forget something. I want you to cover every detail, make it as specific as you can. Take all the time in the world. Be sure you get it right."

"If you want me out of your hair that badly, why don't you just arrest me?"

"Too much paperwork. What I'd like to do is Taser you again but I'll settle for you and Lucy spending the rest of the day with a pad of paper and a pen and bad coffee. Sit tight and I'll find your driver."

I waited until Carter was inside the gallery and then got out of the squad car. I stepped between two sawhorses, putting the front row of spectators between the yellow tape and me, walking the perimeter until I found Lucy sitting alone in the backseat of Carter's unmarked. She turned my way and I signaled her to follow me. A moment later, we had threaded our way through the crowd to the north side of Twentieth.

We walked west toward my car as two cops pulled alongside it and stopped, boxing it in. We ducked behind a van parked at the curb as the cop in the passenger seat got out and scanned the crowd, talking into the radio pinned to his shirt. The driver left him there, leaning against the car.

"What the hell is going on?" Lucy asked.

"Carter wants us to give our statements."

"I know. That's what the detective who questioned me said."

"Yeah, but Carter will make sure it takes the rest of the day and night to get it done."

"He wants us off the street."

"As long as he can get away with it," I said. "Which may be too long for Maggie Brennan and the others. The killer has been sending us down one blind alley after another and I may have just sent Carter down another one."

"What now? We're not getting near your car with that cop on top of it."

A city bus westbound on Twentieth rolled toward us, blocking the cop's view.

"I hope you've got exact change," I said.

We walked alongside the bus until it stopped near the intersection with Oak. The doors opened and a stream of people descended. I looked back to the east. The cop who'd been guarding my car was coming our way. We weren't fugitives but he could hold us long enough for Carter to decide that we were material witnesses and take us in.

A black SUV with tinted windows cut in front of the bus. Rachel Firestone rolled down the passenger window and leaned out.

"Need a ride?"

"As far as you're going," I said, climbing into the backseat with Lucy.

A woman with swimmer's shoulders and close cut brown hair was behind the wheel, her deep brown eyes studying us in the rearview mirror.

"Where to?" the woman asked.

"Just drive," Rachel said.

Chapter Sixty-four

"Why were you and Lucy about to be arrested?" Rachel asked, turning toward the backseat.

"What makes you think we were going to be arrested?"

"I'm a reporter. I notice little things like the cops putting you in separate cars, and the two of you sneaking out of those cars and hiding in the crowd before trying to get on a bus instead of into your car which is being guarded by a cop who was about to nab you when Edie and I saved the day. You know, the kind of details that win Pulitzers."

"We were invited, not arrested," I said.

"That was some RSVP. But I'm glad Edie and I are not accomplices."

"Your conscience is clear."

She laughed. "A reporter with a deadline doesn't have a conscience. What happened back there?"

"I told you that I'd give you the story when it's over and it isn't over."

"And I just saved your ass. That's a deal changer."

"For you, not for me. If you've got a problem with that, pull over and we'll get out."

Edie slowed, swinging the wheel to the curb.

"It's okay, Edie," Rachel said. "He's stubborn enough to get out and then all I'll have is a story I can tell but can't write."

"Thanks," I said.

"Don't mention it because I won't. Not in the paper, anyway. Makes me part of the story and that's no good."

My cell phone rang. Caller ID said it was Quincy Carter.

"Don't answer it. Turn it off," Lucy said. "They can triangulate our location using cell towers."

I shook my head. "I've got enough problems without making Carter chase me."

I flipped the phone open.

"Hey, Carter."

"Man, you are a colossal pain in the ass, you know that!"

"What are you going to do? Taser me again?"

"If McNair doesn't get to you first, only he's gonna shoot you."

"I'll take those odds. He'll probably pull the wrong gun out of his pants."

"Remember you said that. He just had your car towed. I'm asking you the only way I know how, stay out of this. Let me handle Frank Gentry."

Killers, especially serial killers, don't look or act alike. They're the Cub Scout leader who bound, tortured, and killed his victims, the computer programmer who lived down the street until he snatched my son, and the crazy-eyed loner who strangled and gutted the neighbor's cat, bad seeds from worse homes with broken brains and disarming smiles. Knowing all that, I couldn't see Frank Gentry on the list and felt bad that I'd put him on it.

"That's a promise I can make," I said and hung up.

"Where to?" Rachel asked.

I gave her Simon's address. She nodded at Edie and we left it at that.

It was past five when Rachel dropped us off at Simon's brick and limestone ranch house. The driveway and walk had been shoveled but the clean concrete would be a faint memory if the front that was moving in brought more snow. A low, gray cloud layer was pushing dusk into nightfall, the wind picking up.

"Nice job," I told Lucy. "If nothing else works out, you can buy your own shovel and go into business."

She poked me in the arm. "It's good exercise."

Simon opened the door and Lucy swallowed him with a hug. Simon eased her arms down to her side; his eyes and mouth wide open as he looked at me over her shoulder, his expression saying *how about that.* I answered with a nod and smile that said good for you but I'll break both your legs above the knee if you break her heart.

"What's the latest?" he asked, leading us into the bedroom at the front of the house that he'd converted into an office.

I dropped into a chair and told him what we knew, ending with Frank Gentry.

"You really think it could be Gentry?" Lucy asked. "He looked as ordinary as mayonnaise to me. Came to work in a shirt and tie. How do you kill all those people and keep it together like that?"

"I had one case where the killer dumped the victim in the bathtub, poured bleach on the body and then had sex with his girlfriend on the bathroom floor. Coming to work like nothing happened is easy for someone like that but I don't think Gentry is the killer."

"Why not?" she asked.

"Unless we find out that Corliss dreamt he'd be slaughtered on the steps of an art gallery, his murder breaks the killer's pattern of mimicking the victims' nightmares. Corliss was killed for a different reason. Plus, judging from the extensive stab wounds, the killer was out of control. We saw Gentry today. He didn't look like someone who'd gone over the edge."

"Meaning," Lucy said, "the killer stays on the spree until it's over."

"You ask me," Simon said, "things don't look good for Maggie Brennan and the research assistants if they haven't turned up by now."

"I know. That's what worries me. Carter will spend the rest of the night questioning Gentry and the longer this goes, the more likely it is that all we will find is bodies."

"We've been looking for a place the killer could convince Maggie and the others to go without a fight," Lucy said. "But Corliss was the only victim we found at the art gallery. Maybe the killer is picking them off one at a time, finding a place each of them is willing to go."

"Makes sense," I said. "We don't know enough about Janet Casey and Gary Kaufman to know where to look but there's one person who might be able to help us with Maggie Brennan."

"Tom Goodell," Simon said. "And I found him."

"Where is he?"

"Living with his son, like you thought. They're in Olathe."

Chapter Sixty-five

"Olathe is one of the fastest growing cities in the country," Simon said.

"Really," Lucy answered. "Gee, that's fascinating. You know any more cool stuff like that?"

He was driving, Lucy in front, both of them giggling, slapping each other on the arm, drunk on love. It took something that strong to beat back the fear of being too late again. I envied them.

I was in the back, stretched out across the seat, my arm over my eyes. I had been riding the troughs all day, shaking and contorting, brain fog rolling in and out. The thirty-minute car ride was a chance to rest and buy time.

"Does Goodell know why we're coming to see him?" I asked.

"I told him you wanted to talk to him about a cold case. He asked which one. I told him the one about Maggie Brennan."

"What did he say?"

"He said it's about time."

* * *

Tom Goodell had the collapsed build of a tall, once powerful man; his shoulders still broad but rounded, his neck thick but stooped, his chest wide, his belly overflowing his belt. His cheeks were pinwheeled with red spider veins, his hands were age-spotted, and his fingers were gnarled with arthritis but his gaze was sharp and clear when he looked me in the eye.

"Missed you at lunch yesterday," he said.

"Got tied up, sorry."

"Well, come on in."

He led us into the den where there was a fire burning and a television on. A small boy, maybe ten, was sprawled on the floor near the fire, staring at the TV. He motioned us to a couch across from the fireplace.

"Hit it, junior," Goodell said to the boy. "Upstairs and get your homework done before your daddy comes home and kicks both our asses."

"Both our asses, Grandpa?"

"You bet, junior. Yours for not getting your homework done and mine for not making you." The boy scrambled to his feet and headed for the stairs. "Hey, boy! Aren't you forgetting something?"

The boy blushed and smiled, trotted over to Goodell who bent down, offering a rough whiskered cheek for the boy to kiss, hugging the boy and brushing the boy's hair with his hand, the boy returning the gesture, tugging on Goodell's thin white hair, both of them laughing. Goodell waited until the boy was gone.

"Okay, then," he said, settling into his recliner. "Let's talk murder."

"It's a long story," I began.

"You see that," Goodell said, interrupting and pointing to the television. "That thing's on the whole goddamn day. Keeps me company when the kid's in school and my son's on the job, now that he and his wife are split up. I favor MSNBC over those morons at Fox but I've been mostly watching the local news this week."

"That so?"

"It is so. And you see that," he said, pointing to a police scanner sitting on an end table next to the couch. "I'm not one of those old cops who sits around waiting for a heart attack or the balls to stick a gun in my mouth." He sat up in his chair and leaned toward me, speaking slowly. "I pay attention."

"Then you know about the murders," I said.

"You want me to recite their names for you? Your friend there said you wanted to talk about Maggie Brennan. Well, then, let's get to it."

"A woman named Maggie Brennan works at the Harper Institute. The murder victims were involved with the project she's working on. I need to know whether she's the same Maggie Brennan as the one in your cold case."

"Why?" he asked, narrowing his eyes, bearing down on me.

"She's missing. I'm hoping you can help me find her."

He leaned back in his recliner, clasping his hands across his belly. "They're one and the same."

"What makes you so certain?"

"Unsolved case like that doesn't leave you. Not ever. You know that. She was the only survivor. I took an interest, kept up with her as much as I could. Lost track of her for a long time but I found her again when she moved back here."

"Have you been in touch with her?" Lucy asked.

"Just who are you, missy?"

"I'm Lucy Trent."

"What's your interest in this?"

"I'm helping Jack."

"You know what you're doing?"

"I was a cop for five years."

He snorted. "Another ex-cop. Well, I guess we all used to be something else. And, no, I haven't talked to her and don't plan on it."

"Why not?" she asked.

"You ask me that question again when you find her. Her parents, Sam and Gretchen Brennan, owned a place near Spring Hill, that's about twenty miles or so from here. It wasn't much, a few hundred acres. Sam's brother, Charlie, owned a place west of theirs, twice as big. The brothers inherited the land from their parents. Charlie was the favored son so he got the bigger spread. Caused all kind of problems between them but Charlie said they'd patched things up and we never did find anybody who could prove otherwise.

"It was wintertime, fifty years ago this month. Early one morning, old Charlie, he goes over to Sam and Gretchen's place. He said he and Sam were fixin' to work on some fence they shared, get it ready for spring.

"Charlie pulls up in Sam's yard and knocks on the door but he don't get an answer. He tries the door and it's unlocked which wasn't unusual in those days. Folks didn't have so much to be afraid of like they do now. He goes in the house and calls out a hello and he still don't get an answer. So, he goes looking upstairs and he finds Sam and Gretchen lying in bed, cut to pieces and bloody as all hell. Well, the sight of them damn near drives him crazy. He climbs in the bed, puts his arms around them and starts screaming.

"After he calms down a bit, he goes looking for Maggie. Ten years old, she was. Same age as my grandson. He finds her hiding in the bushes outside the house wearing a little slip of a nightgown and near froze to death. That's when he calls the sheriff's dispatcher, crying and crazy, hollerin' that Sam and Gretchen are dead and he's got Maggie. He hangs up before the dispatcher can get anything else out of him. The sheriff, Ed Beedles, he hightails it out to Spring Hill and I'm right behind him. I was Ed's deputy. Been on the job ten years by then but I swear to Jesus I never seen anything like what I saw that morning."

Chapter Sixty-six

"We had a big snow the night before and it was hell getting to Sam's place. Some of the county roads in those days weren't much more than a dirt track.

"By the time I got there, Charlie and Maggie were in the front yard, both of them covered in blood. They looked like something out of one of those slasher movies. Ed's out of his car, walking right up to Charlie, sticking his shotgun in Charlie's face, telling Charlie to let Maggie go only Charlie holds onto her like she's a hostage. I roll my window down, throw my car door open, and get a bead on Charlie. I holler to Ed, are we okay here, Sheriff, and Ed, he asks Charlie are we okay and Charlie says yeah and it's all over. He lets Maggie go and I stay with him until another deputy come and then I went into the house.

"I find Ed in Sam and Gretchen's bedroom, just staring at their bodies. They were a mess. Coroner said each of them was stabbed more than twenty-five times.

Ed, he kept saying over and over, what kind of person does a thing like this and I kept answering Lord only knows."

Lucy asked, "Why do you think the killer spared Maggie?"

"Don't know that he meant to. Maggie was in her bedroom. She had a balcony with double-wide French doors. She said when the killer came for her, she jumped off the balcony and ran and hid in the fields."

"Jumped?" Lucy asked. "How far down was it?"

"Two stories," Goodell said, whistling softly. "Two stories onto hard froze ground, barefoot, and in her nightgown. Sprained her ankle and kept on running. Haven't heard anything like it before or since."

Lucy shook her head. "Doesn't seem possible."

"No, it don't. No, it don't. We never did catch the killer, never even came close. This all happened right after the Clutter family got murdered out near Holcomb. Sheriff Beedles drove out to Garden City to talk to Smith and Hickock after they was captured but there was nothing to link them to the Brennan case."

"Did Charlie's story stand up?" Lucy asked.

"Sure did. He always told the same story and he passed the polygraph."

"What about the physical evidence? Did that match up to Charlie's story?" she asked.

"Well, you got to remember it was 1959 and we were a small operation back then. We didn't know CSI from ABC. There was a blood trail from Sam and Gretchen's bedroom into Maggie's room, led right up to the balcony. Maggie said the killer had hold of her, but his hands were so bloody she was able to squirm her way out. That's when she jumped."

"What about the murder weapon?" Lucy asked.

"Coroner said it was probably a hunting knife and Sam, he was a hunter. Charlie said Sam had a hunting knife but we went through Sam's things and never did find it. Could have been the murder weapon but we don't know for sure."

"Did Charlie take Maggie in?" Lucy asked.

"Nope. He shipped her off to his sister in California. Charlie sold Sam's place and sent his sister the money. The next day, Charlie drove his truck off the road and into a culvert and was killed. We ruled it an accident but I don't know it wasn't on purpose. He was never right again after what happened."

"How did Maggie handle it?" Lucy asked.

"'Course I only seen her a few times after that morning before she went to California. That day, she didn't say much except for what happened. She didn't even cry. I took her to the hospital, had her checked out. The doctor said she was in too much shock to cry. Still, I thought it was a mighty odd thing for a child to go through something like that and never shed a tear. The whole time the doctor talked to her, she just picked the dried blood off her fingernails like it was old paint."

"Sounds like she was one strong little girl," Lucy said.

Goodell looked at her sharply, hesitating. "She was all of that. Squeezed my hand like she was full grown when I walked her into the emergency room."

"You said you've kept up with her," I said. "How did you know she was at the Harper Institute?"

"It was in the Kansas City paper. They run a business section on Tuesdays with announcements of new people being hired."

"The police have been to her home and she wasn't there. Any idea where we might find her," I asked.

He nodded. "Her parents' place. I used to check the county records from time to time, just to see what happened to it, see if anybody would buy a place with that many ghosts. Maggie bought it right after she moved back. That's how I knew for sure it was her."

"She told me that she lived in the country," I said.

"She told you right. She bought her uncle Charlie's old place too. That's where she lived."

"We need the address for Sam Brennan's farm," I said.

"I expect you do," he said, pushing himself to his feet. "Be right back."

He disappeared down a hall and came back carrying the sagging cardboard box he'd brought to lunch the day he presented his case. He put the box on the coffee table, lifting out a three-ring binder.

"Murder book," he said, handing it to me. "You'll find everything you need in there. Best you take a look at it."

I spread the binder open, leafing through the pages. The crime scene photos were faded, more gray than black and white, though the close-ups of Sam and Gretchen's multiple stab wounds stood out in stark relief. The passage of fifty years hadn't diminished the photographs' power.

There were more photographs showing each room in the house and the black spots on the upstairs hallway tracing the blood trail to its endpoint on Maggie's balcony. The coroner's report gave a dry recitation of the cause of death. Charlie Brennan's handwritten statement matched Tom Goodell's memory.

And, there were newspaper articles from the *Kansas*

City Star. The headline of the first read "Parents Murdered, Child Escapes Killer." The story was wrapped around a split-screen photograph; one-half showing the exterior of the farmhouse, the other half a picture of Maggie surrounded by dolls and scattered gift wrap beneath a banner that read HAPPY BIRTHDAY. I read the opening paragraph in the article.

> Early yesterday morning, Charlie Brennan discovered the mutilated bodies of his brother, Sam Brennan, and sister-in-law, Gretchen, in the Brennans' farmhouse in rural Johnson County, Kansas, five miles west of Spring Hill. He also reported finding the Brennans' ten-year-old daughter, Maggie, in the bushes beneath a second-floor balcony. Sheriff Ed Beedles said there was no evidence of a struggle, suggesting that the Brennans were killed in their sleep. He declined to provide further details, citing the need to keep the investigation confidential until a suspect was apprehended. "The Brennan farmhouse is a quarter mile from the nearest road. People who live in isolated areas without any nearby neighbors have to be especially vigilant to protect themselves from criminals," Sheriff Beedles said, noting that the Brennans had left their house unlocked.

A second article a week later highlighted the sheriff's frustration at the lack of any leads and quoted his plea to the public for information that could lead to the capture and conviction of whomever was responsible. The last article, written on the fifth anniversary of the murders, quoted Sheriff Beedles's successor, Tom Goodell, who said that the investigation was still open though authorities had no suspects or hopes of identifying one. The article also quoted Maggie's aunt, Adele Jensen, who declined the reporter's request to interview Maggie, saying that Maggie was a normal teenager except for her recurrent nightmare that she would die the same way as had her parents.

I pointed Lucy and Simon to the newspaper articles and studied Tom Goodell as he avoided me, fidgeting with the fire in the fireplace, poking the burning embers, stirring a shower of sparks. He had never stopped working this cold case, had sought the advice of the retired cops at our monthly lunch, had kept track of Maggie Brennan all these years and, yet, had not contacted her since she moved back to Kansas City. When Lucy asked him why, he ducked the question.

The murder book gave me an idea of what his answer would be but I had to hear it from him. If he were right, his answer would provide the unity of a complex of phenomena that Kate and Simon had talked about a few nights ago, the real truth, not just the directly visible truth, one filled with horror and sadness and none of Einstein's magnificent feeling.

"Tom," I said, "Maggie Brennan has lived here for over a year. Why haven't you talked with her in all that time? Maybe she remembers something that would help you solve the case. She's had a lifetime to think about what happened. A sixty-year-old woman can be a much better witness than a ten-year-old girl, even after all these years."

He jammed the poker into the burning wood, his

back to me. "Like I told missy, ask me after you find her."

"That may be too late. Why haven't you talked to her?"

He faced me, his eyes flickering, his cheeks reddening. He took a deep breath. "That woman scares me more than anyone I've ever known."

Chapter Sixty-seven

"You know what you're saying," Lucy said.

He grabbed a fresh log from a copper bin next to the fireplace and threw it onto the hot coals, watching as it cracked and burst into flames.

"I reckon that's why I've had such a hard time saying it all these years. Can't hardly believe it myself. I had it in my head that someone else would prove me right."

"What did you see that no one else saw?" I asked.

He stirred the fire again, set the poker down and wiped his hands on his pants. "I never seen anyone as cool as that little girl. Doc said she was in shock, that's why she didn't cry, but I watched her when she didn't think anyone was looking. She always had this tight little smile, like she had a secret. And then there was her hands. She had powerful little hands. Sheriff Beedles, the doctors, the DA, everybody felt so bad for her. A week after the murders, I said something to the sheriff maybe we ought to ask her if she did it since we weren't getting anywhere and he looked at me like I was a crazy man, so after that, I shut my mouth."

"But you kept tabs on her."

He nodded. "Read the local papers where she lived. Every jurisdiction has its unsolved murders but a lot of them seemed to happen near where she lived. After she finished her schooling, she moved every two to three years, usually right after there was a run of dead bodies and no suspects."

I thought about how she had asked me if I thought there was a madman on the loose and whether I would protect her and how, when I promised I would, she had squeezed my arm and told me that she was glad and wouldn't worry. I thought about Janet Casey saying that Maggie always wore the same gray overcoat and how I had met Maggie in the elevator the day after Anne Kendall was murdered wearing a new black coat.

She'd interviewed Tom Delaney and Regina Blair and knew as much as Anthony Corliss did about their nightmares, more than enough to convince Delaney to let her into his apartment and Blair to meet her at the parking garage. Corliss must have told her about Walter Enoch stealing the mail, giving her the leverage she needed to make Enoch open the door for her. And she could have learned about Leonard Nagel and Gary Kaufman in the same way I assumed Corliss had.

The difference between her and Corliss that had kept her off my radar was the improbability of a female serial killer, though she had debunked that as well, cautioning me not to confuse the unfamiliar with the improbable. It had all been there in front of me and I had failed to see it, focusing instead on the familiar and the probable.

"I don't believe it," Lucy said. "A ten-year-old girl. I don't believe it."

"It fits," I said, summarizing everything.

Lucy shook her head. "What if the woman in Las Cruces was telling the truth about Gary Kaufman? He fits a lot better than Maggie Brennan."

"Why? Because she's a woman?" Goodell said. "I've seen figures say as many as eight percent of serial killers are women. They're called quiet killers because people have such a hard time believing that about a woman."

"No," Lucy said. "Because she was ten years old, for Christ's sake! How many ten-year-olds murder their parents?"

"Like I told you," Goodell said, "ask me after you find her."

"The address on the incident report is an RFD address," I said, getting to my feet. "How do we get there?"

My knees buckled as I spoke. Lucy grabbed my arm, keeping me upright. Goodell, one eyebrow raised, stared at me.

"You okay?" he asked.

I tried to answer but my vocal cords froze.

"He's fine," Lucy said. "He's got a movement disorder that makes him shake. It's not a big deal."

"Uh-huh," Goodell said. "You carrying a weapon?" he asked me. I nodded. "Let me have a look at it."

I straightened and reached behind my back, handing him my Glock.

"Damn popgun. You take it, Missy," he said, giving the gun to Lucy.

She smiled and slipped the gun into her jacket pocket.

"Hey," I said, my voice restored.

"Don't hey me," Goodell said. "I'm not riding with anyone shaking and carrying at the same time."

"Who said anything about you riding anywhere?" I asked.

"You got as much chance finding the Brennan place in the dark as I do waking up next to Angelina Jolie."

He disappeared again, this time coming back wearing a parka and carrying a shotgun and a box of shells. "Winchester Speed Pump," he said, loading the gun. "The cure for an old man's bad aim. Let's go."

"What about your grandson?" Lucy asked. "You can't leave him here alone. His father will kick your ass."

"Right you are, missy." He turned to Simon. "Did you use to be a cop, too?"

"No. I stick to computers."

"Then you're elected. My grandson likes video games. Don't let him beat you. He can't stand that."

"No way am I staying here on babysitting duty."

Goodell racked the slide on his shotgun and took a step toward Simon who backed away.

"Someone has to stay," Lucy said. "Jack, Tom, and me, this is what we do."

Simon dropped his chin to his chest, reached into his pocket for his car keys, giving them to Lucy who kissed him on the cheek.

"We won't be gone long," she said.

Lucy drove, taking directions from Goodell. The interstate gave way to a state highway that took us onto a county road hard packed with snow and ice, our headlights the only illumination, the countryside invisible in the darkness, no cars coming from the opposite direction to show us what lay ahead. The road was unmarked, turnoffs impossible to see until we were on top of them. Goodell had been right. We'd have been lost on our own.

"Less than half a mile," he said as we rounded a curve on the road. "It'll be on your right, just past the tree line. Start slowing down or we'll miss it sure as hell."

Lucy eased off the gas, the sound of tires crunching snow breaking the silence. The headlights bounced off the tree line, bare branches glistening with ice. Goodell pointed to the trees with one hand, touching Lucy on her arm with the other.

"Here," he said.

The entrance to the farm was a narrow opening in a tangled hedgerow, branches scraping against the side of the car as we passed through. There was no way to make out the path of the drive except for a set of tire tracks that ran ahead of us. The ground opened up on either side, a rolling expanse gradually climbing toward the farmhouse.

A Chevy Suburban was parked in front of the house. Lucy aimed our headlights at the Suburban as I got out and circled it. The doors were locked. I cupped my hands against the glass to get a look inside but the glare from the headlights blinded me.

"Kill the lights," I said.

Lucy and Goodell got out of Simon's car, Lucy popping the trunk and finding a long-handled flashlight. Goodell took a slender Maglite from his coat pocket. They shined their lights inside the Suburban.

"There's some dark spots on the backseat. Could be blood but I can't tell for sure," Lucy said.

The house stood on a rise facing north, trees framing it on both sides, tall branches towering over the roofline from the back, the outline of a small barn visible on the far side of the trees to the east. There were no lights on that we could see.

I borrowed Lucy's flashlight, running the wide beam across the worn clapboard siding where scattered patches of bare wood mixed with the remains of faded paint. The foundation had settled on the west side, giving the sagging porch a funhouse tilt, the second step missing in the set of four leading from the drive to the porch.

I handed the flashlight back to Lucy and looked at Goodell. He was a statue, clutching the shotgun across his body, his breath coming in short, icy puffs, his eyes darting and watering.

"How old are you, Tom?"

"Eighty-two, next month."

"It passes you by, doesn't it?"

He heaved a sigh. "More like it runs you over."

I took out my cell phone. "I'm going to call a KCPD homicide detective named Quincy Carter. You give him the license plate on the Suburban so he can trace it. Then tell him how to get here and stay on the line to make sure he doesn't get lost. We wouldn't have found this place without your help and he won't either."

He nodded, handing me his shotgun. "Can't miss with this even if you're doing the jitterbug. You'll want this too," he said, passing me his Maglite.

"Thanks."

Carter answered on the first ring.

"Where are you?" he asked.

"Out in the country. How'd you do with Frank Gentry?"

"Like you thought we would. He's clean. He can account for every second of every day for his entire life."

"I'm glad. Tell him I'm sorry for putting you on him."

"You can tell him. We found cars registered to Corliss and Maggie Brennan parked in a lot a block north of the Art Gallery and I heard back from the handwriting expert. Gary Kaufman wrote the list of initials you found in Corliss's desk. I'm thinking that drunken old woman was right about him and her cat."

"Maybe. You have a line on him yet?"

"He's in the wind but I'm betting if we find him we'll find his wife and Maggie Brennan. Though I have to tell you, at the rate we're going, it doesn't look good."

"What's he drive?"

"A Chevy Suburban," Carter said.

I stared at the Suburban and the house. "You're right, it doesn't look good."

"What are you doing out in the country?"

"I'm going to let a friend of mine explain that to you," I said and handed the phone to Goodell.

"Listen up, detective. This is Sheriff Tom Goodell, retired."

I turned to Lucy. "Check out the barn. Then take a look around the back of the house. If there's a door, come in that way. I'll meet you inside."

She marched away, holding the Glock at her side, aiming her flashlight into the darkness. I racked the slide on the shotgun and stepped over the missing stair.

Chapter Sixty-eight

Fifty years later, the door was still unlocked, opening without complaint, the top edge clanging against a bell hanging from a rod bolted to the wall, loud enough to tell anyone inside that they had company. A gust of wind followed me across the threshold, the icy air biting the back of my neck.

I swept the entryway with the Maglite, holding the shotgun level, my finger on the trigger. A chandelier missing half its lightbulbs hung from the ceiling. A wall switch made a hollow click without turning anything on.

The entryway opened into rooms on my left and right, pieces of broken furniture littering the floors. A rat ignored me, chewing on the remnants of an upholstered chair. A hallway ran from the entry to the back of the house, a steep flight of stairs breaking into the middle of the hall on the right.

I stood at the foot of the stairs, listening, the only sound coming from the roof as it groaned against the wind. I shined the Maglite up the stairs, the beam bouncing off warped hardwood and peeling wallpaper. The first stair creaked under my weight, as did the second and third. I stopped, waiting for a sign or sound of life, starting again when no one called out, asking who's there or begging me to hurry.

There was a closed door at the top of the stairs. I opened it a fraction, enough to taste the bitter, coppery smell of blood. I raised the shotgun, eased back on the trigger, steadying the stock under my arm, dropped to one knee, and shoved the door open.

Janet Casey and Gary Kaufman lay side-by-side in a four-poster bed, naked, bound, gagged, and dead, their throats cut, their torsos slit open, their intestines gleaming under my flashlight. I stood and leaned against the wall as tremors ripped through me, muscle spasms snapping me at the waist, twisting me to the floor. Using the shotgun as a crutch, I got to my feet and stumbled into the hall.

A dim light shone from beneath a door at the other end of the hall. I staggered toward it, aiming the barrel chest high, and kicked the door off its hinge, stepping into another bedroom. Double-wide French doors on the back wall leading to a balcony swayed open in the wind.

Maggie Brennan stood on the far side of a double bed wearing a nightgown soaked in crimson, her bloody arms hanging at her sides, her hands empty.

"What took you so long?" she asked me.

"Don't move."

A shaded lamp on a nightstand next to a rumpled bed provided the only light. Her gray overcoat lay on the bed, pockmarked with dark stains I was certain were remnants of Anne Kendall's blood. A throw rug was piled in the center of the hardwood floor, three narrow planks, their bent nails aimed at the ceiling, lay alongside the rug, leaving a six-inch by twelve-inch hole in the floor. She took a step toward me.

"I said, don't move."

"I won't."

Her voice was quiet and cold, her face flat, her expression resigned but unafraid. I knelt next to the hole, catching glimpses of a thick book punctured by a bullet, a jeweled tennis bracelet, a severed finger and ear, a knife flecked with flesh and blood, and a single sheet of pink stationery in familiar handwriting, the first words reading *Dear Daddy, I'm so sorry.* I shook again as my heart slammed against my chest. She took another step.

I forced myself to my feet and aimed the shotgun at her chest. "Don't make me tell you again."

I choked on the words, my breath coming hard. She stayed where she was, watching me until the tremors passed.

"Souvenirs," she said. "If you think about it at all, it's the one really stupid thing I did. Especially taking your daughter's letter. But Milo Harper sent the e-mail about you and then I found the letter and it made such sense, it seemed so orderly. Then, when you walked into Anthony's office last week, I knew you were the one."

"What one?"

"The man in my nightmare, the one that would kill me."

"Your aunt said you dreamt that you would die the same way as your parents did. A man didn't kill them. You did."

"You can't blame me, can you? What was I supposed to say? That I dreamed of killing them again? They'd have put me away. I told the sheriff that a man had come and murdered my parents so my dream had to match the story. You know the funny thing about it?"

"There can't be one."

"Ironic then. That became my nightmare. I kill my parents and, afterward, a man comes to kill me. I assume you saw Janet and Gary. We've done our parts. I trust that you will do yours."

"What happened to you? Did your parents abuse you?"

She laughed. "That would make it easier, wouldn't it? You might almost forgive me or at least feel badly for me."

"Did they?"

"No. They couldn't have loved me more and I couldn't have felt it less. I realized that I was different when I was very young and my mother would hug me and I felt nothing. I started experimenting, trying to feel something, anything. I'd do something good and get nothing out of it. So I tried more intense experiments. We lived on a farm and there were always plenty of small animals around. That was no better but at least it was interesting. Killing my parents settled it for me though it was years before I understood why I have no emotions. There's something missing in my brain, in the ventromedial frontal cortex and the amygdala."

"That's a poor excuse."

"I'm a scientist and scientists don't make excuses. We explain the physical world."

"By killing people? What were they to you? Lab rats?"

"Not in the way you imagine, but in my world, yes. The study of trauma will only take us so far in understanding the brain. The real lessons come in controlling and observing the moment of death. Most of my subjects were tortured and tormented long before I chose them."

"How did you choose them?"

"The ones who'd been traumatized when they were young produced the best nightmares. Milo Harper asked Anthony for some good examples and Anthony let me choose them. I put them to a better use than he would have with his silly lucid dreaming nonsense."

"So you killed them in the name of science?"

"You mock me, but, no. Not all. Some were in the name of necessity, like Anthony Corliss. He told me that Gary suspected I was the killer. Gary even made a list with Tom Delaney, Regina Blair, Walter Enoch, and Anne Kendall's initials and gave it to Anthony as if that was somehow proof. I assured Anthony that Gary was more likely the killer after what he'd done to that poor woman's cat. Anthony suggested the four of us meet at the Art Gallery to clear the air. I brought my gun, knife, duct tape, and rope. The rest, as they say, is commentary."

"How many others were there?"

"Let's just say that it's a statistically significant sample of the weak and pathetic." She raised her hands. "And this house is the biggest and best souvenir of them all. This is where it began and this is where it will end."

She turned and walked out to the end of the balcony, her hands on the waist high wooden rail.

"It's over. Come inside."

She ignored me, rising up and down on her toes as if readying to jump. I crossed the space between us, the shotgun under my right arm, and reached for her shoulder. She whirled around, holding a knife in her right hand that must have been laying on the top of the rail, hidden from me, driving it toward my chest in a short, powerful stroke.

I dropped the shotgun, grabbing her wrist with both hands, the blade slicing through my jacket, piercing my chest. She clawed my face with her left hand as my grip slid along her right arm, slick with blood. Spinning again, she broke the grip of one of my hands and pressed her back into me, jerking the knife downward toward my side, jamming it in my thigh. I held on to her wrist with one hand, forcing the knife out of my leg, using my knee to separate us and pushing my other hand against the small of her back, trying to pin her against the rail when the wood snapped and she plunged to the ground.

"Jack!" Lucy called, running from the barn.

I watched from the balcony as Lucy knelt next to her, rolling her onto her back, shining her flashlight on the hilt of the hunting knife sticking out of Maggie Brennan's lifeless chest.

Chapter Sixty-nine

Dear Daddy, I'm so sorry for everything. You and mom tried so hard and you did your best. I used to think I did my best too. Maybe I was just kidding myself or maybe my best just wasn't good enough. I don't know why things turned out this way. You warned me and I wish I had listened. I thought the money would take care of everything but I don't even have that so I guess the joke is on me. Hah, hah. I wish I could come home but I can't. They would send me to jail and that scares me too much to even think about it. Hold onto Monkey Girl. All that's left of me belongs to her. I love you.

Wendy.

I sat on the bed in Maggie Brennan's bedroom, reading and rereading Wendy's letter, holding the page to my face, hoping to catch a scent of her. I closed my eyes, trying to conjure her, summon her, or feel her. I didn't shake but I did ache. When I opened my eyes, Lucy was there. She clasped one corner of the letter between two fingers, read it, and put it with the other souvenirs.

"At least you know," she said.

"Yeah, and I'll tell you something. Knowing isn't all it's cracked up to be. Sometimes, dreaming and hoping is better. Where's Goodell?"

"Standing guard over Maggie's body."

"He must feel pretty good, knowing he was right."

"Unless he's crying for joy, I don't think so."

"He's crying?"

"Buckets. Says it's all his fault she got away with it for so long."

"Getting it wrong or being too late are every cop's nightmares."

"That's more weight than any of us should have to carry. We do our job the best we can with the evidence we've got and let the chips fall."

"The weight comes with the job. If you can't carry it, you should get out. And you and I are out of it."

"The public side, maybe. But that's not all there is."

"You want to go private? Chase deadbeat dads and cheating wives?"

"There's more to it than that and you know it. Simon has enough work to keep both of us busy. He's only sent a little of it to you but there's more. Plus, Milo Harper and Sherry Fritzshall are connected to everyone in town. After the way we cracked this case, people will be standing in line to hire us."

"Look around, kiddo. This doesn't exactly qualify for the victory column."

"Wait till you see what I found in the barn."

"More souvenirs?"

"And lab journals. It was like she was conducting some grand experiment. Some excuse, huh?"

"Scientists don't make excuses."

"Think about it," she said. "That's all I'm saying. We didn't deal these cards but that doesn't mean we can't play them."

I got up, walked onto the balcony, looked at the rocky ground where Maggie's body lay. Lucy stood alongside me. The moon broke through the clouds as Tom Goodell raised his head toward us, moonbeams catching his tears. He ducked his head and turned away.

"Deal me out."

Sirens wailed in the near distance, flashing lights bobbing along the county road visible in the dark from the balcony. Quincy Carter, the Johnson County Sheriff's Department, and the FBI descended on the Brennan farm, not letting us go until close to dawn. I was unconscious the moment my head hit the pillow.

Kevin and Wendy play on the beach, white winged gulls swooping and dipping and dancing overhead. Joy and I watch from the deck of the beach house, the waves breaking in the distance, rolling lazily onto shore, the kids squealing, splashing, and kicking the water. The sun rides across the horizon, red, then yellow and orange, the sky changing from pink to blue to ink, day passing; stars twinkling, planets shining, and the moon sharing and shading its face as a cool wind blows and fireflies christen the night in a phosphorescent shower. Wendy lays her stuffed animal at my feet. Hold on to Monkey Girl, she says. All that's left of me belongs to you. She links arms with Kevin and the wind scours the sand, sweeping them away.

I sat up in bed, glancing at my watch. It was almost eleven. I'd been asleep five hours, not enough to clear the brain fog. I rubbed the dressings on my chest and thigh, feeling the stitches that a paramedic had used to close the wounds.

I tried to untangle Wendy's letter from my dream. Her letter said hold on to Monkey Girl; all that's left of me belongs to *her*. In my dream, she said all that's left of me belongs to *you*, the pronoun making the difference, giving new meaning to her letter.

Monkey Girl occupied its familiar perch on the shelf in my closet. I took it down, kneading its synthetic fur, probing until my finger slipped into a fold along the inseam of one leg, rubbing against an implanted narrow strip of Velcro. I ran my finger along the inside length of the leg, then squeezed and shook the toy without finding whatever had been attached to the Velcro. There were no other hidden pockets.

I was certain that Wendy had left something for me inside the stuffed animal, her letter and my dream the clues. Whatever she had hidden, it had to lead to the stolen money. There would have been no other reason for her cryptic message. My dream had parsed the letter for me.

I sat on my bed, my gut sick at the realization that Lucy had also read Wendy's letter and may have understood its meaning. I was sleeping so soundly I would not have heard her had she taken Monkey Girl, removed whatever Wendy had hidden, and put the stuffed animal back.

I had asked Wendy what she would do the next time she was tempted by an easy, big score and she had asked me what I would do with the money if I found it. They were the same question but our answers were different. I knew what I would do and she was scared of the choice she might make.

I pulled on my clothes and went looking for her. The house was empty and my car was gone. If the dogs knew where she was, they weren't talking. I started to call her cell phone when the doorbell rang. It was Kent and Dolan. I'd forgotten that my forty-eight hours were up.

Chapter Seventy

"We've come for the monkey," Dolan said.

"Anyone else, Dolan, and that would be the dumbest thing they'd ever said."

"C'mon, Jack," Kent said. "We've seen the letter your daughter sent you. Ammara Iverson knew about the stuffed animal. She's the one that put it together."

"You're telling me that you got a judge to sign a search warrant for a stuffed monkey?"

"We can do this the easy way or the hard way," Kent said. "The harder you fight us, the harder we come at you."

He was right and I was buying time until I could find Lucy.

"Wait here."

I ran upstairs, coming back with Monkey Girl.

"You can look at it here. You want to take it with you, get a warrant. Until then, you've got my word I'll take good care of it. Deal?" Kent nodded and I handed it to him. "There's a pocket on the inseam of one of the legs.

There's a piece of Velcro inside. I don't know if something was hidden there, but if there was, it's gone."

Kent handed it to Dolan and stared at me, deciding what to do next when his cell phone rang.

"Kent," he said, listening, the veins in his neck bulging. "You're shitting me! That is total bullshit! All right, all right! Here."

He handed me the phone, grabbed Monkey Girl from Dolan, and threw it on the floor, pulling Dolan to one side, whispering to him, flapping his arms like he was drowning. Dolan's face turned red and he tried to push past Kent who bodychecked him.

"You son-of-a-bitch!" Dolan screamed. "We'll get you for this if it's the last fucking thing we do!"

Kent dragged him into the kitchen. I walked into the living den where I could see them, holding Kent's phone to my ear.

"Hello," I said.

"Jack, it's Ammara. I hope you know what you're doing."

"At the moment, the only thing I'm doing is watching Kent and Dolan pitch a fit. It's a good show but I don't know what it has to do with me."

"Don't play with me, Jack. This is serious shit," she said.

"I'm not playing with you. I have no idea what you're talking about."

She hesitated. "Okay. Here it is. We got an anonymous tip this morning that two and a half million dollars each was wired into Kent's and Dolan's bank accounts. We checked it out and the money came from an account in the Caymans that was closed immediately after the transfer was made. We don't know whose account it was or how the transfer was made but we'll find out and when we do, you better hope you still don't know anything about it."

I looked out the front window as Lucy and Simon pulled into the driveway, Lucy in my car, Simon in his. They got out and waved to me. Simon pointed at the government sedan parked at the curb, his eyes asking the obvious question. I nodded and they high-fived, kissed, and drove away in Simon's car.

"Maybe they won the lottery," I told Ammara.

"That's the best you can do?"

Dolan was on his phone, his eyes popping out of his head, Kent pacing circles around him. Roxy and Ruby raced in through the doggie door, jumped up on them, and peed on their shoes.

"What can I tell you? Every dog has his day."

After Kent and Dolan left, I showered and shaved, went to the grocery store, and came home. A taxi pulled in the driveway behind me and Joy got out of the backseat. She was wearing jeans, a down vest over a turtleneck sweater, her hair tucked behind her head, the only color in her cheeks coming from the cold. The driver pulled her suitcase from the trunk. She paid him and he drove away. We looked at each other, my arms filled with grocery bags, hers hugging her chest.

We were married a long time before we got divorced, long enough to know when something was wrong. I saw it in her flushed-out features, her slumped shoulders. I tilted my head at the front door.

"Let's go inside."

The dogs swarmed her while I put the groceries away. She sat on the floor with them, offering no resistance. I took my coat off and joined her. The dogs exhausted themselves, curling into our laps. I took her hand.

"Tell me," I said.

She cleared her throat. "It's funny. All those years I spent running from doctor to doctor and nothing was wrong with me except that I was a drunk. When I finally quit drinking, I quit running. Then, a few months ago, I felt something in the shower. I decided it was nothing, just my imagination. But it got bigger and I got scared and so I went to a doctor here and she sent me to M. D. Anderson."

"What did they tell you?"

"I have breast cancer, probably stage three or four. They won't know for sure until they get the rest of the tests back."

I let out a long breath. "I'm sorry. Is it curable?"

"Treatable. That's the new mantra. Nobody promises a cure."

"When do you start?"

"Soon. Surgery first, then chemo and radiation." She looked at me, her eyes filled. "If I live long enough, I get new boobs."

She dipped her head to my shoulder and I cradled the back of her neck in my hand. My phone rang. It was Kate. I didn't answer.

Chapter Seventy-one

May 2009

My parents lived in Dallas when I was assigned to the FBI office there. My dad and I had lunch together every Friday. The best part of lunch was arguing over whose turn it was to pay, each of us trying to convince the other to pick up the check. He and my mother stopped by our house one Sunday morning and the conversation turned to whose turn it was to buy, my dad reminding me that he'd bought the week before. I said he would have to pay because I was broke and turned one pant pocket inside out to show that it was empty. He pointed to the other pocket and I turned it out. It was as empty as the first. He looked at me and said wear a different pair of pants, telling me not to make excuses when it was my turn to step up.

I told Kate that story when we had lunch at the end of May. We were sitting at a table on the sidewalk at

Axios. It was my way of explaining why I had gone with Joy to her doctor appointments, sat in the waiting room during her surgery, and moved her into the house Lucy and I shared when she came home from the hospital. Joy's surgery had gone well but she was struggling with chemo and radiation. Her hair was falling out and she was losing weight and hope.

"What's your relationship with her now?" Kate asked.

"I'm taking care of her. When we were married, she went through some pretty hard times when I didn't do that."

"What's that mean for us?"

Sherry Fritzshall had been true to her word, reaching an agreement with Kate to compensate her for the damage Milo Harper had caused her firm. After the ink was dry, she tried to recruit Kate to the institute but Kate told her she had accepted a job in California.

"I don't know. You're moving to San Diego next week so you can take care of Brian. We're both doing what we need to do."

Kate finished the last of her wine, setting her glass down and folding her hands on the table. "Will you come see me?"

"When I can."

She rose from the table. "Don't wait too long."

I watched her drive away. My cell phone rang. It was Lucy.

"It's after one o'clock. Are you planning on coming in to the office today?"

I never asked Lucy or Simon about the money that showed up in Kent's and Dolan's bank accounts and they never said a word about it. Some things are better left unknown and unsaid.

"You and Simon are the partners. You're supposed to be in the office. I'm just a consultant and consultants don't punch a clock."

She laughed. "Well, try to work us in to your schedule. You won't believe who just hired us."